MW00581005

# PIT FIGHTER

# PIT FIGHTER

## VICTOR OF TUCSON ✛ BOOK ONE

## PLUM PARROT

Podium

*To my mother,*
*the first storyteller I knew*
*and my biggest supporter*

Copyright © 2023 by Miles C. Gallup

Cover design by Podium Publishing

ISBN: 978-1-0394-1887-5

Published in 2023 by Podium Publishing, ULC
www.podiumaudio.com

Podium

# PIT FIGHTER

# 1

## SUMMONED

Tucson was hot in the summer; that wasn't anything new, but today the heat coming off the pavement felt particularly nasty to Victor. He was walking home from summer school—fuck Mr. Briggs and his fucking bullshit plagiarism. Victor spat and shook his head. No, he couldn't blame Briggs. He'd paid Tony for that essay; it wasn't Briggs's fault that Tony had gotten it off the internet. "Fucking *pendejo*," Victor said aloud and laughed. That asshole charged him twenty-five bucks and then just cut and pasted it off some website. Why was he thinking about this shit again? Fuck. He'd almost lost his chance to graduate and, along with it, his scholarship to Pima Community College. Yeah, big fucking deal, community college, right? But it was a start, and if he did well on the wrestling team there and kept his grades up, he'd maybe get to transfer to the U of A. Truthfully, he was fucking lucky Briggs had agreed to let him make up the missing credit through summer school. Well, Briggs, Dean Lopez, and Ms. Marshal, the counselor. Damn, but she'd gone to bat for Victor.

"Look out, you fucking dipshit!" The shout accompanied a blaring horn and squealing tires. Victor stumbled back and realized he'd walked into a crosswalk at a red light.

"Fuck you!" he shouted reflexively. The car was already speeding down Dodge Street, and Victor kicked some rocks waiting for the light to change. He almost dropped and did some push-ups, but it was just too hot. He wiped sweat off his brow, shoving it back into his short black hair. The hot wind blowing through the wet hair felt good for a couple of seconds, then it was just hot again. The light changed, and he jogged over Dodge back onto the sidewalk, following Grant Road west. His backpack bounced against his shoulder blades, sweat soaking the fabric of his shirt. The soles of his old Adidas tennies were worn so thin that the hot sidewalk made the rubber super malleable and almost uncomfortably warm. Impulsively, he picked up the pace, pushing himself into a jog, then a run, then a sprint as he came to Chrysler and took a left, his grandparents' neighborhood opening up before him.

"C'mon, just like coach says, 'always finish hard,'" Victor hissed. He sprinted past the Alvarez house, cutting the corner of their overgrown yard into his grandparents' front yard, dove between the two huge old oleander bushes, hopped the little barrel cactus, then slid onto the shaded front porch. He knew his *abuela* would have some juice made, and after he downed a huge glass, he'd take a shower and go see Marcy. She'd been funny lately, kind of distant. He was starting to wonder if she would ditch him when she went to ASU. He opened the screen door and called, "*Abuela!*" He stepped into the living room, and then everything went black.

At first, Victor thought he'd passed out, but he was still conscious, still thinking, while he drifted in darkness. Was he drifting? He supposed he didn't know. He tried to wave his arms around, but he couldn't be sure they even moved. "What the fuck, man?" he tried to say, but no sound came out. He could think it, though, and he did. Just what the fuck was going on? Was he having a stroke? Sunstroke? No, man, he'd overheated before, and he knew what it felt like. He'd been fine, no headache, nothing. Some time passed while he contemplated his fate; he reflected on Marcy for a while, realizing he really didn't think it would be such a bad thing for them to take a break. She had a lot going on, and he needed to focus on getting his shit together. He thought about his grandma and how he needed to make her proud, which made him think about his *abuelo* and how he'd never really done anything to make him proud before he died. Well, that wasn't entirely true: his grandpa had seen him take second at State last year. Still, he'd wanted to do more. He'd always wanted to pay them back for taking him in when his parents died. His mom's parents hadn't given him the time of day.

A pinprick of light pierced the vast expanse of darkness, and it jerked him out of his reverie. He watched as the pinprick expanded to a thumbnail, then a baseball, then a basketball, then it rapidly widened to fill his vision, and Victor found himself standing in a big wooden room. Everything was wood—the floor, the walls, the ceiling, everything. Four guys were standing in front of him wearing baggy brown robes with hoods, and they were all holding glowing metal rods. That's not what made Victor say, "What the fuck?" though. No, it was the strangers' blue skin and fucking fluorescent hair.

"Tshlanet!" one of the blue-skinned guys said.

\*\*\*Integrating non-System entity\*\*\*

\*\*\*Human species recognized and integrated\*\*\*

The messages flashed in front of Victor's eyes, and he swiped a hand over his face, thinking he had on VR goggles or something, but there was nothing there. "What the fuck?" he repeated.

"Silence!" the blue-skinned guy on the left said.

"Well?" a deep voice sounded from Victor's left, and he looked to see a man leaning back against the wooden wall in the shadow of a support beam.

"I can sense a high Energy affinity in this one," one of the blue guys said, "but he's of pitiful rank and racial advancement—I'd say he's Base Zero. He must be from a dead world." This one stood out with his bright green hair and eyes.

"Bah, another. Sell him to the pits."

"Hey, who are you, assholes? How'd you get me out of my *abuela*'s house?" A yellow-haired blue guy stepped forward and swiftly tapped his metal rod on Victor's forearm, and Victor felt cold wash over him. It was a deep, bitter cold that spread through his skin, into his bones, and down to the pit of his stomach. He felt as if the life was being pulled out of him, but he couldn't move; he didn't even think he could breathe. The yellow-haired blue guy waved his rod again and uttered something, then Victor felt himself lift up and float along, the way you might imagine Dracula would glide over the misty ground.

All the color in the world seemed drained, and Victor could mostly only see shades of gray as he floated along behind the blue man. He drifted through some doors, down a wooded forest path, and onto a wide dirt road. Victor panicked at first when he realized he wasn't breathing, but then he noticed he didn't feel any burning in his chest, didn't feel any shadows creeping in on his vision, and he figured something the blue guy had done was keeping his body in a state of suspended animation. He vowed to take that fucker down if he got the chance, though. This was a bullshit way to treat someone.

They followed the road for a while, and eventually they started passing other people going in different directions. People in wagons and on weird mounts—creatures that looked like giant lizard birds, one guy riding a big fucking elk, and a huge hay wagon pulled along by a lizard the size of an elephant.

They came to a tall stone-block wall with a gate in it, and the blue guy leading Victor was waved through by one of the men holding long spears, crackling with electricity. The spearmen stood under the archway, tall and glowering in their military-style uniforms. One of them frowned and spat as Victor's captor walked by.

Victor floated along behind the asshole through busy streets filled with lots of different kinds of people, so many weird-looking people that Victor started to think he must be tripping on acid. There were tall, beautiful women with glistening, magical-looking wings. He saw an eagle-headed guy arguing with a huge dude that looked like an otter. And there were lots and lots of blue and red-skinned people. The red guys were a bit bigger and meaner looking than the blue guys, and some of them had wings—enormous, red dragon-style wings.

They wended their way into back alleys, past very unsavory-looking people, and deeper into the city still, where piled garbage was ubiquitous, and pools of questionable fluids had to be hopped by his blue-skinned escort. After more turns than Victor could keep track of, they finally entered a large wooden building with a giant wagon wheel hung over the barn-style doors. The blue man led Victor past men and women who sparred with fists and weapons. They were punching and wrestling all over the hay- and sawdust-covered floors. They went to the back wall, through a small door, and into an office where an obese, red-skinned man with black hair and black eyes sat at a small desk. He looked up, a wide grin splitting his thick lips and revealing long, gleaming white fangs. "What did you bring me today?"

"We got an item from a colleague at Fainhallow. He thought it might lead to an interesting summon, but we just got this Base Zero runt." The blue guy waved a hand at Victor. "He has a high affinity, though. If you train him, he might be worth something someday."

"Base Zero, you say? He won't make it through one Pit Night. I can't pay much for fodder. I hope the summoning ritual wasn't too costly."

"Master ap'Gravin will take it out of his son's hide; don't you worry about that. Anyway, I'm late for dinner. What'll you give us for him?"

"Oh, here's five. More than that, and I'll be losing money on his upkeep before Pit Night." He pushed a little brown pouch toward the blue guy.

"Eh, it's all the same to me; I didn't put any money into his summon. I'm going to release him now; he's your problem going forward. See you next time." The blue asshole turned and walked past Victor, waving a hand as he went by. Victor felt warm tingles spread through his body, starting with his skin and progressing like a wave of ecstasy toward his stomach.

"Ah, Jesus, fucking *pendejo*!" Victor leaned forward and put his hands on his knees, gathering himself.

"All right, boy. What's your name?" the enormous red devil asked, standing up and shoving his chair back.

"Victor. Where the fuck am I?"

"You're in my pit fighting hall, in a city called Persi Gables. You're not from this world, just in case you were confused about that. Oh, and you're my property now. Don't make me exert dominance over you, because I'd like you to be in one piece for Pit Night."

"What? Assert dominance? The fuck are you talking about, man?"

"Did the language integration fail with you? Are you confused? Listen to my words, boy: you belong to me. You are no longer on your home planet. You will do as I say, or I will beat the piss out of you. Is the meaning of my words coming through?"

"Yes, fuck, man. How the . . ."

"Quiet now. I'm going to take you back to the pens, and one of the other fighters can play question-and-answer with you. I don't have time for that nonsense. Follow me, and if you run, you'll just follow me with a broken leg the next time." Victor followed him. He didn't like the idea of having to try to follow someone around with a broken leg, and the guy was big enough to do it; he had to weigh more than three hundred pounds. For all his size, the man walked briskly, passing over the sparring floor, through a side door, and into a long hallway lined with cages. Some of the cages were big, with several people in them, and some were small and only held one occupant.

"Sir, what's your name?" Victor asked, wondering if he could get anything out of the big man.

"You can call me Boss or Sir." He chuckled to himself as he fumbled with a big key ring, opening the door to a medium-size cage with two other occupants. "I'll put you in here, Victor, because these are my two nicest fighters, and they might give you some pointers before Pit Night. You're welcome." He pulled the metal door open and gestured for Victor to enter. Not seeing any other option, Victor complied, stepping into the cage with a goat-man and a red-skinned woman with bright green-yellow eyes. "Vullu and Yrella, this is Victor. Victor's new around here; where are you from, Victor?"

"Um, Tucson?"

"Ha, okay, this is Victor of Tucson. Show him how things work around here." He slammed the metal door shut, and the two occupants went back to the dice game they'd been playing before Victor's arrival. He sat down on the straw floor and looked out through the bars of his cage, watching the strange prisoners of the other cells pacing around or sleeping or muttering threats at each other. What the fuck had he gotten into?

# 2

### STATUS

Victor had never been religious; sure, his *abuela* was, and she made him go to church when he was little, but Victor had never seen eye to eye with the Catholic idea of life and death. That didn't stop him from falling on his knees in the hay and praying for a while, though. Hands clasped in front of him, eyes squeezed shut, he performed more Hail Marys than he ever had in his life, all the while wishing he had his grandma's rosary. This went on for a while until a cutting feminine voice said, "Kid, I don't know what you're doing, but stop it. You're driving me crazy." Victor opened his scrunched eyes, spots flaring in his vision, to see the lanky, red-skinned woman squatting in front of him, scowling into his face. Her eyes were something else, though: mossy-green with specks of bright yellow and gold. When the lights hanging from the high wooden ceiling caught them just right, they almost glittered.

"Damn, your eyes are pretty," he said before he could catch himself. Her scowl didn't change, but her right hand came up faster than a striking cobra and slapped him on the cheek. Not hard, though, just enough to let him know she could. Victor tipped back onto his butt with momentum as he brought a hand up to his cheek out of reflex. He didn't say anything, though; why let her know it bothered him? "So, anyway, my name's Victor."

"Mmhmm, I'm Yrella. This is Vullu." She gestured to the goat-man, who leaned back into the far corner of the cage.

"Well, I've tried holding my breath, pinching myself, even praying, and

I'm still fucking here, so I'd appreciate it, ma'am, if you could tell me what the fuck is going on."

"Oh?" she smiled and glanced at Vullu, sharing a joke. "So, you're really not from this world, hmm? Old Yund sure has some interesting connections, eh, Vullu?"

"That he does, that he does. You know, I went to his house once, and not as a fighter, as a guest. Well, as the escort to a guest. His villa would send some of the nobility into fits of jealousy. Anyway, the point I'm making is don't judge the man by the stinking cesspool where he works."

"Oh, I wouldn't do that. I'm well aware of his connections." Yrella sat in front of Victor, crossing her legs in front of her, and contemplated him for a few seconds.

"Hey, excuse me? Would you mind just filling me in a little?" Victor couldn't take it anymore.

"Oh, relax, kid. We aren't going anywhere for a while. They won't let us out to exercise until morning, anyway. So, tell me where you're from, Victor."

"Like my planet? It's Earth."

"Hmm, Earth. Not one I've heard before. You, Vullu?" The goat-man shook his head, eyes closed. "Well, what's it like? Does everyone look like you there?"

"Uh, like, as in human? Yeah, but they all don't look like me. Some have whiter skin; some have darker skin. Everyone has different hair. We're all different sizes. Is that what you mean?"

"Human, hmm? Another new one. Well, you seem pretty weak, even if you are bigger than most Shadeni. What's your level?"

"My what, now?"

"Your level. Hello? Maybe he's not understanding everything, Vullu. Maybe the language integration didn't work for him."

"It's possible, I suppose." Vullu nodded, eyes closed, clearly almost asleep.

"Hey, what the fuck are you talking about?"

"Look at your status sheet. Do you see System Language Integration under your skills?"

"*Pendeja*, are you fucking crazy? You're talking like we're playing a video game or something."

Yrella cocked an eyebrow and turned to look at Vullu, who had opened his eyes. "What the Ancestors is going on with this kid?"

"Kid, say 'status' out loud and tell me what you see," Vullu said.

Victor looked from the goat-man to the demon woman, then shrugged. "Status."

| Status | | | |
|---|---|---|---|
| Name: | Victor Sandoval | | |
| Race: | Human: Base 1 | | |
| Class: | – | | |
| Level: | 0 | | |
| Core: | – | | |
| Energy Affinity: | 6.1 | Energy: | 0/0 |
| Strength: | 9 | Vitality: | 10 |
| Dexterity: | 9 | Agility: | 10 |
| Intelligence: | 8 | Will: | 8 |
| Points Available: | 0 | | |
| Titles & Feats: | – | | |
| Skills: | • System Language Integration: Not Upgradeable | | |

"*Chingado . . .*"

"Well?" Yrella pressed.

"All right, what the fuck is this? There's a fucking menu floating in front of my face."

"Are you not familiar with the System?" Vullu asked.

"The what? No, we don't have this system where I'm from. Are there fucking contacts in my eyes or something?"

Vullu and Yrella shared another look, then the goat-man sat up and scooted closer to Victor. "No, I mean the System, not a system. What level are you, Victor?"

"Umm, it says zero."

"How can he be zero? He's a grown man!" Yrella said.

"Victor, is there much Energy in your world?"

"Uh, yeah, even poor people have electricity where I'm from."

"Electricity? Everyone is air-attuned on your world?"

"What? Dude, I don't fucking get what you're asking me."

"How can they summon him from a System void? And from a dead world? He has to be from a dead world, right? How could he grow to his age, be fit physically and mentally, and not at least gain one level?" Yrella sat back, blowing out her breath incredulously.

"What the hell is a dead world? My world is plenty alive—billions of people, plenty of trees and fish and shit."

"No, 'dead world' is a term for a world without Energy."

"We're talking in circles here! There's fucking energy on my world. We have better lights and AC than this dump, that's for sure."

"He doesn't know what we're talking about," Vullu said. "Here, Victor, look at my hand. These cages are warded, but I can get a little Energy out." Vullu held his hand out, palm up, and closed his eyes. A moment later, a flickering blue flame took shape over his palm, growing to about three inches in height. Victor's eyes opened wide, and he leaned forward, stretching out a hand toward the flame. It was hot!

"How the fuck you doing that?"

"Energy!" Vullu shook his hand, and the flame went away. A lightbulb went off in Victor's head just then, and he looked at his status sheet again. There it was: Energy 0/0.

"Okay, I get it. I've played plenty of games; it's like Mana or some other bullshit. Well, I have zero out of zero."

"Zero? It makes sense, I guess. If you don't have Energy in your world, how would you form a Core? Well, don't let that bother you. If you survive a few fights, you should start to build up some Energy, and someone can teach you to form a Core. That's a big if, though, kid. Level Zero? You're probably gonna get killed pretty fast. Sorry." In her defense, she really did look kind of sad, at least in Victor's inexpert opinion.

"So that big asshole is going to make me fight? For real? Like to the death, or are we talking MMA shit?"

"Oh, it's usually to the death. Fighters want to get stronger, which means killing their opponents for an Energy increase." Vullu shook his head while he spoke.

"So, what the fuck? People can just enslave people and make them fight to the death in this world? That's pretty fucked up."

"Ha. There are rules, of course, but might makes right around here, kid, which puts you in a pretty shitty spot."

"Hey, you said 'shitty'—so we have the same slang and everything? Is that the language integration you were talking about?"

"Oh, some of our slang will match, but you say some words I'm not understanding, and I'm sure I could find a word in my language you wouldn't get. It's pretty close, though. The System might be heartless, but it's smart."

"So, what are the rules? How can that guy enslave us and get away with it? Aren't there laws?"

"Oh, sure, that's how he got us. Vullu and I got caught robbing a nobleman's home. You go to prison, and people can buy your sentence. If we had powerful friends, they could have made Yund back off or bought our sentences themselves. We don't have any, though, and you sure as hell don't." Yrella smiled glumly, and shrugged.

"Yeah, but I'm not a criminal!"

"No one in this entire world knows you, kid. Yund can do whatever he wants to you, and not a single soul will know or care. People will be having too much fun wagering on your fight to worry too much about where you came from." Vullu scooted back to his corner and leaned back, crossing his hooved feet out in front of him.

"This is fucking bullshit." Victor slid on his butt into the corner diagonally facing Vullu's and leaned back, stretching out and crossing his arms on his chest. "Does this fucking System have any games? Or just this status shit?"

"Games? No, but we have some bone dice we made. I'll teach you a game tomorrow, but let's get some sleep before the other prisoners start throwing shit at us for talking too loudly." Vullu yawned and nestled his chin down into his chest. Yrella didn't say anything, but she lay on her side, resting her head on Vullu's thigh.

"Did you mean that literally? Are they going to throw actual shit at us?" Victor asked quietly, looking around at the other cages and the sprawled-out inhabitants.

"Oh, I meant it. Good night, Victor." A note of finality in Vullu's voice forestalled any more questions from Victor. Instead, he grunted, rolling onto his side, wishing he had a jacket or his backpack for a pillow.

"At least I wore jeans today instead of shorts. I almost fucking wore shorts to school," he muttered, closing his eyes, and had he been conscious to appreciate it, he would have been surprised at how quickly he fell asleep.

"Get up, Victor. You don't want to miss breakfast." Yrella nudged Victor with her foot, and his eyes popped open. It felt as if he'd just gone to sleep. He groaned and rolled onto his hands and knees. Out of habit, he started pumping out some push-ups. He always did them first thing upon waking up—another thing his wrestling coach had drilled into his mind: before going to the bathroom, before brushing his teeth, before anything: push-ups and sit-ups. A booted foot pressed his shoulder then shoved him sprawling onto his side. "The hell are you doing? You trying to get beat up in the yard? These meatheads don't want to see a runt like you trying to show off. Get up and line up behind me, so we can get out and eat." Yrella's voice was higher than usual, as if she couldn't believe what she was seeing.

"Alright, jeez." Victor hopped up and stood behind Yrella, who stood behind Vullu, waiting for someone to come and open the door, he supposed. He looked up and down the long aisle between the pens, trying to discern if anything had changed, and he noticed the two cages to the left of them, toward the door, were empty. "Is it our turn next?"

"You learn quickly," Vullu said, a distinctly goatlike chuckle escaping his throat.

"After we eat, we get yard time?" Victor felt like he was in a prison VR. Now, he just had to keep his eyes open for some loose bricks or a guard who slipped away to be with his girlfriend, then he could make a break for it. Yeah, right. He was mostly joking with himself, but he did intend to try to get out of this place the first chance he got.

"That's right. We'll try to help you pick up a skill or two while we're out there."

"I know a few moves, but sure, I'm always up to learn something new. I guess fighting to the death is different from a wrestling match." Vullu looked back over his shoulder, up at Victor, and slowly nodded, and something was different in his eyes, almost as if he'd appraised Victor differently. Victor looked down at Yrella's curly black hair, and before he could rein in his mouth, he said, "You seemed taller when we were all sitting in the cage." Yrella turned and looked at him, and Victor saw her right eye narrow slightly as if she was contemplating something, but then she slowly exhaled through her nose and turned around without a word.

The door at the end of the aisle opened, and a large, furry otter-man came through, jangling a ring of keys. "You're up!" he announced, stepping up to their cage door and unlocking it. Victor noticed that he had a metal rod with weird letters inscribed all over it, hanging from a loop on his belt. He stared at Victor with big, moist black eyes as he walked through the cage door. "Don't try anything funny, kid. Just 'cause Boss didn't tag you doesn't mean we won't."

"I won't," Victor said, hurrying after Yrella as she stepped through the door into the central portion of the building. He could smell something cooking, and as he stepped through the door, he saw that on the right, through a broad, short hallway, a cafeteria of sorts had been set up. He followed Yrella and Vullu as they walked around a few long wooden tables to a counter where a blue person in an apron was serving plates of food. Victor took his, noting the buttered piece of round flatbread and the heaping scoop of fatty beans and mystery meat.

The trio sat at one of the tables without anyone else sitting at it and commenced to eat their food. Victor had eaten plenty of beans and eggs with tortillas, so he didn't balk at the lack of silverware; he just scooped his beans onto a hunk of flatbread and wolfed it down. The meat tasted like pork. "It's not bad, actually," he said. "Is there anything to drink?"

"Yeah," Vullu said, gesturing to a barrel and a small table stacked with wooden mugs. "Get us all a scoop, will ya?" Victor shrugged and went over to the barrel, grabbed a wooden mug, and scooped up some room temperature water. He set the cup down by Yrella, then went back for two more.

"Not very refreshing," he said, sitting back down and taking a big gulp.

"Nope, but it does the job." Yrella slammed her empty mug down and burped. Vullu laughed, sipped his water delicately, and set his mug down.

"Well, what sort of fighting can you do, Victor?" Vullu asked, suddenly serious. "I'd like to see you survive your first Pit Night."

# 3

⚜

# PRACTICE

After they ate, Yrella told Victor that they'd have two hours to exercise before they had to go back to their pen. She and Vullu led him out of the cafeteria to the large grappling hall. There were already about twenty others tousling, exercising, and lounging around on benches watching. "What keeps you all from rising up? Fighting your way out of here?"

"Aside from the fact that most of these assholes would kill each other just as soon as they'd work together, most of us that Yund feels threatened by have been tagged."

"Tagged?" Victor looked at her quizzically. Yrella pulled her loose gray blouse up by her waist and showed him a bright blue tattoo on her hard, red stomach.

"Tagged. The ink is infused with an alchemical mixture that binds us to the control rods Yund and his lackeys have. It's an expensive process, so they don't do it to all of the fresh meat." She winked at Victor and tousled his hair.

"Well, you've got some fucking tight abs." He smiled at Yrella's confused face, then looked around the room and said, "Any workout gear? Or I gotta wear my jeans and shit?"

"Your clothes? You'll have to make do with what you have. Yund is a cheap bastard when it comes to us fighters."

"All right, Victor," Vullu cut in, "let's see what kind of fighting you do." They were standing in a relatively quiet corner of the sparring gym, and Vullu sidestepped, facing Victor, beckoning him to come at him with one of his hands. Victor hopped up and down a few times, getting his blood pumping, then he faced Vullu, his center of gravity low, and moved toward him, circling with him, watching him for any forward movement. "Come, Victor, show me . . ." He couldn't finish the sentence because Victor had feinted with his right hand, drawing Vullu's eye, then he'd swept in low, grabbed Vullu's back ankle/hoof, lifted it tight to his chest, and swept his other leg, dropping the goat-man onto his back.

***Congratulations! You've learned Unarmed Combat, Basic.***

"Ancestors! That was smooth! You didn't even see him coming, Vullu!" Yrella laughed, mockingly offering to help Vullu stand, then pulling her hand back. Victor was too astounded by the message floating in his vision to pay them any attention.

"What the fuck is this? I just learned unarmed combat, basic. What the fuck? Basic? I don't think so!"

"Do you feel like you know anything new? Really think about it; concentrate on what you know about fighting," Vullu said, grunting and standing up. Victor did as he said and couldn't find anything new in his head. It was weird, exhaustively trying to contemplate what he knew about something, but nothing was new as far as he could tell.

"Nah, I don't think so."

"I think the System is still trying to categorize what you know, at least with regard to fighting. Let's go, try that again, and if you get it, keep going. Show me what you'd do next." Victor nodded and moved back into circling with Vullu. This time he closed in and grappled with Vullu a bit, reached in, grabbed his neck, pulled on him, grabbed his wrist, pulled it, let him try to grab his wrist, then rolled it out of the grip. Then just as Vullu was starting to get lulled by the push-pull of the grappling rhythm, Victor swept low and forward, grabbed both of Vullu's legs, and drove him backward onto the wooden floor.

Vullu thrashed and tried to flop over, but Victor's ground game was strong. He scrambled up, keeping his center of mass pressing down on Vullu the whole time, then scooped up his head and left arm in a lock, driving his full weight into his shoulder, pressing down on Vullu's chest while he squeezed his head and arm. Vullu was definitely pinned, but now what? They weren't in a wrestling match.

"Uh, you have me immobilized, but now what? What if I start punching you?" Vullu grunted, balling up his free hand into a fist and pounding it into Victor's upper back and side. Victor hunkered down, so his head wouldn't get hit and squeezed harder, going up on his toes to push more of his weight into his shoulder, bearing down on Vullu's chest even more. "Ugh, that's uncomfortable, but it won't stop anyone with any decent points in strength and vitality. What are you going to do?"

"Alright, *pinche*," Victor growled, then he hauled up on the smaller man, scooting his legs under him, so he was behind him, still holding his arm and head in a death grip. This wasn't high school wrestling; why the fuck was he following rules? He let Vullu's arm slip out of his grasp, but then he redoubled his hold on Vullu's neck, wrapping it deep into the crook of his elbow and pressing on the back of his head in a full, rear-naked chokehold. He held it until Vullu stopped thrashing, then he let go, pushing the goat-man off himself and standing up.

***Congratulations! You've learned Grappling, Improved.***

Vullu had started gasping for breath almost the moment Victor let go. He and his buddies had played around plenty with chokeholds; he knew when to let go to avoid hurting someone. "Fuck yeah! Improved grappling that time!"

"That's a more specialized skill, but improved? How can someone without a class learn beyond basic?" Vullu looked at Yrella, and she just shrugged. He looked back at Victor and said, "That was a good choke, but you realize I haven't been fighting back, right?"

"Yeah, well, I kinda could tell." Victor shrugged.

"Hey, I just had a thought," Yrella said. "Victor, do you feel like you know more about grappling now?"

"No, I don't feel any fucking different."

"Uncle's arse, but you use that word a lot—'fuck, fucking, fuck, fuck.' What does it even mean?"

"Fuck? You guys don't have that word? It means a lot of stuff. It can mean the same as shit, or it can mean extremely, like if I said, 'that is fucking cool,' that would mean something is extremely cool. It also means sex. I'm sure there's more to it, but that's all I can think of right now." Victor shrugged.

Yrella looked at him strangely, opened her mouth to say something, then stopped and shook her head slightly. "Anyway, I was thinking the System isn't giving you those skills; it's just recognizing that you have them." She turned to Vullu. "So it didn't give him an improved skill; he already had it."

"Ahh, yes. That makes more sense. If he'd just learned those skills, he'd have gotten Energy with them. Maybe even enough to gain his first level." Vullu was nodding. "Victor, answer me this: have you ever learned to fight with any weapons?"

"No, not really. I mean, me and my buddies used to play around with wooden swords, but we never learned any real skills."

"Yrella, will you go check out a couple of practice axes?"

"Axes? You sure that's best for him to learn with?"

"Well, no. The spear would probably be better, but I like axes, so that's what he's getting." Yrella shrugged and sauntered over through a doorway near Yund's office. Victor watched her go, and Vullu snorted. "Don't let her catch you looking at her like that, kid."

Victor jerked his head away and feigned a stretch. "I don't know what you're talking about, man."

"Good, play it off. That one has teeth, and you have enough problems to deal with, you hear me?"

Victor looked at the little goat-man again, more closely, and he had to admit the older guy could be intimidating when he wanted to be. He had a short gray beard, and a mostly human-looking face, except for those weird yellow-gold eyes with weird-ass irises. "Hey, what are you, er your people, like called?"

"Ahh, no Cadwalli on your world, eh? Makes sense; I've never seen a wingless Ghelli like you."

"The fuck? Ghelli?"

"Well, you look kind of like a Ghelli, though they're very slight people—you're too stocky, and, as I said, they have wings. Ahh, here she comes." Vullu turned and held out a hand, to which Yrella tossed a heavy-looking single-bladed hand axe. He caught it, gave it a twirl, then nodded to Victor. Victor turned and took the axe Yrella was holding out to him. It had a stout wooden handle, and the axe-head was broad and heavy, definitely bigger than his grandpa's hatchet. He held a thumb to the blade and saw that it was rounded and smooth; he couldn't cut butter with this thing.

"All right, Victor. Stand behind me. I'm going to run through some standard axe forms, and I want you to mirror my movements. We'll do each one five times at first, then run through them faster and faster. Victor nodded and took up position behind Vullu. Yrella stood to the side, scrutinizing him as he tried to copy Vullu's movements as precisely as possible. The way Vullu moved reminded Victor of old dudes on VR doing that Tai Chi stuff—he moved slowly and smoothly, and Victor found it easy to mimic him, at least at first. After they'd gone through about ten different movements, repeating each one five times, as Vullu said they would, he picked up the pace, moving a little faster and only repeating the movements four times. Then he moved even faster, cutting the repetitions down to three. By now, Victor's arm and shoulder muscles were starting to burn, and he was breathing heavily. Still, he pushed through—if coach Dorgan had taught him anything, it was to push through the burn, push past the pain. When they were on their next run-through, doing two quick repetitions, a new message appeared in Victor's vision:

***Congratulations! You've learned Axe Mastery, Basic.***

Victor stopped swinging in surprise when he saw a bunch of tiny golden flecks of light start to gather in the air around him. He rubbed his eyes and shook his head, wondering if he was about to pass out or something, but then the little motes of golden light rushed toward him, and he felt as if he'd just popped an E-bomb. He shook his head and put his hands on his knees. "Whoa, fucking hell."

***Congratulations! You've achieved Level 1 Base Human.***

The rush faded quickly, and Victor stood up, feeling fresh, almost as if he hadn't been working out at all that day. "Well, I'm fucking Level One now. Watch out, bitches!"

"That's how things work when you learn a new skill, Victor. Think about the axe and what you know now about fighting." Vullu held up his axe like a visual aid. Victor did as he said and was surprised that he did seem to know an awful lot about axe fighting that he had no business knowing. He knew what angle to hold the blade at for different types of chops, he knew about not extending his center of balance when he swung, and he knew about following through and using momentum to create new opportunities. The number of little facts he knew about axes was simply mind-boggling.

"Well, that's nuts. So, the 'System' just put a bunch of shit in my head? I could've used this during Chemistry class." He held his fingers up, making quotes when he said System, and Yrella and Vullu looked at him quizzically. He shrugged and said, "Eh, never mind. So, like, can I get my axe skill even higher by practicing with you?"

"No, not really. You can get more fluid and increase your ability to the very edge of 'basic,' but you won't be able to move to improved until you have a class that supports it."

"A class? Jesus, this place really is like a game. So, how do I get a class?"

"You live long enough to get to Level Ten. Or, at least that's when most races get their class. I've heard that some of the lower races, like Urghat, get a class much earlier, though they have terrible potential for growth."

"Bro, you're losing me. So, if I'm like you guys, I should get a class around Level Ten. All right, let's hope I can get there. Can you guys teach me more skills that will give me levels?" Victor looked from Yrella to Vullu, and they exchanged glances also, then Yrella shrugged.

"I could teach you some things with knives, spears, and swords. Vullu, you should teach him bludgeons. You'll just have basic skills with them, but you won't be helpless if they put weapons in your pit match. Vullu and I both have some Energy skills we could try to teach you if you had a Core, but you'll need a few levels worth of Energy to build a Core. Oh, look at your status—do you have any Energy now?"

"Um," Victor said, pulling up his status menu and looking at the little Energy label. "I have thirty over zero now."

"Good, your body is absorbing Energy properly. We just need to help you build enough to allow you to form a Core. I doubt we'll get there with just a few skills, though. You'll get a lot more from killing your opponents in the pit."

"Fuck. I keep forgetting about that shit, but I really have to fight to the death, huh? This shit is nuts."

"Unless you want to sit down and die. Trust me; they aren't going to throw you in there with a pacifist," Yrella said, stepping forward and squeezing Victor's shoulder. "You gotta get your head right, kid. This isn't a joke. There are worse places on Fanwath you could be, but not many."

Victor frowned. "Fanwath?"

"This world, Victor. Face it: this is your reality now."

# 4

※

# THE RUSTY NAIL

Victor followed Yrella through the spear forms for the third time, stepping, thrusting, and shouting, "Eyah!" Then he brought the spear shaft around, pushing it with the rear gripping hand, then stepping back, snapping the spear back straight, and moving the spearhead in a small loop. He really didn't know what the fuck all these moves were for, but he could imagine an enemy before him and did his best to mimic Yrella.

\*\*\*Congratulations! You've learned Spear Mastery, Basic.\*\*\*

"That did it!" Victor braced himself for the rush of Energy as the tiny golden motes coalesced in the air and then surged into him. He whooped loudly and shouted, "Fuck yes! That never gets old."

\*\*\*Congratulations! You've achieved Level 2 Base Human. You have 5 attribute points to allocate.\*\*\*

"Oh, nice! I hit Level Two, Yrella!" The spear was the third weapon that he'd gained skill with that day; he'd started with bludgeons with Vullu, then Yrella had taken over and taught him some knife fighting skills before the spear. "I have five attribute points to spend, too!"

"That's good. It seems like your race has similar base properties to mine. The fact that you're leveling off a few simple basic skills shows you have good affinity, too. Celebrate; your people are stronger than Yeksa!"

"The fuck is a Yeksa?"

"You should hope to find out. With any luck, they'll throw some Yeksa against you in the pit for your first few matches; I think you could win."

"So, they're scrubs?"

"They're—" She looked at him closely, squinted her eyes, then continued. "Lesser creatures. They have poor affinity and struggle to gain a few levels in a lifetime."

"Well, what should I do with my points?"

"Five points spread over several attributes will mean very little in tomorrow's pit fight. I'd put them all into one—maybe strength or vitality."

"Hey, you guys have been very helpful to me, and I appreciate it, but I can trust you, right? I mean, like, why have you been so nice? I don't think you'd tell me some bullshit, but I gotta ask." Victor braced himself for an angry reaction, but Yrella just smirked.

"We aren't altruistic." She nodded to Vullu, who was slamming his fists into a wooden post. "Vullu and I get some time knocked off our sentences for each win we get, and if we help out new fighters, we get a little bit of time knocked off if they win."

"Ahh, damn. Well, thanks for letting me know." Victor had a sudden thought. "Hey, so you guys have set amounts of time you belong to Boss." He gestured to the big red man who was berating one of his employees in the far corner of the exercise hall. "But what about me? I don't have a fucking sentence I'm serving. Am I trapped here forever?"

"That's a good question, Victor. I'd focus on solving that problem after dealing with the more immediate issue—you have a pit fight tomorrow, and you're Level Two without a Core." She twirled her spear between her two hands, making it dance between them as she spoke. Victor frowned but didn't argue. He called up his status sheet and decided to dump all five points into strength. Maybe it would let him break a hold or squeeze someone's neck just that extra bit that would make the difference.

A wave of Energy flooded through his body after distributing the points on his status screen, and he took in a deep breath, stretching with his arms held out wide, arching his back as the tingles flooded through him. When it passed, he flexed his biceps, and they definitely popped a lot more than they used to. "Fuck yes!" He'd had very little body fat even before he was summoned, but now, with his strength jacked and after a workout, his muscles felt and looked pumped like never before. Yrella snorted.

"You're still just a baby; don't go getting full of yourself. Some of the monsters in here"—she gestured around the warehouse—"would kill you just for the way you look."

"Oh, like they're fucking racists or something?"

"Racist? Yes, I suppose plenty of Shadeni hate other people just because they're different, and I have bad news for you, Victor: you're more different than anyone I've met."

"Um, I didn't want to be rude, but is that what your race is called? Shadeni?"

"Yes, that's right." She knelt to pick up the spear that Victor had dropped.

"Well, I mean, it's not really true that I'm the most different—I mean, we have different colored skin, but I don't have furry legs and hooves like old Vullu, there." He nodded at the goat-man, who had stopped punching the wooden post and was unwinding the cloth strips around his knuckles.

"Don't be so literal, kid. I meant there's no one else like you in this world, as far as I know. C'mon, let's go turn these spears in. Our time's almost up." She handed him his spear, and he followed her toward the equipment room.

"Do you think there's any way I could get home? I mean, assuming I survive the pit and somehow get free of this place. You think I could find a way?"

"Assuming all that? Sure, why not? Some powerful mages summoned you, but I bet there are powerful mages that can undo it or just help you teleport home. A lot is possible for the higher tier Energy users." That gave Victor plenty to think about, so he didn't reply, just silently followed her as they turned in their gear. Further conversation was cut short when they were shouted at by one of Yund's lackeys to get their asses back to their cage.

Victor was given a hard piece of buttered bread that afternoon, just like on his first day, after they were put back in their cage. As far as he could tell, he was the only one that got this treatment, and Vullu had explained that his low Energy level and lack of a Core meant he had to eat more food than the others to survive. He didn't argue—he was starving like a motherfucker, pretty much all the time. Their water bucket was filled each day, and they all shared the same tin cup, but Victor also drank more than the others.

The afternoons were the most boring for Victor. Everyone else spent time doing something they called "cultivating." They sat around meditating and didn't speak for hours. Yrella tried to explain that once he had a Core, he'd learn how to cultivate Energy to build it up. That might be, but for now, he just had to bide his time, waiting for them to get tired of it so they could talk for a while before lights-out. That afternoon proved worse than usual—Yrella and Vullu spent extra time cultivating, apparently trying to squeeze in as much as possible on the eve of Pit Night.

Victor wrestled with his fears and despair. He was good at bluster and bravado and shoving his feelings where he didn't have to think about them, especially when he had training to do, but here, in the quiet cell, with everyone preparing for battle, he couldn't escape his mental demons. What was going to happen? Was he going to die tomorrow? Was he going to have to kill someone? Could he? Tucson seemed like a million years in the past when he tried to think of his friends or Marcy or his *abuela*.

For the first time in a long while, he thought of his parents. He'd been eight when they died in a car wreck. He'd been in the backseat, but he didn't remember the crash at all. He remembered them arguing, though. His mom had been yelling, her red-brown hair tied up in a bun, her eyes red with tears. His father's hands gripped the steering wheel, staring straight ahead, refusing to answer her. That was the last image he could muster up from the depths of his mind. He didn't remember what they were saying or how the crash had happened; he just remembered his grandma picking him up from the hospital and taking him home. Then there'd been a funeral, and he remembered his aunties talking about how rotten his other grandparents were for not coming.

When Yrella finally stirred and interrupted his reverie, Victor was grateful. He was ready to jump at any excuse to banish the memories, so when she shook her dice, he scooted over in front of her, and they played the simple dice game for a couple of hours before Vullu spoke up and said they should be quiet and go to sleep. Victor groaned, but he was dog tired, so he slid over to his corner and lay down on his side, using his arm for a pillow, and closed his eyes. Sleep came quickly, as it inexplicably usually did in this place, and when he felt Yrella's boot shaking his shoulder, he hopped up, feeling refreshed, if a bit stiff.

They were given their normal breakfast rotation, but then the routine changed. Yund and his goons gathered up almost all the cage occupants and made them stand shoulder to shoulder in two rows of twenty. Then, Yund moved to the front of the hall, near the big barn doors, and addressed them in a booming voice. "All right, you worthless slugs! Time to earn your food. Today we're going to the dockyard, fighting in the Rusty Nail, which means we need to travel. You know what it means when we travel, right?" He paused here, but whatever he'd been hoping Victor's fellow prisoners would say didn't come, so he kept speaking. "That means you better damn well be on your best behavior. Urt, Ponda, and I will be quick on the batons, and I swear to the Ancestors that I'll make you piss blood before I let off the pressure. You get me?"

No one spoke, some of the prisoners shuffled their feet and grumbled, but it seemed that everyone had learned, or inferred, in Victor's case, that

Boss Yund didn't want anyone to answer his questions. Victor wondered if they were going to be allowed to just walk freely toward whatever the Rusty Nail was. Still, his hopes of sprinting away down an alley were dashed when Yund's lackeys, Urt and Ponda, came along the line, somehow producing leather belts out of thin air and handing them to each prisoner. When Ponda, the big furry, otter-looking fucker passed Victor a belt, Victor glanced at Yrella and saw she was already fastening hers around her waist. Victor did the same, noting that the clasp had an iron loop on it.

Urt came along then, leading a long, clinking chain. He went down the row, hooking the chain to each prisoner's belt through the iron loop. When he got to Victor, he reached out and yanked on the belt, making sure it was tight before he slipped the chain through the loop. After this went on for a few minutes, Yund cranked open the big barn doors and led the prisoners, in two lines, out into the dirty street, walking toward the fat orange setting sun. Victor glanced around, happy for his first real look at the city, and he caught his breath when he saw the two moons halfway up the sky opposite the sun. One was huge with rings around it, and the other was small and looked almost like Earth's moon. "*Chingada!*"

"What?" Vullu asked from behind him.

"The moons. Fucking hell, we really aren't on Earth, are we?"

"You didn't believe it until now?" Yrella looked back over her shoulder at him.

"I guess I did, but seeing these fucking moons makes it a little more real."

"Welcome to Fanwath, runt!" a huge, red-skinned man said over Vullu's shoulder. He was a good foot taller than Yrella, and he had big red spikes growing out of his shoulders; otherwise, he looked like one of her people. Victor just swallowed and turned back to the front, following behind Yrella and trying not to get noticed by any of the other prisoners. He glanced from side to side, noting the buildings and how they were different from those in Tucson. Every building was at least two stories high, and they were made from wood and stone blocks. He didn't see any stucco, nor did he see any concrete. The streets were made of bricks or, he supposed, cobbles. Trees were nowhere to be seen at first, but then they passed out of the shitty neighborhood where Yund's building was and he started seeing big tall trees with fucking weird-ass blue leaves. They passed some parks with blue-green grass and some tall stone buildings with actual streetlamps outside them, just starting to click on and give off a warm amber glow in the fading daylight; then they were out of the rich section of town and walking downhill to a more industrial area.

When they crossed through a rather busy square that reminded Victor of a swap meet, something startling happened. A few spots ahead of Victor, one of the other prisoners grunted loudly and hunched over, his broad, muscle-bound red shoulders flexing with strain, then he was suddenly sprinting away from the line. Victor saw his ripped belt fall to the cobbles, but as soon as he realized what had even happened, Ponda leapt through the air, trails of wispy orange smoke in his wake, and smashed down atop the fleeing prisoner. Victor heard the snap of bones and winced. Ponda lifted the large prisoner with one hand, gripping him by the back of the neck, and dragged him back to the line. The man thrashed and cried out, clearly in pain, but Ponda strode doggedly along as if he were hauling a misbehaving toddler. Ponda produced a pair of iron manacles, hooked one to the man's wrist and another to the cable connecting all the other prisoners, and said, "Thanks for letting us know you need a collar. Don't try that again."

"Poor asshole," Victor said.

"Yeah, he'll be stuck now; they'll collar him or put a mark on him like me," Yrella replied.

When they went around a corner and turned down another hill, Victor caught his first glimpse of the shipyard and a vast expanse of water. Victor had never been out of Arizona before, and when he saw the setting sun reflecting over the glittering water as far as he could see, he caught his breath and said, "Holy shit, is that the ocean?"

"No, it's actually a freshwater lake—Lake Beliss," Yrella said quietly, and Victor could see that she was also taking in the view. "My uncle had a ship and crew and fished out there when I was young." She sighed heavily. "Maybe I'll get back out there someday. It's beautiful out on the water this time of day."

"Especially if you have some wine and buttered freshwater qrell, right, beautiful?" Yund boomed from just behind Victor. How the fuck had he snuck up on them? Yrella ignored him, but Yund just laughed and walked up the line, jostling or yelling at various prisoners and laughing at their discomfort. They continued down the slope to the docks then turned to the left, following a crowded wharf street to an even more crowded yard outside a large wooden structure. On the building, above the wide open doors, a huge rusty metal spike had been mounted, and an equally rusted metal sign proclaimed, "The Rusty Nail."

# 5

## PIT NIGHT

The Rusty Nail was like a bad fever dream to Victor. As the sun set and the crowd grew, he and his comrades from Yund's stable were kept sequestered in a roped-off section of the enormous warehouse, but he could see the craziness unfold from behind the ropes just fine. Just as when he'd been led through the streets, he noticed the wide variety of people who cohabitated in this strange world. Red, blue, white, brown, black, tall, thin, short, fat, winged, feathered, furred, hooved, clawed, horned, almost anything he could fucking imagine was represented in the crowd of jostling, drinking, laughing, cussing, and fighting people. As the night outside deepened, the air in the warehouse grew heavy with odors and smoke and heat.

Yund wasn't the only boss who had brought a troupe of fighters. The various groups, some as large as Yund's and others with just one or two fighters, were all kept in roped-off areas on the back periphery of the Rusty Nail. The majority of the thousands of square feet in the warehouse's interior were taken up by stands for spectators, mobile food carts, desks for bookies, and a dozen or so pits. The pits were about twenty feet in diameter, about eight feet deep, and each had a big wooden sign on a post that had a number on it. Victor surprised himself by not being a nervous wreck. He thought part of it was that the warehouse and the pits reminded him of the inside of a big gym during a wrestling invitational. The pits were like different mats, and the pit fighters were like wrestling teams. He knew it was a bullshit comparison, but it was keeping him cool, so he didn't overthink it.

"This is fucking nuts," he said to Vullu as he watched the crowd grow and a band started playing some strange, wild music on a small stage over by the big doors leading to the festival-like yard outside the warehouse. The music reminded him of some fucking weird mix of country bluegrass and mariachi, with lots of stringed instruments and a really upbeat section of horns blaring over the noise in the crowd.

"Oh, aye. People love Pit Night in this city. There are at least four other locations like this. Yund even hosts a smaller gathering at the Wagon Wheel once a month."

"Did I hear you use my name, Cadwalli?" Yund turned from where he'd been talking to a sleazy-looking little blue guy and scowled at Vullu.

"No, boss, I think that came from just behind me. Not sure who it was."

"Right." Yund glowered at him for a moment, then turned back to the clipboard the little blue man was holding. After a few minutes and some grunted curses, Yund chased the guy away and then turned to his gathered troupe of fighter-slaves. "Listen up, you dogs!"

"Are there dogs here?" Victor asked Vullu quietly.

"Of course!" he said, then held a finger to his lips.

"We're overrepresented, and that little asshole just let me know that I need to adjust our roster to make up for it. That means some of you fodder will be fighting as a group against a stronger opponent. It's your chance for glory! You'll get a gold-tier reward when we get back to the Wagon Wheel if you win! Get yourselves ready—you know who you are." Then he turned and walked over to a table where a harried white-haired woman was frantically flipping through some papers.

"That's you, kiddo," Yrella said from behind Victor.

"That didn't sound like good news to me."

"Not really. Just remember: no matter how strong, a fatal wound is a fatal wound. There are no trinkets or potions allowed in the pits. Cut through a neck, pierce a heart, smash a skull, and you can win." Yrella rubbed the outsides of Victor's shoulders briskly, then gave them a good slap. "Get your fire up, kid. You need to win; there's no other option." Victor nodded, scowling, trying to get himself pumped. He slapped his hands together and jogged in place, and then Yund was back.

"All right, listen: Sarl, Turdwater, Asslick, Vel, and Victor, get in front of me!" Victor almost laughed when he heard some of the names, but adrenaline and nerves kept him from really enjoying it, so he ducked under the rope and stood in front of Yund. The others Yund had called jostled him as they came up from behind, pushing and shoving to stand close to Yund. Victor glanced at them and saw two blue guys, one with yellow hair and the other with hair colored bright rust. He saw another otter-person, but he thought it must be a female because she was slight and had some curves that stood differently than he'd seen on Ponda. The fifth member of their impromptu team was a fragile-looking man with lusterless, limp dragonfly wings on his back.

"Here, Boss," Yellow-hair said.

"Right, Asslick. Follow me!" Yund turned and started to wend his way along the wooden pathway between pits, stands, and tables. He shoved people that blocked his way, and generally people scrambled to get out of his way. Victor followed closely, aware of all the eyes on him but still wondering if there was any fucking way at all that he might get out of this mess. Most of the pits were empty, the first fights just getting lined up, but they passed by one with some action going on. As they got close, Victor stared into the pit and almost puked his guts out when a tall, bird-headed guy tore a blue guy's throat out with his oversized beak.

"Fuck me," he said, and strangely, the otter-woman reached forward and squeezed his shoulder reassuringly.

"Courage," she said in a soft, rich voice. Victor looked back into her big moist eyes, and he nodded, drawing his brows together, trying to look fierce. He looked back to Yund's back, followed him around one more empty pit, and then they were there, standing before pit number four. A good-size crowd was standing around the pit's edge, but they cleared the path for Yund, and he waded up to the edge and gestured with one hand.

"In you go, runts. Good luck! Taste some glory in your miserable lives!" Victor walked up to the edge, thinking about jumping down to the sand. Before he did, he glanced over his shoulder at his "team" first. The otter-woman was right behind him, but the bright-yellow-haired blue guy had dropped to his knees in front of Yund.

"Please, Boss! I can be valuable to you in other ways; I'm not cut out for fighting!"

"C'mere, Asslick. Stand up," Yund said in a surprisingly gentle voice. Asslick stood and walked closer to Yund, hope in his eyes, then Yund put one meaty hand around Asslick's neck and yanked him over the edge and into the pit. Asslick landed awkwardly on the packed sand, crying out as his knee buckled under him. "Get in the father-damned pit!" he roared. Victor didn't wait for another invitation and hopped down, landing lightly on his feet. Otter-woman followed, stumbling as she landed, and Victor caught her arm, keeping her from falling. The other blue guy hopped down, a nasty sneer on his face, then the tall, winged guy carefully scooted to the edge and hung down by his hands from the edge until his toes touched the sand. "My team's ready!" Yund hollered from above Victor's head.

A goat-man like Vullu stood on the other side of the pit, and he nodded, gesturing to the pit. The woman who hopped down into the pit from behind the goat-man looked so much like Yrella that, at first, Victor thought Yund would make her fight them. When she straightened up, though, Victor could see the differences. She was taller, more muscular, had little horns poking through her black hair, and her eyes were like smoky orange coals. She stood on her side of the pit, watching the five members of Yund's team coolly. A moment later, a blue guy with violet hair approached the edge of the pit with a spear in each hand.

"This fight will commence on my word. Are both teams ready?" While he listened to Yund and the goat-man answer in the affirmative, he tossed the two spears toward the far side of the pit, toward the middle. He looked at Victor's team, then at the tall Shadeni woman, then he shouted, "Begin!"

Asslick scrambled toward one of the spears; Victor crouched down and moved to his right, keeping the Shadeni woman in view. Otter-woman followed along with Victor, but the other blue guy stumbled back, trying to get to the pit's edge, his knee buckling with each step. The thin winged guy moved toward the horned woman with his hands out in fists. Asslick made it to a spear and turned, grinning, toward the tall red woman. She hadn't yet taken a step, but she smiled at Asslick and strode toward him. He charged with the spear, driving the point toward her stomach, but she smoothly side-stepped, then burst forward so fast that Victor thought she blurred a little, and drove the edge of her hand into Asslick's throat with such force that he flipped backward off his feet to land on his back with a resounding thud.

As Asslick lay writhing, choking, and scrabbling at his neck, the winged guy dove at the woman with surprising grace, dodging her kick then landing a solid punch to the side of her head. She smoothly stepped back, assessing the winged guy anew, then began to circle him. "C'mon," Victor said to Otter-woman. "She'll take us apart if we fight her one by one." Otter-woman nodded, then they started to circle the Shadeni woman, already named Big Red in Victor's mind, making her split her attention from the winged guy. The woman hadn't bothered to pick up the spear that Asslick had dropped, and Victor thought he could get to it pretty easily, but he wondered if he should. Would it just make him her next target? Instead, he moved over toward the spear, keeping his hands out, his center low, ready for the woman to charge him.

"Ghelli, just lie down, and I'll end this quickly," Big Red purred, her voice sending chills down Victor's spine.

"I didn't lie down when ap'Guin's men raped my wife. I didn't stand down when my men and I tore his household limb from limb. I didn't stand down when the Count burned my estate. I didn't stand down when the farcical trial sent me to the mines. I didn't stand down when I was sold to this hell. No, you will have to finish me kicking and screaming the whole way."

"Quite a speech! Did you rehearse that?" She glided over the sandy ground to the winged man like a rattler darting toward a mouse. They exchanged a flurry of blows and blocks that Victor couldn't keep track of, but he didn't care; he'd been waiting for this moment, and he flicked the spear up with the top of his old worn Adidas, grabbed the haft in his right hand and chucked it like a javelin at the woman's back. She must have sensed his movement because she whirled around as though to strike him, but it wasn't him ripping through the air; it was a sharp spear. Her outflung arm deflected the spear's trajectory, but it tore a long gash along her forearm. As she hissed and grabbed at the cut with her other hand, the winged dude landed a thunderous haymaker into the back of her skull.

Victor figured that if the winged guy were stronger, it would have been lights out for Big Red, but though she stumbled forward, shaking her head, she didn't go down. That's when the otter-woman strode forward past Victor, hands outstretched. Victor felt the air temperature drop, then white frost started forming around the otter-woman's hands, and a spray of tiny shards of ice blasted out, tearing into the Shadeni woman. She screamed, holding her arms in front of her face, then she whirled away, rolling over the sand to the spear against the far wall. The spray of ice shards sputtered out, and the otter-woman leaned forward, gasping for breath. Victor ran toward the other spear, looking around to see what the fuck the rest of his team was doing. Asslick was lying still on his back, eyes open and staring. Was he fucking dead? The other blue guy was scrabbling at the pit's edge, trying to climb out.

"You fucking dick! Get down and fight!" Victor screamed as he slid toward the spear feet first like coming in hot to home base. He scooped up the spear, scrambled to his feet, and whirled to face the Shadeni woman. She wasn't where he'd last seen her, though; she was standing over the otter-woman, spear buried in her furry chest. "Fuck!" Victor choked out when he saw the blood bubbling out of the woman's sad-looking mouth and her moist eyes slowly blinking while she scratched fruitlessly at the sand with her little, webbed hands. Big Red twisted the spear a couple of times, then yanked it free, trailing an arc of bright crimson blood.

"What's your name, Shadeni?" the winged guy asked as he circled behind her, trying, Victor thought, to get her to turn her back on him again.

"I'm Thessa-dak. Learn it well, Ghelli; my offer of a quick death has been rescinded." She didn't look at the winged man while she spoke; she hefted her spear and turned to the blue guy who had given up climbing out of the pit and was leaning with his back to the wall, edging sideways. Maybe the laughing, jeering spectators standing above him had something to do with his decision to stop trying to climb. A slow grin spread on Big Red's face, then she took two steps and let the spear fly. It punched through the blue guy's chest and pinned him to the wooden wall of the pit. A short scream tore out of his throat, but it quickly subsided to soft gurgling.

"Hey, *pendeja*, you think it makes you tough to fuck up some people weaker than you?" Victor didn't really give a shit about the chickenshit guy she'd just killed, but he was fucking torn up about that otter-woman. He felt tears stinging his eyes, but they were tears of futile rage, not fear. "This fight is fucking bullshit!" He started striding toward Big Red, reason having fled his mind. He dropped low, spear out, and went through the motions as he had practiced with Yrella and Vullu. At first, a tiny voice in the back of his mind said he was committing suicide, and though he tuned it out, he knew a part of him believed he was about to die. After he'd blinked away his frustrated tears, though, the only thing left in his mind was furious rage. Rage at being tossed into this pit, rage at being summoned to this world, rage at this fucking bitch that killed that soft little otter-woman.

She was fast and strong, but every time she started to push past Victor's guard, the winged guy would dart forward and land a kidney punch or a snap kick, and she'd be forced to back away to regroup. She was getting visibly frustrated; she was more than a match for either of them, but now that they'd found a rhythm, they were beginning to wear her down. Suddenly she hissed loudly and screamed, turning away from Victor and leaping through the air, a move that would have made a pro baller proud, and landed on the winged guy, driving him to the ground. Victor didn't waste a second, though; while she was bearing him to the ground, biting at his neck, Victor charged forward and drove the spear into her lower back, punching it through where he figured her kidney should be. She screamed and writhed, turning toward Victor, but the winged guy grabbed her in a bear hug, wrapping his arms and legs around her and holding her down. Victor yanked the spear out and drove it again and again, filling her back with gushing, spurting holes.

Finally, Thessa-dak stopped thrashing and lay still on top of the bloody, panting man. Victor leaned forward on his spear, lungs heaving for breath.

"I am Sarl, brother. I take it you are Victor?" the man gasped, trying to shove the woman off himself.

"Yeah, Sarl, that's me. Good to meet you. What the fuck . . ." Victor cut himself off as he watched motes of golden Energy start to bead up and coalesce all around Thessa-dak's body. A great swarm of them split into two streams and flooded into him and Sarl.

***Congratulations! You've achieved Level 3 Base Human. You have 5 attribute points to allocate.***

The euphoria of the Energy flooding him filled Victor with strength, and he stood up straight, looking around the edge of the pit. For the first time, he noticed the roaring of the crowd, their cheers and stomping feet. He felt high from the influx of Energy, and the cheers filled him with that old feeling he used to get when he pinned an opponent, so he held up his fist, screaming triumphantly into the face of the crowd.

# 6

AFTERPARTY

Yund practically yanked Victor out of the ring when he finally moved to
climb out. He pulled Victor up into a laughing hug and slapped his back
several times. "By the Lady's swingin' tits! That was well done, boy! You and
that old Ghelli made your Boss several sacks of beads!" He reached down for
Sarl's hand and pulled him out of the pit. "Come on, men! You can rest and
watch the rest of the matches. I'll even buy you each an ale. Dead Gods, but
it was fun to see Tarlen's face when his bitch died."

Yund turned to start stomping his way back to their roped-off area,
but Victor paused, looking out over the pit to the crumpled bodies lying
within. He hadn't cared for the blue guys, but that didn't mean he wanted
them dead. Then there was the little brown corpse of the otter-woman, one
arm stretched to the side, her face turned forlornly up at the dim, smoke-
hazed ceiling. Lastly, he looked at the body of Thessa-dak, the first and
only person Victor had ever killed. His heart lurched toward his throat
momentarily. He'd killed someone. He stared at her long, red-fleshed body,
the darker holes on her back, and the big muddy-maroon puddle that had
spread underneath her. He shook his head, turned, and followed after Sarl
and Yund.

When they got back to their area, Victor noticed that many of Yund's
prisoners were gone. He scanned the twenty or so faces sitting and standing around behind the rope, but he didn't see Yrella or Vullu. "Hey, Boss, are
Yrella and Vullu fighting?"

"That's right, runt. If you see Urt or Ponda, they can tell you which pits."
He turned and started talking to another member of the Rusty Nail's staff,
writing something on a clipboard as Yund rattled off some numbers. Victor
looked up and down the line but couldn't see Ponda or Urt, so he started
looking around the nearby pits, but the crowds were thick, and it was impossible to make them out. He decided to just wait around by the ropes, hoping
they'd be back by to pick up or drop off a fighter.

"That was good teamwork, Victor," Sarl said, walking toward him with
a big wooden mug in each hand. "Boss said we could have one, so I picked
these up on his credit." He smiled, and Victor took the mug he held out.

"Damn, thanks." Victor took a sip of the stuff, and it tasted like warm, flat
beer, but in that moment, it was one of the best things he'd ever tasted. He
took a long drink and sighed. "Man, who would think some warm beer could
be so damn good?"

"It's not the beer that's good; it's your hard work and your joy in being
alive—they'd make anything taste good right now. To living!" he said, knocking his mug against Victor's, and they both took another long pull. Some of
the other fighters gave them sour looks, but Victor pointedly avoided eye
contact.

"The hell do you two think you're doing?" Ponda waddled toward them,
his two center teeth jutting out of his half-open, scowling mouth.

"Easy, Boss. Big Boss said we could have an ale for winning our match,"
Sarl said, a lazy smile on his narrow face.

"Ha, he musta won some good bets." Ponda shrugged.

"Hey, Ponda, Boss said we could watch some matches. Can you tell me
where Vullu and Yrella are fighting?" Victor asked, noticing a slight buzz
already hitting him.

"Vullu is in seven, but I don't know about Yrella; Urt took her."

"All right, thanks!"

"Hang on, boys. If you're going off to watch fights, then I gotta collar
you. I only got two collars with me, so don't be gone long in case Boss wants
to let some others watch. Just watch a fight or two." Seemingly by magic, he
produced two black metal collars that he held out. Sarl backed away, though.

"I think I'll just wait here. I don't really want to watch any fights anyway,
and I hate the idea of wearing a collar."

"Who do you think you're fooling? Collar or not, you belong to Boss."
Ponda snorted, smirking. Sarl just shrugged, raised his mug to Victor, then
turned and walked back under the rope.

"Well, I wanna see Vullu fight, so go ahead, slap it on me."

"Smart lad," Ponda said, snapping the cold, heavy collar around his neck. Victor didn't notice feeling any different.

"What's it do, anyway?"

"If you disappear, Boss can use a linked amulet to make it so hot it melts through your neck."

"Fucking hell," Victor spat but then turned and scanned the pit signs for number seven. He saw six and figured seven would be close, so he worked his way over there. It seemed that most of the races in this world were generally smaller than the average human, but every now and then, he'd bump into a person who just seemed larger than life. They were physically imposing, but also, a certain presence seemed to bleed out of them that just made Victor feel insignificant and small. He tried to avoid those people simply because they made him feel shitty and because he figured that if he felt that way, his instincts were trying to tell him something, so he'd treat it like a warning.

He had finished his ale by the time he found pit seven, and he surreptitiously tried to make his way toward the edge so he could see in. Most spectators had to jostle for space on the floor, but a few sat in little bleacherlike stands and had an unobstructed view from one side of the pit. Victor knew better than to try to get into the stands, seeing as he was wearing a fucking slave collar, but he managed to worm his way close enough to the edge to see over the heads of a couple of blue guys who were shouting and cheering excitedly. When he finally saw into the pit, he could see why—Vullu was punching the shit out of a big Shadeni, and there were three other mutilated corpses in the pit. Victor saw discarded axes, knives, and a long pole with a small sword blade affixed to one end lying on the sandy ground. As the Shadeni staggered and fell against the pit wall, Vullu didn't back off, and he didn't pick up a weapon; he just kept pummeling him in the head. He smashed him into the side of the pit until golden motes started to coalesce around the bodies, and four streams of Energy slammed into Vullu. He stood, bloody fists in the air, and howled.

Victor started to cheer for Vullu, but then it hit him that he had just watched another guy beat the fuck out of someone until they died. He was looking at four corpses. Again. It all started to feel a little too crazy for him, so he turned and made his way back to the roped-off area where his fellow prisoners were waiting for their turns to fight or die. His earlier euphoria had faded with a suddenness that left him reeling. When he slipped under the ropes, Ponda wandered by and took the collar off his neck, admonishing him to stay put behind the rope. Victor stood there, looking around the hazy, noisy warehouse at all the strange people and listening to people screaming and roaring, and he wondered if this could possibly be real.

"You won!" Yrella's voice cut through his inner turmoil, and when she grabbed his shoulder, jostling it in excitement, he couldn't stop the smile that turned up the corners of his mouth, especially when he looked at her and saw huge raccoon-eye bruises around her eyes. The dark bruises looked positively black through her red skin, and he almost laughed aloud.

"Yeah, but what the fuck happened to you?"

She reached a hand up and tenderly touched the flesh under her left eye. "It shows?"

"Oh yeah! You look like a raccoon."

"What's a raccoon?"

"Uh, a small animal, but it has black fur around its eyes."

"Ugh, that asshole pounded my face like seven times before I slipped free."

"Jesus! Fucking prick, but you got him, right?"

"I did! But tell me about your fight; Vullu and I thought you were doomed!"

"Psshh." Victor made the leaky tire sound, then laughed. "Well, me and that winged guy, Sarl, ended up making a pretty good team."

"Winged guy? He's a Ghelli. Now that you've survived a Pit Night, I'm going to have to expand your education."

"Anyway, yeah, we managed to double-team this big red bitch . . ." He trailed off, then corrected himself. "Er, we managed to beat this really tough, respectable, Shadeni woman."

"Is that how you think of us? Red people? I guess to someone new here, that would stand out the most. What do you call the Ardeni? Blue people?"

"Uh, is that what they're called? Thanks, Yrella. I'm not trying to sound like an idiot, but sometimes that's what comes out. I spend too much time with my buddies, I think."

"Well, you used to. Now you're stuck with us." She smiled and slapped his shoulder, and Victor swallowed the lump that had stuck in his throat at her words and forced himself to smile back. They stood quietly for a few minutes, Yrella slowly massaging the skin around the bruises on her face. A few minutes later, Vullu arrived, and they all congratulated each other on their victories again. Victor zoned out a lot after that, and the hours blended together while they waited for all of Yund's fights to finish up. It was after midnight when they were all chained together and led back to the Wagon Wheel. Victor counted only twenty-eight fighters in the line going back, which meant that twelve had died at the Rusty Nail.

When they got back to the Wagon Wheel, the last thing Victor felt like doing was partying. He wanted to crawl into a corner, bury his head in some hay and go to sleep, hopefully dreaming about someplace other than here, about doing things other than killing. Yund had other ideas, though—his bets had gone very well, and he wanted to share the wealth, such as it was. He'd sent Ponda back ahead of the fighters, and when they came into the big exercise hall, there were three barrels of ale and a tabletop covered with meat, cheese, and bread. The fighters cheered and rushed forward, and Victor followed along with Yrella and Vullu.

Victor had been drunk a few times in his life. It wasn't all that hard for a guy to find a party where no one was checking IDs in Tucson; it was a university town, after all, and Victor had made a lot of friends on the wrestling team, being on varsity since he was a freshman. At that moment, if he couldn't fall into a sleep coma, he figured a drunken stupor would do just fine, so he grabbed a tin cup and set to it, downing three full cups of the bitter, warm ale before Yrella pulled him away from the table.

"Trying to black out the night's events?" she asked wryly.

"Easy to see through me, huh?" His head was buzzing pretty hard already, and he always talked too much when he'd had some beers, so he tried to really think about his words before letting them come out of his mouth.

"It's normal, Victor. A lot of the people put into the pits aren't killers—just criminals or people caught on the wrong side of a war. Me and Vullu were ready for this place, though—we were up to a lot of bad stuff, to be honest."

"Well, you seem pretty cool to me."

"Easy to be 'cool' when we get paid for it." She shrugged.

"Hey! You're using my words now. That means we're friends." Victor nudged her with his shoulder, grinning down at her.

"Ha, don't get ahead of yourself, kid. Sure, we're friends, though, unless Yund finds a way to make money putting us in the pit against each other." When she grinned at him this time, she was sure to show her long, sharp canines. Victor knew she was teasing, but still, a little cold shiver crossed over the nape of his neck because he realized there was a vein of truth in what she said. He shoved the thought to the back of his mind, though. Instead, he admired the way her lips curled up and the little crinkles around her eyes. She took a step back.

"Easy, kid. Just enjoy being alive for now, eh? Drink a few more cups, but just be ready to work your ass off tomorrow; Yund doesn't give days off." She turned and walked away, presumably to find Vullu and hang out with him. Victor went back to the table, a little annoyed that she was treating him like a kid but well aware that he wasn't exactly a match for her. He shrugged and filled his cup.

He glanced around the big exercise hall and noticed that, while they were being given some liberties, Yund was careful not to let his guard down—he had Ponda sitting on a stool next to the big open doors, and Victor could see a couple more of his lackeys lurking around outside. One of them was smoking something from a pipe, but they looked very alert. Not for the first time, Victor studied the walls, looking for another way out of the place, a way he could slip through some boards or anything. There was no way he meant to spend the rest of his life in this shithole, but he couldn't see an easy way out. He took a big gulp of his drink while trying to imagine a way past Ponda.

"Hey, Victor!" Sarl approached him from the other side of the table. "Why not come and sit with me and a couple of friends from my cage? I'd like to introduce you, seeing as I already told them what a great team you and I were!" The thin, wan-looking man looked different to Victor; he wasn't sure if it was because of an actual change or if it was that Victor had seen him fight and knew that under that unassuming appearance, he was a tough bastard.

"All right, man, let's get wasted."

# 7

※

# CORE

Yrella hadn't been lying about Yund not giving days off. The next morning and day went just the same as any of the others Victor had experienced in the Wagon Wheel. Wake up, get breakfast, work out, and go back to your cage to be bored shitless until the next day. At least it seemed to be going that way until the Boss himself approached Victor's little trio as they were working on his axe forms. "Runt! What level have you managed to get to?" he hollered as he got close.

"Uh, Level Three, Boss."

"Huh, not terrible. Listen, I may be a right scoundrel, but I keep my promises, and I offered your group a gold reward if you won. I already gave the old Ghelli his prize; now it's your turn, and I'm going to give you a choice."

"Okaaay . . ." Victor didn't know what to expect, so he looked from Yrella to Vullu, and they both maintained neutral expressions, so he just looked at Yund expectantly.

"Well, you came here at Level Zero, right?" Victor nodded, "Well, I doubt either of these two geniuses have helped you build a Core yet, eh?"

"No, I don't have a Core. I'm also holding five attribute points if you could give me . . ."

"That's not important right now; listen, I can either pay one of those book-brains from the academy a fee to come and help you make a good Core, or I can buy you a racial upgrade fruit. You're at the lowest level for your race, right?"

"Uh, how do I see that?"

"On your status sheet. What the runny shits have you two been teaching this kid?" He glared at Yrella and Vullu.

"Only to keep himself alive in a lopsided pit fight, no big deal!" Yrella retorted.

"Huh. Look at your status sheet, kid, where it lists your race. What does it say after it?"

"Um, Base One."

"Right, that's the lowest. I can get you a fruit to lift it to Base Two, or I can help you make a good Core. What's it gonna be?" He stared pointedly at Victor, who had no idea what the correct answer was, so he looked at Yrella. She mouthed the word "Core" pretty clearly, so Victor shrugged and turned back to Yund.

"The Core, I guess."

"Smart man. One racial upgrade probably won't save your ass during the next Pit Night but using Energy just might."

"Hey, Boss." Victor licked his lips nervously; he'd wanted to ask this question for days now.

"Yeah? I gotta go schedule this thing; what is it?"

"Well, I kinda got fucking kidnapped and forced to come here, and I have no idea how long you own me for. Is there any way I can get free?" He cringed back as the massive, red-skinned man frowned down at him.

"Huh, I'd call you ungrateful, but I guess you have a point. Listen, kid, most of the dregs I buy from those mages don't last more than a fight or two. No point talking about freedom when that's the case, right? Tell you what: you win five matches, and we'll make a contract. Nobody ever better say I ain't fair, right, Vullu?" Vullu nodded his head, but he wasn't smiling. "Right, well, I've got a business meeting, then I'll see about getting you some help with your Core. Get back to work!" He turned and walked away, not glancing at Victor, let alone waiting to see if he was amenable to his terms.

"That could have gone worse," Yrella said, slapping Victor on the shoulder. "Smart move asking him right after a big win."

"I didn't plan it that way, but yeah. I'm not really excited about having to fight four more times, but I guess it's something to shoot for." Victor looked around the big exercise room and, for the hundredth time, wondered if there was another way out of this predicament. What if he ran to the police or whatever and told them what had happened to him? It couldn't be fucking legal just to summon innocent people and then sell them. Every time his mind went down that road, he remembered the warnings about getting "tagged." He knew Ponda, Urt, or one of the other lackeys was always watching the door. Then he thought about how it was his word against Yund's and that no one, literally no one, in this entire world knew him or could vouch for him.

Shortly after that, they had to return to their cage, and Victor played around with Yrella's dice while she and Vullu did their meditation thing. They had just finished and were getting ready to teach Victor a new dice game when Ponda slammed open the main door and walked over to their cage. "Kid, follow me. Boss got your reward." He unlocked the metal gate and motioned for Victor to follow.

"See you later, Victor," Vullu called. Yrella just waved and leaned back against the metal frame of the cage, letting her eyes close lazily. Victor nodded to Vullu and then followed Ponda. He didn't know why, but it felt as if he were going somewhere to be punished. He hoped he was just being paranoid.

"Boss has that wizard waiting for you in his office. He said I have to leave you alone in there, but I'll be right outside the door. Don't mess with any of Boss's shit. Clear?"

"Yeah, I'm not going to mess with that dude's shit. You think I'm interested in his old socks and diaries and shit?" Victor scowled at Ponda; the big furry guy was acting like his friend Mike's dad, and it rubbed him the wrong way. Mike's dad was always assuming Mike and Victor were up to no good, and, while it was true a lot of the time, it was shitty to assume the worst of people. Then again, Ponda was a hired guard for a bunch of criminals they were forcing to fight to the death. It was probably healthy for him to assume the worst.

They got to Yund's office door, and Ponda opened it, giving Victor a little shove, then he pulled it closed. Victor looked around in the dim light, glad to see Yund wasn't present. Instead, a man the size of his six-year-old cousin sat in Yund's chair. The guy was wearing a shiny silver robe and had painted his entire bald head royal blue. There was a leaf painted in white on his blue left cheek. He cleared his throat and, in a surprisingly deep voice, said, "Ahh, Victor, I presume. Take a seat." He gestured to the wooden chair in front of Lund's desk.

Victor sat down, keeping his eyes on the strange man, and as he got closer, he saw that what he had at first taken for sparkly blue eyes were actually gemstones. The man had glittering little gems where his eyes should be! "Uh, hello," he said as he sat down.

"Hello. I'll cut to the chase, Victor. I was paid to perform a service, and I'm going to do it, then I'm going to get out of here. I'm not here to waste any time. Is all that clear?" His eyes stared at Victor, not blinking as normal eyes should, and it was unnerving as hell.

"Yeah, fine. What do we do?" He slouched in his chair, feeling like he was in front of an annoyed Dean of Students for the thirtieth time.

"I'm going to perform some diagnostics, and then I'll help you, with the aid of some tools, to form your Core. First, how much Energy have you banked?" Victor looked at his status screen.

"Two-twenty," he replied.

"That should be more than sufficient; I've helped Bogoli children form Cores with only forty-five."

"Bogoli?"

"My race. Now please don't interrupt my process with questions." He closed his eyes and twiddled his fingers around in the air in front of him, then a blue sparkly sphere appeared in his hand. He set it on the desk.

"How did you do that? I've seen a bunch of people pull shit outta nowhere in this world!"

"You don't have dimensional containers where you come from? My ring— it's also a storage device." He closed his eyes again and wiggled his fingers, frowning as if trying to find something. Victor thought about his answer, and he would have been a bit more shocked, but the truth was, he expected something like that. He'd been fucking summoned by wizards to get here, after all. The blue-painted guy grinned, and a pair of thick, lavender glasses appeared in his hand. Victor caught himself thinking of him as "the blue-painted guy" and remembered his foot-in-mouth conversation with Yrella after the Pit Night.

"Hey, what's your name, mister?"

"You may call me Dolo. It is an honorific meant for teachers and elders among my people."

"Er, okay. Thank you, Dolo." The little blue man nodded, then pointed to the sparkly, blue crystal-looking sphere.

"Please pick that up and hold it between your hands." Victor did as he instructed, picking up the heavy, cold ball and holding it in his two palms. It reminded him of a snow globe, and, as he looked into the glassy surface, he saw that the little sparkles were moving around. He stared into it, growing ever more fascinated by how the tiny lights flickered and flashed. The closer he looked, the more he realized the sparkles were all different colors, and they seemed to follow a secret pattern. He felt that if he just watched it long enough, maybe the right little stars, he'd start to learn the design. He snapped to himself when he felt a long strand of drool run down his chin and fall onto the thigh of his jeans. He shook his head and looked at Dolo.

"The fuck is this thing?" he asked, swallowing all the spit that had accumulated while he'd sat there with his jaw hanging open. Dolo, for his part, seemed unaware of Victor or his embarrassing drooling incident. He had on his violet sunglasses with brass-colored frames, and he was staring at the ball in Victor's hands. He didn't respond to the question, and Victor wondered if he'd been dumbstruck too. "Dude, you there?" He waited for an answer for at least a full count to sixty, then started to wonder if he should shake the guy. He was just beginning to move to set down the ball when Dolo cleared his throat.

"Wait! Don't set it down yet." That cleared that up. He wasn't dumbstruck; he was just an asshole who responded when he felt like it. Victor felt sorely tempted to set the ball down in spite of his request, but then he wondered if that would mess up the test or whatever he was doing, and then maybe he'd get pissed and leave Victor hanging with no Core. So he swallowed his irritation and held onto the ball, waiting for Dolo to snap out of it. Eventually, he said, "You may set the ball down now. What an interesting alignment. It looks like spirit might be the way to go with your Core class. Just a moment while I sort the proper tool."

"Why's that interesting? Is it good? Bad?"

"Hmm, it could be either, but it's interesting because it's quite unusual for the civilized races of this world to have a spirit marker for their Core alignment."

"Well, I don't know what you're talking about, so I'll take your word for it." Victor drummed his fingers, watching the little guy mentally going through his things. After a moment, a flat black stone, as wide as Victor's old school tablet, appeared in his hands, and he set it on the desk in front of Victor.

"This will sound rather obscene, but please put some spit on this slate." Dolo looked down, as if he was embarrassed.

"You want me to spit on it?"

"That's right. Just a few drops, please, no need to gather any phlegm." Victor sighed and leaned forward, squeezing some saliva out between his lips to let it drop onto the center of the slate.

"Excellent, thank you," Dolo said, then he pressed his index finger against a corner of the slate and closed his eyes. A moment later, the little puddle of Victor's saliva started to bubble, then it flashed into a bright red cloud of steam. Dolo nodded, staring at the cloud through his glasses, then he said, "Quite interesting, indeed! A rage affinity!"

"A rage what?" Victor leaned forward, watching the red smoke dissipate.

"An affinity. Listen, I'll need you to make a decision now."

"Wait a second! Can you tell me what affinity even means? Like on my status sheet, I have an Energy affinity line, and I don't even know what it is."

"Oh, bother," the little man sighed heavily. "I'm going to help you out here, Victor. Energy affinity is a touchy subject among the peoples of this world. Primarily because some people see races with low natural affinity as less-than. They believe that those born with a high affinity are chosen somehow and destined for greatness and dominance over those with lower affinity. Some creatures, like Yeksa, don't have enough natural Energy affinity for the System even to recognize them, hence their lack of language integration."

"All right, so I shouldn't talk about it? What's a 'high' or 'low' affinity?"

"Well, for instance, races like the Yeksa have generally less than one affinity. We Bogoli are quite gifted, and many of us have affinities in the sixes or sevens, though the average is quite lower. Now, I can tell your affinity for rage-attuned Energy will be quite high, and that's all you should ever tell anyone—that it's high. Only people you trust, mind you. I wouldn't ever mention that to someone in a position to do you harm." He looked toward the door pointedly.

"Huh, I get it," Victor said, looking again at his status sheet and his six-point-one Energy affinity.

"Now, are you ready to make a decision?"

"What kinda decision?" Victor frowned.

"You have a close alignment to spirit with a very strong rage affinity," he said, then looked at Victor's confused expression and said, more slowly, "You have a chance to have a powerful, specialized Core. It comes with some strings attached, though—such a strong rage affinity would mean that you'd struggle to channel unattuned Energy. Rage-attuned Energy is very potent, so that wouldn't be such a bad thing; it's just that the types of skills and spells that you can easily manage with such Energy are often violent and destructive. Hence the choice: create a specialized Spirit Core or forget about your affinities and create a very neutral generalist Core. I think you could easily form a Pearl Class Core."

"Why can I make a Spirit Core?"

"You are strongly aligned with spirit, which allows . . ."

"No, I mean, why am I aligned like that? What is the spirit?"

"Spirit is where our emotions, our feelings dwell. It's the part of us that isn't physical. Surely you must at least have some sense of it?" Dolo looked at Victor, a blue painted eyebrow raised up in an arch. He wasn't sure why, but unbidden memories came to his mind—memories of his mom and how he'd spent so much time talking to her long after the car accident. He'd spoken to her while he lay in bed, unable to sleep in his new room at his grandparents'. He'd told her about how he was scared at school, about how he missed his dad. He'd raged at her for dying. The thing was, Victor swore, even now, years later, that she'd spoken back to him. He swore he'd heard her saying, "Everything will be all right. Everything's going to get normal again." Did he have a sense of his spirit? Yeah, he'd say he did. He knew what Dolo was talking about.

"So it's because I'm close to my feelings?"

"Not necessarily close to them; maybe they influence you more than normal. Or maybe it has nothing to do with any of that, and the Ancestors have chosen to give you this alignment."

"Ancestors? You mean like my genetics?" Dolo looked at him blankly. "Like it runs in my family?"

"Oh, perhaps. Members of the same family often have similar affinities and Core alignments."

"When you say 'Ancestors,' are you, like, praying? Do you all worship your ancestors?"

"Praying? No. We Bogoli know better than that." He looked offended.

"Yeah, well, I don't want some generic bullshit; let's do that Spirit Core."

"Yes, that's an interesting choice." He paused and looked around the pit-master's office, then continued, "I think it will serve you well." He concentrated on the air in front of his face for a moment, then he started setting items down on the table: a little blue bag, a red candle, and a long golden chain and amulet. "Put this chain around your neck and lean back in your chair so the medallion rests on your navel." Then he opened the little blue pouch and took out a red crystal lens. While he was positioning the candle, Victor looped the chain over his head and pulled it down so the round, glinting medallion rested on the center of his stomach.

"What the fuck are we doing, actually? This is looking a little weird."

"Don't balk now, Victor; this was the right choice. Mediocrity never writes history!" He stared at the candle for a moment, and it flared to life with a crackling red flame at the end of its wick. He held the red crystal out in front of the candle flame, and as the light from the candle hit the angles of the crystal lens, a beam of red light came out the other side. Dolo angled the lens so that the red beam hit the center of the amulet on Victor's stomach. "Do you feel that warmth, Victor?"

"Ahh, yes! You're burning the shit out of me, dude!"

"No, Victor, it's just the Energy I had stored in this candle; it's fire-attuned, which is the closest I had to rage. It will work, though. It should work. Victor! Concentrate on the heat, feel how it echoes into your body, feel that heat flowing through your flesh. Now pull it to that hot spot where the amulet is."

Victor listened to Dolo, and not wanting to fuck up this procedure, he tried his hardest to do exactly as he said. He concentrated on the hot spot in the center of his belly, then he traced that burning feeling and felt the tiny echoes of it around his body, flowing around through veins or something. He tried to imagine scooping up all those little hot spots and pulling them down to the center of his stomach.

"That's it, Victor, good. Just keep pressing all that Energy in; feel where it passes through your body. The amulet will help you create your pathways, too, don't worry—once we trigger it with enough Energy." Just then, the amulet on Victor's stomach lifted into the air, flared a brilliant crimson, and began to pulse with a red light over Victor's stomach. Victor felt a hot, angry flare in his stomach with each pulse. The heat spread out, radiating into his body, limbs, and head. He was transfixed by the process, unable to contemplate moving, outside his body, watching the red rivers of anger spread through himself.

Victor focused his attention on that central point of heat in his stomach, and after a few seconds, his surroundings seemed to fade away, and it felt as if he was seeing inside himself. A hot, pulsing red star lay in the center of his being—his Core. He watched the red Energy from the candle rushing into him to meet with the more crimson Energy flowing through the channels in his body, collapsing into the hungry, pulsing star. Suddenly the star, his Core, seemed to collapse in on itself, shrinking to a tiny point of brilliant red light, then it surged out, like a star exploding, only in slow motion. A wave of red Energy expanded from the center of his being, spreading through his entire body, through every cell. Victor went even more rigid with the slow cascade of Energy, and when the wave finally passed through his extremities, he collapsed back into the chair. A sheen of sweat instantly coated his body, and he panted as if he'd just sprinted a mile after doing circuits.

***Congratulations! You've formed a Spirit Class Core, Base 1.***

"Well, that's my job done. I appreciate you making this tedious bit of shady business at least a little interesting. Good luck with your endeavors." Dolo scooped up his candle and other paraphernalia, then stood. All the while, Victor tried to get his breath back and take stock of his situation.

"It worked?" he finally croaked out as Dolo was walking around the desk, his little blue-painted head just a few inches higher than the top.

"Oh yes, I'd say you must have a powerful rage affinity after that display. I'd be careful using too many Energy abilities unless you want to lose yourself in it. I'm sure you'll gain more and more control with practice and, hopefully, a class that helps you refine your talents." Once again, he looked around the filthy office with a frown, then said, "Good luck," and knocked on the door. Ponda opened the door immediately, and Dolo walked out. Victor stood shakily and started to leave as well. Ponda blocked his path at the doorway, though.

"Well, what did that little weirdo do for you?" he asked with a note of genuine curiosity in his voice.

"Helped me form my Core."

"Ahh, you were that far behind, huh? I knew you were shit level, but I didn't know you didn't even have a Core. Well, back to your cage, runt. Two more days until the next Pit Night!" Victor nodded and walked toward the pens, calling up his status sheet as he moved.

| Status | | | |
|---|---|---|---|
| Name: | Victor Sandoval | | |
| Race: | Human: Base 1 | | |
| Class: | – | | |
| Level: | 3 | | |
| Core: | Spirit Class: Base 1 | | |
| Energy Affinity: | 3.1, Rage 9.1 | Energy: | 93/93 |
| Strength: | 14 | Vitality: | 10 |
| Dexterity: | 9 | Agility: | 10 |
| Intelligence: | 8 | Will: | 8 |

| Points Available: | 5 | |
|---|---|---|
| Titles & Feats: | – | |
| Skills: | • System Language Integration: Not Upgradeable<br>• Unarmed Combat: Basic<br>• Knife Combat: Basic<br>• Axe Mastery: Basic<br>• Spear Mastery: Basic<br>• Bludgeon Mastery: Basic<br>• Grappling: Improved | |

That little guy hadn't been lying about his rage affinity, whatever the hell that was. It looked as though his normal Energy affinity had gone down. "Well, here's hoping that guy didn't fuck me over."

# 8

## RAGE

Victor had to tiptoe when he returned to his cage with Ponda because he didn't want some pissed-off pit fighter to toss shit at him for waking them up. He didn't know if they'd actually do that, but Vullu had seemed serious about the risk, so he figured he wouldn't take chances. He crept to his corner of the cage, curled up on some straw, and went to sleep, listening to Yrella and Vullu breathing and the soft, deceptively soothing sounds of prisoners shifting around, snoring, and mumbling in their sleep.

"A Spirit Core, huh?" Yrella asked when he told her about his experience the next morning. She wore a frown and looked a little skeptical.

"Yeah, it was either that or some generic all-purpose Core, at least according to that Bogoli guy."

"Any affinity?" Vullu asked.

"Yeah, um, rage." Victor shrugged helplessly.

"That sounds portentous!" Yrella laughed.

"Portentous?" Victor wasn't bad at English, but he'd definitely done more wrestling than reading the last few years.

"Let's just say rage might not be a bad affinity for a pit fighter," Vullu joined Yrella in her chuckling.

"All right, all right, now that I have a Core, what do I do with these ninety-three Energy points?" They were sitting in the mess hall, waiting to be dismissed to practice.

"I can show you how to channel Energy into your strikes," Vullu said, mopping up the last of his eggs with a corner of his flatbread. "It should help you a lot, and as you experiment and fight and gain levels, hopefully you'll gain some skills or spells that utilize your particular brand of Energy."

"Yeah, and tonight, we can try to help you figure out how to cultivate," Yrella chimed in. Ponda's bulk filled the doorway, and he hollered for everyone to get out of the mess hall, so the three of them hustled out to the exercise hall. They moved to their usual corner, but a large Ardeni man—that's what the blue guys were called, if Victor recalled correctly—was occupying the space, twirling a large staff around.

"Zan, this is our space," Vullu said flatly. Zan stopped swinging the staff around and looked at Vullu for a few seconds, visibly contemplating his response, but then he just shrugged and walked toward the center of the gym, as Victor had taken to calling the space. "All right, kid, let's practice with fists first."

"Okay, what do I do?"

"Settle down; let me try to explain this. Hmm." He tapped his furry chin as he spoke.

"He needs to be able to feel his Core and his Energy first," Yrella said, resting a hand on Victor's shoulder.

"I think I can feel it. When that guy was helping me form it, I kinda looked inside myself and could even see it." As he spoke, Victor heard his words and blushed, realizing he sounded like some kind of New Age nutjob.

"Oh, that's good, Victor! Your affinity must be pretty high—I couldn't see my Core until I'd practiced meditation and found my center after quite a few days of practice." Yrella smiled encouragingly.

"Yes, good, Victor; can you see your Core now?" Vullu asked. Victor closed his eyes and felt the heat at the center of his body, turning his "eyes" inward toward it. There it was—a bright, pulsing, crimson star.

"Yeah, I see it." His voice sounded far away from himself.

"Good. Now, you know how you turned your vision into yourself? Now you have to imagine you have a presence there, that you can push and pull things around. Use your presence to pull some of the Energy from your Core into the channels around it. Let me know if you can do that." Vullu's voice also seemed far away, and Victor found himself more and more wrapped up in his study of his Core. Still, he heard what Vullu said, so he tried to imagine pulling on some of that red Energy, and as he did so, a strand of it broke away

and illuminated the pathways near it. Victor smiled and pushed the strand
into the nearest pathway.

"Okay, done it."

"Good!" Vullu's voice had a touch of excitement that Victor rarely heard
from the dour goat-man. "Now, visualize that Energy traveling up the pathway
toward your right fist. When you've got it, say so." Once again, Victor followed
Vullu's directions, pushing that strand of Energy farther into the pathway,
guiding it along his stomach, up his chest, down his arm, and into his fist. All
the way, it felt hot, pulsing with a heat that was more than temperature.

"Got it!" There was an edge to Victor's voice like a snarl lurked beneath
the surface.

"Now, open your eyes and punch the post!" Vullu said quickly. Victor
opened his eyes, and it seemed like a very faint red haze obscured his vision.
He glanced to his left, saw the wooden post, and punched it with his throbbing, itching right hand. He felt his body's muscle memory as he stepped
into the punch, twisted his hips, and drove his fist into the wooden post. A
resounding crack rang out as a flash of red Energy splashed out of Victor's
fist. Unbidden, a savage grunt rose from Victor's throat.

"First try! And he split the post!" Yrella cheered.

"Uh." Victor's voice was thick, and only his deepest vocal cords seemed
to want to engage, "Goddamn, I feel like punching more shit!" He stood up
straight, looked away from the post and his friends, and shook his head, taking several deep breaths.

"You all right, Victor?" Yrella started to reach a hand out to his shoulder,
but Vullu grabbed her wrist.

"I think his rage affinity is extreme, Yrella. This will be something he
needs to get used to slowly."

"I'm all right, but yeah, I was feeling a little nuts for a second there. Like
I wanted to fight, and it didn't matter who."

"Sorry, Victor; I don't know much about Spirit Cores. We had one woman
in my hometown with one, but she had a love affinity. She was well sought
after for her services . . ." Vullu trailed off, then continued, "The point is, I
have no idea how those sorts of affinities work."

"The good news is you smashed that post!" Yrella said, clapping Victor's
shoulder. "I think you just need to keep practicing, as Vullu said. When you
feel normal, throw another punch; hopefully, it'll get easier to control."

"Right, let's do some grappling in between. What do you guys say?" Victor asked, dropping to the sawdust to stretch. They agreed, and their hours

of practice were spent alternating between grappling, with Victor helping them get better at takedowns, and Victor channeling rage-attuned Energy into his fist and punching something. Each time, he felt the emotion rising in him, but never enough to entirely lose control. Victor knew if he channeled more than one rage-fuelled strike, he'd run the risk of losing himself in it. He hoped it got easier to control; otherwise, he didn't know how useful it would be.

That afternoon, Victor got to join in the "cultivating" that all the other prisoners did. Yrella took the lead in trying to explain it to him. "First, you need to understand that Energy is everywhere. It wasn't always so dense around our world, but when the System and the great oceans of Energy came to our part of the universe, it became a very tangible, important part of life." She paused to look into Victor's eyes to see if he was following her.

"Yeah, okay."

"Well, so the next thing you need to know is that the Energy in your Core is probably different from the Energy around us. Energy can have lots of different affinities. Some of the most common ones that you'll run into are elemental affinities—some Energy is attuned to fire, wind, or other elements. Other, less common affinities might be something like death or life or pestilence. I'm sure there are more than I know of and more than I can list. Like your affinity, for instance, I hadn't heard of a rage affinity before, though I knew things like that existed."

"Okay, everything you said makes sense, I guess, but I'm not sure how people end up with affinities." He gestured at himself to make his point.

"People who claim to understand that are probably lying," Vullu said from his corner of the cage.

"Right, let's focus on what we know: because of the different Cores and affinities, it's very common for people to cultivate Energy differently. These cultivation methods are often called 'drills' because it's a routine you repeatedly follow, slowly building your Core and thus your strength with Energy. You can even gain levels through cultivating if you're good at it and do it enough."

"So, you guys don't know how I'm supposed to cultivate, do you?" Victor could see where this was going.

"No, not exactly. We can describe our process, though, and maybe you can figure things out. Over time, you'll hopefully perfect your method, or maybe you can buy a cultivation manual for your type of Core down the road." Yrella smiled, giving him a chagrined shrug. "I'll do my best." Victor smiled back at her. She might be older and think of him as a kid, but she was fine as hell, and when she smiled like that, he was just grateful Yund put him in this cage when he'd first arrived.

"Hey, I appreciate any help you guys can give me."

"All right, so sit like I am, with your legs crossed and your palms open on your knees. Most people have Energy pathways open to the world on their palms. I'm pretty sure you do, too, judging by how your Energy-infused punch worked." Victor did as she said, feeling silly sitting there like he was going to do yoga or something, but Yrella nodded, reassuring him, and he settled into the pose. "Now, turn your mind inward, and look at your Core." She waited a moment and then continued, "When I cultivate, I move some of my Energy from my Core into my pathways and let it cycle through, all the way to my hands, and then back toward my Core. As I send it back to my Core, I try to pull some of the Energy out of the world with it, adding to my Core a tiny bit with each cycle."

"Huh, let me see . . ." Victor trailed off as he tried to do what Yrella described. He had no problem pushing a strand of his Energy into his pathway and then nudging it out along his pathways. It circled through a winding path around his abdomen, then out toward his left hand, and when he felt the burning, furious Energy bubbling up around his palm, he pushed it back toward his Core. Almost too late, he realized the thin strand of Energy he'd pulled from his Core had become a thick, surging river. He could feel it and see it with his inner eye, like a roiling red torrent that struggled to push out into the world, but he gritted his teeth and growled, pushing his will against the flood and forcing it around into a return pathway toward his Core. He tried to do what Yrella said and pull some Energy out of the air with it, but he wasn't sure he got any because his own Energy was so bright, hot, and full of roiling emotion that whatever Energy might be in the air around him seemed to pale into non-existence.

"Are you all right, Victor?" Yrella's voice sounded small, distant, and irritating, and Victor growled again, bearing down on the Energy flowing through his pathways, pushing it back toward his Core. It bucked and surged, trying to turn down other routes to find an outlet, but he fought it, sweat breaking out on his forehead and soaking his filthy green T-shirt. While he struggled, thoughts came floating out of the back of his mind into his consciousness, making him look at memories that he'd rather stay buried. He remembered his cousin on his mom's side texting him after his parents had died, "Why don't you come to grandma's house anymore?" He remembered asking to visit them and having his auntie tell him that his mom's family didn't want to see him anymore. Victor growled, clenching his fist and pushing against the surge of Energy. The flood of Energy had made a complete circuit now and was starting to return to his Core. Annoying little memories started to pile on; he remembered when he'd asked Paul to let him use his deodorant, reaching into his locker to grab it before he answered, and how Paul had slammed his locker on Victor's hand. He remembered the fight that ensued and growled savagely.

He felt a hand on his shoulder, and he opened red, bloodshot eyes and bared his teeth at Yrella, who had moved to kneel in front of him. "Victor! Push the Energy back to your Core! Don't cycle anymore." With a monumental effort, Victor closed his eyes, burying the murderous thoughts that had come out of nowhere. He turned his mind to his Energy and continued to push and bully it back into his Core. Finally, he felt the red, angry heat start to fade from his flesh, and he breathed deeply, burying all the infuriating memories back into the depths of his mind, so he could open his eyes without hate glowing balefully forth from them.

"Sorry," he said in a throaty voice and wiped his face, hoping the tears that had pooled in his bloodshot eyes would blend with the sweat that soaked him.

"Don't apologize, Victor," Vullu said from his corner. "You did a good job containing that surge. I think you'll need a lot of practice, and we need to learn more about Spirit Cores. Your Energy might not be cultivated the same as mine and Yrella's."

# 9

❖

# MASSACRE

That's right, pull that rope next to Lesha!" Ponda shouted at Victor. He wasn't sure who Lesha was, but he figured it was probably the Ardeni woman standing nearby. He grabbed the rope and yanked, and Ponda hollered, "Good!" He bent and pulled on a brass latch, and a massive section of the floor started sliding toward Victor, slipping underneath the wooden planks where he was standing. He kept pulling the rope, and he heard Vullu and another guy grunting as they pulled theirs, and the floor kept sliding, revealing the deep pit that had lain hidden the whole time Victor had been training at the Wagon Wheel. Pit Night was happening at the Wagon Wheel that night.

The venue wasn't nearly as large as the Rusty Nail, but there wouldn't be as many fighters here; according to Ponda, there'd just be another fighting troupe coming here to compete with Yund's stable. These were terms Victor was starting to pick up. Stable—like they were horses or something. Fighting troupe—a nice name for slaves who had to fight for your amusement. He felt some red heat start to spread through his body, and he clamped down on his Core, trying to think of something happy. His fuse seemed shorter now that he had actual rage Energy boiling at the center of his being.

It was funny how a person's living conditions could change their outlook. Over the last few days, as they practiced fighting, and Victor practiced using his Energy and trying to figure out how to cultivate his Core, he'd begun to look forward to the next fight. He'd put another point into strength, a point into dexterity to bring it up with agility, and the rest into vitality. He felt great, despite his shitty living conditions and boring diet. His muscles were ripped, his endurance was easily as good as when he'd prepped for State, and he felt vital—more alive than he could remember, and he was an eighteen-year-old athlete, so that was saying a lot. "Hey, Ponda, what's next?" he called after the pit was fully open.

"Now, you five over there need to get your asses out back; bring in the stands and set 'em up. Vullu, you know how it's done. Show the others." Victor followed along, helping Vullu or Yrella with one chore after another. They'd been at it all day, converting the practice gym into an exhibition hall. When they were finally done, and Yund announced that they would be in their cages until match time, Victor was tired but impressed by the transformation. The pit was bigger than the ones at the Rusty Nail, though there was only one. It was a good forty feet by forty and had tall wooden stands on three sides. The side that faced the open barn doors of the Wagon Wheel was open so that the riffraff without the funds to buy a seat could crowd around to watch the fights.

The afternoon passed quickly as Victor and his cage-mates rolled dice or dozed away their exhaustion. Sometime during the afternoon, lying on his back in the scratchy hay and sweating in the hot, stuffy air, Victor tried to think about his life back home. He was disturbed by how distant it seemed; by his reckoning, he'd been gone only about a week, maybe a little more, but it felt a lot longer. He wondered how his *abuela* was. He knew one or both of his aunties would be taking care of her, but she must be worried sick about him. He'd never been away for this long. Even when he'd "run away" in high school, he'd only stayed the weekend at a friend's house. He tried to picture Marcy and found he kept picturing a different girl he'd had a crush on during his sophomore year. What a weird thing to happen! He strained his mind for several minutes, picturing one friend after another, all the girls he could remember from his classes, and finally, it clicked—there was Marcy. He'd never had that happen before, and he wondered what was happening. He figured it must be a combination of his mind being amped up about the fight and all the stress he'd been under since he'd gotten kidnapped.

"Hey, Victor, just win," Yrella said. "They won't put you against anyone too high level—there's no sport in it. Well, unless they put you in a group against a stronger enemy like last time, I guess." Yrella smiled at him from her corner of the cage, and he blew out his breath, trying to banish the memories he'd purposefully been calling out of the depths of his mind.

"Yeah, I just want to get it started. I hate waiting around for my match."

"You'll have more fun during this Pit Night—since there's only one pit, you'll get to watch all the fighting," Vullu said, speaking into the air as he lay on his back with his eyes closed. Victor grunted and rolled over, cranking out some push-ups. He had so much nervous energy that he felt like crawling out of his skin. Vullu sat up, grunting, and laughed at Victor. "Imagine getting as fit as he is without any Energy, Yrella. You have to give him credit; I don't know how I'd cope if I didn't have my levels and Core."

"True. Your people must have strong wills to thrive in a dead world."

"Nah. First of all, not everyone thrives, and secondly, we have a shitload more tech than this world. We have all kinds of gadgets to help us cope with our weak-ass bodies."

"I think you're being modest," Yrella snorted. "Which is very unusual for you, I might add." Victor sat up and laughed with her.

"You're busting on me? Does that mean we're becoming real friends, Yrella? You're not just helping me for a bonus from the Boss?"

"Don't get too sure of yourself, kid." She laughed, though, and Victor could see she was happy with the banter. The door slammed open, and Yund came striding down the central aisle, banging his long, inscribed metal rod against the cages as he walked.

"Get ready to fight! I only need twenty-four fighters tonight, so line up by your cage door when you hear your name!"

"Aww, boss! Can't we watch the fights if we ain't fighting?" A tall goat-person, or Cadwalli, bawled out from a cage near the back wall.

"No! I barely have room out there for the paying customers and the fighters. Now shut up!" Yund yelled, then he lifted a clipboard and started calling names. Victor and Yrella got called, but Vullu didn't.

"Good luck, you two."

"He probably didn't have a suitable opponent for you, Vullu," Yrella said, reaching out and clasping hands with him. Vullu nodded, then held a fist out toward Victor. Victor nodded and bumped his fist, standing behind Yrella by the gate. Ponda and Urt went down the row of cages, letting out the fighters, then led them all out the door into the crowded, smoke-hazed, steaming hot exhibition hall. He led them to a roped-off area where the corners of two bleachers met. Just enough room between the two corners for a fighter to slip through and drop into the pit.

Yund was standing on one of the bleachers about halfway up, where he could look over his fighters and see into the pit easily. He looked down at the twenty-four fighters and shouted, "Yrella, you're up first. Into the pit!" Victor held his fist out for her, and she bumped it, smiling in that way of hers that made her yellow-green eyes twinkle, then she hopped down into the pit. Victor was taller than most of the other combatants, so when he pushed as far forward as possible, he could see most of the pit. He saw Yrella standing down in the sand, stretching her arms behind her back. A moment later, from the opposite corner, a lanky, blue-skinned Ardeni man dropped into the pit.

"First match!" A black-furred goatlike Cadwalli man shouted from a tall wooden stand overseeing the pit. He reached behind him and spun a crude-looking wagon wheel with pictures of various weapons drawn in charcoal around its circumference. The wheel stopped spinning, and the little arrow pointed at a picture of crossed axes. "Axes!" he shouted, and a person near each corner threw an axe down to their fighter. On Victor's side, the weapon was supplied by Ponda. Yrella knelt and picked up the single-bladed hand axe. Victor groaned quietly—she didn't like fighting with axes. The Ardeni man picked up his axe and flipped it easily between his hands. "Begin!" shouted the judge.

Yrella was fast, and this was the first time Victor had seen her go all out. She moved like a blur, gliding over the sandy bottom of the pit, dropping into a low slide, as she swung her axe, aiming to relieve her opponent of his leg below the knee. He saw it coming, though, and dodged to the side, flinging his axe. It tumbled through the air to land with a wet thud in the back of Yrella's skull. She fell to the side, twitching in the manner bodies do when they haven't yet realized they're dead.

"Victory! One match for the Broken Rope!" the judge screamed. Yund cursed and spat, uttering words Victor didn't have a translation for, though it wouldn't have mattered because Victor couldn't hear anything. His vision had gone red, and his heart had started beating like a runaway drum solo, pounding in his ears like the rushing of a waterfall. Yrella was dead, just like that. He couldn't believe it, he couldn't accept it, but he kept seeing her body topple and twitch. He felt himself suffocating and had to lean over, holding onto his knees and trying to breathe. Air wouldn't come, though, and the redness in his vision continued to deepen. His hands began to shake, gripping his knees tightly, squeezing the denim of his jeans into his flesh.

"I said you're up, kid!" Yund hollered. "Put him in, Ponda!" Victor thrashed and jerked away from the hands that grabbed his shoulders, but they were huge and strong, and though he struggled, he was tossed into the pit and fell sprawling into the sand. He struggled to his hands and knees, looking out over the sandy pit, wondering at how red everything was. There she was, her corpse just ten feet away. They hadn't even taken her out before they started the next fight? He gripped the sand, grinding it into his fists. He was still on his hands and knees, still shaking and grinding sand into his fists, when he felt the ground shudder slightly. He looked away from Yrella's body to see that his opponent had dropped in.

He stared at the big otter-man. He looked a lot like Ponda, but his fur was darker, with a slight red sheen. He was younger than Ponda, Victor figured, but he didn't care. All he cared about was that Yrella had just been slaughtered like one of his auntie's chickens. The idea of going back to that cage to just Vullu, of spending time here in this troupe of prisoners without Yrella, was unbearable. A choked scream of rage started to come out of his throat. "We have a rowdy one there, folks!" the goat-man judge yelled. A moment later, he shouted, "Maces!" Victor wasn't listening, though; he was pushing Energy out of his Core, into his pathways, letting it run rampant. He didn't try to control the flow; he didn't aim to turn it back to his Core. He just let it surge through his pathways, toward his hands, and into his mind. His vision had turned a deep red, and in his inner eye, replaying over and over, he saw Yrella dying, falling over to twitch like a broken thing.

"Begin!" the judge hollered, and Victor didn't even look at the mace that had been tossed near him. He exploded up from all fours, a wake of sand following behind, and smashed into his huge opponent. He moved like a wolverine, with no regard for himself or defense, simply lashing out like a wild, furious animal. His Energy-infused fists smashed into the otter-man, cracking bones and pulverizing flesh, pounding it into jelly. The otter-man's one feeble attempt to hit him with a mace was woefully too slow. Victor's right fist destroyed the otter-man's left knee. Victor slid around, dragging himself in close, using his opponent's thick leather belt as a handle, and landed a devastating left hook into his blubbery kidney. After that, everything was a red-hazed blur, with Victor simply pushing as much Energy out of his Core and into his fists as possible, savoring all the dark images that filled his mind as rage consumed him.

When he came back to himself, Victor was lying in a curled-up ball in the roped-off area behind the other fighters. He had a message from the System in his vision:

***Congratulations! You've achieved Level 5 Base Human. You have 10 attribute points to allocate. You have learned the skill: Berserk, Basic.***

***Berserk, Basic: Prerequisite Affinity, Rage. You double your strength and speed for a short while, losing yourself in the glory of combat. Your body becomes more resilient, and you benefit from rapid regeneration during the duration, though you lose all sense of self-preservation. You may suffer from the inability to discern friend from foe while under the effects of Berserk. Energy cost: minimum 75, scalable. Cooldown: long.***

Victor dismissed the notifications, then sat up, looking at the backs of the other fighters, cheering and hollering. Yrella was gone. Victor pressed his fists into his eyes, completely drained of emotion and exhausted; he didn't feel any tears, but he didn't want to look at the world.

"Thunderak shit, kid, that was a massacre!" Ponda said, squatting down beside him. "You all right? I had to drag you off that guy's corpse."

"No, I'm not fucking all right, dude. I'm not fucking all right at all."

# 10

## ALONE

"It's a shame, but it's the reality we live in, Victor." Vullu was trying to sound composed, but Victor could see the pain in his eyes. He felt guilty for making the older guy feel as though he had to comfort him. Vullu should be dealing with his own grief, not trying to console someone he hardly knew.

"Yeah. It sucks. Anyway, I'm sorry for your loss, Vullu." Victor moved to his corner of the cage and put his face toward the corner post, resting his forehead on the iron. He closed his eyes and tried to think of anything other than Yrella's twitching corpse.

"She was your friend, Victor. Just so you know. She joked a lot, but she told me she was glad Yund threw you in our cage."

"Jesus, man. I don't wanna hear that! What good does it do anyone? She's fucking gone!"

"She's not gone if we carry her with us, Victor. Your relationships with the people you meet shape you, you know. Knowing she was fond of you changes the paths you will walk, whether you realize it or not. So, it's good that you know." Victor gently banged his forehead against the iron post, feeling the way it vibrated his skull.

"If you say so, dude." He heard a cell door clang, and he looked up the aisle to see Ponda walking away from a cage toward the exit. "Hey, Ponda," he called.

"What, kid?" The big furry man glanced at him as he strode by.

"When's the next fucking fight? I need to get five done as soon as possible."

"I wouldn't wish too hard, kid. Boss saw you massacre that guy, you know; he's gonna try to make some money off you. Your next match might get a little uglier, if you get my meaning."

"*Chingado*! Of course he is. Well, I don't care; when is it?"

"Four days, and it's at the Nail, so you might get more than one fight. Boss's stable is running light." Ponda didn't wait to see if that answer satisfied Victor; he kept walking, slamming the door behind himself.

"Well, I got ten points to spend. Any advice, Vullu?" He turned and slid down onto his ass, folding his legs in the position that Yrella had taught him.

"I know it might seem counterintuitive, but you might want to put some points into will and intelligence; they help with Energy manipulation. It might help you figure out a cultivation drill if you increase those attributes." Vullu sat down, lay back, and closed his eyes, apparently done talking. Victor looked at his status sheet and decided to put two points each into intelligence and will, bringing them to an even ten. Then he dumped his other six points into strength. The System had said his Berserk skill would double his strength and speed for the duration—might as well capitalize on that. He knew that if Yrella were there right now, she'd nag him to try to figure out his cultivation method, so he rubbed a knuckle into his forehead, trying to focus, and then he took a deep breath and looked into his Core.

As he studied the throbbing red star, he began to make out details about it that he hadn't noticed before. The pulsing almost seemed like breathing, and as it swelled and contracted, he saw little waving tendrils of Energy that existed only briefly. As he studied those tendrils, his mind began to wander, and it went where it always seemed to go since the pit fight: Yrella. He saw Yrella smiling, her eyes lighting up. Then he saw her scowl when he complimented those eyes. He remembered her laughing when he lost over and over at dice. He remembered her standing next to him after the first Pit Night, drinking warm ale like it was Christmas dinner. Then he remembered her getting killed, and all of his memories began to run red in his mind.

Victor jerked out of his memory of Yrella when he noticed his Core was pulsing more rapidly and brightly, then he felt something subtle at the edge of his awareness, and he tried to track it down with his mind. He traced his pathways, then he became aware of the Energy outside his body. He could feel the warmth of it as it drew near, slowly changing from bright, yellow Energy into red, angry Energy that slipped into his pathways, drifting slowly toward his Core. Was he cultivating? What had triggered it? Had it been his thinking about Yrella? Victor blinked back tears as he thought how happy she'd be if she knew he'd figured something out.

He determined that he needed to prove his hypothesis, so Victor started reminiscing about things that pissed him off. His old gold standard had been his parents' deaths, but that had grown dull over the years, no longer the cutting blade that filled him with rage. Instead, he thought about the pit fights; he thought of that friendly otter-woman. He thought about how he never learned her name or even bothered to learn what her race was called. He dealt with those otter-people every day, and he didn't even know their proper name. What a self-centered asshole! He felt his Core throb, and a wave of hot rage surged through his pathways.

Victor remembered what it felt like to be helpless while that wizard asshole had dragged him through the streets and sold him to his place. He remembered his dismissive, snobby attitude and how he'd made him feel as helpless as a little kid. Victor imagined breaking out of his spell and beating the shit out of him, and his Core pulsed. This time he was ready for the surge of rage, and he watched it as it cycled his pathways, drawing ambient Energy into him as it circulated back to his Core. He was doing it! Victor spent the next hour dredging up painful memories, really examining them, and soaking in the rage that boiled out of his Core. He was startled out of his meditation when a System message appeared in his vision:

***Congratulations! Your Core has advanced to: Spirit Class, Base 2***

He studied his pulsing, burning Core and could see that it was larger and the flames more violent than when he'd started. He began to take deep breaths and think calming thoughts, but it took a good half an hour before his vision was no longer tinted red and he could breathe without wanting to snarl.

"You figured something out, didn't you?" Vullu asked. Victor looked at him; he'd sat up in his corner. He sat, watching Victor, waiting for an answer.

"Yeah. Seems I need to focus on shit that pisses me off, and then my Core starts to pull Energy from around me, converting it to rage Energy." Victor sat back, feeling exhausted and, for once, able to close his eyes without picturing Yrella.

"Is that healthy?"

"I don't fucking know, man. I doubt it, but I'm kinda fucked anyway, right? Not like I can take this Core out." Victor couldn't help snapping, his frustration rapidly reigniting his anger.

"No, I suppose you can't. Not with the resources available to us, that's for sure. How do you feel now?"

"A little annoyed at the twenty questions, but I was feeling better. I can close my eyes without thinking of, well, you know." Victor shrugged and sighed deeply, lying back and throwing an arm over his eyes. "Anyway, I gained a Core level, so that's something. Let's talk more in the morning; I'm wiped, bro."

"All right, Victor." It sounded as though Vullu had lain back down, but Victor didn't open his eyes to check. He just focused on the blackness behind his eyes and tried to drift into it. Before he knew it, he was asleep.

For the first time since he'd been brought to this world, Yrella didn't wake him up the next day. Victor and Vullu went through their routine as usual, and when they returned to their cages in the afternoon, Victor spent another few hours steeped in memories that filled him with frustration and rage. When he finished, his Core was hot and dense, and he felt it might level again soon. He was spent and slept again, not chatting with Vullu and not playing dice. This cycle repeated for two days. On the third day, Victor's Core leveled again, and he noticed he had more than three hundred Energy points available to him now. He opened his eyes, breathed deeply, and painstakingly began the process of pushing all his rage-attuned Energy into his Core, slowly coming out of the fury his cultivation drill seemed to induce.

"Your Core leveled again." Vullu didn't phrase it as a question, so Victor didn't answer. They hadn't spoken much over the last few days—something was off with their dynamic that Victor didn't think could be fixed. The piece that made them connect had been Yrella. Maybe that wasn't true, but Victor believed it, and so did Vullu, which made it true enough. His rage contained and his vision clear again, he exhaled slowly and looked at Vullu. The Cadwalli was a dangerous fighter; Victor knew he held back a great deal when they sparred. He looked miserable, though, and Victor wondered what the old guy had to live for if he ever got out of here. Did he have a family? He'd known Yrella outside this place; had they built plans together for when they might someday be free? Were those plans dead now?

"You doing all right, Vullu?" He didn't know where the question had come from, but Victor was glad he said it. Sometimes stupid things escaped his mouth, but this had been right—he could feel it.

"I think I'm going to leave, Victor. I earned my freedom a while ago; I'd been staying to help Yrella pay down her debt."

"Oh? Well, shit, man. I can't blame you. I'd wanna get out of here, too." Victor was screaming inside his mind, but he managed to keep it out of his voice.

"Really, Victor? I'm worried about you, but my heart is broken, and I think I need to seek out loved ones." Victor's mind spasmed at this latest statement. Was he a complete bonehead? Had Yrella and Vullu been, like, together the whole time? He thought they were something like friends or partners in crime; he hadn't noticed romance between the two. His mind flashed back to how Yrella used to sleep with her head on Vullu's thigh, and he groaned inwardly. He was an idiot.

"Vullu, you've been through hell, bro. You should get the fuck out while you can. I'll fight my way free; I'm determined. If nothing else, I'll do it for Yrella." Victor knew it was bravado, but he didn't care. He couldn't stomach the idea of Vullu sticking around this place because he was worried about him. Vullu studied Victor for a few long moments, then he stood up and started kicking at the cage door, making it rattle loudly with each blow of his hoof.

"Victor, I'm not going to forget about you. Keep working on getting out, and I'll see what I can figure out from the outside." The exit door slammed open, and Ponda came waddling down the aisle.

"What?" he barked.

"I'm checking out, Ponda. Take me to Yund."

"Ha, we was betting on when you'd do this. Urt's gonna be happy." While Ponda fiddled with the cage door, Vullu stepped over to Victor and held out a hand. Victor took it and, for maybe the last time, gripped his sparring partner's hand, wincing at his iron grip.

"Take care," Victor said. He wanted to say more, but he didn't trust himself. He'd almost choked up on "take care."

"Remember what I said—keep working for it. I'll try to help you out." With that, he strode out of the cage and down the aisle with Ponda, and when the heavy door slammed shut, it felt more final than ever before. Victor sat down, looked at his empty cell, and wondered what he could have done to change things, what he could have done not to be alone.

# 11

# BERSERK

Victor didn't sleep well the night Vullu left. He lay in his cage, feeling he had way too much room to himself, and listened to the sounds of all the other prisoners. They came drifting over the wooden slats, between the bars of his cage, snoring, mumbling, farting, and rustling around in the scratchy hay. Victor used the piss bucket twice, always looking back and forth in the dim room, trying to see if any of the cages had wakeful occupants. There was one thing he could praise Yund's prisoners for; they minded their own business when someone was using the bucket.

Victor, bored in the middle of the night, decided to count the other prisoners, so he quietly moved around his cage, counting the slumbering, dark shadows in the other enclosures, and came up with only nineteen. Hadn't there been more than forty when he first arrived? More than fifty percent dead in a week or so? Even someone who wasn't a math whiz could see those odds weren't great. The stark reality added to the thoughts keeping him awake, and he lay on his back, staring at the ceiling until the door crashed open and Ponda came in, screaming at everyone to wake up.

"Big night at the Nail, vagabonds! Boss needs you to perform—make up for the dead and wounded from the last one. He's offering rewards; time to find your guts!" He stomped on the wooden planks and howled with his big furry fists pumping in the air.

"Hey, Ponda," Victor said when the furry, rotund man approached his cage. "Can you tell me what your people are called? I keep calling you an otter-man in my head 'cause we don't have people like you in my world."

"Ha, kid, you always surprise me with what comes outta your mouth. My people are the Vodkin, and we're the toughest damned people on Fanwath; remember that!" He unlocked Victor's cage and said, "Now go eat some breakfast, then go to Boss's office; he wants a word with you. You know the way, right? You're not a lost little huldii without your friends, are you?"

"If that's a joke, I don't get it; I don't know what the fuck a huldii is. I know the way," Victor replied, slipping out of the cage, under Ponda's big arm.

"Hurry up, runt!" he growled after him, and Victor picked up his pace, despite trying to walk out coolly. He picked up his usual plate of slop and flatbread and sat down by himself, ignoring the glares he felt from the other prisoners in the mess hall. Ponda might have been teasing, but Victor did feel the absence of his friends. He'd been missing Yrella, but even when they hadn't been talking much, he'd taken some comfort in having Vullu to hang around. He wolfed down his food, then left the mess and tapped on Yund's wooden office door.

"Come in!" the boss's voice bellowed, vibrating the flimsy door in its frame. Victor opened it and stepped into the cramped, messy space. Noting the distinct scent of grease and spices, he looked at Yund's desk and saw a big wooden platter covered in congealed, moldy food scraps.

"Boss, you wanted to see me?"

"That's right, kid. You've got two fights under your belt now, and I didn't forget my promise to you. Win today, and you'll be closer to a contract with me. We're short fighters, and I don't have new 'recruits' coming for another week, so I'm scheduling more than one match for most of you. Because you're Tier Zero, I think I can get you into three or four. You up for it? It's your chance for glory and to win a contract from me."

"Do I have a choice?" Victor, truth be told, wanted to kick some ass. He knew that he was thinking of these Pit Nights like wrestling matches, at least subconsciously, and if he slowed down and really analyzed what was coming, he'd be less enthused: death and bloodshed and maiming weren't as appetizing as pinning an opposing school's wrestler.

"No. I wanted to gauge your enthusiasm, though—might have some bearing on what kinda fights I get you into."

"I just want to earn a contract; I don't give a fuck anymore. Put me in with the asshole that killed Yrella."

"Ha, you'd be dead before you picked up a weapon. You're not ready for that kind of speed; he was Tier Two. So was Yrella, by the way."

"Tier Two?"

"Yeah, kid, higher than Level Twenty. You sure don't know shit, do you? Don't worry; if you live, you'll have some new cage mates soon, and you can ask them all the dumb questions you want. Now get outta here, so I can figure out this lineup." He picked up his clipboard and waved it around. Victor turned and walked out, going over to the corner of the gym where he and Vullu had been practicing the last few days. The big Ardeni guy, Zan, was already there, punching the wooden beam that Vullu used to like to use. Victor ignored him and started doing a little circuit of push-ups, crunches, and pull-ups on the nearby bar.

"Your daddy's not here anymore, huh?" Zan said after a while, watching Victor finish a set of pull-ups.

"Fuck you, man." Victor dropped and went into his next circuit, sweat already pouring out of him, soaking the filthy, stinking shirt he'd worn now for over a week. Zan snorted and turned to punch his post, apparently not wanting to push the matter further. Victor hadn't been bullied in a long time—not since middle school when he'd hit a growth spurt and joined the eighth-grade wrestling team. He knew there were people in the Wagon Wheel that could beat his ass without any struggle. Vullu had made that clear to him, trying to help him learn to keep his mouth shut, so he didn't offend any of the "monsters" in the place. He figured the best way to deal with guys like Zan was to act as if he wasn't scared but not to do anything to piss them off. Zan seemed content to ignore him after the jab about Vullu, so he kept working out, moving to weapon practice, starting with knives.

It wasn't nearly as much fun stabbing and thrusting into the air without Vullu or Yrella to encourage him or even mockingly correct his form. He'd decided to turn in the knife and get a spear when Ponda screamed at everyone to get all the gear put away and line up. Victor was one of the first in line, and he watched the others filter in from the cage room or the mess hall; he'd never seen the fighters looking more bedraggled, tired, and low energy. "Time to chain up!" Ponda yelled. "Fights are starting earlier today." He and Urt moved among them, handing out belts and connecting the chain, then they were off, just a single column of eighteen fighters. Yund wasn't to be seen, but Victor supposed he'd probably gone ahead to finalize the matchups.

It was bright out while they took their circuitous route through the city and down to the docks. Victor kept his head up, meeting the glares of the people that scurried out of their way or openly judged; the average citizens took pride in looking down on the prisoner-fighters. At least that's the way it seemed to Victor. He saw a lot of beautiful women; the Ardeni had especially bright eyes with exotic colors, and they caught him staring a few times. Looks of disgust chased his eyes away, and he almost blushed, but a cold sliver of anger kept the blood out of his cheeks. Who the fuck were these pretty people to judge him? He wasn't a criminal and hadn't done anything to deserve his treatment. Or had he? His friend Tracy liked to talk about "karma"—had he done something to deserve getting summoned to this place?

He tried to pay more attention to the kinds of buildings they went by this time. He saw a lot of houses, places that looked like restaurants, shops, a few big government buildings, and, of course, all the warehouses down by the docks. The Rusty Nail wasn't as crowded as last time when they arrived. The sun was still far above the eastern horizon, so Victor figured more people would be coming as the night progressed. Ponda led them around the walkways bordering the various pits and then put them into their roped-off area near the back wall. Victor leaned back against the wall, trying to avoid looking at or talking to any other prisoners. He wasn't in a mood to mess with those guys on a good day, and he was feeling particularly moody.

He leaned there with his eyes closed, arms folded on his chest, until the buzz in the air grew in volume and a different kind of energy permeated the atmosphere. When he opened his eyes, he saw that the crowd had filled out, and people were starting to lead fighters to pits. Victor looked around the periphery of their holding area, trying to spot Yund, and finally saw him striding toward the Wagon Wheel fighters.

"Listen for your names, lads!" he hollered, ignoring that a third of his fighters were women. Ponda and Urt started calling names, but Yund pointed at Victor and beckoned him forward. "You've got four fights. If you win, kid, I'll set you up a sweet contract when we get back. I know you might be worried about the terms, and I want you to feel motivated, so you can count on a gold level reward in addition to your contract. Sound good?"

"Uh," Victor started. No, it didn't fucking sound good. Four *pinche* fights in one day? Was he trying to get rid of him? Still, Victor knew he couldn't argue or change the man's mind, and he'd always been game for a challenge. He couldn't help feeling the parallels between Yund's little speech and what his coach often did before a big meet. Did he ever act like he couldn't win when his coach spoke to him? Hell no. "Yeah, it sounds fucking good."

"That's the spirit! Follow me." Yund turned and started wending his way toward one of the bigger pits near the center of the warehouse. When they came up to the edge of ring number two, Victor stopped in his tracks.

"What the fuck are those?" Pacing around and hissing up at the spectators in the center of the sandy pit were five gray-skinned little men with long black nails and stringy, patchy white hair. They were wearing rags and waving clubs and knives, trying to intimidate the crowd. Their thin lips pulled back when they hissed, revealing mouths filled with pointy, jagged rows of teeth.

"Those are Yeksa, kid. Your first match."

"Uh, who else is going in there with me?" Victor looked around, guessing some other low-level fighters would be going in against the Yeksa with him.

"Ha, you're on your own! Just go crazy—they're weak. Don't let them swarm ya! Now get up to the pit's edge and wait for the word."

"You signed me up for four fights, and the first one is against five fucking dudes?" Victor scowled at Yund, but he stepped up to the edge, staring down at the gray little savages. They didn't seem to speak, just hissed and growled, brandishing their weapons.

"Choose a weapon," said a smooth-shaven Ardeni. In each of his blue hands, he held a different weapon—a club and an axe. Victor reached for the axe out of reflex; he'd spent a lot more time with it than other weapons because Vullu favored it over other weapons. The Ardeni looked at Yund. "Ready?" Yund nodded, and the man shouted, "Begin!" Victor stepped forward and thought about his Berserk ability, using the knowledge the System had put in his head to activate it, sending a surge of rage-attuned Energy flooding out of his Core and into his body. His vision turned a deep crimson, fury filled his mind, and, as he fell to the sand, his back arched, his muscles visibly convulsed, he roared like a caveman.

He landed in the sand on all fours, his mouth hanging open in a maniacal grin, a crazed look in his eyes. The axe was still nestled in his grip, and he lifted it in front of his face, where he studied the blade for a moment, his brow furrowing in fury. The Yeksa, for their part, hissed and, as one, charged over the sand toward Victor. He was still transfixed by something, staring at the axe, when the Yeksa fell upon him, clubs and knives pummeling and perforating his flesh.

The image of Yrella falling and twitching when the axe hit her head faded, and Victor confronted his reality as little wooden clubs smacked down onto his skull, shoulders, and back. At least two knives bit into his back. Boiling heat had filled his flesh, and Victor roared with the terrible fury that suffused his being, lashing out with the axe and surging to his feet. The steel blade of the axe caught one Yeksa on the shoulder and severed its arm. Victor roared and began to lay about himself with the axe, ignoring the clubs and knives coming toward him. As the little knives sank into him, and the Yeksa pulled them back for another strike, his flesh pulled together, and almost no blood seeped out. The clubs' contusions healed even as the Yeksa lifted them for another strike. Victor screamed and willed more rage Energy out of his Core and into his muscles, and he smashed his axe back and forth, wading through the little savage men like a reaper at harvest.

As quickly as the fight began, it was over, and only pieces of the Yeksa remained. When Victor saw no more immediate enemies, he looked around outside the pit, and when a particular face triggered his rage, he hurled his axe at him. Luckily for Victor, far more powerful people watched the fights than he, and his axe was easily intercepted. He paced and growled, visible steam rising from his blood-soaked clothing, and then it was over, and he fell to his knees, limply staring at the sand. He remembered the fight, but it was hazy like snatches of a dream. He looked around the pit, saw the broken, dismembered bodies, and almost vomited, but then thin streams of yellow Energy motes began to flow into him from the five different corpses, and his nausea retreated, his exhaustion faded. As he climbed from the pit, he waved away his notification:

***Congratulations! You've achieved Level 6 Base Human. You have 5 attribute points to allocate.***

# 12

✦

# CROWD FAVORITE

Yund clapped Victor on the back, put his big meaty arm over his shoulders, and led him back to their staging area. On the way, he said, "I told you those things are weak. You made minced cutlets of 'em. Listen, your next fight isn't in this bracket; we gotta wait for the first bracket fights to wrap up, so you might have twenty minutes or an hour. Go shake out the cobwebs, get some water, and be ready!" Then he propelled him toward the rope, and Victor slipped under, looking for their big water barrel.

Sarl was standing near the barrel, and he handed Victor a cup. Victor drank deeply, sighed, then scooped the cup into the barrel to refill it. While he poured water over his head, shirt, and arms, trying to get some of the blood off, Sarl said, "Hey, Victor, I wanted to say I was sorry to see what happened to Yrella." Victor looked up sharply, squinting at Sarl's face, and he saw only sincerity.

"Thanks, man." He felt guilty inside that he should have a nice thing to say about Yrella whenever she came up, but he just didn't have those kinds of words. Not right now, in the middle of a Fight Night and covered in blood.

"I take it you won your fight, eh?"

"Yeah, one of 'em."

"You have more than one? As far as I know, I only have one today."

"Yeah, you heard him. They're short or some bullshit. I have four fights. Well, three now." Victor shook his arms off, then downed a third cup of water, loudly sighing as he hung the cup back on the peg.

"Four? That seems extreme; I'd be tempted to wonder if Boss was trying to get rid of you."

"Nah, man. I think he knows about my Core. He saw me fuck that guy up the other night, and I think the guy who helped me make my Core told him about it." Victor had been thinking about Yund's change of attitude toward him, and it only made sense that the guy whom Yund paid would tell him whether he'd had any success. It seemed that a rage-attuned Core was perfect for Victor's situation. All Yund had to do was drop him in a pit with only enemies and tell him to go nuts. Victor didn't know how effective something like Berserk would be among high-tier fighters, but it seemed to be overpowering at his current level.

"Your Core?"

"Yeah, he paid some guy to help me figure out what kind of Core to form, then help me with it. Didn't you get a reward for winning that fight with me?"

"Oh, he offered me a racial upgrade fruit or extra time off my sentence. I took the time off."

"Does that motherfucker ever let us take a shower or something?" Victor asked, looking down at his shirt and jeans.

"Aye, if you win enough fights, he'll reward you with things like baths, extra meals, prostitutes, even, as you've seen, special things like racial upgrades. He's more generous with fighters with long contracts." Sarl clapped Victor's shoulder. "It's good that you have won your first three fights. It means you've got a fighting spirit, and that's half of what you need to survive the pits, or so Kurl says. He's been fighting the longest among those in my pen—there are seven of us."

"What's the other half?" Victor almost didn't want to ask.

"Luck! You need to be lucky with who you get matched against, with injuries, with sickness, with your manager; is he poisoning you so he can make you throw a fight? Did he do any of a hundred other things to ruin your chances?"

"Fuck, man, I just want to get outta this mess. I wanna win my freedom, then find a wizard or something to figure out how I can get home."

"Good, keep your goals manageable!" Sarl laughed, and Victor kind of saw the humor in his words, so he chuckled along. Then Ponda's huge paw was on his shoulder, and the big Vodkin pulled him toward the ropes.

"Hurry up; we're almost late," Ponda said, shoving people out of his way as he dragged Victor between the pits toward the center again. What was with him getting the big pits tonight? Victor hustled after him, and when they came to the edge of pit one, he stood on the little fighter's platform and was relieved to see no swarming monsters waiting for him within.

"Just another fighter, then," he said softly to himself. Trying to get pumped up, he hopped in place and closed his eyes, thinking of things that got his blood boiling, trying to avoid the most harrowing memories. He remembered how Zan had referred to Vullu as his "daddy." He was mocking Victor's relationship with Yrella and Vullu, totally making a mockery of his memories with them! Victor felt red heat start to pour out of his Core, and a cruel smile twisted his lips.

"Fighters are ready!" a booming voice sounded from the left, and Victor opened his eyes, noting the Vodkin judge looming in his red-tinted vision. He looked down into the sandy pit and saw spiked clubs here and there in the sand, three of them. He looked around the perimeter and realized he was one of three fighters standing on the edge, ready to jump in. He stood with his legs partially flexed, listening for the signal, his thighs trembling with anticipation. "Begin!" The judge roared, and Victor launched himself forward and to the left toward a club handle sticking out of the sand.

As he flew through the air, Victor saw that the other two also had jumped toward weapons. When he landed, he grabbed the club's handle in one hand, spinning to face his opponents and preparing to activate Berserk. The other two fighters were both Shadeni—their red faces snarled in menacing grimaces as they stalked one another and Victor. Both men wore tattered leather clothing, and neither looked particularly graceful in the sand, but Victor didn't let his guard down, choosing the one on his right to start to circle. The other Shadeni saw what he was doing and flanked Victor's target, forcing him to split his attention. None of them charged the others, though, and Victor slowly inched closer, keeping his club ready, moving on the balls of his feet, his center low and primed to react. Victor could feel the tension, feel the knife's edge their inaction was balanced on, and said, "Let's go, assholes!" as he triggered his Berserk.

Burning rage surged out of his Core into his body, and as before, Victor's vision went crimson. His body convulsed as his muscles thrashed and swelled, then he was roaring and charging into the Shadeni, swinging his spiked club in an arcing blur. The Shadeni, remarkably, managed to lift his club to block, but Victor smashed into him so hard that their clubs' spikes married the two wooden weapons. The momentum of Victor's swing continued forward, ripping the club from the Shadeni's hand and burying the long nails of both clubs into his chest. He was thrown backward, stumbling into the other Shadeni, and they both scrambled for balance, falling away from Victor.

"Come on!" Victor roared and leaped at the uninjured Shadeni, smoothly stepping inside the arc of his club and scooping him up in a double leg take-down. Victor pressed his chest into the Shadeni, using his mass to hold him down, while he scrambled up his legs to kneel on his arms, then he began to punch his face. He hit him once, twice, three thunderous blows to his face, then Victor's vision darkened, and stars exploded in front of his eyes. He top-pled to the left, his face planting in the sand and grinding for several inches. The other Shadeni had extracted the clubs from his chest and smashed Vic-tor in the back of the head.

Victor didn't quite understand how, but his vision started to clear, and through the red haze of his vision, he saw the sandy floor and one wooden wall of the pit. Dimly, he was aware of the screaming and shouting and cheer-ing coming from around him, but he just grunted and scooted his knees up under himself and pushed up onto his hands. He glanced to the right, and there were the two Shadeni. Both looked winded and bloodied, circling each other, having dismissed Victor as a goner. Victor didn't pause to consider his rationality when he got pissed that they'd written him off. Instead, he pushed on that rage, pulling more Energy from his Core. He began to pant heavily, and drool was pouring out of his snarling mouth when he jumped to his feet and slammed into the nearest Shadeni—the one he'd hit in the chest earlier.

He body-checked the Shadeni into the wooden wall, and Victor heard ribs crack. He grabbed the guy's wrist and twisted it with all his strength until the man screamed and dropped the club. As he reached for the fallen weapon, the other Shadeni charged at him and brought his club down for Victor's skull. Victor grabbed the club's handle and rolled over his shoulder, away from his enemy's swing. He smoothly rolled onto his feet, then screamed and charged at the two Shadeni, smashing his club from left to right and right to left, the ferocity of his blows overpowering their attempts at defense. He completely ignored their punches and half-formed club swings. And as his brutal smashes broke through, their defense crumbled, and he hit them again and again until they were still, and golden motes of Energy were streaming into him.

***Congratulations! You've achieved Level 7 Base Human. You have 10 attribute points to allocate.***

Victor waited for his vision to clear, but he realized it already had. Some-time while he'd been smashing those two guys, his Berserk had worn off, and he hadn't even noticed. What did that say about him? What was he becoming? He shook his head and looked at his notification. "Fuck me; I forgot to spend my last five points." He reached his hand back and felt his skull. It was tender, and his hair was soaked with blood, but he couldn't find any big lumps or broken bits. Whatever cut had bled was also closed up. Slowly he became aware of the crowd standing up around the pit, screaming and cheering. Several of them held paper slips in the air, howling with glee. They were all fixated on him, waiting for him to do something, maybe? He let go of his head and raised his gory, bloody spiked club into the air, over his head. The screaming and cheering began anew, with increased fervor. "Fucking chill out, you psychos," he said under his breath, but he still grinned and shook his club in the air while he walked over to the little platform where Ponda was waiting.

"Kid, I thought you died when he smashed your head!" Ponda said as he hauled him up to the edge.

"No such luck, big guy." Victor realized he still held his club, and a lot of people had eyes on him, so he dropped it down into the pit. "Fuck, I'm thirsty."

"Let's go; you'll have a little time before you have to fight again. Can you go crazy like that as much as you want?" Ponda started walking back to their section, clearing a path for Victor as long as he stayed near the big man's back.

"What do you mean, 'go crazy?'"

"You know." Ponda looked back over his shoulder, "When your eyes get all full of blood, steam rises off you, and you scream and smash people around."

"Ha, well, today's the first time I've had a skill for it, so I'm still learning its limits. It says it has a long cooldown, but I've used it in both fights, so it can't be that long."

"'Long' can mean anything from a few minutes to a few days. It sounds like your skill is usable after a few minutes. I think the System calls it 'long' because in a fight, twenty minutes is the same as forever."

"That's the fucking truth." Victor had never known how long six minutes could be until he'd started wrestling. They were back at their section, and Victor made a beeline for the water. Ponda clapped him on the shoulder as he went by, and Victor actually felt that the big guy was being friendly. Sarl wasn't there this time, and Victor figured he was probably off fighting. For a minute, Victor wondered if he'd be back. Would he die in this fight? At that moment, Victor decided he didn't want to get close to any more fighters. He already felt he'd be gutted if Sarl died, and he hardly knew the guy. He couldn't handle any more Yrellas, that was for sure. He grabbed a cup and began the process of hydrating.

After drinking his fill and washing some of the blood from his hands and arms, he sat back against the wall and contemplated his attributes. It was evident that his Berserk ability was the only reason he was alive right now. It allowed him to go all-out offensively while holding his body together against the stabs and pummeling he'd inevitably take. He decided to stick with his strengths for now and spread the points around his physical attributes. When he was done, his strength was up to twenty-five, his vitality was a solid fifteen, and his dexterity and agility were both at twelve. When he applied the ten attribute points he'd banked, the surge of Energy that flooded through him, presumably making the improvements, was intoxicating, and he closed his eyes, just absorbing the good vibes.

Victor's third fight for the night took a little longer to come around. According to Ponda, a few fights had turned into real brawls, dragging on for a while. He said that some of the Tier Two and Three fighters had abilities that made them very hard to kill. In any case, the time finally came, and Ponda led him back toward pit number two again, right near the center of the warehouse. However, something new happened this time when Victor stepped onto the platform: people started cheering and clapping. A few of the spectators even shouted his name. "Don't get too excited," Ponda said, standing next to him. "They cheer for you because they've already seen you bleed tonight, and they're happy you didn't slink away to the infirmary."

"Is that an option?" Victor couldn't stop himself from smiling along when Ponda laughed and shook his head.

"Not unless you can't walk."

"Fighters ready?" Victor looked at the familiar judge and nodded along with Ponda. He glanced around the pit and saw he only had to fight one opponent: a tall, striking woman with blue skin and pale green hair and eyes. She wore leather pants and a tight cloth shirt, and she looked as if she'd just come out of a beauty salon—she was so clean, her hair so lustrous. She frowned and nodded in Victor's general direction.

"What the fuck?" was all he had time to ask before the judge shouted for them to fight. Ponda gave him a little shove, and he fell toward the sand and mortal combat with the most beautiful person he'd ever seen.

"Victor, hmm? I heard the crowd—they like you." Her green hair bobbed in a high ponytail as she circled him. He licked his lips nervously, not liking the idea of beating up, or killing, a beautiful girl. So far, there weren't any weapons in the pit, so he moved in close to grapple; he wanted to test the waters. She met his attempts to grab her neck or wrists with easy deflections, and when he tried to slip in for a single-leg takedown, she hopped back and gave him a shove, so he stumbled to one knee. He smiled, enjoying the competition, and when he started to stand, turning to face her, her snap kick caught him on the forehead, and he stumbled back onto his ass, bright stars blooming in his vision.

The kick caught him by surprise, and Victor knew he was being dumb, taking her more lightly as a threat just because she was hot, so when she flashed in with a straight punch aimed at his throat, he pivoted and swept her legs, sending her crashing into the sand. Victor had always had a strong ground game, and he was on her before she'd gotten her hands under her. He slid around behind her, grabbing her head in a chokehold. Somewhere in the back of his mind, he was recoiling at the idea of choking this girl to death, but more immediately, he just wanted to immobilize her. That's when an ear-shattering sound ripped out of her throat, sending a visceral shockwave of piercing needles into Victor. He felt as if someone was peeling his skin off as he rolled away from the girl in the sand, thrashing like a man on fire.

This time when his vision went red, it wasn't from rage but from blood. Blood was sheeting down into his eyes, coating his face, arms, and chest. Had she actually shot him with a thousand needles? Where the fuck did they come from? He groaned, rolling in the sand, then he felt a thunderous concussion as her foot slammed into his kidney. He gagged, rolling again, trying to get some distance. The deep throbbing pain from his lower back told him he'd taken an injury unlike anything he'd experienced before. Something inside him was broken. He pulled his knees up to his chest, turtling up while struggling for breath. That's when he heard her giggles. She was fucking giggling while she stalked around him in the sand. He caught a glimpse of her as she darted in front of him, then she was behind him, and he tried to spin to keep his legs between them, but she didn't come in for a kick or punch; she screamed again, and thousands of tiny, fiery points of pain ignited along his shins and knees. Blood darkened the denim of his jeans, soaking them through, and Victor inhaled sharply, wanting to let out a scream, but the fiery pain was too intense; his scream choked in his throat.

"Does it hurt, boy? I've heard from reliable sources that it does." Her voice had a lilting quality, lighthearted and teasing. She giggled, and Victor closed his eyes and activated his Berserk ability. Instantly the fiery pain all over his body went silent, and he thrashed onto his back as his body surged with

burning rage-attuned Energy. "Dying already, boy? I haven't finished enter-
taining the crowd yet." She screamed again, and Victor felt the tiny needles
hitting him all along his stomach, arms, chest, and neck. They didn't hurt,
though; he just knew they'd hit him, the way you'd notice water running over
your hand at the same temperature as your body. It didn't burn or feel cold;
it was just there. He hopped to his feet, his face a terrible visage of steaming
blood, baleful red eyes, and snarling blood-flecked teeth.

The beautiful Ardeni woman's smile fell away, and she took a step back.
She raised her hands and screamed again, and once more, Victor felt the
pressure of something hitting him, though it didn't bother him anymore. He
roared in a fury and was on her in a heartbeat. She tried to drive him aside
with a spinning round kick, but Victor punched her shin as it came at him,
cracking the bone. She wailed in pain, but before she could fall, Victor was
sliding behind her, one powerful arm around her neck, squeezing her larynx
into the crook of his elbow. He roared up at the sky while he crushed the life
from her, and the crowd roared back. Her body went limp, and Victor paced
around in the sand, still holding her tight in his arm, looking for something
more to fight.

When he came back to himself, he noticed the notification in his vision:

***Congratulations! You've achieved Level 8 Base Human. You have 5
attribute points to allocate.***

When he reached up to dismiss it, the girl's corpse fell away, and he realized he'd been holding her this whole time. The crowd was going wild, chanting his name, cheering the blood-soaked monster in the middle of the pit.
Victor took two steps away from the body and vomited.

# 13

## UNDERDOG

Victor didn't remember a lot between climbing out of the ring and slumping down against the wall in the roped-off area. There was only a handful of fighters standing around or lying on the wooden floor, everyone else presumably dead, injured, or off fighting in a pit. He remembered Ponda's big meaty hand on the back of his neck, guiding him along the walkways above the pits, then his gruff, "You got maybe an hour till your last fight." Then Victor had stumbled, still soaked in sticky blood, to the wall and collapsed.

His mind was blissfully blank; he'd started with some self-loathing about killing that girl, but it didn't stick. He hardly remembered doing it, for one thing, and for the other, he very clearly remembered her mocking, nasty tone as she tried to bleed him to death with whatever magic she'd been using. No, even when he looked at his brown-red stained blue jeans, he couldn't get too disgusted. His mind was just too tired. Had he been using Berserk too much? Did it have some sort of effect on his mental state? What if it didn't work in the next fight? He couldn't find the energy to give a shit. He just sat there, eyes closed, staring into the black void behind his eyelids.

"You look wrung out, Victor." Sarl had come to stand near him, leaning against the wall while he sipped a cup of water.

"I am, bro. Hey, you won your fight?" Sarl didn't look bad—his usual wan self, with maybe a new bruise or two.

"Aye, I did. Thank Nature."

"Nature? Do Ghelli worship nature?"

"Hmm, I don't think 'worship' is the right word. Maybe 'revere' would be more fitting. We recognize nature's power and potential, and we pay respect to it. What troubles you, though, Victor? You've won three fights now, correct?"

"Yeah, man, but I don't feel great about it. I have an ability that sends me into kind of an enraged frenzy for a while, and fuck; there's no getting around the fact that I've fucking slaughtered quite a few people now. What am I becoming? Jesus, can I ever go back home? How many freshmen at community college have killed a bunch of people? I guess it happens, but my old life just seems so distant and small now. I feel like I'm losing myself. Does that make sense?" Victor was pissed at himself for spilling his guts to Sarl. Hadn't he just resolved not to get closer to anybody? Here he was asking this guy for advice like he was some kind of counselor.

"It makes sense, Victor, more than you know. I walked that road long before I was put into these pit fights. I took a leap for vengeance that forever separated me from my old life. I chose that road, but you didn't—you're just trying to survive. You can't blame yourself for that."

"What do you mean, you took a leap?"

"I mean just that. I stepped out of my comfortable life of submission and purposefully crossed a line. I killed people outside the law to make them pay for what they'd done to my loved ones. There was no going back from that. Even when I was done and I submitted, my old life was dead. Now I live for the unknown. Will I live through enough fights to be free again? What will I make of myself then? I stopped caring the moment my wife died. I suppose that's rather liberating."

"Heavy shit, bro." Victor had a hard time feeling sorry for himself when he heard Sarl's story, as vague as it was. He looked around at the eight or so fighters hanging around behind the ropes and studied their faces. Everyone was fighting demons, he supposed. He wasn't the only one suffering this shitty existence. Sure, he'd been kidnapped, but judging from what he'd seen of this world's legal system, he doubted he was the only one unjustly thrown to the pits.

"Here comes Boss," Sarl said, nodding to the big Shadeni purposefully stomping toward their section.

"Kid, your fight's coming up. Come on." He waved for Victor and held up the rope so he could easily duck under it. "Lady's tits, boy—you're completely soaked in blood. You win this one, and I'll throw a trip to the baths into the pot." Victor didn't reply, just followed in Yund's wake as he pushed through the crowds toward the central pits again.

"Damn, why are all my fights in the center tonight?"

"Because I secured some interesting fights for you. You're welcome! This next one is a bit out of your league, but he's a straight brawler—nothing flashy as far as I can tell."

"What do you mean, 'out of my league?'" Victor had to shout at Yund's back to be heard over the cheering, stomping crowds they were walking through.

"Well, the last fight you won was against a Tier One. I think she was Level Twelve. This guy is closer to Tier Two."

"What the fuck, dude? I'm Level Seven!" As he said it, Victor remembered his five attribute points, and he hurriedly put them into vitality.

"This guy is strong and tough but not particularly fast, and his Energy ability is almost non-existent. You can do it!" Yund had slowed to turn toward Victor while he spoke, and Victor could see in his eyes that he wished he hadn't told him anything about his opponent. Was he really hoping Victor could win, or did he build him up with those other three fights just so he could bet against him in this one?

"Yo, are you fucking me over, Boss?"

"Just get your ass in there and beat this guy to hell. If you win, things will look up for you around here, get me?" Yund leaned down, his big black eyes squinted in a scowl, brooking no argument. Victor just nodded. As they approached pit one in the warehouse center, the crowd started to clap, and Victor realized that many of them were chanting his name again. Had Yund told them his name? Did they get some sort of fighter list? He'd be lying if he said he didn't enjoy the adulation. He always liked it when he won a match, and the audience cheered, but this was on another level. These people were hyped to hell, stomping, cheering, pumping their fists. They also had a rabid, almost insane look in their eyes, but who can be picky when it comes to adoring fans?

He stood on his little platform, waiting for the judge's word, while staring across the pit, trying to get a glimpse of his opponent. He saw Ponda walking around over there, or he thought he did, but then the huge Vodkin stepped onto the platform, and Victor saw the white stripe running down the center of his fur from his forehead to his chin. "Definitely not Ponda."

"Fighters ready?" Victor didn't get a chance to respond because Yund did it for him.

"Ready!" he hollered. The Vodkin lifted a ham-size fist and roared.

"Begin!" the Judge shouted, and Victor jumped in before someone got the satisfaction of pushing him. The ground shook slightly as the Vodkin dropped down, with a grunt catching himself on a fist as he fell forward. Victor glanced around, making sure he hadn't missed any weapons, and then he backed away, wanting some distance between him and his opponent so he could try to gauge what he was dealing with in terms of speed and surprises. The big white-striped, otter-looking asshole stomped directly at Victor, his fists raised and nothing but business on his face. The guy had to weigh more than three hundred pounds, and Victor didn't think he was strong enough to take him down; certainly, he couldn't throw him.

"Quit running, rat," the big man growled as he stomped after Victor. Victor didn't know what to do; he was hesitant to pull the trigger on his Berserk skill right away. What if this guy lived through the punishment he could dish out? Would Victor have any fight left in him after it wore off? He wanted to try to wear this guy down a little first, but he was out of ideas. The Vodkin charged him suddenly, his huge thighs bunching and rippling with the effort of driving such a big body forward. Victor dove to his left, rolling over his shoulder and back up onto his feet, altogether avoiding the charge.

"You have rats in this world?" Victor asked, laughing at the absurdity of that thought being at the forefront of his mind.

"Fight me! Fight Durn!" The Vodkin had nearly smashed into the wall in his charge, and when he turned and screamed this challenge, saliva fluttered out of his gaping mouth with the force of his lungs. The crowd cheered and began to chant, "Durn, Durn, Durn!" Victor was losing them, it seemed.

"Spears!" the Judge cried, and someone was quick to comply, tossing spears down, both of them landing near Durn.

"That's bullshit!" Victor yelled. Then, as Durn stooped to scoop up a spear, he sprinted for the other one. Something in the back of his mind tickled, and, as he bent to pick up the spear, Victor dropped flat. Durn's spear ripped through the air where he'd been standing, struck the pit wall, and smashed through one of the sturdy boards, vibrating in place for a moment. "That woulda fucked me up," Victor hissed, rolling to his knees and diving away, spear in hand, as Durn stomped toward where he'd lain.

Victor began, then, to really test Durn. He used his spear to keep him at bay, trying little feints and jabs with it, seeing what he could get through the big man's guard. Durn might not be the fastest guy Victor had ever met, but he was tough as hell and not exactly bad at fighting. He slapped the spear aside most of the time, but when Victor got a jab through, here and there, it only seemed to enrage the big man. Soon he was bleeding from four or five minor puncture wounds and one long gash along his forearm, but he wasn't any slower or less aggressive. Victor, on the other hand, was starting to run out of steam, and he began to wonder if this fight was hopeless. If this guy really had ten or so levels on him, that seemed like a huge attribute advantage. What if he had something like fifty vitality? Could Victor keep this dance up long enough to wear the big guy down?

Victor, always on his back foot, moving away in a constant retreating circle, tried to figure out a pattern to open Durn's guard. He found that if he feinted low, stepped left, then feinted high, he could almost be sure to have a clean shot at Durn's belly. He repeated the process three times, never taking the shot, just to be sure, then Victor began to channel Energy out of his Core, into his pathways, leading to his arms. He instantly noticed the red tint to the light, his heart beating faster, and his breath roughly tickling his vocal cords into a growl as he exhaled. Then he used his feint combo to open Durn's guard and pushed with all his will at the Energy in his pathways, driving the spear forward. It moved like a bolt of red lightning, catching Durn on the left side of his belly and exploding through his layers of fat, muscle, and organs to punch out through his back.

Durn screamed, but it wasn't a death knell; no, he screamed in fury and disbelief, and his black eyes blazed with sudden red light. He charged forward into the spear that Victor still held, dumbstruck by Durn's reaction, and swiped one massive fist with such terrible force that it dislocated Victor's shoulder, lifted him from the ground, and sent him tumbling through the air to smash into the pit wall. Durn roared, raising his arms in the air, careless of the fluids gushing out around the terrible spear wound in his gut. The crowd roared back, stomping their feet and chanting Durn's name.

Victor was stunned but not out. He'd fallen along the wall to lay slumped against it. His forehead was bleeding into his eyes again, and his arm was pure agony. He thought something else might have broken in the crash with the wall, but he couldn't be sure. He closed his eyes, took a deep breath, and activated Berserk. His searing pain faded to just a feeling that was there but not important. He stood up, careless of how his left leg bowed inward, and the only thing he could see was Durn. In the center of Victor's vision, he stood there, a red-soaked obstacle that needed to be knocked down. Something was funny with Victor's left arm; it didn't want to move as he intended, flopping with a strange grinding sensation in his shoulder. He didn't care; the other arm worked fine. He stomped toward Durn, who was just refocusing on Victor after his open-mouthed roar of dominance toward the spectators. Durn growled when he saw Victor striding toward him with a terrible expression on his face. A little of the heat faded from Durn's eyes as though he could read the intentions playing across Victor's mind, and rather than charge forward, he took a half-step back.

Victor didn't wait to see what Durn was doing; he reached with his right arm and grabbed the spear shaft protruding from Durn's stomach. Durn swiped at him with an oversized fist, but Victor ducked under it, stepping forward to Durn's left and shoving the spear to the right, forcing him to twist away barking and coughing blood; then he stomped into the side of Durn's knee. It was like kicking a small tree, but Victor's rage-fueled blow elicited a loud *pop* from the joint, and he knew he'd torn at least one tendon. Durn howled in fury and pain, but the noise only made Victor's wicked grin widen. He let go of the spear shaft and continued past Durn, grabbing it where it protruded from his back, just below the spearhead, and as Durn stumbled forward, Victor strode in the opposite direction, yanking the full length of the spear through Durn's body.

The crowd was exploding with energy, screaming and cheering, stomping, fighting, and trying to change bets. Victor didn't hear them, though; to him, it was a distant buzzing. He only had ears and eyes for Durn, who was coughing blood and pressing his hands to the large hole in his stomach, trying to keep his insides on the inside. Victor tossed the spear up, caught it in his right hand, and, in one smooth motion, fired it like a javelin into Durn's back. Durn roared anew, stumbling forward on his bad knee and falling into the sand like an old, rotting tree. Victor, blood-flecked teeth exposed in a wide, crazed grin, strode forward, planted a foot on Durn's back, and yanked the spear out, a spray of blood arcing along with it. Victor stabbed Durn again and again until he was standing on the large man's back, his tennies soaked in blood, panting and looking around for his next opponent.

After a few moments, while the crowd roared and stomped, Victor's vision returned to normal, and he was swallowed by pain. He barely had time to register the message in his view before he slipped from Durn's blood-soaked back, painfully twisting his injured knee and falling into the sand, unable to catch himself with his unresponsive arm.

\*\*\*Congratulations! You've achieved Level 10 Base Human. You have 10 attribute points to allocate. Your first class selection is available to you.\*\*\*

# 14

⁘

# CLEANING UP

Ponda ended up having to jump down into the pit and help Victor out. He lifted him by his good arm and swung him over his shoulder, then clambered up the side, with Yund giving him a hand. "Take him to the infirmary; we'll pick you guys up after Zan's fight." Yund reached out to clap Victor on the shoulder but thought better of it, pulling his hand back. "We'll get you to a bath tonight, kid. You did good." Victor just closed his eyes, hanging over Ponda's shoulder; he didn't feel that he'd be able to look around and still keep his stomach contents to himself. He tried to lose himself in the bumps and sways of the big Vodkin's stride. After a while, he heard a door swing open, slam against a wall, then swing closed behind him.

"Put him on that cot," a smooth, all-business voice said, and Victor opened his eyes to see an Ardeni woman pulling a needle and thread through the forehead skin of a short, stocky man. He watched her for a moment, admiring how she quickly jabbed the needle in and out without eliciting any curses from the patient. Then Ponda swung him around and helped him scoot onto a low wooden cot with no mattress or blanket. It was stiff, but at least it looked clean, so Victor lay back and tried to zone out, closing his eyes and trying to remember the words to the songs that had been popular back in another world, in a different lifetime.

"... wouldn't you say?" Victor's eyes opened, and he looked around, feeling panicked, but then he saw the infirmary and the Ardeni woman, and he remembered where he was.

"Uh, what?" he mumbled through dry lips.

"You've made a mess of your shoulder."

"Yeah, I can't move it."

"It's dislocated, and there are ligament remnants in the joint. Did you level after you got this injury?"

"Uh, yeah. How can you tell?"

Because your ligament was shredded, but the Energy that leveled you healed it up. The old bits are still in there, though. Don't worry; I have a spell for it." Something was off about this woman, and Victor was trying to figure it out when he realized what it was—she had kind, undamaged, unhaunted eyes.

"I think you're the first person in this world I've met that wasn't mentally fucked up or just plain mean."

"Hmm? You have some interesting slang. I'm sorry you've seen a lot of trauma; let's see if I can make you more comfortable at least, okay?" Victor closed his mouth and nodded. "My name's Lita, and I'm going to heal you, so don't resist my Energy, okay?" Again, Victor nodded, and Lita reached one hand into the filthy collar of his T-shirt and rested it, tenderly, above the swollen upper portion of his shoulder. Then, she took the other and grabbed ahold of Victor's tricep. When she closed her eyes, he felt some warmth under her hands, then some tingling spread into his shoulder. It didn't hurt at all, but he knew what she meant—he could feel her invading Energy, and he had a subconscious urge to push it out with his own Energy. He held himself back, clamping his will down on his Core. Soon his shoulder was vibrating, and warm, buzzing waves pulsed through it. Then with a *pop*, his shoulder reset, and a wave of relief ran through his body as muscles he didn't know he'd been tensing up relaxed. "There we go! Anything else really bothering you?" Her eyes were the craziest shade of bluish pink that Victor had ever seen, and she had matching hair cut short and pulled back out of her eyes with silvery clips.

"Uh, do all Ardeni have matching hair and eyes?" She smiled and leaned back, caught by surprise by the question.

"Oh, not all. Most of us, though. Our original world was very vibrant. Some of our plants died off with the merge, and the other worlds weren't so bright and colorful. Oh, I'm babbling."

"No! I don't know anything about this place! Thank you for talking to me." Victor reached out and almost took her hand, but he pulled back, not wanting to alarm her.

"Just where are you from, pit fighter?" She said "pit fighter" teasingly, not judging, and Victor found a smile creeping onto his lips.

"Uh, another world; I got summoned by some assholes."

"I figured you were from another world, but I thought perhaps you came through a City Stone."

"Nah, summoned. I don't know where this world is, even. I'm from a place called Earth, and I bet your eyes are prettier than any girl's in my whole world." Victor didn't know why he was flirting with this woman, but something felt good in his head, as if he'd lost a heavy weight. He hoped it was him really feeling good and not some temporary side effect of her healing. He grinned when she smiled and looked down, embarrassed. "Hey, don't hide 'em from me."

"Well." She looked at him again. "Your eyes are nice, too. They're like warm honey and seem deeper than the bright eyes of my kin."

"Maybe we're both enjoying seeing something different," he said, widening his smile. She opened her mouth to reply, but then the door slammed open again, and Ponda strode in.

"Got him patched up?" Lita scooted back from Victor, clearing her throat.

"Ahem, yes. Just finished."

"Good! Put it on Yund's tab. C'mon kid. Time to hit the baths." Ponda gestured for Victor to get up, then turned to open the door. Victor sat up from the cot, then swung his arms around from back to front.

"Nice job, Doc. Thanks for fixing me up." He held out a hand, saw it was caked with dried blood, pulled it back, and just sheepishly waved.

"You're welcome. What's your name?" Ponda looked back sharply, an eyebrow raised, but Victor didn't care.

"Victor. Hope I see you again, Lita." Then Ponda's meaty hand was on his shoulder, and they were walking briskly out through a wooden hallway, past some concession carts, and then through the vast, open doors of the Rusty Nail. They found Yund and the other fourteen surviving fighters waiting near a beer cart where Yund was, unbelievably, buying every fighter a mug. He saw Ponda and Victor striding up and ordered two more.

"What a night, boys! What a night!" The four surviving female fighters exchanged glances but didn't correct Yund. "You all deserve this! We came with the fewest fighters but won the most fights. Now four of those wins were on young Victor's back, but that doesn't discount the wins the rest of you racked up. Good work! Drink that ale, and we'll head back at a leisurely pace." Victor savored the ale, marveling at the icy temperature. Apparently, this world had refrigeration tech or at least magic, but Yund didn't often spring for it.

Victor was eager to get back to the peace and quiet of his cage to look over his menu for selecting a class. He hadn't told anyone about leveling to ten, though he figured Yund would figure it out sooner rather than later. He seemed to have a way of gauging a person's strength. Maybe it was a skill or spell or some kind of magical item. While they walked, drank their big mugs of cool ale, and joked about fighting to the death, Victor almost felt normal. What did it say about him that this sort of thing seemed normal to him now?

"Take him in there, Ponda. Treat yourself too. See you in the morning," Yund said, waving at a white stone building with several chimneys pumping out steam in the bright moonlight. Ponda grabbed Victor's shoulder and steered him toward the building, and as they got close, Victor saw the unmistakable image of a bathtub silver-embossed on a big copper door.

"Bath time," Ponda announced superfluously. Victor followed him through the door, noting how it swung noiselessly open and closed behind them. They walked into a clean, tiled foyer, and an Ardeni woman with orange hair, wearing a white robe, handed them both towels and bars of soap. Ponda slapped some little colored beads on the counter and said, "Two private baths." The woman nodded and moved to the side of the room, pulling aside a curtain, revealing a hallway.

"Rooms one and two. Shall I arrange for some attendants?" She looked from Ponda to Victor and raised an eyebrow.

"Nah, just the baths. Just a minute, kid." Ponda reached a hand to his belt and produced a metal collar. "Sorry, but you're gonna have to clean around this thing. I don't wanna be worried about you bolting while I'm relaxing in the bath." He opened the collar and snapped it shut around Victor's neck.

"Don't trust me, huh?"

"Of course not. You don't get to where I am by trusting people, kid." Victor was going to crack a joke, but he could see that Ponda was taking himself seriously, so he decided to keep his mouth shut. He was still in a good mood from the ale and his time with the pretty healer, so it wasn't hard to fake a smile. He followed Ponda into the short hallway, and the doors to "Bath 1" and "Bath 2" were immediately to their left. Ponda gestured to the second door, and Victor nodded, opening it and stepping in.

The room wasn't large, maybe ten feet by ten, and the back five square feet were all taken up by a sunken bath. Victor stepped up to the edge of the first step leading down to the water and marveled to see it flowing like a river. The water came in through a grate on one side of the tub, falling down the wall like a little waterfall, then pooling in the tub to flow out through a grate on the other side. He touched the water and found it hot, but not unpleasantly so. Green plants with long flat-leafed vines lined the far wall, and steam hung cloyingly in the air.

Victor took a look at himself and his blood-soaked clothes and shuddered to imagine putting them back on after he bathed. He stepped into the hot water, fully clothed, then stripped his articles of clothing off, one by one. As he took off his shirt, he held it under the hot steamy water for a moment, softening up the crusted blood, then he used the bar of soap to wash it, squeezed it as dry as possible, and laid it out on the tile to dry. Then he repeated the process with his jeans, underwear, socks, and even his shoes. Sure, his clothes were soaked and still stained, but they were "clean." Then Victor spent a few minutes washing himself, scrubbing till his skin was more pink than tan.

The soap smelled like some kind of flower and maybe vanilla. Whatever it was, it was better than old blood. After he'd worn the bar of soap down to just a fraction of its former glory, he set it on the edge of the bath and fell back into the warm, gently flowing water, letting it caress and murmur to him as it passed along his ears. Victor had no idea how long Ponda would let him relax like this, so he intended to make the most of it.

It turned out that Ponda really enjoyed bath time. Victor drifted into sleep floating in that tub, and when Ponda finally came for him, he felt as if he'd had almost a whole night's sleep. He couldn't be sure, but some time had definitely passed because his clothes were nearly dry. Ponda barked at him to get out, so he did, drying himself with the towel, then pulling on his slightly damp clothes. He followed Ponda out of the bathhouse, his tennies squeaking and squelching on the tile floors.

"Feeling better, kid? You smell better."

"Yeah, Ponda. I needed that, thanks."

"Don't thank me. Yund told me to take you."

"Yeah, but I don't think we had to spend that much time in there. So, thanks." Ponda looked at him but didn't argue; he just nodded and kept walking. They got back to the Wagon Wheel before the sun started to rise, and Ponda locked Victor into his cage with a finger over his fur-lined lips.

"Boss is gonna be busy today. Sleep in if you can."

"All right," Victor replied, moving to his usual corner of the cage and lying down on his back, arms behind his head. It was time for him to take a look at his class selection.

# 15

## CONTRACT

Victor looked at his status page and the flashing green button labeled "Class Selection." He touched the button, and a message overlaid his current view:

***Level 10 class selection. Class selection is permanent. Human Energy cultivators will next be offered a class refinement selection at Level 20. To view your options and make your selection, use the arrows to page through this interface.***

Victor had talked to Vullu and Yrella about classes quite a lot during his first few days with them. They'd explained that the System put together packages of skills and attribute allocations to help people focus and apply the growth they experienced through Energy cultivation. He didn't quite understand it, but he knew about classes or archetypes from playing VR games. It seemed like the same kind of concept. Clicking the first arrow, he saw:

***Class selection option 1: Bruiser, Basic. You use might and brutal tactics to overwhelm your enemies. Class attributes: Strength and Vitality.***

Victor almost swore aloud, but he remembered all the fighters still snoozing around him and kept his outburst down to a quiet scoff. The idea of being a Bruiser didn't exactly excite Victor, but he couldn't lie—he'd already been fighting the way it described. Sighing heavily, he pushed the arrow to see what was next:

***Class selection option 2: Fighter, Basic. You use physical prowess to best your foes with remarkable feats of combat skill. Master weapons and your body to become a force that can change the tide of a battle. Class attributes: Strength, Agility, and Vitality.***

It was another basic class, but it appealed more to Victor. It seemed to have more potential for growth than the Bruiser option. He touched the "next" arrow:

***Class selection option 3: Berserker, Improved. Fury and overwhelming force guide you on the battlefield. With little concern for your safety, you put the domination of your foes first. Class attributes: Strength, Vitality, Agility, Will.***

"What the fuck?" he said in a hushed voice. Wasn't he already a Berserker because of his Berserk ability? Maybe taking the class would help him improve his ability to control his rage or give him different types of skills to go with it? It was an improved class, also, whatever that meant. He was trying to imagine what other talents he might get with the class when he saw the "next" arrow was still blinking. Another choice then; he touched it:

***Class selection option 4: Spirit Champion, Advanced. Prerequisite: Spirit Core. You hone your will to control the surging tide of your spirit affinity, learning to use it without succumbing to the force of its pull. Class attributes: Will, Vitality, Unbound.***

"Fucking hell," Victor hissed. Wasn't this exactly what he needed? He was sorely tempted to push the "select" button, but doubt held him transfixed. It sounded too good to be true. What would he give up by not taking one of the "basic" or "improved" classes? It seemed they had less to offer, but maybe there were other perks. Would he get more skills? Faster levels? Maybe Berserker wasn't what he wanted as much as Spirit Champion, but what if it allowed him to survive longer in this fucking hellhole? Did he just want to survive, though? Victor thought about how he'd felt, standing in the center of the pit, coming back to himself, and finding the Ardeni girl's corpse held tightly in the crook of his arm. He vaguely remembered the fight, remembered grabbing her, but it was like snippets of a dream. What if Spirit Champion let him hold onto himself a little better and kept him from becoming an absolute monster while in the pit? What if it didn't? What if it just gave him more skills that utilized his rage affinity? The description sounded promising, but it was maddeningly vague.

Victor's mind turned to Yund and what he would want Victor to choose. Victor was pretty damn sure Yund would tell him to select the Berserker option. Then he thought of Yrella, and a smile spread on his face. Yrella would tell him to choose Spirit Champion, no question. Feeling a wave of relief, he reached up and made the selection.

\*\*\*Congratulations! You've gained your first Class: Spirit Champion. Class skill gained: Sovereign Will, Basic. Class skill gained: Channel Spirit, Basic\*\*\*

\*\*\*Sovereign Will, Basic: As an act of concentration, you can apply up to 25% of your total will to any physical attribute.\*\*\*

\*\*\*Channel Spirit, Basic: Apply your Core's Energy to your physical attacks, manifesting your attuned Energy as a destructive force. This skill will bypass the usual effect spirit affinities have on the cultivator's emotional state. Energy cost: 25. Cooldown: minimal\*\*\*

Victor lay there on the straw-covered floorboards, thinking about the notifications he'd just read. Everything sounded great to him, but he was plagued by doubt. Had he been too impulsive? Should he have picked the Berserker? His immediate future seemed to have a lot of fighting in store for him, and maybe it would have been wiser. Still, the skills sounded great—one that would allow him to improve his strength or speed and another that would make channeling Energy into his attacks a lot easier. Or so it seemed based on the descriptions.

The Sovereign Will ability got him thinking about his attributes, and he remembered he had ten points to spend. Should he bump up his strength, or should he push it into his will? It seemed that if he could use will to improve his strength, dexterity, or agility, maybe he should keep building it up. Perhaps when he got a higher-tier version of the skill, it would allow for a higher percentage. Ultimately, he decided against it—according to his class description, he'd be getting more will with each level. He'd want to make sure his base fighting stats were good with or without his new ability. He decided to put five into agility and five into dexterity as they'd been lagging behind his strength and vitality.

When he got done, Victor felt incredible. He was clean for the first time in a long while, and his physical attributes were all more than double what they'd been when he came to this world. He flipped over in the dim, nearly dark light of the closed-up pen hall and cranked out more push-ups than he'd ever been able to do at his peak wrestling shape. When he stopped, he wasn't even that winded, and he felt that he could do another set after just a couple of minutes. Would he keep these improvements if he somehow returned to Earth? Would the Energy in his Core sustain him? Would he slowly bleed off his Core's power and lose his gains if there wasn't Energy around Earth? He had no way of knowing, and he wondered if anyone did. "Great; one more thing to worry about," he grumbled, becoming aware that many of the prisoners were stirring, yawning, and talking quietly in the other cages.

Victor sat quietly, using his unorthodox method of concentrating on stuff that pissed him off to cultivate more rage-attuned Energy, and the morning hours slipped away. He'd made good progress when the door slammed open, and Urt, Ponda's less friendly contemporary, strode into the pen hall, hocking up a great gob of phlegm and spitting it on the floor. "All right, lazy time's over. Victor, Boss wants to see you. Everyone else, line up for mess hall and exercise rounds!" Victor stood up and waited for the crabby, clean-shaven Ardeni to open his cage. "Come on. Move quick; I have a lot of shit to do." Urt strode to the other door, and Victor kept close to his heels, not wanting to piss the guy off any more. They crossed the exercise hall, then Urt rapped lightly on Yund's door, pulled it open, and waved Victor through.

Once again, Victor sat down across from the large red man, trying to determine if he was angry or just always had that expression on his face. "You wanted to see me, Boss? This about my contract?"

"Oh, want to make sure I remember what I promised, eh?" Yund snorted and leaned his wooden chair back precariously under his bulk. "Well, you're in luck. I've got one written up here. Now, I tried to be fair, thinking about how you got here. I also had to think about my bottom line and how I've lost a lot of good fighters. Not to mention all the help I've given you—putting you with my best fighters for some training, buying you help with your Core, and arranging good fights for you. That said, here's the contract." He opened a drawer and pulled out a sheet of thick, cream-colored paper. He pushed it across the desk and Victor read it:

*Contract of service between Yund's Wagon Wheel Fighting Troupe (the Wagon Wheel) and Victor of Tucson (Victor),*

"How'd you know how to spell Tucson?" Victor couldn't help asking.

"I got it right? Honestly, I don't know. The System Language Integration is some strange magic." Yund shrugged, and Victor kept reading:

*Contract of service between Yund's Wagon Wheel Fighting Troupe (the Wagon Wheel) and Victor of Tucson (Victor), wherein Victor agrees to fight for Yund's Wagon Wheel Fighting Troupe for no less than five years, and wherein the Wagon Wheel agrees to remove one month of Victor's term of indenture for each of his victories. Additionally, the Wagon Wheel agrees to provide opportunities for Victor to improve his combat prowess and readiness as rewards for exceptional accomplishments.*

*Signed:*

*Yund, Owner and responsible party for the Wagon Wheel* _____

*Victor of Tucson* _____

"Five fucking years, man?"

"Well, don't forget you can subtract a month for each of your wins! If you fight twelve times, that's a year off your time! You've been here less than two weeks and already fought six times!"

"Look, man, I'm not a genius, but I'm not a dumbass, either. I feel like this language is kinda vague. What does it mean you'll 'provide opportunities' for 'exceptional accomplishments?'"

"For instance, last night—when you fought that guy outside your tier—I'd reward you for that. Maybe a racial upgrade fruit or an attribute boost. Maybe if you had a maiming injury, I'd pay for healing." Victor grunted at this and leaned back in his chair, thinking. Five years sounded like a hell of a long time to have to fight for his freedom. If he fought once a day, which was impossible, he'd still need two months to clear his debt. Still, it was a goal to work toward.

"Fuck, man. Five years. My friends will be finishing college. Well, not most of them, but they'll be starting their lives, having kids. My *abuela* might be dead by then. This fucking sucks, dude. I already won you some fights, and you know I'm not a criminal."

"Victor, there are a lot worse people that you could have been sold to. This isn't a bad contract. Now, I think I need you to make a decision before I lose too much patience and just scrap the deal."

"Hang on." Victor knew that Yund had him over a barrel, but he also knew he had a little leverage—he was a moneymaker as long as he kept winning. "Can we clarify some language? I want my first six fights to count against my time, and I've heard you talking about different types of rewards: silver, gold, etc. Can we put some language in that says you'll give me a fight that can earn me a gold reward at least once a month?"

"Kinda pushy for someone who lives in my cage." Yund frowned, but he pulled the contract over in front of himself and produced a long quill and a pot of red ink. He struck through a couple of lines and scribbled some notes, then he showed the changes to Victor. They were exactly the changes he'd asked for. "Fighters do better when they feel incentivized, Victor. I usually have real scum in my cages, but the ones that aren't scum, I try to motivate. Your friends Yrella and Vullu were examples of those kinds of fighters. Ponda is another. Did you know he used to be one of my fighters? Tell me something, kid: have you picked your class yet?"

The question caught Victor a little off guard, and for some reason, he felt a little guilty when he replied. "Yeah, this morning."

"My own fault, I guess. I should have told you to wait. I could've given you some advice. What did you pick?"

"Spirit Champion. It's supposed to help me gain more control of my Spirit Core."

"Spirit Champion? I'm not familiar with it! I thought for sure you'd get Berserker or Gladiator. It sounds like it might be what you need, though. This brings me to another problem, though."

"What's that?" Victor felt a couple of butterflies start to flutter in his gut.

"Well, you're getting a little too strong to run around unbound." He drummed his thick red fingers on the desk.

"But we have a contract now," Victor replied weakly. He didn't want to get some kind of fucking tattoo that bound him to these assholes.

"I'll think on it. Trust me when I say you'd regret making a run for it. Ponda's Tier Three and my other managers are all Tier Two. Don't get yourself into a mess by trying to run for it."

"I won't. You know, I don't know a single person in this world." Victor would have said anything at that moment to try to reassure Yund; if he were going to make a break from this place, he absolutely didn't want a collar or one of those tattoo things. So far, he hadn't seen his moment, his chance to run for it, but he knew sooner or later they'd let their guard down at the wrong moment, and then he'd fucking be gone. No goddamn way was he going to spend five years in this place!

"Well, let's sign this, and you can go get some practice in," Yund said after a long, quiet moment. He scribbled his name on his line and passed the quill to Victor. Victor, heart thumping with the implications, signed his name on the contract.

# 16

JUSTICE

Several days passed at the Wagon Wheel before anything new or remarkable happened to change up the doldrums of Victor's days. He'd just finished with a particularly infuriating bout of cultivating, managing to level his Core again when the door to the main exercise room slammed open and Ponda came striding in, holding the end of the chain they used to bind the prisoners for travel. However, this time, he wasn't there to chain up Victor and the other fighters; he was delivering a line of new "talent." He strode down the aisle until the train of people following him had cleared the door, then he went back, counting them off as he passed, and slammed the door shut. Victor saw twelve new fighters, ranging in age from kids to senior citizens and in size from tiny to massive.

Ponda unchained their belts, told them to take them off, then started ushering them into cages, introducing them to their new roommates. Victor felt his stomach make a little nervous loop when Ponda approached his cage with a small, red-skinned Shadeni girl. She was shorter than Yrella had been and lacked her lean hard muscles. She seemed like a kid. "Victor, this is, uh, what's your name again?"

"Belsa," she said in a quiet voice, looking down.

"Right, Belsa. I need you to show her how things work."

"C'mon, Ponda. Don't do this to me."

"What, killer?"

"I can't show her what's up without learning what she's like, and then I'm going to get depressed when she dies in a week or so." Victor tried to say it quietly, but he knew the girl heard him. She didn't say anything, though, just looked at the ground, quietly shuffling her feet.

"Sorry, kid, but your cage has plenty of room, and I need you to step up. If you don't want her to die, teach her a thing or two." Apparently, that was the end of Ponda's desire to talk because he opened the cage, gave Belsa a nudge through it, and slammed it behind her. Victor looked at Belsa standing awkwardly in the middle of the cage, and he pointed to the corner where Vullu used to sit.

"That's your corner. Sleep over there." She wore dark brown leather pants, no shoes, and a matching leather vest with blue and green beads sewn onto the front panels, making little zig-zagging designs. She didn't look at Victor, but she walked over to her corner, sat down on her knees, and seemed to meditate or pray, still facing the corner. "Hey, if you didn't hear, my name's Victor, and I'm sorry if I came off as an asshole. I just can't deal really well with this place, so I'm fucked as to why they'd put you in here with me."

"It's all right," she said softly but didn't move or speak beyond that. Victor sat down and looked at his status sheet. Just as he'd hoped, leveling his Core had given him another hundred Energy points.

"Hey, um, if you need to go to the bathroom, there's a bucket there. It's gross, I know, but people are cool about not watching each other when we use it."

"Thank you." Again, she spoke softly and didn't look up. Victor was starting to feel really shitty about how he'd acted when she first got there. She seemed younger than him, and he began to wonder how the hell she'd ended up in this place.

"Um, you're Shadeni, right?" Suddenly she turned, glaring at Victor with bright green eyes that reminded him very much of Yrella. She lifted her lips in a snarl and inhaled sharply.

"Why do you talk to me, boy? I thought you wanted to avoid getting to know me before I die?" Her voice was cutting and sharp, and Victor knew it carried around to the other cages because it got quiet as others tuned in to hear the drama.

"Whatever. I said I was sorry for that, but if you don't wanna talk, that's cool." He refused to yell or get upset. She was hurting, and he knew what it felt like, so he just sat down and went back to cultivating. She didn't say anything more, and when he couldn't take any more processing of his rage and stopped for the night, he saw her curled into a ball, sleeping in her corner. He stood, stretched, and then lay down in his corner, staring at the ceiling for a long time before falling asleep.

"Hey, wake up." The voice intruded on his dreams, and he groggily opened his eyes. Belsa was kneeling near his head, and when she saw his eyes open, she leaned close, "Someone's fighting in the big cage over there. It sounds like they're killing someone!" Victor's heart started to hammer, and he jumped to his feet, looking out through the cage's bars, trying to see what Belsa was talking about. He heard a gurgling sound and a wet *thwap*.

"Hey, what the fuck's going on there?" he called.

"Mind your business, kid," a dark shadow leaning against the other cell said.

"That you, Zan? C'mon, man, you know we'll all catch hell if we're caught fighting."

"Quiet down, and no one will get caught; he's dying in his sleep, is all."

"Fucking hell, *pendejo*! You guys killing one of the newbies?"

"He had it coming, trust me; now shut up before Ponda hears your whimpering."

Victor slumped against the bars and turned to Belsa. "I can't do anything about it. Do you know who it is they're attacking?" She shook her head. "Well, unless we wanna be targets to the old monsters in here, we need to shut up." Her eyes blinked slowly, then she nodded and moved back to her corner. Victor did the same and was glad that he didn't hear any more sounds from the other cell. Apparently, they'd finished their business, and he could rationalize that it would've been too late for him to get the victim any help, even if he'd wanted to risk enraging the other fighters. He closed his eyes, and it felt as if he'd only just started to drift into sleep when he heard the main door slam open. He sat up, saw daylight streaming into the cages through the gaps in the warehouse boards, and looked to see who had come in. Ponda was striding down the aisle, and he shouted, "Mealtime, line up!"

Victor stood and moved to nudge Belsa with his toe. When she stirred, pushing her black hair out of her face, he said, "Hey, time for us to get some breakfast. Line up behind me by the door." He and Belsa were waiting their turn as Ponda let the closer cages go first when one of the guys from the pen across the way ran up to the bars and yelled.

"Ponda! Something's wrong with this guy. He's not getting up!"

"Shut up! It's too early for yelling. I'll check it out in a minute." A moment later, Ponda opened Victor's cage, and he led Belsa out and showed her the mess hall, glad that he wouldn't be in the pens when Ponda discovered the dead guy.

"This place is fucking savage, Belsa," he said as they sat down with their food. She didn't reply, just took a bite of her congealed pork fat and beans. "How'd you end up in here?"

"So, now you want to get to know me?"

"Am I going to pay for that comment for the rest of my life? I'm sorry, all right? For the third fucking time." She stared at him for a moment, then took another bite.

"Well, I got captured. My tribe was raiding a town in Spinecut Gorge. Most of my family got killed; a few of us lived, some court sentenced us to prison, and they sold our sentences at auction."

"*Madre!* Any of your people here with you?" He gestured around, indicating the Wagon Wheel.

"No, most of us got split up at the auction."

"Well, you got a shitty deal. Sorry. I've been here a couple of weeks, and more than half the people I've met here are dead. I hope things go better for you, though. Do you know how to fight at all?" She snorted and nodded.

"I'm Shadeni. I was born with a spear in my hand."

"Oh, well, that's good. I, uh, well, the first person I met here who was really kind to me was a Shadeni. Her name was Yrella." Something about saying her name aloud made water well up in Victor's eyes, and he looked down, busying himself with eating his breakfast.

"Where are you from, Vic-tor?" She said his name slowly, as if she was feeling how it came out of her mouth.

"Well, some assholes summoned me for some reason from my world. I think it was a mistake because they didn't seem happy to see me, then they sold me to this guy who runs these pit fights." Victor shrugged, polishing off his flatbread. "Shall we go get some exercise in? It's the best part of the day unless you like lying around in the hay and feeling bored." She nodded, and they walked out into the exercise hall. Since she'd said she was "born with a spear," Victor checked out a spear, and they practiced with that weapon for a while. Belsa wasn't slow or weak, but she was no Yrella or Vullu, and Victor didn't find himself learning anything from her. Still, it was good to have a partner to go through the spear forms with, and they had a good workout going when Yund's office door slammed open and the big Shadeni man hollered for Victor to come over. Victor handed Belsa his practice spear and jogged over to Yund.

"Kid!"

"Yeah?" he panted, slightly out of breath.

"I got you a special fight tonight. Private exhibition. Some rich bitch has a thief she wants punished. She hired the Wagon Wheel to put a fighter in the pit with him."

"Why me?"

"Cause you're the right tier, and I said so. Wait for me here a minute, and we'll get going. Gotta take a coach; her estate is outside the city." Victor nodded and stood there in his bloodstained clothes, sweat dripping down from his hair, and wondering at the strange, impossible turn his life had taken. Belsa walked over toward him, still holding the practice spears and raising her eyebrows in a questioning look.

"Uh, I have to go to some fight with the Boss. Just turn those in, and then it'll be almost time to go back to the cages. See you later. Well, I hope." Victor grinned at his dark humor. Belsa waved, choosing not to reply. He'd found she was a girl with a decided penchant for speaking as little as possible.

"Let's go, kid!" Yund said, loudly banging his door open. Victor waited for him to lead the way and then followed him out of the Wagon Wheel, down the narrow, trash-filled alley to a busier, wider street, where Yund started looking around for a coach for hire. As always, Victor was kept fascinated watching the people and the strange animals they used for transportation. The coach Yund ended up hiring was a small shiny black box pulled by two bird-lizard things, with the driver sitting up high on a springy seat.

The inside of the coach had once been plush, Victor could tell, but the red upholstered seats were threadbare, and the carpeted floor was mud-stained and patchy. He sat back in the deep cushion and caught the distinct scent of weed clinging to the fabric. "Boss, people smoke weed here?"

"Weed?"

"You know, pot. Marijuana? I can smell it in the cushions."

"Oh, sure, that's ban blossom. Banban."

"Huh, sure smells like weed. Does it make you high?"

"Sure, kid, but I'm not getting you any, so quit bugging me about it." He produced a clipboard from some secret container and started flipping through papers while Victor sat back and let the rumbling of the coach lull him into a nap. "Get up, Victor." Yund's voice cut through his dreams, and Victor sat up, blinking his eyes rapidly. "We're here; get your fight face on." Victor almost laughed at the idiom, but he snorted, stretched, and waited for the coach to come to a halt. After a moment, its wheels came to a stop, and Yund popped open the door, squeezing his bulk through the narrow opening.

Victor followed and was immediately grabbed by the fresh, cool air. No more stink of garbage or excrement, just fresh air. Victor had never been out of Arizona, and he'd never breathed such cool, clean air. Even up in the Santa Ritas, there was the ever-present taste of dust.

He saw he was standing on cobbles, and they'd been dropped in front of a large white manor. It was constructed of stone blocks and sprawled out into lots of different buildings with tall, peaked roofs. An Ardeni man in a red and black uniform waited for them near the door, and when they approached, he looked at Yund briefly but then stared at Victor for a long while before finally announcing, "He won't do."

"Oh, think again, lad," Yund said, not fazed in the least.

"Excuse me, Sir Yund, but he's only Tier One, and he looks like he's been dragged through a charnel pit."

"Well, you guys can put something fresh on him, and as for his tier, you needn't worry; he's up for the task."

"Sir, the criminal is Tier Two."

"Exactly. Not a problem. Now go ahead and take my fighter where you need him. I'll find the festivities." Yund didn't wait for a response but strode straight to the door and into the manor. The uniformed man looked at Victor with an air of defeat and then beckoned for him to follow.

"This way. We'll have to give you some clean clothes. You realize you are representing the Lady's Justice tonight. I hope you don't let her down."

"Justice? What do you mean?" The inside of the manor was fancy, like the rich people's houses on VR. The floors were smooth white stone, the walls were smooth white plaster, and art, furniture, and plants were everywhere. Where did rich people get so much shit to put around their houses? They had to be constantly shopping or something.

"I mean just that. Rather than send this man to trial and then prison, she offered him a trial of combat. The fact that you are under-ranked is not going to make her happy. If you lose, your master will have a very unhappy customer."

"Well, I don't want to lose either, bud. Also, he's not my master." They'd come into a long narrow room with several beds lined up along each side. Each bed had a chest at its foot. Were these servants' quarters or maybe soldiers' barracks?

"Wait here." He moved to a large chest at the end of the room, opened it, and started rummaging inside. "White, black or red clothes? The only boots I have are black leather." He threw a pair of black shoes that looked like a cross between cowboy boots and hiking boots at Victor's feet.

"Uh, just black, I guess."

"Yes, it should hide stains the best. Though they have minor cleaning enchantments." He straightened up and held out some heavy garments to Victor. They felt almost like denim, but they were black and looked more like cotton. Victor held up the shirt and saw that it had tiny letters or figures stitched around the cuffs in a shiny black thread.

"Yo, these look way too big. Same for the boots."

"Yes, fool, do you think we size all of our servants and custom tailor their garments? These will fit you perfectly after you bond with them."

"Bond with them?"

"Ancestors! Where did they find you? Put on the clothes, and channel some of your Energy into them. They'll bond with you." He stood there, watching Victor expectantly. Victor shrugged and stripped out of his crusty, stained T-shirt and jeans, kicking his tennies off and noticing the new holes in the soles. He stood there in stained boxers and hole-filled socks.

"Man, you got any clean underwear and socks by any chance?"

"If the Lady hears of this . . ." the man grumbled, but he walked back to the chest and came back with some soft, white underwear and thick woolen socks. Victor wasted no time slipping out of his filthy undergarments and trying on the new ones. They were too big, but he did as the guy said and tried to push a little bit of Energy out his pathway into them. To his astonishment, they immediately shrank to fit him snugly. Excited by the prospect of magical clothes, he pulled on the pants and shirt, then slipped on the big boots. He performed the same trick, channeling Energy into the clothes and boots, and soon he was standing with clothes that fit him perfectly for the first time in his life. The shirt had a low collar and clung flatteringly to his chest and arms. The pants were about as similar to black jeans as he could imagine, even having pockets as he was used to. The boots were the most kickass thing, though. They felt more comfortable than any tennies he'd ever owned, snugly hugging his feet. The soles seemed like rugged leather or wood, but they somehow cushioned his feet perfectly, and he wondered if they had some sort of comfort enchantment. The thing he liked the most about them, though, was that they were tough, with a metal-plated heel that clicked on the marble floors when he walked.

"That certainly made a world of difference," the uniformed servant said. "Now, you look like someone who could represent Justice. Please drop your old clothes in that chute."

"Is that the laundry?"

"No, the incinerator." Victor opened his mouth to argue, but then he realized that if they burned his old clothes, they would have to let him keep these, so he dumped his old belongings into the chute, belatedly realizing that he had nothing left of his life on Earth. "Good, follow me." Swallowing the lump in his throat, Victor turned away from the chute and followed the servant. They passed through several hallways, across a breezeway, into another building, then out into a garden and along another path that opened onto a lawn lit by glowing yellow orbs and a large bonfire. People stood around drinking from glasses and talking, and a tall Ghelli with glorious wings that shed sparkles of light was singing and playing a stringed instrument.

Her voice was ethereal, and the music was unlike anything Victor had ever heard, seeming to push right into his mind, triggering emotions and memories from distant corners of his life. On a primal level, he recognized that he was being influenced by Energy, and he tried to focus his will to push the music out. The music didn't resist him, and he soon heard it normally, without its unnatural influence. "Is that singer trying to cast spells on me, man?"

"Energy enhances her song—it's a skill of hers," the servant said. "You should easily be able to avoid the effect if you don't like it. Come, I'll introduce you to the Lady." Victor followed the man across the lawn to a group of Ardeni women standing around wearing slinky dresses and sizing each other up. The guy who'd been showing Victor around stopped a few feet away, so Victor did, too. They stood there for a while, then one of the ladies, the tallest one with bright yellow hair and eyes, looked their way. The servant seemed to recognize a signal and stepped forward to say, "Lady ap'Brellin, may I present your representative of Justice." He gestured, and Victor moved up to stand at his side. He had no idea what to say, so he just cleared his throat and nodded.

"What a tall and striking Justice we have tonight. Is that my household livery I recognize?" She stepped forward and reached up to rest a hand on Victor's chest, tracing a finger over the fabric of his shirt.

"Ahem, yes, my Lady; I felt he would more appropriately represent you wearing these garments."

"Hmm, yes. Very good, Pel. Well, you're a quiet one, aren't you? Are you ready to deliver Justice?" She turned from the servant to stare into Victor's face, her hand still on his chest. He'd be lying if he said he didn't like her warm hand resting there, but he was also a little flustered with all the other people around and the ladies visibly snickering behind their napkins or drinks.

"Yes. Uh, yes, I'm ready." His voice had cracked at first, and he couldn't help the embarrassed grin that parted his lips. The lady also smiled, and, allowing her fingers to drum upon his chest one last time, she pulled her hand away and called out to the people milling about the lawn.

"It's time for the trial; our Justice is here and ready to perform!"

# 17

### ❧❧❧

# PRIZES

The liveried servant led Victor down another pathway through the gardens to yet another lawn, where a fighting pit had been dug and lined with fresh wood; the smell of sawdust and paint still hung in the air. The Lady and her guests came in twos and threes to find spots around the pit's edge while Victor stood off to the side, waiting for instructions. Yund appeared after a few moments, a clutch of snacks held in a napkin in one hand and a delicate wine glass in the other. The glass looked comically small in his massive hand, and Victor snorted an involuntary chuckle at the sight.

"Friends, thank you for coming. As you're no doubt aware by now, my household suffered an affront that left us shaken and inconsolable last week. A vagabond took it upon himself to break into our home." She gestured around her to the grounds and the manor in the background. "To steal from us, assault us, and even try to take my daughter's innocence." She paused for the crowd to gasp, exclaim, and even swear threats of vengeance. "I took the matter to Magistrate Dorl; he cautioned patience. He counseled a measured and restrained response. He spoke of politics and influence! Our representative for Justice in the city spoke of politics! My blood boiled; I fumed; I raged at those who love me, shaken by my impotence. If only I'd had the guards kill him in the act! If only I'd made him disappear before approaching the authorities! Those are the mad thoughts that whispered in the back of my mind. Then dear Larl here found a solution." She paused again and gestured to a tall, thin Ardeni man wearing a sharp-looking suit.

"That's right! It might be archaic and out of fashion, but trials by combat are still perfectly legal, regardless of the political connections of your offender!" he said loudly, obviously reciting words that he'd been practicing.

"Precisely!" the Lady continued, "It is my right; nay, it is everyone's right to put an offender that they've captured in their own home into a trial of combat. All we need are witnesses." She smiled and waved around at the crowd. "To ensure a fair combat, and a willing"—she pointed at Victor—"Champion of Justice. Why, Magistrate Dorl's assistant, Lisell, is even here to bear witness to the legality of our proceedings." A thin, severe-looking Shadeni woman wearing a black robe and a strange, square golden hat that reminded Victor of an old lady's purse, nodded to the crowd, not a hint of emotion on her face.

A commotion broke out from the other side of the pit as a man wearing nothing but a pair of loose black pants and chains was pulled toward the pit by two servants wearing the Lady's livery. He was an Ardeni, but big, larger than many the Shadeni Victor had met. He was as tall as Yund, though not nearly as heavy. He struggled and strained against the servants, but they had some control over him with the chains and managed to get him to the pit's edge, where they held him, looking expectantly at the Lady.

"Gweld ap'Horrin! Your time for justice is at hand!" the Lady shouted, pointing at the bound man. He glared at her, eyes hooded by heavy, black brows, scowling with his lips pulled back in a sneer. He started to answer, perhaps to offer a retort, but the Lady yelled, "Put him in!" The two servants gave him a shove, sending him down the eight feet to the hard dirt bottom of the pit. Then she whirled on Victor. "Your time is nigh, Justice! Do your work!" Victor felt a big meaty hand on his shoulder, nudging him toward the pit, and when he looked behind him, he saw that Yund had made his way over. Victor snorted and walked toward the pit; no doubt Yund wanted to make sure he didn't make a run for it.

"Bitch! Wench of a lesser house! You call this fair? Me fighting bound by magical chains?" Gweld was shouting as Victor approached the edge.

"Your chains will be removed when our Justice has taken his position in the pit," Lady ap'Brellin said, striding to a big wooden chair positioned on a small dais to provide her an unobstructed view of the pit. Victor stood at the edge and looked at the Lady. When she nodded, he hopped down into the dirt, staring at the guy he was supposed to fight and kill. He wasn't a pleasant guy, that was for sure. Still fuming and straining against his chains, he had an ugly expression on his face, snarling and nearly frothing at the mouth with agitation. His hair was black, which was strange to Victor—every Ardeni he'd met had bright, colorful hair. Was he not Ardeni? Could the races of this world mix, perhaps?

"Are you ready, Justice?" the Lady asked from her perch. Victor formed his hands into fists and nodded. "Release his chains!" she shouted to someone; Victor had no idea who. A brief flash of light and a puff of smoke signaled the destruction of Gweld's chains, and the big man flexed his fists, looked at Victor, and grinned.

"No weapons for us, then?" he called up at the crowd, suddenly charming. The frothing, raging face was gone, though his eyes were still obscured, hidden in the shadows of his brows.

"Justice?" The Lady looked at Victor questioningly. He didn't know how to respond. The guy was bigger than he was and at a lot higher level. Maybe a weapon would even the playing field, or maybe it would just get Victor killed faster. According to the System, his skill with weapons was only "basic"—what if this guy was an expert? He looked at the Lady and shook his head. She smiled, looked at Gweld, and said, "No, dear thug. You will die by the bare hands of Justice."

"This lady really hates you, *pendejo*," Victor quietly said as he started to circle the larger man. For his part, Gweld growled, rubbing his hands together, staring at Victor. Victor felt a surge of something like paranoia, and he wondered what strange fucking thing this guy was going to do. He didn't want to give him time to do something wild, so he used his Channel Spirit ability to launch a rage-fueled leg sweep. He slid forward gracefully, bringing his left shin, throbbing and pulsing with red-hot Energy, toward Gweld's legs. Gweld had been standing straight, not a muscle tensed, and Victor hoped to catch him off-guard. He was partially successful; Gweld cursed some word Victor hadn't heard before and pulled his hands apart, pointing one palm down toward Victor's sliding body. A wave of cold poured over him, cooling the rage-attuned Energy in his leg and slowing his movement immensely. His shin collided with Gweld's and bounced off painfully.

"Fuck!" Victor grunted and tried to roll away, but he felt as if he were in slow motion. He'd just dipped down to his shoulder when Gweld's foot snapped into his hip, throwing him off balance and tumbling into the dirt. The crowd hissed, and Victor knew if he could see the Lady's face, he would recognize the look of uncertainty and abstract frustration. He rolled again, nearly running into the pit's wall, trying to get some distance between himself and the other man. He scrambled to his feet, arms held in a guard position in front of his face and neck, but Gweld hadn't pursued him. He was standing in the center of the right, concentrating on the space around his hands again. Victor saw white smoke or steam rising from them, and he was just getting ready to launch himself at Gweld again when white crystals erupted around Gweld's hands, spreading up over his arms, chest, head, and down his legs. After an instant, Victor faced a man encased in steaming white ice crystals. "Oh, this is bullshit!"

Victor had barely finished his objection when Gweld was on him, moving with the inevitability of a juggernaut; he stomped up to Victor and started punching as if his arms and fists were pistons on a machine. Victor tried to block the strikes, but it was like trying to block burning logs; wherever he touched Gweld's icy carapace, he was singed, and when he put enough force into his blocks to actually stop a punch, he felt his flesh getting smashed and torn, and the impact jarred him deep in his bones. Victor retreated around the edge of the pit, realizing he was in over his head. Again. Rather than panic or terror, though, he started to feel angry. Yund had known this fucking guy was Tier Two. What was this bullshit ability that coated him in fucking freezing ice? How was he supposed to fight that? Should he have asked for a weapon? Maybe a damn hammer would have been the right move. All these thoughts raced through Victor's mind as he backpedaled away from the juggernaut.

The other half of Victor's mind, the part that hadn't been spouting a string of pointless questions and complaints, had noted that Gweld might be nigh invincible and able to throw endless, painful punches, but he was also predictable. As he pursued Victor, he followed the same pattern: step, punch, step, punch-punch, step, punch, step, punch-punch. Victor avoided most of the punches, painfully deflecting one now and then to keep Gweld feeling like he was accomplishing something. As he backed away from a punch-punch combo, Victor channeled Energy into his right fist, used his Sovereign Will ability to pump up his strength, and stepped into Gweld's left jab, taking the blow on the shoulder but delivering a savage right hook to Gweld's hard, icy chest.

A thunderous crack echoed up out of the pit as Gweld's carapace shattered, and he was flung back to the pit wall as if a wrecking ball had struck him. Victor had no idea what kinds of tricks someone over Level Twenty might have in store, so he didn't think it would be smart to let up the pressure. Instead, he went Berserk; he lifted his face to the night sky and roared, his muscles convulsing as rage-attuned Energy poured into them, making his back arch. As shades of red clouded his vision, Victor looked at the man sitting up out of the crumbled chunks of ice, and fury filled his mind. Here was his enemy; here was the one who'd been burning and smashing him. Here was the thing he needed to destroy.

Victor leaped at Gweld, hands clenched into rocklike fists, and they collided in a flurry of punches, explosions of ice, snarls, and screams. Gweld wasn't done—he conjured hunks of ice to block punches and sent shards of ice stabbing into Victor's body, eliciting cries of fury and even more frenzied punches and kicks and headbutts. As soon as the ice fragments pierced his flesh, his body pushed them out, flesh pulling together with hardly any blood loss. Gweld's smug grin was long gone; panic stared out of the deep hollows of his bloodied eyes.

Victor could feel the rage waning, feel the fury in his muscles starting to cool, and he roared in denial, pulling more Energy out of his Core and sending it surging along his pathways. Dimly he was aware that his Core was more a flickering light than a raging sun, his Energy nearly spent. Still, he didn't care; the only thing that mattered was that Gweld was still moving, still trying to fight back. He drove him from one wall to another, punching, grabbing, throwing, pursuing. After a time, his mind came back to him, and he felt his hands hefting something heavy. He followed through with the motion, throwing it against the wall, and when he saw Gweld's mutilated corpse slide down into the dirt, Victor stumbled backward, looking around in a panic.

The Lady's guests were standing around the pit. Some held napkins or handkerchiefs in front of their mouths, looks of horror in their eyes; others leered openly, words of encouragement sent Victor's way. Victor stumbled backward to the center of the pit and looked up to the Lady. She sat in her chair, beauty personified, with her hair perfectly coiffed and her hands folded in her lap, but in her eyes, in her bright, yellow eyes, Victor could see despair. At first, he thought she was upset by his savagery. He was certainly upset about it; why shouldn't she be? But then she spoke, "Well done, Justice. Friends, please return to the estate; dinner will be served shortly. I apologize, but I'll need a few moments—I'd hoped this swine's death would bring me closure, but I feel nothing." She stood and walked away. Some of the other ladies followed after, but most of the guests moved away from the pit, talking in hushed or excited conversations about the fight.

"Well, come on, kid. I'll give you a hand out." Yund had approached the pit behind Victor. Victor reached up and took his hand, allowing him to hoist him up to the edge. "I knew you were fighting above your rank, but that was better than I'd hoped. Nice work." He patted Victor's shoulder and steered him toward a dark path in the garden. "Let's walk around the manor to get to the coach. I'd rather not go through that house with all those fancy shits. I already got my payment."

They walked in silence for a while, then Victor said, "I'm glad he turned out to be a bad guy. Yund, I don't ever want to fight someone like Belsa."

"First of all, kid, 'bad' is relative. Just because all these nobles at this house hated that asshole doesn't make him 'bad.' Don't get me wrong, he probably was, but don't believe people just because they're beautiful and clean. That 'Lady' has a lot of blood on her hands, believe me." Yund reached up and put a hand on Victor's shoulder while they walked. "Second of all, Belsa's that new girl I got at auction yesterday, right?" Victor nodded. "Yeah, well, I'm an asshole, but I know you by now, kid. I'm not going to arrange a fight like that for you. What good would it do me for you to get yourself killed 'cause you feel sorry for your opponent?" He shook Victor's shoulder and continued, "Now, enough moping. You won an impressive victory here, which means I owe you a reward. I already got it for you, too. Hang on; let me see here." He held a hand to one of his pouches, concentrating for a moment while they walked along the garden path. "Aha!" A rolled-up piece of paper with a hunk of red waxy stuff holding it closed appeared in his hand. He handed it to Victor and said, "It's a general cultivation method for Spirit Cores. When we get back, break the seal and stare at the runes—the System will trigger it, and the knowledge will go into you."

"Seriously? I wish I had scrolls like that in high school."

"Listen, that was pretty expensive—not many people are interested in Spirit Cores, at least not in this part of the world. After you learn it and get a few more levels, I'm going to need you to either get tagged or start wearing a collar between fights. Nothing personal, but I have an investment to protect."

"Whatever. If I have to do it, I will, but I'd rather not get the tag—it seems too permanent. Hey, I didn't level from that guy."

"Your new class takes more effort to level. Maybe next time, or maybe now that you have a cultivation guide, you'll be able to advance that way, too." Ahead of them, Victor could see a light on a brick post, signaling a gateway. When they approached, he saw that they'd come out of the gardens near the front of the house by the stables and waiting carriages. Victor followed Yund toward one of the carriages, but a figure stepped out from the shadows nearby as they approached. Lady ap'Brellin walked up to them, a small package in her hands.

"I know you've been paid, Mr. Yund. I wanted to give a gift to our young representative of Justice."

"Oh, of course, Lady," Yund said, bowing low and stepping to the side.

"I'll see that he takes full possession before you leave, sir. I know how cutthroat your business is." Yund's obsequious smile faltered momentarily, but then it was back, and he nodded enthusiastically, taking yet another step back. She nodded and stepped closer to Victor, holding out the package. Self-conscious of his bloodstained hands, Victor reached out and took the paper-wrapped box. It was about three inches square and as heavy as a paperback book.

"Um, what is it?" he asked.

"Open it." She nodded toward the box, indicating that she'd be staying around until he complied. Victor peeled off the brown paper, revealing a light brown wooden box. He lifted the lid to find a straw-filled interior on which a deep purple plumlike fruit sat. "This fruit will advance your race. If you want to achieve levels beyond fifteen, you'll need at least one advancement. This fruit should get you as many as four."

"Lady! This is too valuable for someone like him! I can't see you wasting such a prize!" Yund stepped forward, reaching for the box in Victor's hands.

"Sir! You will back away and allow him to consume this fruit! I have paid for his services for the evening, and I will reward him as I see fit."

"He could die in a day! Why such a rare fruit? You could give him a Wyrdla berry for a hundredth of the price!"

"That is the last outburst I'll tolerate from you, Mr. Yund." She didn't even look at him, trusting that her words would suffice. They worked, though. Yund turned away and paced in a small circle, visibly clenching his mouth shut to avoid saying anything. "Come, Justice. Sit in your coach and eat the fruit. You won't want to be standing when the effects hit you."

"Um, okay. Thank you." Victor was at a loss for words. What the hell did it even mean to "advance your race?" He knew these guys used the word "race" differently than the humans back home. When there were actually different species of people, it made worrying about the color of someone's skin seem a little dumb. He stepped past the Lady, opened the coach door, and climbed up onto his seat. He looked at the woman's beautiful, cold face one more time. She nodded, and he ate the fruit.

# 18

## CULTIVATING

Victor sank back into the cushions of the coach, the scents of perfume, sweat, and old smoke wafting up around him. As he swallowed the fruit, which hadn't tasted like a plum, more like an orange with the texture of a banana, warmth pulsed through the flesh that it touched, and then in a wave from the center of his belly out to his limbs. He felt a buzzing sensation all over his body, and then he felt heavy, as if he were sinking into the center of the world, pulling the coach and everything else along with him. Waves of pink light, darkening to violet, rolled over his vision, and he lost himself watching the patterns of shifting colors. When he started to feel himself again, began to remember that he was a person, he became aware of the rattling clatter of the coach wheels outside the window and the bump and sway it made as it rolled down the street. "What happened?" he muttered, his mouth feeling as though he'd tried to swallow a cup of dusty sand.

"What happened? You got a tip worth more than I made at the last three Fight Nights." Yund sat across from him, eyes narrowed as he studied Victor. "Well, what happened? I can see your race advanced. How much?"

"You can tell?" Victor coughed. "Hold on," he said and thought about this status page:

| Status | | | |
|---|---|---|---|
| Name: | Victor Sandoval | | |
| Race: | Human: Base 4 | | |
| Class: | Spirit Champion | | |
| Level: | 10 | | |
| Core: | Spirit Class: Base 4 | | |
| Energy Affinity: | 3.1, Rage 9.1 | Energy: | 420/420 |
| Strength: | 25 | Vitality: | 20 |
| Dexterity: | 17 | Agility: | 17 |
| Intelligence: | 10 | Will: | 10 |
| Points Available: | 0 | | |
| Titles & Feats: | – | | |
| Skills: | • System Language Integration: Not Upgradeable<br>• Unarmed Combat: Basic<br>• Knife Combat: Basic<br>• Axe Mastery: Basic<br>• Spear Mastery: Basic<br>• Bludgeon Mastery: Basic<br>• Grappling: Improved | | • Berserk: Basic<br>• Sovereign Will: Basic<br>• Channel Spirit: Basic |

"It says Base Four next to my race now."

"Three ranks. From one fruit. Well, nicely done, kid. I hope you live long enough to appreciate it." Yund folded his arms on his chest and visibly sulked.

"What's the point of racial advancements anyway?" Victor held up his hands and noticed that some of the scars he'd accumulated recently were gone, and almost all of them had faded to faint white marks.

"If I had a mirror, you'd know. When you stand up, you'll notice. You're bigger, taller. More than that, your body has improved from your blood to your heart to your bones. It can hold more Energy now, which means a higher level cap. If you had a peaceful life, you'd live a lot longer now, too."

"Awesome," Victor said, running his fingers along his face, trying to notice anything different. He felt good, but other than that, he seemed the same. When they got back to the Wagon Wheel and Victor clambered out of the coach, he noticed a remarkable difference: he was looking at Yund almost eye to eye. "Fucking hell, I *did* grow!"

"Ponda!" Yund barked as they strode through the door. The big Vodkin came waddling out of the mess hall.

"Yeah, Boss?"

"Put him back in his cage and put a collar on him. He's grown a bit much to be wandering without a leash." Victor felt a little surge of heat in his Core when Yund spoke about him like a dog, and he snarled involuntarily. "Here, kid." Yund held out his hand. "You dropped this when you ate the fruit." Victor reached out, and Yund pressed the scroll with his cultivation method on it to him.

"Oh, thanks, Yund."

"You mean Boss."

"Right. Thanks, Boss." Victor walked over to Ponda and followed him to the pens. He was pleased to see that Ponda didn't seem so big to him anymore, either.

"Getting bigger, eh, kid?" Ponda asked as he unlocked his cage.

"Yeah, got a prize for winning." Victor shrugged and ducked into the cage. Ponda didn't close it right away but pulled out a dull iron ring about four inches in diameter, holding it up to Victor's neck. "I think that's too small, dude."

"Nah, it'll stretch when I activate it. Hold still." He pressed one edge of the ring to Victor's neck, then Victor felt it get warm, then hot, then it seemed to flow around his skin, stretching itself into a ring of metal that snugly wrapped around his neck. "Don't do anything dumb with this on, kid. Boss can kill you from a mile away as long as you're wearing this."

"All right." Victor didn't like the sound of that. It made him think of a VR flick he saw where prisoners' heads exploded if they tried to run away from the warden. Ponda didn't seem to care to stick around to hear his concerns, though; he slammed the gate shut and walked out of the pens without a backward glance.

"Where'd they take you? Did you really have to grow even taller? You were already a freak compared to most Shadeni." Victor turned to see Belsa sitting in her corner of the cage, green eyes glinting brightly in the shadows.

"I had to go to this rich lady's house and fight a criminal. I won, so she gave me a prize." Victor gestured at his body. "Racial upgrade."

"You really know how to paint the scene with your words." Belsa laughed.

"Damn, you're in a better mood. Teasing me, huh?" Victor moved to his corner and sat down, wondering if he could use the scroll in such dim lighting.

"I guess I'm relieved that I don't have to get to know a new cellmate yet. You might be rude, but at least I know you. Who knows what I'd get next! What's that?"

"All right, nosy *chica*, it's a cultivation method, I guess. I'm supposed to stare at the runes or whatever." Victor ran a finger along the loose edge of the scroll, pulling it under the red seal, and it broke away into little crumbles. Victor had a sudden thought, "Hey, when I say 'girl,' what word do you hear?"

"Girl?"

"What about when I say '*chica*?'"

"Girl?"

"That shit's crazy. I just said 'girl' in two different languages, and you heard only one."

"It's the language integration. The System makes us all hear our native language when others speak."

"Yeah, I get it. It's just fucking weird."

"Fucking?"

"C'mon, you can guess what it means." Victor unrolled the scroll and saw that the runes were faintly shimmering symbols of letters that he'd never seen in his life. Belsa said something, but he'd tuned her out, staring at the runes as they shifted ever so slightly on the page. Suddenly one of them moved more than the others, then it popped out into the air. Victor almost dropped the scroll in surprise, but he held on, and then more runes popped off the paper and began to flow into a glowing line that streamed toward Victor's eyes. As the runes hit his eyes, they became a pulsing beam in his vision. A dull ache started to throb at the base of his skull. Just as he began to fear his head would burst, it came to a stop.

\*\*\*Congratulations, you've learned a new skill: Spirit Core Cultivation Drill, Basic.\*\*\*

"I mean, that was cool, but I don't know if I really like the feeling," he said, mostly to himself. He thought about cultivating Energy and found that he suddenly understood a great deal more about the subject. Thanks to Yrella's guidance and his experimentation, he'd figured out a lot of the process. One thing he knew now was that Spirit Cores couldn't absorb unattuned Energy.

He had to process any Energy he cultivated into rage-attuned Energy. There were ways to do so, and it turned out the one he'd figured out was the crudest, most dangerous method recorded in the manual.

There was a method to memorize and imprint the feelings associated with memories that evoked strong emotion so that you could study those feelings but not relive your trauma over and over—the pure essence of rage rather than rage-soaked memories. Victor found he hadn't done everything wrong, though—you needed those memories to study in order to develop your meditation on the feelings and essence of the emotion. Because the manual was for general Spirit Core cultivation, it didn't deal explicitly with rage. Rather, it spoke in generalities about "emotions" and their essence.

Another thing the manual provided was the drill for cultivation itself. It was an exercise that began with Victor studying the essence of his attunement, creating a self-propagating feedback loop within his Core. As the Energy became too intense, he was supposed to push it through his pathways in a specific pattern, to create a loop that brought in external Energy, converted it to rage-attuned Energy, then directed it back to his Core. It was similar to what Victor had been doing but far more efficient.

"Did it work?" Belsa had scooted closer to him and was staring expectantly.

"Yeah. Got a cultivation drill." He moved to sit in the position Yrella had taught him and closed his eyes, ready to begin the possibly arduous process of developing rage constructs to study so that he could stop reliving all of his most painful memories.

"What are you doing?"

"I'm gonna try it out! Chill out, please. Go do some meditating or something." He spoke sharply, and regretted it when she looked down quickly and scooted back. He almost took the words back, saying he was sorry, but he didn't, and it pissed him off that he was being such an asshole. He decided to use that feeling and quickly started following the cultivation manual's process for studying a feeling and turning it into a pure construct. It was like a mnemonic trick or self-hypnosis, but he understood it so thoroughly, thanks to the way the System put it in his head, that he performed it flawlessly. He found that he could study the construct of the feeling caused by his interaction with Belsa to start a hot pulse in his Core, actually generating Energy with his rage. The best part was that he could study that feeling, experience the rage, and feed off it without the emotional baggage of remembering Belsa's crestfallen face. It was as if he pulled the feeling out and could leave the memory in his subconscious.

Victor stopped, letting his Core wind down, then he purposefully thought about how he'd snapped at Belsa. The shame and guilt were still there, but not the rage. Had he really separated that feeling from the memory? "How fucking weird!" Belsa shifted but didn't say anything. "Hey, I'm sorry I snapped at you. I have a lot on my mind, and I couldn't think."

"It's fine."

Victor knew very well that it wasn't "fine," but he figured he could try to cheer her up tomorrow. He'd said he was sorry, and she could sleep on that. If that little surge of anger allowed him to cultivate rage, how would a bigger memory work? Could he separate the rage from a truly white-hot fury-inducing episode in his life? He was too chicken to even contemplate thinking about Yrella's death right now, and he was tired of soaking in the frustration of his parents' car wreck, so he picked something a little less tender: the time he'd been hanging at his aunty's house with his cousin Tricia and her friends. The time they'd been speaking Spanish, and Victor, barely able to follow a slowly worded directive from his *abuela*, couldn't follow along. His cousin had said, "Better speak English; his mom was white." Her friends had laughed and said something in Spanish that, again, Victor hadn't been able to follow. He'd been embarrassed and angry at being singled out, so he'd lashed out. He was a nine-year-old boy, and he'd cussed at his cousin, called her a bitch, and run to hide.

Victor focused on the memory, studied the rage, and used the method in the manual to create a construct from it. He was fascinated to see that most of the anger he felt in that memory was aimed at himself. He'd been angry for not being better at Spanish. He'd been angry at himself for not being able to defend his mom; he'd been angry at himself for feeling small and unable to stick up for himself. Most of all, he'd been angry at himself for reacting so harshly to his cousin; they'd never gotten along the same since that day. When Victor built the construct of all that rage, he found it flamed hotter and quickly started pulsing in his Core.

On a whim, he added the construct from his interaction with Belsa, and he found that their ability to generate rage complemented each other. Victor ran through his drill twice, noting that he'd built his Core far more significantly than in an entire afternoon of cultivation with his old method. He wanted to stop, though, and analyze the memory from which he'd built the rage construct. When he thought about that day, all he felt was guilt and a sense of loss. He really had pulled the anger out of the memory. Was it hypnosis? Was it magic? There was so much to learn and understand about how the System and Energy worked, and Victor knew he was only scratching the surface.

Not wanting to tangle with any more memories, Victor spent the evening cultivating around the two constructs he'd made. When he received a message announcing he'd improved his Core by another rank, he almost whooped aloud but caught himself when he noticed Belsa's sleeping form. He found that he wasn't tired at all; in fact, he felt energized, and he knew it was from the racial upgrades he'd just gone through. He went back to cultivating and didn't stop until he got another System message and saw the sunlight poking in through the high boards on the east wall of the building.

***Congratulations! You've achieved Level 11 Spirit Champion. You have gained 7 will, 7 vitality, and have 7 attribute points to allocate.***

# 19

## PRIVATE PARTY

"You know, I really didn't think much about escaping until they put this fucking collar on my neck," Victor said, trying to squeeze a finger between his skin and the thick metal band; he had an itch developing that was fast becoming a new source of rage Energy for him.

"Why didn't you ask for the tag?" Belsa sat up from where Victor had tossed her, trying to teach her to manage her momentum better.

"I dunno. Something about it reminded me of how ranchers brand their cows and shit." Again, he rubbed at the collar. "Of course, this isn't much better. Collars are for dogs, not people, you know?"

"Oh, I agree. You think they'll put one on me?"

"When you get to Tier Two, or are a tough Tier One like me." Victor jammed a thumb into his chest and flexed his other arm, hamming it up. She laughed, in a much better mood today than she'd been the night before. He supposed that was a direct result of him not being an asshole today. Victor felt this revelation should be written somewhere: people tended to react to you similarly to how you treat them.

"You joke, but I guess it shows they're afraid of you. Or afraid of what you might do, at least."

"Yeah, of course, I didn't realize it in time." He flicked the metal collar again.

"What about your clothes? Did Boss give those to you?"

"No, and you can call him Yund when it's just you and me. It bugs me that he makes us call him Boss." Victor rubbed the sleeve of his black shirt between his fingers, marveling at the garment for at least the tenth time that day. When he'd woken, he'd been stunned to see that all the little rips had mended, and the blood that had matted the fabric was gone entirely. "Nah, the Lady at the house we fought at gave 'em to me. I guess her servant did, actually. Seemed like a decent guy."

"Well, that shirt isn't as nice as my vest, but it looks better than those bloody rags you had on before." She gestured to her beaded vest proudly while she spoke, and Victor got the feeling she was fishing for a compliment.

"Yeah, that vest is nice. Did you, uh, sew those designs on it?"

"Yes, I did the beadwork. An artisan in my clan made these beads—they're all polished stones and shells."

"Yeah, they're, um, they're real nice."

"Victor! Kid! Come over here!" Yund had poked his head out of his office door, saving Victor from an awkward conversation about fashion.

"Keep working on your falls," he said as he jogged away, past a few other sparring fighters, and up to Yund's door. "Yeah?"

"You ain't going to Pit Night tonight."

"What? Why?"

"Another private fight. I'm going to have Urt take you. You'll have to leave soon because the fight's outside the city again."

"Oh, c'mon, Boss. Do I have to be a 'Justice' again?"

"Nah, but it's related—one of the guests liked what they saw and wanted to enter you in a private tournament." Yund looked down, and to the side, kind of shiftily, and Victor knew he wasn't telling him everything.

"Anything else I should know?"

"No, kid. Well, actually, yes—don't mess around or get any ideas. Urt's going to have control of that collar, and he's a lot less patient than I am!" He slammed the door in Victor's face after he finished speaking, and Victor turned back to the exercise hall. Yund was definitely acting shifty, but he was a shifty guy in a dirty business. Was it anything unusual? Unfortunately, there wasn't any way for Victor to know. Maybe Urt would let something slip on the way to the fight. Victor wandered back over to Belsa, and she seemed to pick up on his mood right away.

"What's wrong?" Her green eyes crinkled in her round face, a look crossing her face that Victor couldn't place—was she scared? He supposed it would be scary for her; she didn't know anyone else in the Wagon Wheel. If things were bad for Victor, her little bit of stability could disappear.

"Oh, Yund just told me I have to go to another private fight. No Fight Night at the Rusty Nail for me."

"So I'll have to go alone?" she asked, her voice soft and her eyes unfocusing, staring into space.

"No, you won't be alone! Everyone here is going, except Urt and me, I guess. Ponda will be there, and he won't let anyone mess with you. Well, outside your fight at least." He reached out and held out a fist to her. After a moment, she scrunched up her knuckles and knocked them against his. "That's the spirit. You're going to do fine—Yund will put you with someone you can beat; I'm sure of it." Victor felt a little bad because, in the back of his mind, he was thinking that his little field trip with Urt might be a perfect opportunity to make a break for it. Urt wasn't as strong or as smart as Ponda, and they'd be away from Yund and all his other lackeys. He couldn't think of a better opportunity, collar or not.

They sparred for a while with spears, then did an exercise circuit, and then Ponda was screaming at everyone to get back to their cages. It was time for the next round of prisoners to come out for exercise. They'd barely gotten back in their cage, Ponda slamming it shut and stomping out, when Urt came in, slamming the door open against the wall. Victor briefly congratulated the guy who'd built that door—it saw a hell of a lot of abuse. He stomped up to Victor's cage, hocked a huge loogie, spit it into the hay, and said, "Looks like you got a special night ahead, boy."

"Not my choice." Victor shrugged and walked over to the cage door. Urt fumbled with the lock, and Victor looked over to Belsa. "Hey, good luck tonight. You'll do fine. We'll swap stories tomorrow, all right?"

"Right. Good luck, Victor." She nodded her head, mouth held in a straight line, and her eyes did not betray any emotion. Victor had to admire her guts. He'd at least had Yrella and Vullu at his first Fight Night. Urt pulled the cage open and gestured for Victor to follow. He held up a little silver rod as they walked.

"With this, I can make that collar so hot it melts through your neck. Don't cock about, got it?"

"Yeah. Fuck, man. Have I ever caused you trouble?"

"Just keep it in mind." Urt walked to the door, slamming it open again, then motioning Victor through. They strode through the big exercise hall. Ponda had a group of the newer fighters assembled near the far wall and was yelling at them about some rule or another they'd broken. Yund's door was closed, and no one looked at them or said anything as they walked through the big doors and out into the street. A coach much like the one Victor had ridden in with Yund was already waiting, and they clambered up into it.

The coach's interior was in much better repair than the other one. Victor saw that right away—there wasn't any mud on the black lacquered floor, the red seat cushions weren't threadbare, and it didn't smell of anything in particular. "Not too bad," he said to Urt, partially trying to make conversation and partially trying to irritate the recalcitrant manager. Victor laughed at himself, thinking of Urt as a manager. Sure, he "managed" the fighters, but he was more like a prison guard than a coach.

"Huh. Yeah, I didn't hire it. The guy paying for you to fight did." That was interesting. Victor looked around more closely, but he didn't see any identifying marks on the coach's interior.

"Do you think it's his coach? Or did he hire it and send it to us?"

"How the shit would I know? Quiet now and let me snooze." Urt leaned back, closed his eyes, and crossed his arms on his chest, the rod that controlled Victor's collar clutched firmly in his left fist. Victor briefly entertained the idea of trying to grab the rod and jump out the coach's door. He reached out and tried the latch, not really surprised when he couldn't move it. He was locked in here. These guys seemed dumb and lazy, but they weren't new at the whole kidnapping and enslaving part of their lives. He pulled the curtain aside to at least get a view of the journey through town, but the glass was black. He couldn't see anything outside. The light coming from the little glowing orb in the coach's ceiling looked so much like daylight that Victor hadn't realized at first that the windows were covered.

"Great. Guess it's going to be a boring ride." He looked at his status page and decided to allocate his seven free points. He'd debated it for a while, not sure what was the smart move, but he figured he'd been winning fights by being able to finish people quickly while he was Berserk. Since that seemed to be a winning strategy, he decided to put three into strength, two into agility, and two into dexterity. He figured that would be a good distribution to follow for a while. His class levels gave him plenty of will and vitality; he just thought he should keep his other physical stats improving with the free points. He stared around the coach's interior, stared at Urt, and wondered which of his rings and belts were the mysterious "dimensional containers" that all the non-enslaved people in this world seemed to have.

A dark thought crossed his mind; could he strike Urt hard enough to knock him unconscious or kill him before he could activate the collar? He was just lying there, helpless. What if he channeled his rage and really let him have it, right in the head or neck? Victor ran through it in his head over and over. What would happen if he killed him? Could he take the rod, hopefully, get this collar off, then try to break out of the coach? Should he sit in the coach and wait for the driver to open it? Then he could make a run for it. What if he failed to knock Urt out? The guy was an ex-fighter and supposedly pretty high level. If he didn't incapacitate him, he'd be in trouble for sure. What if he couldn't get out of the coach or if they had guards waiting? What if the driver was some kind of powerful Energy user?

Victor shook his head, sitting back in his seat and closing his eyes. "Chickenshit," he said, lightly banging his knuckles into his forehead.

"Quiet!" Urt grumbled, snorting and swallowing a mouthful of phlegm.

"That's fucking gross, bro." Urt didn't respond, and Victor decided to pass the time with some cultivation. He'd run through his entire drill four times when the coach's rattling, swaying travel slowed, and the sound of the wheels transitioned from softly grinding dirt roads to clattering, grinding cobbles again. After a few moments of this, they came to a stop, and Urt sat up as though he'd never closed his eyes.

"All right, look tough." Urt scooted up in his seat, facing the door, and when someone rapped on the dark glass, Urt knocked back in a similar pattern.

"You guys have a secret knock?" Urt didn't answer, just shrugged. The door opened, and the coachman held it while Urt scrambled out. Victor followed, stepping onto rounded cobbles into the cold night air. He looked around, noting the dark shadows of thick tree canopies on either side of the cobbled path. A stone wall and gate were nearby on this side of the lane, and Urt motioned for Victor to follow him to it. The coachman didn't say anything, but Victor heard him close the door, and, as they stepped through the shadowed gateway, he heard it clatter a short way down the lane and then stop. The path they walked along was bedded in small, round stones and roughly ten feet wide. On either side of it, tall, looming trees made the night feel exceptionally deep and heavy. As they walked, Victor's and Urt's feet crunching in the gravel filled the air, nearly drowning out the chirping and droning of all the nighttime insects lurking in the thick foliage. They walked for about five minutes, every now and then passing lampposts that shed yellow islands of light in the darkness. When they followed a final curve in the path and a stone wall with a black, iron door mounted in it came into view, Victor felt a little surge of relief—he'd been a bit unnerved walking through the dark forest, regardless of the well-maintained path and the intermittent lamps.

Two Ardeni men stood outside the door; both wore black and blue uniforms, had swords on their belts, and sported shiny metal helmets. As Urt approached, Victor in tow, one of them stepped forward. "From the Wagon Wheel?"

"Aye," Urt said.

"You have the contract and the control rod?"

"Aye." Urt pulled a rolled-up parchment out of "somewhere" and handed it and the control rod for Victor's collar to the uniformed servant or guard. He turned to look at Victor, then shrugged. "Sorry, kid."

"Here's for your boss." The guard handed Urt a heavy-looking sack about the size of a bag of sugar.

"The fuck is going on, Urt?" Victor looked at Urt with wide eyes, but he refused to make eye contact.

"Shut up and move with us." The guard turned and opened the metal door with a grinding squeal, signaling seldom used hinges. Urt, for his part, turned and walked up the gravel path, his feet crunching loudly at first and then fading as the night swallowed him. "I said let's go. I don't want to have to use this." He waved the rod in front of Victor. Victor looked from one stony-faced guard to the other and followed through the doorway. They were in a narrow, low-ceilinged stone hallway. Victor had to stoop to walk along behind the first Ardeni, and the other took up position behind him. Yellow light globes appeared in the tunnel every twenty feet or so, just bright enough to keep the space dimly lit. Victor didn't note any doors in the tunnel, and he could feel that they were slowly moving down a slope.

"Can you guys tell me what the fuck is going on? Am I here to fight in a tournament?" The guard in front of him laughed, a short, mocking sound.

"That what your owner said? Sure, that's what it is. We're taking you down here to a 'tournament.'" He snickered again, and the guard behind Victor snorted also. Victor knew he wouldn't get any answers from these assholes, so he just readied himself, figuring he'd have answers soon enough. They finally came to a T in the tunnel, and the guards led Victor to the left. After a while, they arrived at another heavy, iron door. The guard put a big metal key into the door, grunted as he twisted it, broke away some rust, and then pulled the door open, hinges squealing.

They walked into a round room with a convex stone ceiling and mortared stone walls. In the center of the room, a lone table sat on a sturdy metal frame. The first guard touched something on the wall, and cool white-blue light filled the air, almost as if it was exuded from the stone ceiling. He walked to the table and turned a crank, and it rotated on its pedestal on some sort of hinge until it was perpendicular to the floor. The rear guard gave Victor a shove. "Stand with your back against the table," he said gruffly.

"The fuck is this?" Victor began to panic and started to reach for his Core.

"Don't even think about it, shithead. I'll melt your head right off." Suddenly the collar around Victor's neck grew warm, then uncomfortably hot, and he reached up in a panic, trying to squeeze his fingers in between it and his tender throat. "Just do what I said, and I'll cool it off." Victor complied, walking up to the table. As soon as he was standing with his back touching the metal surface, the collar started to cool, and the guards each pulled one of Victor's hands down to the table, clasping something around his wrists. Then the guards backed away, and the first one stepped around to crank the little wheel again. Victor rotated backward ninety degrees so that he was now lying facing the round dome of the ceiling. "All right. I'll watch him. Go let Lord ap'Horrin know he's here."

Victor's mind raced as the other guard walked away, pulling open and then closing the squealing metal door. He'd heard that name before— ap'Horrin. He couldn't place it, though. It might have been a name he heard at one of the Fight Nights or someone that Vullu or Yrella had mentioned. He couldn't figure it out. He knew one thing, though: Yund had fucked him over. Yund, Ponda, Urt—they'd all known this was going down. Ponda hadn't looked at him when he was leaving. Urt had said, "Sorry, kid." Obviously, Yund knew—he'd been paid a fat sack of whatever passed for money in this world. What were these assholes planning for him? He couldn't think of any sort of good scenario where someone is strapped to a metal table deep underground. Sure, maybe they were going to do some cosmetic modifications—give him a tattoo and some fangs. He snorted a short laugh.

"Good that you can have a sense of humor. I'll be honest with you; I hope the Lord's quick with you 'cause I don't have the same kind of stomach he does." Victor had almost forgotten the other guard was still in the room.

"Dude, can't you tell me what the fuck is going on?"

"Shouldn't be that hard to figure out. How many lord's kids have you killed?"

"What the fuck? I only fight in pits, dude, and I sure as hell don't get to pick my opponents."

"True, it's not really a fair deal for you, but Lord ap'Horrin has to save face somehow, and he can't very well kill Lady ap'Brellin, can he? Now shut up; I'm not supposed to talk to you." Lady ap'Brellin, the Lady that hired him to be a "Justice?" Images of the garden party and the newly constructed pit filled Victor's mind. The man thrown in the pit with him had been a noble, the "criminal" he'd killed because the courts wouldn't do what the Lady wanted.

"Oh, God." Victor strained against his restraints, but they were immovable. He knew if he tried to use his Energy abilities, the guard would use the collar, but he couldn't help the panic rising in his chest. What was this fucking guy going to do to him?

# 20

---

# FRACTURED

Victor felt that the lord that the guard had gone to fetch would arrive any moment, so he lay there tensely, his mind providing detailed fantasies about what kind of hell was waiting for him. He lay like that for a long time, tense, sweating, even twitching with nerves. When long minutes went by, then hours, he thrashed about, trying to get even a tiny amount of wiggle room in his wrists so that he could turn or look behind him. His restraints wouldn't budge, though, and though he tried, he couldn't get his head turned far enough to see the guard that was presumably still sitting or standing behind him. He tried to engage the guard in conversation a few times, but after a few grunts of "Quiet!" or "Just wait," he gave up.

After a while, he tried to find some solace in dozing off. He closed his eyes and tried to focus on things that made him happy, or at least places that made him happy. He imagined walking around the big wash where he and his buddies had built a fort every summer. He remembered how it smelled out there during monsoon season, how the water would flow for a few hours after each storm, and then he and his friends would go out and find tadpoles in the big puddles left behind. Where did those toads go during the rest of the year? His friend James had said they hibernated, but Victor couldn't picture toads sleeping underground for most of the year, just coming out during a month or two when the rains really pounded the desert. He supposed anything was possible, though.

"Creosote," he mumbled. "That's what smelled so good around the washes during the rains." He lifted his head off the table and brought it down with a thud. He did it again, harder, with a louder thud.

"Cut that shit out." The guard didn't sound happy. Maybe he was as bored as Victor.

"Oh, you're still there? Fuck you, *pendejo*." Victor closed his eyes and let himself drift again. Memories and dreams blurred together for a while, and then he really did sleep, deep, sinking into the earth sleep, with no dreams to bother him. Then he felt a gentle hand on his cheek, caressing it lightly, and he opened his eyes to the cool, sterile light of the domed stone ceiling. He blinked a few times and saw that an Ardeni man with a neatly trimmed black beard was standing next to him, his hand resting on Victor's cheek.

"Ahh, there he is. There's our young *Justice*." He patted Victor's cheek twice more, then pulled his hand away. He didn't have a smile on his face, but his voice didn't sound particularly angry or cruel. Victor saw that he had dark eyes like the guy he'd fought in the pit. Another Ardeni without bright hair and eyes? He wanted to ask about it but knew he had to play this smart, so he kept his mouth shut. "Well, have anything to say for yourself?"

"Um, are you the father of the man I had to fight, um, at that Lady's house?"

"Oh, just an innocent victim of circumstance, hmm?" The man's brow furrowed, and a glint of cruelty entered his eyes.

"You can say what you want, man, but I didn't fucking choose to be there, or even in this goddamned world!"

"Is that right? So, some stranger, some *victim*, just a Tier One nobody, managed to kill my Tier Two son in a pit fight?"

"Actually, yes. I didn't even want to fight there. I had no idea who your son was."

"What do you say to that, Drelk?" He looked past Victor toward the part of the room behind his head.

"Well, I told you about his savagery. I don't think I need to say more. I can't imagine anyone unwillingly doing what this beast did to your son, to your son's corpse."

"And that"—a hard glint entered the lord's eyes, and his voice became icy—"is why you must be gentled and put somewhere away from society, Victor. Did I say that right? Your name? It's a new one to me, but I saw it on the contract I purchased."

"The fuck do you mean, gentled? Dude, just let me go, and I won't bother you or your society." Victor strained against his bindings again, but he made no headway.

"Victor, I'm going to watch what my friend Tkelvic does to you, and I'm going to enjoy it. It's the least I can do for myself as consolation for the loss of a child, however misbehaved he was. When Tkelvic is done with you, I will sell your contract to a place often equated to hell. Do they have a concept of hell where you come from? A place for terrible souls to go after life? Don't bother answering me, Victor. I'm not interested, really." He stepped back from Victor and looked around. "Drelk, you may go. Hols, please get Tkelvic; he's in the next oubliette."

Victor lay there, paralyzed by panic. He heard people moving around and then the scraping of chains on stone, accompanied by the click-clack sound of something big moving around on stilts or wooden shoes. He stared at the ceiling, trying to will himself out of his predicament, but then a long, dark shadow fell over him, and he looked up in the face of horror. A man loomed over him, but not a man like any he'd ever seen. This man was naked and had gray skin and a long angular face with huge black saucers for eyes. His mouth and jaw reminded him of an insect's mandibles. The freakiest part of him, though, was that he didn't have arms. No, he had long, thick spider legs coming out of his shoulders and back, allowing him to loom over Victor's table. Victor opened his mouth to scream, and that's when he saw the tentacles. The man had a nest of tentacles at the base of his abdomen, and two of them shot forward and wrapped around Victor's face, clamping his mouth shut.

"No noise, meat," the gray man-spider said in a grinding, discordant voice that registered deep in Victor's gut. Victor strained against the tentacles but couldn't move his head at all. He darted his eyes around, trying to find some sort of solution, some hint of hope. That's when he noticed the collar and chains on the creature. So, he was enslaved, too?

"Do not kill him, Tkelvic!" the lord's voice came from behind Victor. "I want him to feel what you do to him, and I want him to live with it."

"Yes, Lord," the horrifying creature said in that deep grinding voice. "I feel his Core. He's a spirit wielder. I've never broken a Spirit Core."

"I don't care what his Core looks like or if he's got twenty affinities. Shatter it!" Hearing those words, Victor felt real panic enter his mind, and he thrashed against his restraints, thrashed against the tentacles holding his head. He arched his back, reached into his Core, and pushed his Energy into his pathways, trying to activate Berserk. He didn't care about the collar anymore; he had to do something. Just as the Energy left his Core, he felt it dragged along his pathways and into the restraints at his wrists. His body's weak thrashing couldn't dislodge the tentacles and didn't affect the bonds. "The restraints flashed; he's trying something!"

"He cannot break free. I must concentrate," the looming, gray man-spider said as if to dismiss a child's worries. Victor's head was being held so that he could only stare at the ceiling, but he felt more of the tentacles start to wrap around his abdomen, squeezing him uncomfortably tight. Suddenly he felt a heavy pressure, right above his navel. Then it was like something was digging into his flesh, driving into his stomach, pulling apart his abdominal muscles and slipping between them. He screamed as he'd never screamed before. The pain was horrifying, but his inability to move and the invasive way the creature was probing into his body magnified his pain and discomfort. He kicked and thrashed, but the creature's weight and death grip with its tentacles kept his torso still.

The pain in his stomach grew as a hot buildup of some sort of foreign Energy began to throb right where his Core was. Victor stopped trying to see anything with his eyes, closed them, and turned his vision inward, trying to see what was happening to his Core. There it was, dim, low on Energy, but still whole, a red sun drifting in a vast void. Then Victor saw what the alien creature was doing: a bright spot of Energy was taking shape near his Core, slowly growing, pulsing with a sickly green radiance. He weakly thrashed with his body, but he knew he was on his last dregs of consciousness. He watched helplessly as the foreign Energy grew to eclipse his Core, and then with a white-hot, searing, acidic burn, it flashed into his Core and tore it apart. Victor screamed as though someone were peeling the flesh from his bones and then sank into the endless void, drifting without a coherent thought.

An eternity later, Victor opened his eyes to gray daylight. He was lying in straw on a wooden floor. The floor bumped and jostled, and, as he blearily rubbed at the crust binding his eyelashes, he foggily surmised he might be in a wagon. His right hand felt heavy, and he looked at it, noticing the metal cuff and chain hanging off it. "Fuck," he groaned, trying to push himself to a sitting position. He felt so weak, his arms could barely manage the motion.

"Oh, you're alive after all," a dry, wispy voice said from behind him. He managed to scoot to a sitting position and looked toward the voice. An old, gray-haired Ardeni man was chained to the floor a few feet away from him. A few other hunched individuals shared a similar fate farther into the wagon.

"Damn, dude, where the fuck are we?" His voice was scratchy, his throat sore and raw.

"In a wagon! Ha!" The old guy grinned, showing an alarming lack of teeth. Victor felt like shit. He felt worse than he had since coming to this world, worse than that time he'd had the flu and couldn't eat for five days.

"I get it. A wagon. Where's it going? Who chained us in here?" Victor tried to gather some spit and swallow it to make his throat a little less scratchy. His mouth was like the inside of a cotton ball, though, and he could barely dampen his tongue.

"We're bound for Greatbone Mine. I imagine the Greatbone Mining Consortium put us in the wagon—that's who bought us at auction." How the fuck had Victor missed an entire auction? He tried to remember the last thing that he'd done. There'd been some practice with Belsa, then the private fight.

"Oh, fuck." All the memories came to him—the metal table, the huge insect man, his Core. His Core! Victor looked inward, and there, where the bright, blazing sun of his Core used to pulse, he saw scattered bits of Energy, some yellow, some faintly flickering red, but none of it responded to him; it just floated listlessly in the void. "What did that fucker do to me?" He called up his status page:

| Status | | | |
|---|---|---|---|
| Name: | Victor Sandoval | | |
| Race: | Human: Base 4 | | |
| Class: | Spirit Champion | | |
| Level: | 11 | | |
| Core: | Spirit Class: Base 5 (fractured) | | |
| Energy Affinity: | 3.1, Rage 9.1 | Energy: | 5/5 |
| Strength: | 28 | Vitality: | 27 |
| Dexterity: | 19 | Agility: | 19 |
| Intelligence: | 10 | Will: | 17 |

| Points Available: | 0 | |
|---|---|---|
| Titles & Feats: | – | |
| Skills: | • System Language Integration: Not Upgradeable<br>• Unarmed Combat: Basic<br>• Knife Combat: Basic<br>• Axe Mastery: Basic<br>• Spear Mastery: Basic<br>• Bludgeon Mastery: Basic<br>• Grappling: Improved<br>• Spirit Core Cultivation Drill: Basic | • Berserk: Basic<br>• Sovereign Will: Basic<br>• Channel Spirit: Basic |

His Core now said it was "fractured" and he had a maximum of five Energy. In other words, he couldn't do shit. He reached up to scratch his neck and noticed the collar was gone. "I guess they don't need to collar a guy with a fractured Core." He couldn't even activate Berserk or Channel Spirit. He supposed he might be able to use his Sovereign Will skill, but he couldn't be sure until he tried. A wave of nausea rose from his stomach, and he bent over, shivering for a few minutes. When the discomfort faded, he attempted to straighten up, but a sharp pain from his stomach stopped him. He lifted his shirt and shivered at the sight. He had an eight-inch cut, crudely stitched and scabbed with puffy red flesh running laterally along the center of his abdomen. Thin, jagged black lines ran off into his tanned flesh from the incision.

"That looks infected, friend," the strange old man said.

"Yeah, it sure does, man." Victor leaned back, groaning and shaking, a sheen of sweat coating his face and forehead.

"When we stop, tell the wagon master. He won't want you dead before delivery." The older man sniffed and started picking at something on one of his bare feet. Victor looked down at his own feet and saw that his new boots and socks were gone. He still had on his black pants and shirt, though. If he could just activate his Berserk, it might heal his stomach, and he might be able to break the chain. He knew it wouldn't work—he was seventy Energy shy of the minimum to activate it, but he wanted to try. He concentrated on the ability and tried to activate it as he'd always done. He felt a little flutter in his gut, but nothing happened. He didn't feel it fail or pain or anything; it just didn't work. He leaned his head back against the bumping wagon and closed his eyes.

"I'm fucked, man." While he waited for something in his world to change, Victor thought about the people he'd met in this world. He thought about Yrella and savored the deep knot of discomfort that formed somewhere around his heart. It was nice to have a good, clean moment of sadness, a memory untainted by his current predicament. He tried to imagine what Yrella would say to him right now. It would probably be something about keeping his head up, staying ready for anything. Did he have that kind of fight left in him? What did it mean that his Core was fractured? Would he ever be able to gain power again? Would he be a broken person in this world? He supposed it made trying to get home an easier choice; if his Core was shot, there wasn't much point in not trying to get back to Earth. That thought surprised him a little—he hadn't consciously admitted that he'd been thinking about staying in this world, but there it was. He'd been gaining a lot of new abilities and a feeling of power that he'd never replicate back on Earth. He supposed that he'd hoped to break free of the pit fighting and then see what he could figure out. He laughed bitterly. "You're a fucking idiot. You can't do shit; how are you going to get home or anything?"

"Hey, don't get too down—just because someone bought your contract doesn't mean they have to follow it. How long was your contract for?" The old man nudged him with his bare, calloused foot.

"Somewhere between four and five years, I guess. You really think they'll let us go after our time's up?"

"It's the law! We're in the Ridonne Empire now—no slavery is allowed, only indentured service." The old man had a manic tone to his voice, and it set Victor a little on edge.

"Dude, I hate to break it to you, but it ain't much different. We're going to some mine? You think they keep good records of their miners and their service terms? Is there some sort of government inspection to keep them honest?"

"Ha ha! Smart questions, young man! I've been indentured eleven times in my life. Guess what that means? I've been set free ten times! Have some optimism! It's important for surviving times like this. My name's Pel, by the way. What can I call you?" Whether he wanted to admit it or not, the old man had managed to ignite a tiny spark of hope in Victor's heart. He might be down, but maybe it wasn't forever. Five years was a long time, but he had a long life to live if what he'd heard about racial improvements were true.

"I'm Victor." He closed his eyes again, and he didn't try to think about anything this time. However, some images still came into his dozing mind: Belsa smiling as he showed her how to do an armbar, the healer at the Rusty Nail when they'd flirted while she fixed his shoulder, Vullu laughing at Victor when Yrella snatched his flatbread off his plate. He smiled but couldn't help the little pools of tears that started to fill the corners of his eyes.

# 21

## GREATBONE MINE

When the wagons creaked to a halt that evening and the wooden door at the back rattled with the efforts of someone to remove a heavy lock, Victor sat up, painfully, to get a good look outside. His efforts were largely wasted, though, as a man, broad in girth, stood in the doorway. He set down a basket of hard rolls and a bucket of water with a ladle and said, "If ya don't share, I'll beat the snot out of three of you at random." Then he collected the disgusting bucket full of piss, shit, and vomit the prisoners had been sharing and slammed the door shut. Victor had started to open his mouth to voice a complaint about his stomach wound, but only a croak had escaped his throat.

"That's no way to get yourself seen to," the old man said to him with a wink. Victor snorted and waited his turn for a hard roll. When it came his way, it was truly hard. He couldn't eat it until the water bucket made its way back to him, and he drank a few ladles. After he'd lubricated his mouth a bit, he was able to suck on the roll until he could scrape it off by fractions with his teeth. When he'd finished his meager dinner, he looked at Pel and cleared his throat.

"Hey, how long have we been out of the city? Out of Persi Gables?"

"Oh, that's a funny one. We were auctioned off in Gelica. We've been in the wagon two days since." This threw Victor for a loop. How long had he been out since that fucking monster destroyed his Core?

"How far is Gelica from Persi Gables?"

"Oh, hmm. Maybe a week with a mount. You really got put through the grinder, eh, Victor?"

"You're damn right, my man. You're damn right."

"Hey! Hey, big Vodkin!" Pel called out to the big furry guy near the wagon's door. "Can you knock on the door? This guy has a badly infected wound—we should tell the wagon master." The Vodkin studied him for a minute. His impassive black eyes blinked twice, then he nodded and thumped on the door three times. After a minute, the lock clattered around and the wagon's door opened.

"This better be good, you mongrels!" the large shadow of the wagon master said. Victor couldn't make out his features in the dim light.

"Sir! Pel, here! Um, this guy you've had passed out back here? He has a badly infected wound, but he's awake. You might want to put something on it if you don't want him to croak before you get paid."

"Bah, which one is he? Send him out here." Victor could see his head dipping down so he could peer into the dim interior of the wagon.

"He's chained, sir," Pel supplied.

"I am not crawling in there. Come here, old man. I'll give you the salve." He motioned, and Pel eagerly scrambled to the door, bowing and scraping obsequiously when he got close to the wagon master. "Wait a minute." The shadow departed for a moment, and Pel crouched in the doorway, then sand crunched under boots, and the wagon master was back. Pel came scurrying back into the wagon as the door slammed, and he squatted in front of Victor.

"You want me to put it on?"

"Uh, no. I'll do it; thank you, Pel." Victor took the little clay pot in the palm of his hand. He unscrewed the lid, catching a whiff of something pungent, then lifted the hem of his shirt to expose his swollen, bloody, pus-filled wound. He took a generous dab of the cream and rubbed it along one corner of his injury. He'd expected it to sting but hadn't quite been ready for the lance of fire that shot through to his spine. He squeezed his eyes shut, inhaling through his nose, then took another dab and continued to spread it along the cut. He dabbed some around the puckered holes where the thick thread used to stitch him up stood out from his flesh. If he had a knife, he'd cut those stitches out—they looked disgusting and seemed too loose to be doing any good. By the time he was done, his eyes were red and bloodshot, and sweat was pouring off his brow.

The little clay pot was still half full, so he capped it and stuck it between himself and the wagon wall. His stomach had stopped stinging, and the throbbing ache had subsided a lot, so he had a good feeling that the ointment was doing what it needed to. "Better?" Pel asked, leaning forward eagerly.

"Yes, Pel. Thanks again for speaking up." Victor took a deep breath, and for the first time since waking up, he didn't feel like he was in excruciating pain. When he lay back and closed his eyes, though, he found he couldn't sleep, and as the night wore on, he grew more and more uncomfortable, alternating between sweating and shivering. At one point, Pel came over to him and felt his head.

"You're feverish, Victor. Can I ask you a personal question?" Victor, delirious, just nodded his head, staring glassy eyed at Pel. "Do you have a Core? Have you cultivated and gained levels? I'm not familiar with your race, but someone with Energy and a few levels should be resistant to sickness." Victor could only laugh at the statement or try, but it came out more like a croaking cough.

After that, the night became a blur of strange memories, dreams, and sweat-soaked reality. Victor was vaguely aware of the passage of time, with the wagon moving again and the sun shining between the boards in the ceiling and then stopping again. He'd never be sure exactly how many days passed that way, but sometime after the third or thirtieth day, he snapped out of his fever and ravenously drank from the water bucket that had been left beside him. Pel noticed his movement and scurried over. "Victor! You live! I spread that ointment on you twice more! Your wound looks a lot better," he said and held a finger to his lips, showing Victor a tiny sliver of sharp metal in his other hand. "I cut them nasty stitches out, too." Victor lifted his shirt, noticing that his stomach was sunken and his ribs were protruding, but that the wound was just an angry red, raised scar now.

"Thanks, Pel. I owe ya one."

"No, you don't, Victor. I caught a glimpse of some of the threads around you in one of my dreams, and I'd rather you didn't bind yourself to me. No offense, my friend, but I saw a lot of bloodshed in your path."

"You can see the future?"

"Not that neatly, no. I see potential, and I can see some of the paths you've taken and some of the paths you might take. It's not easy to explain. My class is Augur, but I'm rather hobbled at the moment." He shrank back to the wagon wall and pulled his knees to his chest. Victor didn't know how to react to what he'd said. Was he doomed? He shook his head and decided not to dwell on it; he already knew he had a shitload of problems—it was nothing new.

That evening he ate his roll, drank a lot of water, then slept like he'd never slept before. When he woke, the wagon was moving, and he felt a lot better. Pel was scraping something into the boards of the wagon with his small, jagged scrap of metal, and Victor watched him for a while. Eventually, he asked, "What are you doing, Pel?"

"Oh!" He jumped, startled by the question. "I'm, well, I'm recording our experiences here. In case we disappear or die, at least some part of our life is written here on this board. I've put all our names here and written a little about where we all came from and what we've been through. For you, Victor, I mentioned that you came from Persi Gables and that you recovered from a terrible injury."

"Could you change that? Or add to it? I was summoned, against my will, from a town called Tucson, and I'm a fighter. Can you mention that? I'm a fighter, Pel." Victor didn't know why he cared what Pel wrote about him on the floorboards of a wagon in the middle of nowhere, but he did.

"Of course! I'll be your chronicler, Victor." He busily went back to scratching into the wood, and Victor smiled. The wagon stopped early that day, and when the door was flung open, Victor realized why—they'd arrived at the mine.

"C'mere, Pel!" the wagon master hollered, and Pel hurried to the door. "Take this key, unlock the rowdy ones, then bring it back to me. Listen, you mutts! Once you get unlocked, you will slowly, one by one, exit the wagon and line up before me." Pel took the key and started unlocking the manacles from the three or four prisoners that the wagon master had deemed risky enough to warrant them. Victor had no idea why he'd been locked in—he was weak as a baby and not ready to fight anyone, let alone break out of a wagon. After Pel unlocked his manacle, he rubbed his raw, itchy wrist for a few minutes before slowly, shakily crawling out of the wagon behind everyone else.

When he dropped down onto his bare feet, Victor noticed that the dusty dirt was hot, hot as it was back in Arizona. He had to squint his eyes against the sun, but as they slowly adjusted, he saw that the wagon had pulled to a stop on the crest of a big dusty hill. There was a dirt road back behind the wagon leading down the hillside, and as Victor followed it with his eyes, he saw a vista, unlike anything he'd ever witnessed. The road led down into a green expanse of tall grass that stretched as far as his eyes could see. When he turned to where the other prisoners were lined up on the other side of the wagon, he suddenly realized that he wasn't on a "hill" per se—it was a pile of mine tailings. The dirt road continued down the side of the mountain of packed dirt into a deep open-pit mine that was stepped like an inverse pyramid. He saw people walking up and down the different levels of the pit, carrying buckets and other tools; they looked like ants from this vantage. At the bottom of the pit, a massive black archway led into the ground, and Victor could see carts and beasts of burden moving along a wide road that went into the darkness. "Holy shit," was all he could say as he shuffled over in the hot dirt to line up with the others.

"Impressive, isn't it?" the wagon master asked. Victor looked at him for the first time and wasn't surprised to see he was a Vodkin. Victor had guessed as much because of his size. That was one thing the asshole that broke his Core didn't take away—Victor still had his racial advancements and was nearly as tall as the big wagon master.

"It's cool, but I'm not looking forward to working in it," Victor muttered.

"Ha, I don't suppose you are. No, I don't suppose you are." The Vodkin turned and looked down the road that led into the mine. "All right, here he comes. Stand up straight. Look healthy. If you don't get bought, I'm going to take you somewhere far worse, believe me!" The seven prisoners straightened and stood in a line. Victor didn't really do anything to try to look more appealing. He still hadn't made up his mind that he could do anything about his predicament. He wasn't sure there was anything that could be done for him. He'd been scared to look at or feel his Core since that first time he woke, and he didn't know if there was any hope for him when it came to Energy use. All that said, he didn't really give a fuck if these assholes wanted to buy his contract so he could work in their mine. Fuck them.

A cart gradually made its way up the steep slope from the mine, and when it got close, Victor was intrigued by the animal pulling it—it looked a lot like a giant monitor lizard. It was almost as tall as a pony, but it was a lot wider with big fat legs and strong, clawed feet. A red-skinned Shadeni man was driving the wagon, and when he jumped out, Victor could see that he wore fancy clothing. He had shiny black boots with silver-tipped toes and a gray suit made of flowing, cool-looking material. He looked very comfortable in the heat. He strutted up to the wagon master, and Victor noticed he had a leather cord coiled up and hooked to his black leather belt.

"Well, what've you got for me, Glethwid?"

"Foreman, good to see you. Take a look, take a look. I have some strong laborers in this group. None with strong Energy auras—one less thing to worry about, eh?" The foreman hummed to himself as he pulled out a little lens and held it to his eye. He looked closely at each prisoner through the lens, pausing on Victor for a long time.

"What's this one's story?" He gestured at Victor. "Someone did a number on him, eh?"

"Bought him off an auction out of Persi Gables. Non-native, obviously, hardly any Energy aura. He's got most of a five-year contract left—plenty of muscle on him. I'm sure you'll get more than your money out of him."

"Hmm, I'll be the judge of that." He moved to the far end of the line and started carefully going over each of the prisoners, asking to see their hands, making little teasing comments, or asking questions about their past. Victor couldn't figure it out at first but eventually decided the guy was trying to see if anyone would be more trouble than they were worth. A little voice in his head said he should mess with the guy and try to piss him off, but then he thought about how the wagon master said the next stop would be worse. So far, people who'd said something was rotten in this world hadn't lied to Victor; he decided to play it cool. "Well, big lad, aren't you?" Victor didn't respond, just stood still under the man's scrutiny. "Not much of a talker?"

"What should I say?"

"Have you always been so weak with Energy?"

"Most of my life, I didn't know what Energy was." Victor wasn't sure why he was being deceptive, but something told him that the less this guy knew about his Core or his abilities, the better.

"What's your name?"

"Victor."

"Can you dig, Victor? Let me see your hands."

"Sure. I've dug plenty of holes." Victor held up his hands, and the man turned them over to see the calluses on his palms.

"These aren't digging calluses, Victor. Are you scared of the dark?"

"No."

"You're an odd-looking man, Victor. Where are you from?"

"Tucson." Victor shrugged.

"Huh, never heard of it. Do you have people that are looking for you?"

"Uh, probably, but they don't have a clue where I am."

"Well, welcome to Greatbone Mine, Victor." He turned to the wagon master. "I'll take them all." Turning back to the group of prisoners, he raised his voice and announced, "This is the greatest amber-ore excavation site on this continent. You're going to see great things in this mine and be part of something even greater. You'll have to earn your freedom here, but if you work hard, I'll be fair to you. Now, get into the wagon."

Victor clambered up into the mine wagon behind Pel and sat on one of the side benches so he could look into the massive excavation while the wagon slowly trundled along behind the giant lizard. The mine truly was incredible in its scope. He was admiring the size of the long, stepped slopes leading down to the bottom, imagining how many trucks could drive down it side by side, when he caught sight of the giant bones sticking out of the side of the excavated hill. "What are those bones from?"

"Nobody knows, new employee. Nobody knows. We've dug up a lot of very "great" bones here. That's where the name comes from!" Victor could hear the smug laughter in the man's voice; clearly, he was his own biggest fan.

"Is it true that there are ancient ruins in the depths?" Pel asked.

"Oh, yes, old one. Yes, indeed. We've run across quite a few ancient structures in the vast depths. I doubt you'll all get that deep. Well, depending on how you perform and where your talents are. We'll see. Now, I'm going to smoke a pipe before we get down there in the dust and heat, so sit back and enjoy the ride." He pulled a white pipe that looked as if it had been carved from a piece of ivory out of "somewhere," then proceeded to tamp in a leafy substance and light it up.

Victor inhaled the sweet smoke that wafted his way and looked out over the wagon's side at the huge excavation and the massive black tunnel at the bottom. He might be here to do slave labor, but he couldn't help feeling a little excitement at the mystery of finding ancient ruins in the depths. He imagined finding an ancient dwarven hall or something out of a fantasy VR, and a little spark ignited in his heart. He smiled; maybe things weren't completely hopeless. Then it hit him: that spark had been more than excitement. It had burned and was warming him physically. He could still feel it, and it wasn't his heart; it was farther down, more toward his center. His Core.

# 22

※

# LAM'S FURIES

Victor still hadn't taken a look inward to his Core by the time the wagon trundled to a stop at the bottom of the long, hard-packed gravel road. He was afraid of what he'd find; right now, he had a little hope that something good was happening, and he knew that if he looked and still just saw his shattered remnant of a Core, he'd fall into a pit of despair that would be tough to climb out of. Meanwhile, the foreman shouted for them to get out of the wagon and line up in a more literal sort of pit. He wondered just how bad a turn his life had taken by coming here; he didn't know it would be all that bad, but he figured it would be. The asshole that had destroyed his Core for him sure thought he was sending Victor someplace shitty.

"I said line up, shoulder to shoulder. No talking!" The foreman's voice had risen in volume noticeably, and Victor thought he heard irritation bleeding into his "I'm too cool for this place" demeanor. Victor hopped out of the wagon and hustled over to the hastily forming line. Once again, he stood next to Pel, towering over the little blue man. The foreman consulted a clipboard and spoke quietly to an Ardeni man wearing khaki-colored pants and a long-sleeved shirt. He had orange hair cut very short under a wide-brimmed hat, obviously designed to provide maximum protection from the sun. Victor looked around; they were at the bottom of the enormous open pit, and as they'd descended, it only grew larger in perspective. Victor saw hundreds of people moving around down there, carrying buckets, pushing carts, and leading animals. Even with so many people working busily, the space seemed enormous. The entrance to the colossal tunnel had to be almost a mile away.

"All right, listen up. I'm going to call you up here one at a time. We'll go over your contract, so the imperial auditors don't give me any headaches, and then I'll give you your first assignment. Don't waste my time with questions—there'll be someone at your worksite to fill you in." He looked at his line of newly acquired workers for a moment, then continued, "Pel ap'Drom." Pel hustled forward with a wheezy grunt of excitement. Standing there, not allowed to move, Victor let his attention turn inward and looked at his Core without thinking about it.

At first, he almost opened his eyes with disgust, seeing the same landscape of scattered tiny drops and shimmers of Energy, but he forced himself to really look. A lot of the Energy had that red shimmer of rage, but a lot of it was the pure, rich golden yellow hue of unattuned Energy. While he let his inner eye's gaze sweep back and forth over the scattered remnants of his Core, he caught a brief flicker and saw that one of the tiny little pools of rage-attuned Energy was very slightly spinning. While he studied it, he caught the flicker again and realized it was a tiny pulse. Was this what was left of his Core? Victor used his will to urge the little spark to flare brighter, for the slightly spinning drop of Energy to spin faster. He almost laughed aloud when it responded; it flared brightly for a fraction of a second, and its movement seemed to flicker just a touch more rapidly. To his delight, Victor saw a tiny droplet of rage-attuned Energy nearby slowly start to drift into the pulsing little fragment of his Core and join with it.

"Victor! Victor of Tucson!" The foreman's voice yanked Victor back into reality. He opened his eyes and stepped toward the foreman quickly, unsure if he'd already been called and missed it.

"Here, sir!" He stumbled up in front of the foreman.

"Not time for dozing yet, Victor. All right, I have your contract here. What a mess! I've never seen so many scribbles and initials. There's no witness or official notary mark for either the original signatures or any of the alterations. Lucky I have Tyn here. He'll make sure our portion of the contract with you is up to imperial standards, don't worry. Now, it looks like you were initially contracted for some sort of fighting sport, hmm? Let's see, then you were sold to a private party, one ap'Horrin? Right, well, then your contract was bought by the Greatbone Mining Consortium. Now, I'm not sure you're aware, but all the provisions added to your contract initially were stricken out at the sale to ap'Horrin. Here we have a simple agreement of four years and six months of unspecified labor. That sound right?"

"No, not really. I didn't get any say in those contract changes, and I had some things promised to me—opportunities for earning awards and stuff like that."

"Right, but how do I know that? Maybe you breached some terms of service, and that's why it was stricken, hmm?" Victor felt some heat rising in his neck at the man's words.

"That's bullshit, man." He couldn't keep the frustration and bitterness from dripping some venom into the words. The neatly dressed, perfectly coiffed man narrowed his eyes and looked Victor up and down, resting his right palm on the handle of the coiled whip on his belt.

"Take a breath, Victor. Think about what you say to me, and really consider your tone. Now, I have to work with what I've been given, and this contract is a joke, but one thing is clear—the length of commitment. Tyn, do you agree?"

"Agreed, sir. You're doing your best to stick to fair terms with this inhabitant of the Ridonne Empire. I think your diligence will be admired by any auditors that happen to pull this ill-conceived contract."

"Excellent." He flicked his hand up to his ear, pulled a quill from behind it, touched the tip to his tongue, and signed the paper attached to his clipboard. "Put your signature or X here," he said, holding out the quill to Victor and pointing to a line on the bottom of his old contract. Victor ran his eyes over all the crossed-out lines and little signatures and initials, shook his head, and took the quill. He knew very well that this guy could kill him if he wanted to. He could kill him and make up some bullshit story about how Victor went crazy and tried to escape and kill all the guards. He doubted the "imperial auditors" were very hard to please. He wrote his name next to the spot where the foreman pointed. "Good. You're a quick learner, Victor. I think you'll go far in the Greatbone operation. See that tent over there with the big red axe painted on it? That's where you're to report. You'll learn the rules there but let me give you a quick primer: don't try to run. We have guards with bows and mages with spells stationed all over. You'll stand out like a feyris to a redhood hawk."

"All right." Victor didn't trust himself to say more without getting in trouble, so he just nodded and started walking toward the big tent the foreman had gestured to. It looked almost like what Victor imagined a circus tent would look like. It appeared to be made from gray canvas and had a red flag flapping at its peak in the dusty wind. On the side facing Victor, a big red axe had been painted, and Victor wondered just what that meant. He saw several other tents nearby with different symbols painted on them: a pick, a cart, a crudely drawn lizard, and a shovel. He shrugged and scanned ahead and behind him for any sign of where Pel had gone, but he didn't see the old man, and he briefly mourned the loss of yet another friend; something made him feel that he wouldn't see him again.

When he got to the tent, he had to walk around the side to find the big open flaps to enter it. A small wooden ramp led up out of the dust onto a decklike floor. Victor walked up and saw that large open trunks lined the wall on his left. Several men and women clustered around posts with different designs carved into them on the right-hand side. Each cluster had one of the mine employees wearing khaki standing nearby. Along the back wall, several mine employees sat behind a long table. Victor walked up to the table and looked at the employee sitting nearest the middle, a pale-blue-haired Ardeni woman. She cleared her throat, sat up a bit straighter, and motioned for Victor to come forward.

"I was told to come to this tent," he said by way of greeting.

"Mmhmm," she said, pulling out a flat black slate. "Put your right hand on this slate and say your name." Victor shrugged and leaned forward to lay his hand on the slate. It was warm and seemed to buzz slightly at his touch.

"Victor Sandoval."

"All right, you're registered with the deep delvers. Are you new to the mine or been here before?"

"Uh, I'm new. What's a fuckin' deep delver?" Victor tried to cut off his words, but they came out too fast. The woman didn't seem offended, though, just looked at Victor quizzically for a moment, then answered him.

"Well, you've been chosen to be in the group that enters the deeper dig sites ahead of the workers to make sure they're clear of hazards. That means you must have some fighting experience, hmm? Either that or Foreman Venz-dak decided you're going to be more trouble than you're worth and wants you in a hazardous job." She shrugged as though it was a fifty-fifty chance. She glanced over at the little groups of people clustered around the different poles. "Pick a number between one and four."

"Huh?"

"Our reinforcement crews all have four people in them. Pick a number, and that'll be your new crew."

"Um, three, I guess." Victor didn't think it mattered, and he liked the number three.

"Right, that's Captain Lam's group. Okay, before I can get you some equipment, I'll have to get you collared. Let's measure your strength."

"Uh, what?"

"For your collar—we don't want to waste an expensive amber-ore collar on you if you don't need it, right?" She produced a smooth, white crystal that reminded Victor of one of his *abuela*'s Christmas candles. It glowed with a brilliant, warm radiance. "Hold that." She held it out to Victor, and he took it in his hand. The glow immediately subsided to the point where Victor thought it was gone completely. When he really looked, though, he saw a very small, almost imperceptible luminescence. "Oh, great, we'll just need a Tier One for you. I bet I could even use a Tier Zero if I had one."

"Oh, great." Victor let the crystal roll out of his hand onto the table. The woman looked up at him sharply, eyes squinted in anger, but didn't say anything. She scooped up the crystal, then stood and walked around to the row of chests, motioning Victor to follow. He was surprised to see a line had formed behind him, and when he turned to follow the Ardeni woman, one of the other employees at the table called the next prisoner forward. Victor didn't recognize the people in line, and he wondered where they'd come from. Did they have to pull prisoners from other parts of the operation to fill this duty? The woman was rummaging through a chest, and she stood with a smooth black ring in her hands.

"It's iron, but the artificer took the time to smooth it out. You should be grateful. I've seen some delvers wearing much rougher work." She handed it to Victor and motioned toward her neck that she wanted him to put it on.

"Uh, how do I put it on?" He couldn't feel any seams in the metal.

"Oh, just hold it to your neck; I'll do the rest." She'd pulled a thin, silvery rod from somewhere and held it, waiting for Victor to comply. Once again, feeling as if he should see another option but unable to find it, Victor pressed the cool metal against his neck. The woman reached forward and tapped the ring of iron with her rod, and suddenly it was around his neck. "Now, you seem new to this stuff, so listen: because of your assignment, you're allowed to carry a baton and to use Energy abilities if you have them, but only for self-defense against the creatures in the depths. That collar will suppress your Energy if you try to leave the mine. It will allow us to track you. It will allow us to kill you remotely if we must, and, finally, it will be impossible for you to remove—it's designed to resist someone with far more Energy than you possess. Understand all that?"

"Yeah, I get it."

"Good!" She smiled brightly and moved over to the next chest. She reached in and lifted out a gray metal rod about two and a half feet long, perfectly cylindrical with a worn, sweat-stained leather handle wrapped around one end. She handed it to Victor, and it felt very heavy and sturdy. "This is your weapon for deep delving. You're allowed to carry it around with you, but it must always be held down next to your side. If you raise it in a threatening manner outside of your duties, any of the Greatbone Consortium employees have permission to summarily execute you. We all carry one of these control rods. Do you understand?"

"Yeah, I get it. Can I get a belt or something to hang it on? I don't want to accidentally fuck up and lift it up where I shouldn't."

"There's a Contribution Store at the camp Settlement Stone. You'll see it when you go into the main cavern. Indentured workers are allowed to earn contribution points at a reduced rate. You should visit the store when you have your free hour each evening to pick up quests. Okay, that's it from me; have you got any questions? Last chance!" This time, she gave him a genuine smile, and Victor wondered how pissed he should be at her. Was it her fault she had this job? Did she see the wrong they were doing to people like Victor? He decided that he couldn't let her slide, so he didn't return her smile, just shrugged.

"I can't think of anything right now."

"All right, go stand next to the post with the pultii carved on it." She gestured at the other side of the tent.

"What's a pultii?" Victor glanced at the posts and just saw various strange-looking animals carved on them. She sighed heavily and walked past him, pointing at the pole that was second from the right. He nodded and walked toward it. When he got closer, he saw that the most prominently carved animal looked kind of like a turkey. Was that a pultii? The employee standing next to the group clapped his hands when he walked up.

"Right! That's our fifth walking up. C'mon then, dogs; I'll deliver you to Captain Lam." He started walking out of the tent, and the three Ardeni and one Shadeni that had been clustered around the pole followed him out. Victor brought up the rear, noticing that they all held the same gray metal batons, pointed to the ground. The employee was walking straight for the gaping maw of the enormous tunnel. In the sun's bright glare, he couldn't see far into it, but he got a sense of depth from the shadows that hung under the high stony ceiling. It took them a good ten minutes to cross the hard-packed dirt of the open pit to the first shadows of the cavern, and when the sun finally was obscured and Victor slipped into the tunnel's domain, he caught his breath at the scale of what he saw.

The enormous central tunnel of Greatbone Mine stretched into the distance farther than he could see, brightly lit with Energy lamps that hung from the soaring ceiling and stood on wooden posts at regular intervals. All along the sides of the vast tunnel, ramps carved into the stone switchbacked and ran in a dizzying maze, a honeycomb of smaller tunnel openings leading away into God knew where. Ramshackle huts and tents lined the sides of the great hall, interspersed with larger, more sturdily built buildings. "C'mon, quit gawkin', you vermin. Captain Lam's barracks are deep into phase two. We gotta pick up the pace if I'm gonna make my date." He laughed as if he'd just said the funniest thing in the world. They walked past people pulling carts, hauling buckets, and lounging on wooden crates. They walked by large barracks-type buildings, some with smoke coming from chimneys and dozens and dozens of little buildings. Here and there, they passed fires burning with people cooking something on sticks over the flames, and Victor looked up wondering if smoke was a problem, but wherever it went, it was lost to his eyes. After about a mile, they had to circumvent a large crowd forming into multiple queues around a tall, black stone covered in strange writing. "That's the Settlement Stone, you vagabonds," the employee called back over his shoulder. "When you get settled, you should ask Captain Lam to let you come pick up quests. I'll give ya that tip for free, you brigands!"

"He's a funny guy," the little red-haired Ardeni man in front of Victor said out of the side of his mouth.

"Yeah. Real comedian." Victor snorted, and the man laughed.

"I'm Tyge," the man said, turning slightly and offering his hand. Victor took it and nodded.

"I'm Victor." They continued for another fifteen minutes, and the number of ramshackle buildings dwindled off to only one here and there. The tunnel was still the same enormous size, though, making the structures seem all the smaller. Their leader stopped outside a building that reminded Victor of a Viking longhouse. It had large metal braziers hung from the overhanging lintel, and they burned with a blue-white, smokeless flame.

"This is Lam's longhouse," their guide announced, then walked up to the big wooden door and pounded. He didn't wait for an answer, though, depressing the iron latch and pushing the big door inward. It swung smoothly on big metal hinges, and Victor saw the inside from where he stood, looking over the employee's shoulder. A stone hearth sat in the middle of the big hall, and

Victor could see heat waves rising off it and faint smoke rising to the opening in the center of the building's ceiling. All along both walls were narrow
wooden beds, each with an identical gray blanket and single white pillow. On
the far side of the open hearth was a long table, and Victor could see a dozen
or so people sitting at the table, apparently sharing a meal.

A tall woman stood up at the far end of the table and walked around it,
toward the door and the group of new recruits. Victor struggled with his
grasp on reality when he saw her; everything about her seemed unreal in one
way or another. She was easily seven feet tall but thin as a rail. She had pale
skin and huge almond eyes that glittered like cut emeralds, and sprouting
from the center of her back were four enormous dragonfly wings that seemed
to be dripping with glittering fairy dust. She wore a dull, copper-colored
breastplate and dark leather pants, with similar armor plates on her thighs
and shins. When she was just a few paces away, her strident tenor voice cut
through the cobwebs in Victor's mind, sounding like a trumpet calling him
to battle. "Ahh, my new recruits. Wonderful! Thank you, Bilun. I've got it
from here."

"You're quite welcome, ma'am." Their escort turned smartly on his heel
and, without a parting insult for the prisoners, marched away.

"Well, well. Come forward, recruits! Welcome to Lam's Furies, the toughest bunch of deep delvers in all of Greatbone!" She regarded the five of them
with a warm smile, and Victor noticed, now that he was able to jerk his eyes
away from her glittering wings, that she was as badass looking as she was
beautiful. She was covered in little scars and had weird, colorful tattoos all
over her arms and neck, and probably elsewhere, but she had on too much
armor to be sure. With her long blonde hair pulled back in a knotted braid,
she regarded each of them coolly for a few moments, and when she looked at
Victor, she glanced up and down his frame, a slight frown above her pointed
chin.

"I haven't seen your paperwork yet. Tell me your names, please." She
looked at them one by one, and everyone said their names, but Victor was
still too stunned by this woman's otherworldly appearance to hear them. She
seemed to exude a power or energy that was unlike any of the people he'd yet
met. She was simply larger than life. Finally, she rested her gaze on Victor
and raised a sharp blonde eyebrow.

"Um." Victor had to swallow several times to moisten his vocal cords. "I'm
Victor."

"Where are you from, Victor?"

"From Earth. Another world. Um." She kept staring at him, and he felt that he had to fill the silence. "From a town called Tucson. I, uh, I was summoned and fought in some pits in a city called Persi Gables."

"Now I'm getting the picture. All right! Enough for now. Our day's duty is over, so come and sit at the table and get to know the rest of my crew. I'll assign you each a buddy to tell you how things work, and by tomorrow morning, I'll expect you to be ready for duty. We start early, recruits, very early."

# 23

⊰⧊⊱

# DELVE SIX-FOURTEEN

Victor followed the old blue Ardeni man to the back of Lam's barracks, where he'd promised to hook him up with a belt. It was cool that he was allowed to have a club, considering he was basically a slave, but he didn't like carrying it all the time. When he'd mentioned it to Gris, the guy that Captain Lam had ordered to show Victor around, the man had laughed and said that Victor just needed a belt. "All right, Victor, let's see here," Gris said, throwing open a big wooden chest and rooting through leather scraps, burlap, tattered old clothes, and worn-down boots. He finally pulled out a length of leather with a tarnished, bent tin buckle. He tossed it to Victor, who ran it through the loops on his black pants and buckled it with about seven inches of leather to spare.

"Yo, how about a pair of old boots? The assholes that sold me took my good ones." Gris looked Victor up and down, then shrugged.

"Ain't coming out of my pocket!" He laughed, digging around and throwing a bunch of boots at Victor to try on. Victor held a few that looked about right to his feet and, after trying on several pairs, settled on two boots that were mismatched but fit him passably. "Look at that! You're ready for delving!"

"All right, thanks, Gris. So, what's next? We supposed to go get some 'quests' or some shit?"

"That's right," the old guy reached up to scratch his white stubble, running his fingers around inside his collar to let his skin breathe. Victor noticed that his collar was a lot more ornate than his own, made from something more like a bronze alloy than iron, and covered with a lot more weird letters. "Yeah, let's go do that now. I need to turn one in, anyway." He started walking back through the hall, past a bunch of the others in Lam's unit, including other veterans giving newbies their version of orientations. Lam wasn't around, having left to handle some business shortly after Victor and the others had arrived. When they got outside and started back toward the tunnel entrance, Victor was surprised that he couldn't see the enormous tunnel exit. It had felt as if they'd walked straight in, but the slope was deceptive, and, in the distance, the only thing he could see was more tunnel and the ceiling with huge globes of glowing Energy throwing orange-yellow light down.

"Dude, this tunnel is fucking huge."

"Ha, wait till you see the deep vaults." Gris strode ahead, moving quickly for a guy with such short legs.

"Hey, is Lam one of those, um, Ghelli? You know the people with the dragonfly wings?"

"Oh, aye. She's a rare sight, though. Her race is up into advanced stages; she can even fly with them wings."

"That's pretty badass. What's she doing in these mines?"

"Ha, you got a lot to learn, Victor. These mines run deep. When they chased the amber-ore vein with this tunnel, they started running into ruins, and the deeper they went, the bigger the ruins got. All kinds of ancient shit was buried down here. Lam works for the Greatbone Mining Consortium, but she's also hunting artifacts for herself." That made sense to Victor; she'd been something from another league compared to all the other people he'd met in this world. Even the lady at her mansion hadn't had anyone around that resonated like Captain Lam. They started running into other mine workers as they walked up the tunnel, and after a few more minutes, they came up the curving path to the big central area where most of the shanties and buildings were concentrated and where the weird black stone rose into the air.

"What is that thing, anyway?"

"What?"

"That big fucking stone with all the weird letters all over it."

"Really? You didn't have a Village or Town Stone where you came from?"

"No, man. I'm not from this world." Gris gave Victor a good long stare with his bright red eyes, then grinned.

"I guess that makes sense. Well, it's a Settlement Stone, where this 'community' is directly connected to the System. It lets the people running the place buy things from the System, build structures, and set up stuff like a Contribution Store for us workers."

"Ahh, gotcha. So that's where we get the quests?"

"Right, because we're not free employees, our rewards are pretty small, but it all adds up." Gris led Victor down the slope to the cleared area around the Stone, and they joined one of the queues of people waiting to interact with it. Victor passed the time waiting by people watching, and he saw plenty to keep him entertained. He noticed that many of the people milling around wore belts with pouches attached and that the pouches all had a pickaxe branded on them.

"What's with those bags with the pickaxes?"

"Those are people on mining detail. They get a dimensional container to carry what they dig out each day. Those bags are enchanted specially, though; they keep track of what the miners put in them, so there's no funny business when they drop off their haul each day."

"They think of everything, huh? Hey." Victor slapped the metal baton sticking out of his belt. "What kinda shit we gonna have to fight down there?"

"I've seen all kinds of creatures deep down: giant rats, Yeksa, zombies, ghouls, the list goes on and on. Captain Lam killed a Yovashi the other day, too." Victor didn't know what the fuck some of those things were, but he was a little tired of playing the dummy, so he just grunted and acted impressed.

"So, am I going to be fucked? I mean, my Core got basically destroyed. I can't do much beyond swinging this club around."

"Ahh, I was going to ask you about that collar but didn't want to be rude. So, you really don't have much Energy, huh?"

"Yeah, that's right."

"Well, Lam's a good Captain. She'll probably put you with some of the stronger guys and just expect you to help out as best you can. Um, I won't lie to you; deep delvers suffer a lot of casualties. Hey, here we go! Our turn." He laughed and walked up to the vacant facet of the octagonal Settlement Stone. "I'll go first. You just put your palm on the Stone, and you'll see some menus and stuff that you can go through. You want to go to the quests section; it's the second option on the first page." Victor nodded and watched as Gris went about his business, and when the old man stepped back and nodded to the Stone, Victor slapped his palm against the flat surface.

He immediately saw a menu screen pop up in his vision, much like when he looked at his status page. He only had two items on his menu: Contribution Store and Quests. He touched the Contribution Store first, just to see what it was, and he found a menu with a dozen subheadings from things like food to clothing to approved weaponry. Victor clicked on the weaponry list and found a menu with three different items: basic baton, artificed baton, and heavy artificed baton. Victor grunted and said, "Just batons?"

"Oh, you're checking out the store? Yeah, they don't like us with real weapons up here, even though some of the guys in our unit could really massacre a lot of people with a baton. It doesn't make sense, but it keeps the administrators happy." Victor looked at the prices: the cheapest baton was fifty credits, and the heavy artificed baton was five hundred. His balance was zero, so he shrugged and backed out of the Contribution Store and clicked on the Quests button. A menu appeared:

| Quests for Victor Sandoval in Greatbone Mine: | |
|---|---|
| 1. Slay 100 denizens of the deep | Reward: 1-3 credits per kill based on creatures slain, determined by System calculation. |
| 2. Recover Energy-rich materials | Reward: 1-1000 credits based on Energy level, determined by System calculation. |

"One hundred? I have to kill a hundred fucking things down there? Are there that many monsters?"

"Ha! Yes, and then some. They keep coming, too, no matter how many times we kill them and beat them back. I suppose if we stopped going deeper, chasing ore, they might stop coming. Who knows?" Victor sighed, pushed the green "accept" button next to each quest, then turned back to Gris.

"All done, man. What's next?"

"Now we should go get some shut-eye because Captain Lam doesn't hardly ever sleep, and she likes to wake our asses up early." He turned to leave, and Victor followed. They returned the way they came, meandering through the little clusters of soiled humanoids. Some of the denizens of the mine cast sidelong glances Victor's way, and a few even seemed outright hostile. He felt out of place, as usual in this world, but more vulnerable than ever. At least when he'd been in Yund's warehouse, he'd had Yrella and Vullu watching his back at first. He tried to avoid making eye contact with the larger, more dangerously crazy-looking individuals. He felt some relief when they finally passed out of the more crowded central settlement area and into the quieter, darker stretch of tunnel that led to Lam's barracks.

When they walked up to the doors of the barracks building, Gris motioned for Victor to be quiet and then opened the door slowly to avoid making any noise. A few dim lights showed members of the unit huddled over whatever sort of strange hobbies kept them busy during the bedtime hours, but most everyone was sleeping already. Gris pointed to an empty cot near the door, and Victor took his meaning, going over to it. The mattress was thin, like burlap stretched over scratchy hay or grass, but he had two wool blankets, so he lay down on one and pulled the other over himself. He'd kicked his boots off and looped his belt with his cudgel over the little bedpost but otherwise slept with his clothes on. When he closed his eyes and stretched out, Victor realized it was the first time he'd slept in a bed since coming to this world. It might have been a shitty, uncomfortable bed, but it beat sleeping on a hard, hay-covered floor.

He was deeply asleep, dreaming of watching his grandma cook breakfast, when someone gave his cot a good shake and said, "Time to move out! Get up!" Victor yawned hugely and rolled onto his back, looking around. The barracks hall was brightly lit, and the entire unit was lining up by the door, a few people still straggling into the line. He didn't know what would happen to people slow to move, so Victor jumped up and jammed his feet into his boots. Gris walked up while he was pulling his belt tight.

"Don't forget to make your bed. Captain Lam doesn't like a sloppy barracks." He helped Victor fold his blankets and said, "Just fold them neatly at the foot of the cot every morning."

"Got it, thanks." Victor hustled over to the line, following Gris, and was happy that he wasn't the last person; a thickly built, red-skinned Shadeni guy lined up behind him, looking disheveled and stressed.

"I didn't sleep at all!" he groused quietly to the back of Victor's neck.

"That sucks, dude. You'll do better tonight."

"If I live that long! I can't believe I was assigned to the delvers!" Victor glanced over his shoulder at the stout man and shrugged.

"Yeah, here's hoping." They'd only been lined up for about a minute when the far door opened and closed, and then Captain Lam was striding through the barracks toward them.

"Good! I don't have to beat anyone this morning. Yet. The beds look all right, and you're all lined up. This is how we do it every morning. Now move out! Sergeant Fath, lead them to forward delve six-fourteen."

"Right, Captain Lam!" a massive, hulking Shadeni man with an eyepatch shouted, pushing open the door and marching out. The line of club-wielding prisoners followed him out, and Victor was surprised when the sergeant started booming out a march cadence, and the veterans echoed him. It reminded him of an army VR he'd watched a few years ago, some comedy about a rich guy who had to sign up for basic training.

*Marching through the deep dark!*

*Always in the deep dark!*

*People know us!*

*Monsters fear us!*

*We are the delvers!*

*The mighty Lam's delvers!*

*We drive back the darkness*

*and the hiding creeps!*

*Tough Lam's delvers!*

*Rough Lam's delvers!*

*Marching through the deep dark!*

Victor had never marched before, but it wasn't hard to figure out that he was supposed to step with his left foot when the guys in front of him did so. He didn't know the words to the march, but it was easy enough to repeat after the humongous voice of the sergeant. They made good time, and he had to admit that the cadence made it more fun than just walking along in a bunch. They went through a dozen different verses before repeating, and Victor started to think the sergeant was just making them up off the top of his head and felt rather impressed.

After an hour or so of marching, he noticed that the lights were less frequently hung in the high tunnel ceiling and that the tunnel was growing more narrow. It was still large enough to drive a few trains through, but it was definitely tapering. Another twenty minutes brought them to a circular wooden platform surrounding a massive vertical shaft that descended into even greater depths. Captain Lam, whom Victor hadn't seen on the entire march, was standing on the platform and gestured to a long rope hung through some pulleys. Sergeant Fath screamed, "Grab hold, unit!" pulling the rope's loose end toward the column. Victor hustled to comply, grabbing the rope with a dozen other sets of hands, then the sergeant screamed again, "Pull!" Victor pulled along with everyone else, and they started to haul the rope back down the tunnel. They hauled it for what had to be five hundred yards before the word came from down the line to stop.

"The fuck is this for?" Victor asked Gris, who had also helped haul the rope.

"Whatever delver unit went down last night didn't return. They left the lift at the bottom, and it ran out of Energy, so we had to pull it up by hand."

"They didn't return?"

"Yeah." Gris shook his head. "Probably found a nest of something nasty."

"Jesus." They walked back to the shaft, and Victor saw that a circular platform was now hovering in the open shaft. Captain Lam was standing on the platform, holding her hands against a shimmering white and yellow crystal about the size of a basketball mounted at its center.

"She's recharging it," Gris said.

"Huh," Victor grunted and moved over to the crowd of other delvers waiting for further instructions. After about five minutes, Captain Lam straightened and motioned for everyone to board. Victor followed after the others, hopping over the two-foot gap between the deck and the floating platform. He didn't look down while he jumped because he had a feeling he didn't want to see just how deep the shaft was. The platform hardly moved with each additional delver, bobbing almost imperceptibly under their combined weight. When Captain Lam and her twenty-two delvers were all standing on the platform, she touched the crystal, and Victor's stomach dropped as they descended. It was like riding on a huge open-air elevator, and he wondered how many people fell off to their deaths every year.

Victor watched the stony sides of the shaft blur past for a few seconds, then they were slowing, and the platform came into a huge underground space that boggled Victor's mind. Energy globes hung from massive chains shedding light over the broken, stony landscape filled with strange fungi and glistening plant life. A river cut through one corner of the cavern, flowing quickly enough to form rapids on the tumbled stones scattered in its bed. As the platform gently came to a stop atop a small hill next to a large rectangular building, Victor noticed movement out among the giant fungi stalks. He strained to see what it was but only caught glimpses of something pale and furtive. "What's moving around out there?"

"Probably mulsii," Gris responded. "They're like fat, pale worms with legs, and they have the temperament of a rabid dog. They'll eat anything."

"Sounds great."

"Good news is, we can grill 'em up. They're pretty good." Gris smacked his lips.

"All right, time to look sharp! Get your sticks in your hands!" the sergeant hollered. Victor, happy to comply, gripped his baton in his right hand and looked around nervously. "We need to cross to tunnel fourteen, and that means we're going through those shrooms. Be on the lookout for mulsii." He turned and started marching, and the unit followed, keeping the same line order as when they'd been up in the tunnel. This time, however, there wasn't a loud marching cadence. When they started across the massive cavern, Victor became aware that his bird's eye view from the platform hadn't given him an accurate perception of its size. They hiked for nearly fifteen minutes before coming to the first fungi stalks, and as they approached, Victor could see that they were like big, pale, creamy-gray trees.

When the column moved into the fungi forest, Victor reached out and touched one of the rubbery stalks, amazed by its size. "Careful, youngster," one of the other veterans said. "Some of the shit that grows down here is poisonous to touch. That one's all right, but don't go grabbing everything you see."

"Right, thanks." Victor wiped his hand on his pants, though there wasn't anything on it. They hiked for a few minutes, but then a rumbling sound accompanied by a strange chorus of hoots brought the column to a halt as the sergeant screamed, "Mulsii pack!" Victor lifted his club and stood shoulder to shoulder with two others as the unit formed a loose circle, facing into the mushrooms. The rumbling grew louder, then Victor saw the long, pale-white forms of the mulsii charging between the stalks. They had wormlike bodies, six long sticklike legs, and broad heads that reminded Victor of his cousin's pit bull, though without the fur and friendly mammalian eyes. If these things had eyes, they were too narrow and pale for Victor to spot, though he saw their long nostril slits flexing as they surged over the spongy ground.

He couldn't make any more observations because the things were on them then, and Victor became too busy methodically smashing his baton into hard skulls, bendy bodies, and brittle legs. The two members of Lam's unit on either side of him seemed to know what they were doing, and Victor found himself able to focus entirely on anything that approached him directly, ignoring his flanks. The baton might have been a simple weapon, but it was heavy, and Victor was strong, and he had no trouble smashing the occasional mulsii that charged him and sending it skittering off along the ground. The furious melee was over as soon as it began, and the delvers were left heaving for breath while the surviving mulsii hooted and howled, charging away into the fungi stalks.

Victor looked around and was surprised to see that one of the delvers was down; a massive chunk of his neck above his collar was gone. Several others sported bite wounds on their arms and legs, and some of the veterans were starting to move among them, passing out bandages. Victor cracked his back and felt a surge of Energy as the downed creatures began to emit golden motes. He looked at his Energy attribute on his status page and saw that he now had forty-four over seven. Hadn't he had a maximum of five before? Once again, he felt a little surge of hope that his Core wasn't wholly destroyed. Maybe it was healing, and maybe he could do something to help it along. He resolved to spend some time trying to cultivate or at least manipulate the little pools of Energy where his Core used to be next time they rested.

Sergeant Fath was exhorting the delvers to move faster as they buried their downed comrade when, with a gust of wind and a shower of glittering Energy, Captain Lam came out of the darkness and landed among them. "Damn! Already lost one, Sergeant?"

"Aye, Captain. It was a bigger pack than we expected."

"Well, finish the burial, then we need to get moving. We're supposed to clear six-fourteen today, and you're not halfway there yet."

"Aye, ma'am! You heard the captain, worms! Dig faster!" Victor tuned the sergeant out as he watched Captain Lam walk down the line past him and then up the path toward whatever tunnel was their goal.

"Don't let her catch you staring like that, Victor," Gris said with a chuckle.

"I can't help it; she's amazing."

"Yeah, she's something to see, that's for sure, but she's the most dangerous thing in this mine, so mind your manners."

"Right," Victor said as he knelt to pull up another handful of airy soil to toss into the pit where they'd planted the dead delver. Victor felt a little bad that he didn't even know the guy's name and that he was disappearing into an unmarked grave, but there wasn't anything he could do about it. When they resumed their march, the sergeant made them move a lot faster than previously, and it was only a few minutes later when they moved out of the fungi forest and into a big stone tunnel, but not nearly as massive as the tunnel up above. This tunnel didn't have light globes in the ceiling, so a few of the delvers were given bright, glowing lamps to hold. Victor figured one of the veterans must have a dimensional container because he never saw anyone carrying gear. Still, somehow things like these lamps and shovels seemed to appear out of nowhere when needed.

They followed the tunnel on a winding path, past several other tunnel openings, and always on a downward slope. They'd been traveling for about an hour when word made its way down the line that they were almost to delve six-fourteen and should get ready for a fight. Victor looked ahead and thought he saw Lam talking to the delvers in the front, and he wondered if the captain would be fighting with them. Thinking about Lam fighting made him smile, and it was with some surprise that he noticed his lack of stress or anxiety. He supposed part of it was that he didn't know what to expect, so he couldn't properly freak himself out, but a significant factor had to be that he'd been fighting for his life for weeks now, and this just didn't seem like anything worse than what he'd already been through many times in the pits.

Victor gripped his baton and surged forward with the rest of them, happy to see Lam's glittering wings up in the lead. Suddenly the sergeant started chanting, in his huge, bass voice, "Now we kill! We kill for Lam! Now we kill! We kill for Lam!" The other veterans picked up the chant, and Victor, feeling the mob frenzy, screamed along with them. They charged, chanting, roaring, batons waving in the air, down the tunnel and into a wide, open cavern filled with half-buried stone buildings. A bright orb of Energy blazed, hanging from a chain in the vaulted ceiling, shedding light on the scene, and skitters and shrieks echoed from the shadows as they burst into the open area in front of the tunnel.

Swarming, dark forms poured from the collapsed buildings and surged toward the band of baton-wielding delvers. "Form up! Shoulder to shoulder!" the sergeant boomed, and Victor found himself once again in a loose circle, facing out toward a much larger force of enemies. He still hadn't gotten a good look at them, but as he crouched, baton ready to swing, he saw a cluster of dark shadows erupt from a nearby collapsed building toward his side of the circle. They were about as big as a person and moved almost like shadows, sliding along the ground with gleaming red eyes. Still, they were definitely solid because he brought his baton down on the first one to slide toward him, and he felt it crack, and a shower of hot liquid sprayed onto his fist and forearm as he pulled his baton back for another swing. He smashed it into the creature again, and as it twitched and thrashed, Victor realized they were like long sticklike men with perfectly black carapaces. Their heads reminded him of something he'd see on a praying mantis or a grasshopper.

"Stickmen!" one of his neighbors grunted, swinging his baton. Victor smashed aside another one and another. He wanted to ask what the fuck a stickman was but never got a moment to catch his breath; they just kept coming, sliding over the ground in waves, and now that Victor had seen one up close, their movement freaked him out even more. They were crawling along the ground the way a person would crawl up a ladder. While he was fighting, he heard a tremendous shriek, and when Victor glanced toward it, he saw a massive black-carapaced form crawling out of a dark crevice about halfway through the cavern. He didn't have time to worry about it, though, as more stickmen came at him.

As he battled on, he heard a clear, piercing shout echo through the cavern, and when he looked, he saw Lam diving through the air, streaks of glittering light trailing behind her. She smashed into the top of the giant carapaced head emerging from the crevice, and a tremendous crack resonated through the cavern. Victor had to look away to fight again, but throughout the battle, whenever he got a moment of respite, he'd glance toward where he'd seen Lam, hoping to watch her do something cool again, but she just stood at the edge of the crevice, a colossal hammer resting on her shoulder, watching the fight. None of the smaller stickmen approached her.

Victor grew tired, and he found himself wishing he could call on his old rage, but he had to settle for his weapon skill and good old-fashioned strength and endurance. He'd just smashed aside another wave of the creatures when the guy on his left fell to his knee, a stickman crawling up onto his back, gripping with its hooked hands and biting into his shoulder with its black, razor-sharp mandibles. Victor cracked it on its hard head with his baton but then fell back to fight off another two that were coming for the gap in the line. He screamed, "Get that off him!" to the girl fighting on the other side of the downed man. She kicked out at the stickman she was fighting, sending it sprawling, then she turned and helped to finish the one on the guy's back. By the time they were both back in line, another wave of the creatures was coming. "Where the fuck? How many of these fucking things are there?" he yelled to no one in particular, and no one bothered to answer.

Victor's arms were numb, and he felt as if he was swinging a lead telephone pole by the time he smashed the last of the creatures, looked around for his next victim, and found nothing more coming his way. He turned and looked around the scene. Piles of black-carapaced bodies surrounded the knot of delvers. They stood with hands on knees, huffing and puffing for air or kneeling over fallen comrades, trying to staunch bleeding. Just then, a thick fog of golden motes coalesced over the mounds of defeated creatures and began to stream toward all of the survivors. While Victor stood transfixed, absorbing a thick stream of Energy, he saw a shimmering golden and sparkling purple river of Energy come out of the crevice and smash into Captain Lam's chest. She rose off the ground, her entire body glowing and sparking with golden-purple light. He'd long since finished absorbing his little stream of Energy when Lam finally floated back to the ground, and her glow subsided.

He'd been so amazed by the sight of Lam's Energy absorption that he hadn't noticed the System message that had popped up in his vision:

***Congratulations! You've achieved Level 12 Spirit Champion. You have gained 7 will, 7 vitality, and have 7 attribute points to allocate.***

"Holy shit," he said, despite himself.

"What, Victor?" Gris asked, limping over and holding a hand to a bleeding bite on his shoulder.

"Oh, nothing," Victor didn't know if he should mention that he'd leveled, so he deflected, "I mean, did you see Lam floating in the air?" Gris started talking about something like high-tier Energy rewards, but Victor tuned him out, looking at his status sheet. He'd somehow convinced himself that he was broken, that he couldn't level anymore while his Core was "fractured." He'd leveled, though, and when he turned his eye inward, he saw that more of those red droplets of rage-attuned Energy had moved toward his tiny, pulsing Core. He looked at his Energy and attributes on his status sheet:

| Energy Affinity: | 3.1, Rage 9.1 | Energy: | 289/23 |
|---|---|---|---|
| Strength: | 28 | Vitality: | 34 |
| Dexterity: | 19 | Agility: | 19 |
| Intelligence: | 10 | Will: | 24 |
| Points Available: | 7 | | |

His Core was healing; there wasn't any other explanation. He had a shit-load more Energy in his body than his broken Core could hold, but he knew he could work with it. If he got a chance to do some cultivating, he thought he could really start to heal, and then maybe he'd have a surprise for the fuckers that put the collar around his neck. He was thinking about where to throw his seven free points when the sergeant hollered, "All right! Let's bury our dead, clear the corpses, and we'll rest before heading back for the day. Good fight, Lam's Furies!"

# 24

## BEETLES

Three of Lam's Furies had died fighting the stickmen. Nobody seemed particularly broken up about it, and Victor couldn't help imagining himself in their shoes; one minute, they were marching along, joking and laughing with other prisoners, and the next they were buried under some rubble, forgotten at the bottom of a deep pit in the ground. "If this is the fucking bottom," he said, spitting into the dirt.

"What?" Gris asked.

"Just thinking about how shitty this is. Those dudes we just buried—nobody's gonna remember them. Their families probably already considered them lost, right? I mean, I can't imagine people are happy to hear about their loved ones coming to Greatbone Mine. Here one minute, alive and fighting, gone the next, forgotten so they can be replaced by the next poor suckers the foreman sends down." They were sitting on some rubble, eating hard rolls and dried meat that one of the veterans had handed out.

"Welcome to life, kid. Work as hard as you want, be as important as you want, but when you die, the world moves on." Gris handed a skin of watery wine to Victor, and he took a long drink. It wasn't strong enough to give him even a slight buzz, but at least it was something different.

"Yeah, it's just bullshit, that's all. I'm sick of being led around like a dog, told to fight one thing after another." He spoke softly so as not to draw attention to himself, but he had to say something to someone. Gris chewed his hard, crunchy bread, staring at Victor for a moment before he replied.

"Victor, you know I'm not really your friend, right? I'll have your back in a fight, as long as we're fighting what Lam tells us to, but don't get any ideas that I'm going to help you escape or some crazy thing. I've been down here three years and have five more months to go. I'm going to make it, and I won't do anything that'll stick my neck out. You understand me?"

"Yeah, I feel you." Victor sat back against the stone and stared up at the ceiling, a hundred feet above. He studied the little sparkles in the rock that had to be reflections of the glowing Energy lamp. What made the reflections? Gemstones? Eyes? Flakes of ore? He had no idea, so he stopped worrying about it. "Hey, how long we gonna get to rest?"

"Probably until Captain Lam comes back. She's scouting ahead into the ruins around here. Could be ten minutes, could be a couple hours." Gris stretched out and hung an arm over his eyes. Victor sat up and cleared his mind, focusing inward on his Core. If he was going to get out of this place, he needed to be stronger, and he couldn't get much stronger until he fixed his Core. Could he fix it? He decided he had to; he was tired of being told what to do, and there was no way he'd be spending five years in this place. What would happen if he ran through his cultivation drill with his Core the way it was?

"One way to find out," he muttered very softly and began the process. He called up one of his rage constructs and focused on it, feeling the heat start to spread at the very center of his being. It was working! He was so pleased that he almost interrupted the process. With the build-up of rage-attuned Energy, his little Core fragment started to pulse and flare very rapidly, and Victor had to begin the process of pushing Energy out and through his pathways right away. However, this proved beneficial because as he cycled the Energy around in his pathways, it started to absorb some of the little red pools of Energy that floated around his burgeoning Core. He pushed the Energy in an ever-widening circuit of his pathways, spread out from his Core all the way to his extremities and then back again. When the wave of hot, red Energy surged back into his little Core, it felt as if a fire had ignited in the center of his body, and he watched with his inner eye as his little Core swelled, started to crack, then slowly stabilized. The cracks healed over, and it pulsed more slowly and steadily. Looking at it, Victor thought it was easily twice as big as it had been when he'd started. He paused, took a long breath, then looked at the Energy numbers on his status sheet:

| Energy Affinity: | 3.1, Rage 9.1 | Energy: | 118/49 |
|---|---|---|---|

"Oh, fuck yes," he muttered. His Energy cap had more than doubled. Could it really be this easy? Just some cultivating, and his Core would be fixed? The asshole who'd fragmented his Core had acted as if what he was doing was permanent. Thinking back to when he'd been strapped to the table while the weird-ass tentacled guy had reached into his stomach, he shuddered, but a vivid memory came to him—hadn't the tentacled guy said something like he hadn't broken a Spirit Core before?

He looked into his Core again and saw the little pulsing, red sun still surrounded by tiny pools of Energy. The red, rage-attuned pools were significantly reduced, but the other white-yellow Energy pools seemed as numerous as ever. What was the deal with those? When his Core was fragmented, why had part of it lost its rage affinity? Not for the first time, he wished that he had an expert to consult. He wondered how much Lam could teach him; she was the most powerful being he'd ever met and had to know things that could help him. He shoved the thought aside, though; there was no way he was going to let anyone know his Core was recovering, even a little. Not to mention, he had no real reason to trust her; just because she was awe-inspiring didn't mean she would want to help him. The last thing he wanted was for her or someone else to decide he needed a stronger collar.

"You cultivating, Victor?" Gris asked as if on cue. "I'm surprised it does you any good with such a weak Energy level. I suppose everyone can improve a little, eh?"

"Ha, yeah, everyone always makes fun of me, but I figure it's relaxing if nothing else." Victor grinned, then stood up to stretch. It wasn't much longer until Captain Lam came out of the deep crevice, glittering sparkles streaking after her as she flew over to the group and landed.

"Good news, delvers! I found another vein and even more ruins. We'll set up a forward camp tomorrow so the diggers can come down and get started. Sergeant! Bring them back to the barracks!"

"Right, Captain!" Sergeant Fath shouted. "You heard the captain! Line up, cockroaches!" Victor snorted with laughter at being called a cockroach; part of him was pleased that the dirty little bastards were on this world too. They lined up and began the long march back to the barracks. Victor was glad for the distraction of the march cadence that Sergeant Fath began; this one had some colorful lyrics about people's mothers, and, with the positive results with his Core, he was in just enough of a good mood to laugh at the absurdity. At the start of the march, he applied his seven free points to his strength, dexterity, and agility attributes, figuring that he needed the extra physical ability while his Core was on the mend.

Their return to the barracks was uneventful; nothing attacked them, and their only stop was to ride the levitating platform back up to the main tunnel. When they got back, some of the delvers wanted to go to the Settlement Stone to turn in their quests, but Victor saw that he only had thirty-nine kills when he checked the status of his quest. He opted to sit on his bunk and do another round of cultivating. He'd gathered from Gris's reaction that people couldn't tell how much Energy he was moving around when he cultivated, so he figured it was safe to do. He was a little worried that someone as powerful as Lam would know what was going on with him, but she didn't hang around in the main barracks, so he sat down on his bunk, folded his legs the way Yrella had taught him, and began the process.

He'd managed to complete two full rotations of his cultivation drill when he became aware of a lot of activity and opened his eyes. People were gathering at the table for their evening meal, so he stretched and looked at his Energy stats:

| Energy Affinity: | 3.1, Rage 9.1 | Energy: | 125/125 |
|---|---|---|---|

He'd processed all the extra Energy he'd gained from his kills, and his Core now pulsed with deep, red Energy, sending warmth and a sense of potential through his body. He looked inward and saw that he'd gathered more than half of the little fragmented pools of rage-attuned Energy, though the unattuned Energy pools were still there. He was missing something when it came to those; he was sure of it. He had a small hope that they'd start to become absorbed once all of the rage-attuned Energy was gone, but he felt there was more to it.

The unit's dinner consisted of mystery meat drenched in fatty gravy, more hard biscuits, this time with butter, and a generous slice of some sort of melon. It reminded Victor of cantaloupe, but it was red with round, green seeds. Gris told him to eat the seeds when he saw Victor collecting them on his plate, so Victor gave it a try; they were tough, chewy, and spicy. Combined with the fruit's natural sweetness, they were a surprising treat. After they ate, Captain Lam ordered everyone to sleep. She said they'd be starting extra early, and she didn't want any noise coming from the barracks. The surviving members of the unit were exhausted, and respect for the captain and her sergeants ran deep, so everyone quickly complied, clearing off the table and quickly moving to their bunks to get what little sleep they could. Everyone except Victor, that is. He waited for those near him to fall asleep, then he silently sat up and began cultivating. He didn't care how tired he would be; he was going to cultivate all night if possible.

Victor woke to someone kicking his bed. He jerked up and looked around; apparently, his exhaustion had overcome his desire to cultivate at some point. He looked at his Energy numbers:

| Energy Affinity: | 3.1, Rage 9.1 | Energy: | 274/274 |
|---|---|---|---|

He almost cussed at Gris in surprise, but he bit his tongue and stood up to fold his blankets. Then he hustled over to the line of delvers. He turned his attention to his Core and saw that it was swirling around, pulsing and glowing almost like it used to before he'd been damaged. He remembered having about five hundred Energy before they fucked his Core over, though, so something still wasn't right. He studied the space around his Core and found that there were still tons of fragmented little pools of yellow-white Energy. Whatever that tentacle dude had done to him, his rage-attuned Core was not absorbing those fragments, and his cultivation drill wasn't converting them. It was a problem, but one he could take his time to figure out; right now, he was just pleased that he wasn't helpless when it came to Energy use anymore. Still, he'd have to be careful; he didn't want any of the Greatbone employees to know what he was capable of, and Victor knew that the other prisoners were just as likely to rat him out as help him.

The march down to where they'd fought the horde of stickmen went smoothly. They ran into a couple packs of the mulsii, but they were small groups and fled from the delvers. This time Victor was marching behind Gris, but a thin Ghelli woman, only about five feet tall, was in line behind him, and she kept trying to chat with him during the march. With the sergeant chanting a cadence, and everyone shouting it out in refrain, Victor had a hard time hearing her, but she was persistent. "I said, how'd you manage to not get any bites or anything during that last fight?" They'd just gotten to the site of their previous battle, and the sergeant had ordered them to drink and rest while they waited for Captain Lam to show up.

"What? Oh, I just watched my spot on the line and didn't let any through. Why? Did you get bitten?" He looked at her thin, pale limbs and fragile little wings and tried to wrap his head around the idea that she was the same type of person as Captain Lam.

"Yes! One of them got around and bit me right on my butt cheek. No, I'm not showing you! It hurts when I walk, though. I wish they weren't so stingy with the healing salves."

"Ouch, that sucks." Victor took a deep swig from the wineskin someone passed him and gave it to the girl. "What's your name, anyway?"

"Edeya. You're Victor, right? I heard the old white-bearded man talking to you." Victor smiled at the description of Gris.

"Yeah, that's right. Anyway, nice to meet you, and remember, when you're fighting shoulder to shoulder, you gotta trust the people next to you to have your back, so you can focus on the shit in front of you. Don't let anything through and leave it to them to do the same. I'm not trying to be a know-it-all; Gris told me this stuff."

"Oh, thanks, but I already got an earful about that. You're right, though; that was my problem." She smiled, and Victor thought she was cute in a way. Her features were very fine and pointed, but she had big green eyes and a friendly smile. She kept her hair cut short, almost as short as his. He couldn't help thinking she seemed extremely fragile, and he had the dark thought lurking in his mind that he shouldn't bother getting to know her because she'd probably be dead soon. He tried to think of something to talk about with her almost to spite that mean, bitter voice he seemed to be hearing in his head more and more.

"Hey," Victor said, "I'm kinda new to this world and don't know much about Energy and Cores and stuff. Is it rude for me to ask what kind of Core you have?"

"Oh, I don't think it's rude, not when you put it that way. I have a Pith Class Core—It's a nature-affinity Core very attuned to trees and plants."

"That's pretty cool. Can you make plants grow or something?"

"Hmm, yes!" Her grin broadened, showing off straight, white teeth, and Victor couldn't help smiling back. "If I can get some levels, someday I'll be able to craft living wood and even travel the Tree Road."

"The Tree Road?"

"Yes! Some Ghelli with a Core like mine and with a suitable class can get a skill that lets them touch one tree in a forest and travel through it, traveling along the intertwining roots, to come out through any other tree in the forest!"

"That's actually pretty badass. Nice!"

"Well, now it's your turn. What's your Core like? I noticed from your collar that it's not, um, never mind." Victor shrugged, reaching up to run his fingers around the circular iron band on his neck. Edeya had a collar that looked more like steel, and like the one Gris wore, it had dozens of intricate figures carved into it.

"Nah, don't worry. It's true. I'm from a world without any Energy, and before I came here, some asshole destroyed the Core I had." He'd already rehearsed what he'd say to people inquiring about his Core. "I mean, I have a tiny little Core fragment left, but when I cultivate, nothing much happens."

"Oh, that's terrible! What savages! What kind of Core did you have?"

"Um, Spirit."

"Oh, no! Spirit Cores are so rare among my people! One of our elders had a Spirit Core with a Courage affinity! She was sought after by generals in Ridonne to encourage their troops before big battles. She made a fortune that she brought back to invest in our town."

"Courage? That sounds pretty cool."

"You have a funny way of speaking, Victor. I kind of like it!" She looked down, a bright rosy tint flooding her cheeks, and Victor suddenly imagined a mulsii sinking its long teeth into her shoulder and dragging her away. He shook his head and squeezed his hand into a fist until his nails bit into his palm. Just because she was delicate and just because she was friendly didn't mean that she had to die. "Are you all right?"

"Um, just a headache. Sorry." Victor was rescued from any further conversation when Captain Lam came streaking out of the dark crevice in the middle of the cavern. She strode over to the group of delvers, looking perfectly clean and coiffed as if she'd just come out of a salon.

"Well, I killed a Tier Four salamander. There's some trash for you all to clear out, but you should manage. Set up a barricade and the forward camp when the foothold is secure. I'm going to report my findings and let the foreman know to schedule a mining crew." Lam spoke to Sergeant Fath, but it was easy to hear her clear, ringing voice. She strode past the delver unit, nodding to anyone that made eye contact, and Victor nodded back to her, standing up straight subconsciously.

"She's amazing, isn't she?" Edeya asked in a hushed voice.

"Yeah, that's for sure. Fucking A." Victor looked down and smiled when Edeya giggled at his words. "Yeah, I talk funny. I get it."

"All right, let's move out," Sergeant Fath said. "Captain says we gotta climb a pretty steep slope for about two hundred feet, then we're going to be in the shit. Heads on a swivel, batons ready!"

"Here we go!" Edeya said, gripping her little baton and rushing over to line up. Victor frowned and hurried after her.

"Great," he muttered, "now I feel like I have to watch her back."

"You good, Victor?" Gris asked, coming up behind him.

"Yeah, about to crawl into a deep pit full of man-size bugs and shit. Feeling great!"

"Aw, come on! We don't know if it's bugs; it could be spiders or giant lizards; it could be ghouls or imps. Heck, it's probably not bugs!" He laughed and slapped Victor's shoulder. Victor shook his head and followed Edeya into the crevice. The delvers slid and scurried down a loose slope of scree, keeping to the near side of the shaft. Every now and then, an Energy globe was attached to a wall or a rocky outcropping, and Gris said the captain had put those there for them.

"Must be nice to be able to fly," Victor said almost wistfully.

"Oh, I hope I can advance my race that far someday!" Edeya said over her shoulder.

"Are there many Ghelli that advanced?"

"No, not many. Only two in my hometown, and we had . . ."

"Quiet!" one of the veterans ahead of Edeya hissed.

"Aye, let's hush," Gris said from behind Victor. Victor looked around at the shadowy rift, wondering what lurked up in the high, rocky gloom. The captain's lights allowed them to see where they walked, but they didn't shed much light on the far side of the crevice. After a few minutes more, the word was passed up the line to get ready. They came around a bend, and Victor saw another large Energy globe spilling its yellow-orange light into a wide, low-ceilinged cavern, one wall of which gleamed and glittered in reflected light. "Damn me!" Gris whispered, "That's the biggest amber-ore vein I've seen."

The crevice opened into the cavern, and on the far side, perhaps two hundred paces away, a broad, dark tunnel continued into the depths. A howling, hissing, clacking cacophony erupted from that tunnel, and a wave of creatures rushed toward them out of the shadows. "Beetle riders!" Sergeant Fath screamed. "No holding back! Use your Energy! Captain Lam ain't here to save us! C'mon down the slope; let's get our backs to that wall!" Sergeant Fath charged down the remaining slope, and the line of delvers surged after him. Victor followed, of course, trying not to pass up the shorter-legged people in front of him but also wanting to hurry so he didn't get caught out in the middle of the cavern when the "beetle riders" fell upon them. When they got off the scree-covered slope, Victor let his legs really stretch out, and he grabbed Edeya's wrist, pulling her along with him. He'd barely gotten into position and pulled her next to him when the creatures, howling and skittering, closed the distance and attacked.

Victor raised his baton and smashed the head of a yellow and red beetle the size of a mastiff as it tried to jump onto Gris's back. Gris, panting and red-faced, lined up next to Victor and offered him a nod of thanks, then the battle took his attention away. The eighteen delvers were lined up against a solid wall of rock, and a skittering, hissing, clicking horde of beetles spread out before them. Every fifth beetle or so was ridden by a little manlike creature with skin so pale that it looked transparent. They bore spears and crude clubs and axes, and they hissed and howled with mouths gaping open to display snakelike fangs. Victor wasn't an expert on combat logistics, but in his amateur opinion, they were fucked.

At first, it didn't go as badly as he feared; some of the delvers had pretty amazing Energy skills, and they turned the tide in their favor for a while. Sergeant Fath roared out a battle chant that seemed to invigorate the delvers, making Victor's arms surge with buzzing energy. He felt confident and sure and laughed while he smashed his baton out in heavy overhead strikes at anything within range. He was careful to keep his place in the line and felt so good with the sergeant's chant bolstering him that he had time to spare between opponents to throw an occasional smash at the creatures in front of Edeya. She didn't complain, though she'd held her own so far.

One of the veterans a few spots down the line would roar every couple of minutes and breathe out a long, liquid belch of flames that would drench the beetles in front of him for a good ten paces, lighting them on fire and sending them hissing and squealing in a panicked, frenzied rampage through the horde. Some of the beetles they touched would also start to burn, and they'd go mad with pain and panic, lashing out at each other. Another delver was able to discharge electric shocks with his baton blows, though it seemed to drain him considerably. For his part, Gris would occasionally speed up to superhuman levels, smashing everything in front of him, sending shards of carapace flying, and driving into the horde for several seconds before rushing back, panting, to take up his position again.

Victor just plodded along, swinging and swinging, blocking and kicking with his old worn boots whenever a beetle got too close. After seeing the fireworks some of the delvers were able to dish out, he began to have some hope that they had a chance. Still, the horde of beetles and their riders seemed to keep coming, and after several minutes of fighting, when his arm was burning from swinging his baton, one of the riders managed to slip a thin, stone-tipped spear past his guard and punch a hole about two inches deep under his left collarbone. Victor roared in pain and snatched the spear, pulling the pale, creepy little man close and bringing his baton down on his flat, hairless head. The creature's skull deformed under the blow, and it dropped at Victor's feet among the broken and smashed beetle corpses.

The corpses were starting to be a problem as they piled up; the fresh waves of enemies were crawling over them and coming at Victor and the other delvers from a greater height. On top of that, the space for maneuvering was becoming more and more cramped. Victor was starting to feel more and more exhausted, and his frustration at the situation was mounting. His shoulder and triceps were screaming with fire after swinging that heavy baton for the thousandth time, and, still, the creatures came pouring out of the tunnel.

Hissing like a snake, a beetle rider jumped off its mount toward him, swinging its axe in a two-handed overhead strike. Victor stepped forward, inside its swing, and smashed it in the side with his baton, sending it flying to his left, where it crashed into Edeya. She stumbled back, then several beetles broke through and started swarming over her. A surge of guilt and panic hit Victor as he realized he'd caused her to fall, and he simply snapped, activating his Berserk ability for the first time since his Core had been fractured. Red washed over his vision, and his muscles sang with Energy. He howled in exuberance, smashing his way through the beetles that were snapping at Edeya's legs, and then, with a monumental effort of will, turned away from Edeya and the delvers. He waded into the horde of beetles and their riders, swinging his heavy metal baton like a thin reed.

Victor's baton whistled and shrieked as it split the air, blasting through carapaces and sending the lithe beetle rider bodies flying. He laughed maniacally, his mouth open in a leering grin as fluids and shell fragments splattered him. He had a plentitude of targets to brutalize, and at some point, in the midst of his rage, the sergeant started up his chant again, adding more fuel to his frenzied rampage. He mowed his way deep into the horde, laying waste to a wide circle of insects and their pale riders.

Victor was only aware of the need to destroy his enemies and didn't have any sense of how the tide of the battle was flowing, but his rampage had given the other delvers a much-needed respite and chance to regroup. While he pushed ever farther into the horde, accumulating cuts and bruises that seemed to heal as fast as they appeared, the other delvers, led by the sergeant's bellowed commands, pulled in tighter. They moved down the wall away from the piled corpses, readying themselves for the inevitable wave that would come when Victor finally fell.

Dimly, Victor was aware that his Berserk was fading. Though he was still in battle and tried to push more and more rage-attuned Energy into his body to keep the ability stoked, his Core was flickering and sputtering, having fed him everything it had. With a final surge, he smashed his way through a thin line of beetles so that he could mount the slippery, rubble-strewn ramp that led up out of the cavern. He'd just gotten through and gained a bit of ground when his Berserk finally faded, and he almost collapsed as the exhaustion hit him. He fell to one knee, and a beetle clambered up, snapping at his face. He managed to thrust out with his left hand, punching it under its snapping mandibles and flipping it back down the slope. Something sharp on its carapace ripped a jagged gash over his knuckles, but he'd gained enough room to struggle to his feet.

"Where the fuck?" Coming out of his rage-induced Berserk was like waking up from a dream. He had a dim memory of the fighting, but now, as he stood on the slope and looked over the chittering, clacking horde, he was utterly disoriented. He saw the delvers a hundred paces away fighting against the wall, and he saw a swath of dead beetles and riders, but there still had to be hundreds of the things. He weakly lifted his baton because some of the creatures were starting to surge up the rocky slope to him. "This is it? I'm going to be beetle food?" He was exhausted, his arms were numb and heavy, and his vision was dim, as if his eyes weren't getting enough blood. "Come on!" he screamed, trying to pump himself up, hoping to spark some adrenaline. A beetle came within reach, and he smashed down on it with his baton, nearly stumbling on a loose rock.

He'd just lifted his baton for another blow, grunting with the effort, when a gust of wind rushed past him, trailing a line of glittering sparks. "What the fuck?" Then his brain caught up with his eyes, and he saw Captain Lam streak down to the cavern floor, directly in the middle of the horde of beetles. A burst of crackling silver-tipped flames rolled out from her impact point, completely incinerating a hundred or more beetles in a perfect circle around her. She shouted in a pure, ringing voice, swinging her two-handed hammer around in great arcs, sending broken beetles flying with each swing. She carved a swath through the remaining insects to the line of delvers, and Victor, though he had another beetle in front of him to deal with, laughed in excitement at seeing something so utterly badass. His baton suddenly felt lighter, and his muscles less exhausted, and he beat the beetle and two more after it into broken carcasses.

By then, the other delvers and the captain had moved on to mopping up stragglers, and Gris helped Victor with the last few beetles near the ramp. When Victor saw Gris and saw that no more beetles were coming, he fell to his knees in exhaustion and smiled up at the old veteran. "Hey, I thought Lam wasn't coming to save us? Somebody needs to tell the sergeant to quit being so pessimistic." Gris was helping him to his feet when the air around them suddenly filled with a mist of golden motes. "Oh shit," Victor said when he saw how much Energy was coalescing from the hundreds and hundreds of corpses. A massive stream of Energy surged toward him, and though he felt transfixed by the rush of vigor and well-being, he managed to see that his stream was broader and brighter than anyone else's, including the captain's.

***Congratulations! You've achieved Level 14 Spirit Champion. You have gained 14 will, 14 vitality, and have 14 attribute points to allocate.***

"So much for not getting noticed," he muttered, though Gris seemed preoccupied with his own Energy surge. He looked around the cavern and saw that nearly everyone was dealing with their own problems, and for a second, he thought he'd skate under the radar. But then he glanced at Captain Lam and felt the weight of her gaze as it bored into him.

# 25

# SECRETS

After sorting through the wounded delvers and seeing to their injuries the best they could, Sergeant Fath directed the able-bodied prisoners in the construction of a barrier over the tunnel that led farther into the depths. One of the veterans had a rune-inscribed bag from which he pulled all the boards, hammers, nails, pickaxes, and saws that they needed for the construction. Victor worked hard, all the while wondering when he'd be singled out and called over to speak to Captain Lam about his prodigious Energy gains at the end of the fight. Nothing happened, though, save for a few of the delvers looking at him with more respect and clapping him on the shoulder, saying things like, "You really took it to those bastards! Nice fighting!" Edeya, who'd suffered a badly twisted knee, didn't seem to blame him for getting knocked down and overrun, but he wondered if she even realized he'd been the one to throw that beetle rider onto her.

After they'd built a sturdy barricade over the tunnel, complete with mounted ballistae and ramparts for the defenders, Sergeant Fath handed a sack to Victor and another one to Gris and told them to get started collecting beetle corpses. "Um, how do I use this thing?" Victor asked Gris after the sergeant had walked away.

"You never used a dimensional container? The ones they let us use are enchanted so that multiple people can access them. Just concentrate on it and send some of your Energy out to it. You'll understand what to do after that."

"Uh, right," Victor said, looking at the big floppy sack he'd been handed. How was he supposed to "send Energy into it? " He concentrated on his Core, and just as he did with his cultivation drill, he pushed Energy out along his pathways, feeling the hot simmering rage tickle the back of his mind. He continued to push, as thin a stream of the Energy as he could, until it moved along into his hand, then he pushed harder, trying to shove it into the bag. Suddenly he became aware of the bag and the enormous space within it. He could see that it was empty without even opening it. Holding the bag in his left hand, he reached out to touch one of the beetle corpses and willed it into the bag. Like magic, the crumpled, gooey carapace poofed out of existence, and Victor became aware of it sitting in the bag's dimensional space. "That's pretty fucking cool."

"Glad you like it," said a strong, clear voice that sent shivers down his spine. Victor jerked his head around and saw that Captain Lam was standing just behind and to the right of him, watching him with her glittering emerald eyes. She'd put away her massive hammer but still wore her armor, which, combined with her height, made Victor feel insignificant in her presence.

"Um, yeah. I've never used one before," Victor muttered, holding up the sack.

"Sergeant Fath tells me you might be responsible for the delvers living long enough for me to make it back in time. You think that's true?"

"Oh, uh, no, I don't think so. Most of the veterans had some pretty awesome abilities. I just went a little crazy at one point and charged into the horde. I bet I would have done more good if I'd stayed in the line." Victor watched her face while he spoke, wondering if she'd see through him. Her eyes narrowed a little, but her lips quirked in a smile.

"Being modest? Or are you hoping I won't take note of your ability? I think it's the latter; you don't seem the modest sort." She stood with her arms folded, and she tapped one long finger against her opposite elbow, studying him. Victor swallowed and stood up straighter. She wasn't all that much taller than him, six or eight inches, but she just had a certain presence that made him feel small. He supposed it had a lot to do with her level and how much Energy she had.

"Well, to be honest," he said, deciding that it might be wise to mix some truth with his dissembling, "I have an ability that causes me to kind of go berserk, but I don't remember a lot after I do that."

"Oh?" She looked at him and nodded. "When I read your contract, it made note of you having a dysfunctional Core. Surely your Berserking ability requires a significant amount of Energy?"

"Well, yeah, but I had a lot of Energy saved up from yesterday's fights. It doesn't go to my Core, just kinda sits in my pathways and stuff."

"Mmhmm. And you just received another large influx, correct?"

"Yeah." He couldn't see a way to hide that fact; she'd seen it with her own eyes.

"Your affinity must be high. Well, that's beside the point. You have enough Energy to activate your berserking skill again, right?"

"Uh, yeah."

"Good. I can make use of you. Carry on; clean up this mess. I'll let you know when you're needed." She turned and walked over to where Sergeant Fath was berating another delver who'd done something wrong, and Victor, though he struggled not to, watched her walk away with a very stupid expression on his face. He finally pulled his eyes back into his head and got to work cleaning up the beetle corpses. It took him the better part of an hour, even with another delver helping, so big were the piles of corpses and beetle parts in the wide cavern. When he and Gris finished, Sergeant Fath hollered at them to "eat something," so they went over to where the wounded delvers were propped up near the amber-ore vein, and Victor sat down next to Edeya.

"How's the knee?" he asked. He munched on the hunk of "rations" that one of the veterans had passed out. It was a chewy square of animal fat, dried meat, and dried berries and nuts. If you didn't think about it too much and just ate it without wondering where the meat came from, it didn't taste all that bad, and it was certainly filling.

"It's sore, but Captain Lam told Fath to break out the good salve for it, and I can feel it getting better already. I think I'll be able to walk pretty soon."

"Well, that's good!"

"It is! Victor, I thought I was going to die in that fight. I thought we all were. When I fell and those beetles started crawling on my legs, I was sure it was over."

"Yeah, um, I'm sorry about that."

"What? Why? You're the one that cleared them off!"

"Shit, you're kidding, right? I hit the asshole rider-guy onto you. I'm the one that knocked you down." He took another bite of his ration and stared at her, daring her to react.

"You're too honest," she said. "I mean, you didn't have to tell me that. It doesn't matter anyway; it's not like you meant to knock me down, and you made up for it." She shrugged, pushing herself up a bit higher against the stone wall, and then reached out and snatched the rest of Victor's ration bar. "I'll take this as payment."

"Hey, what the hell?" Victor laughed and mock-snatched at the ration, and Edeya giggled, cramming it into her mouth. Her cheeks bulged out, her eyes wide, and Victor laughed even harder. "Ahh, I needed that. It's good to laugh, you know?" Victor sighed deeply, stretching out his legs and knocking the heels of his boots against the hard ground, trying to get some of the crusty bits of carapace to fall off. He thought it was strange how he could laugh and joke around while stuck in his current mess. He was in a strange world, deep under the earth with a collar on his neck, being forced to fight monsters. "But I can laugh and joke around," he said aloud.

"What?"

"Talking to myself. I'm weird, remember?" He bumped her bony shoulder with his elbow and smiled down at her.

"Well, what about?"

"Just thinking about how strange it is that people can find things to laugh about in the worst fucking situations. How long are you stuck in this place?"

"I owe two years. I took on some of my parents' debt so they could avoid prison. My little sisters needed them home."

"Jesus." Once again, Victor was reminded that he wasn't the only one with a raw deal in this place. "If I ever get out of here, I'm going to work to gain enough clout to put this fucking indentured servant bullshit out of business."

"Hah, gonna take on the whole Ridonne Empire, hmm?"

"All right, I know I don't know shit, but I'm going to do something. Seriously. This system is garbage. I mean, it's basically like allowing slavery without calling it slavery."

"True. On the Beneset Steppes, some tribes openly enslave people they capture, but at least they're honest about it. It's awful, but you know what I mean."

"I guess. After living like this, though, I couldn't be okay with it for anyone."

"Victor!" He turned to see Sergeant Fath staring at him and motioning for him to come over.

"Catch you later," he said to Edeya, then got up and walked over to the big sergeant. "Yeah?"

"Go stand over by the barricade and wait; Captain Lam has a job for you." He turned from Victor, looked up and down the line, then shouted, "Heng! Come here!" He saw Victor still standing there and made a shooing motion toward the big wooden barrier. Victor shrugged and walked over to it, sighing with some relief when he saw the big Vodkin veteran coming over; at least he wasn't being singled out. A moment later, they were joined by another veteran that Victor didn't know the name of, a short but very stout, angry-faced Cadwalli with red and yellow irises in his weird goatlike face. Heng nodded to him when he walked up, but neither of them spoke.

"Uh, I'm Victor," he said, looking at the two men.

"Heng. That's Fenlale; he doesn't talk."

"Any idea what this is?"

"Nope." Heng leaned his broad, leather-clad body against the barricade and spat off to the side. Victor noticed that both of the veterans had some decently thick-looking boots and vests, and their batons were larger and had those little System letters all over them.

"You guys buy your gear at that big stone thing with the shop in it?"

"Yeah, the Contribution Store. You pick up quests?" Heng asked.

"Uh-huh. Got one to turn in."

"Yep." Victor didn't respond; he wasn't really interested in pulling more grunts out of the recalcitrant fellow, and besides, he could see Captain Lam coming down the ramp. He watched her, wondering why she didn't fly everywhere, but admiring the grace with which she traversed the ground. It was like watching a dancer; everything she did was smooth and perfect. He wondered just how high her dexterity and agility were. She didn't pause by the other delvers, just walked straight up to the trio of them standing by the barrier and nodded in greeting.

"All right, I found some ruins I want to explore, and I need you guys to watch my back while I dig around. Let's go; I want us back here in a couple of hours." She climbed the short stack of steps leading to the little rampart and leaped over the side, and the two veterans hurried after. Victor followed in their footsteps, once again feeling caught in the wake of the events happening around him. He knew, logically, that he didn't have a choice but still felt he should be resisting somehow. While he dropped off the side, hanging from the rail to break his fall, he determined that his resistance would have to be mental for now. He'd continue to grow stronger, lie about his abilities, and take every opportunity to plan his escape. Surely, he wasn't the only prisoner down in the mines who felt that way, and they obviously weren't having much success, but that didn't mean he couldn't make something happen. Fuck anyone who said otherwise.

Captain Lam and the others were standing a few feet away; she was looking at a document, tracing something with her finger, and the other two stood with batons in their hands, looking around nervously. Victor lifted his baton and looked around, walking over to them. The tunnel on this side of the barrier was about two feet higher than his head and a good ten paces wide with a reasonably steep, descending slope. They were still in a part of the tunnel illuminated by the big orb that Captain Lam had hung from the ceiling in the cavern, but it was dark just a bit farther on. Victor was about to ask about the light, but Lam put the paper away and produced a glowing yellow orb, passing it to the burly Cadwalli veteran. "All right, follow me. Victor, you bring up the rear. If you get attacked, use your Berserking ability; don't hold back."

"All right," he said, squeezing his baton more tightly, glad for the leather grip that soaked up his sweat. Lam didn't set an easy pace, striding quickly with her long legs down the tunnel. She turned down a side tunnel that Victor didn't even see until he'd walked right up to it. The opening was a narrow crevice behind a protruding elbow of solid stone, and when the light winked out as Fenlale turned into it, Victor had a momentary panic but realized what had happened and hustled after them. What the hell would he do if he got separated down here without a light? They followed the narrow, natural-seeming series of cavelike tunnels for a while, turning and descending several times until Victor was sure he'd struggle to find his way back with or without a light. Remarkably, nothing attacked them by the time the captain stopped, and Victor caught up to the trio.

They were standing in a tunnel mouth, looking out on another vast cavern. Fenlale had covered his glowing orb with his leather shirt, and Victor could see that the cavern was dimly illuminated by hanging moss that glowed with an eerie green-white luminescence. "Glow-moss," Heng matter-of-factly said when he saw Victor staring around. An underground stream rushed through the cavern, and stone structures lined both sides of the stream, including a partially intact stone bridge. While they watched, a rumbling sound signaled some movement on the far side of the stream, and Victor saw a taillike appendage disappear beneath a pile of rubble that might once have been another building.

"There it is," Captain Lam said, pointing to the rubble pile. "It's a greater rot fiend, Tier Three or so. I'll deal with it; you three need to make sure nothing jumps me while I'm fighting. If it's something you can't handle, try to keep it busy awhile, and I'll try to hurry with the rot fiend." The tunnel opened onto the cavern a good twenty feet from the ground, so Captain Lam produced a rope and piton, which glowed red when she pressed it against the tunnel floor and sank four inches into the rock with a soft hiss. As quickly as it had begun to glow, it returned to normal, and she hooked the rope to it, throwing it down toward the floor. "After I fly down there, hurry down the rope and take up positions around that pile of rubble so you can watch my back."

Captain Lam looked at each of them, making sure they acknowledged what she said, then produced her huge hammer from some hidden container, hefting it in both hands. Victor had never seen it up close before, and he admired its craftsmanship. It had a long, black wooden handle topped with a silvery metal hammerhead pointed on one side and flat on the other. He figured it would weigh a good twenty-five pounds if the hammerhead were steel. Either she was ridiculously strong, or it was lighter than it looked because he'd seen her swinging it around like a broomstick. "Good luck," he said, feeling like an idiot. Captain Lam didn't make fun, though, just nodded her head and fell backward off the ledge.

Her abrupt departure caught Victor by surprise, but she rotated smoothly, and her brilliant, enormous dragonfly wings started to beat rapidly, throwing motes of sparkling light behind her as she raced toward the buried creature. "C'mon," Heng said, grabbing the rope and dropping over the edge. Fenlale followed close behind, and Victor brought up the rear. They descended quickly, then hurried over the broken stones on the cavern floor, moving between ancient buildings toward the sounds of crashing rocks and hissing shrieks that had erupted in the distance. "Matron! She could have waited for us to get closer!" The big otter-man leaped over a collapsed stone pillar, and Victor almost laughed at how funny it was to see such a wide man move so nimbly.

"I'll go left!" Victor shouted at the backs of the other two delvers, then turned left around a large stone structure blocking their path; the other two went right. He figured that they shouldn't all be in one spot if the captain wanted them to watch her back. He rounded the building and had a short stretch of open ground ahead of him, down which he could see the stream flowing. He sprinted for it, wondering if he could make the jump or if he'd need to traverse the ancient bridge. While running, he sped past stone buildings, some intact, others nearly completely collapsed. He heard another tremendous crash and then a roar that vibrated his body; he clapped his free hand over his ear and tucked the other one against his shoulder, trying to spare them from the outburst. The sound cut off with an almost comical squeak, and Victor resumed his dash to the river.

When he passed by the last of the structures on his right and could see
clearly over the bridge, he finally caught sight of Captain Lam and the creature she was battling. Lam moved in dashes and leaps that carried her a
dozen feet in the air; Victor, again, wished he had wings like that. The creature was the size of a hippopotamus and built similarly, though it was shorter
with six legs, a long flailing tail, and a nest of probing, spiked tentacles surrounding a slender, pointed beak. Victor watched Captain Lam leap over its
back, avoiding its thrashing tail, land near its left rear haunch, and smash her
hammer into its hip with a thunderous crack. Still trying to watch the fight,
Victor began to trot along the river toward the partially crumbled stone arch.
He was moving past a low-walled ruin when something burst up from the
riverbank and slammed into him, knocking him through an ancient door,
disintegrating it into a cloud of desiccated wood dust. Whatever hit him was
growling and slobbering, its hot, wet mouth worrying at his shoulder as they
tumbled together into the ruin.

When they smashed into the far stone wall, coming to a halt, Victor, still
madly gripping his baton, began to thrash down at whatever was digging and
clawing at him. It was dark in the small structure, but he caught glimpses
of dark fur and gleaming yellow eyes. The creature finally secured a good
hold on his shoulder and crunched down, and Victor screamed as long fangs
punctured his shoulder, and the beast began to shake its head back and forth,
like a terrier killing a rat. It hurt so badly that he lost track of his thoughts
and simply activated Berserk. Suddenly red rage flooded his vision, and he no
longer felt any discomfort from the horrible bite on his shoulder; he just felt
the annoying pressure and wanted to be rid of it.

Victor stopped screaming and thrashing and got his feet beneath him,
standing up and lifting the heavy beast with him. He charged forward, carrying it, still clinging to his shoulder, and bodily slammed it into the stone wall.
He felt its heavy, scrabbling body compress under his weight against the wall,
and its jaws sprang open, releasing his shoulder. Victor took a step back and
began to methodically and mechanically smash his baton into an area where he
could see the creature's eyes reflecting light. His first blow cracked something,
and the next ten or twelve began to spray wet, warm fluid on each backswing.
When nothing came looking for round two, Victor started to pant and look
around, wondering, in his rage, what else he could kill. He paced around in the
dark interior of the building, growling and grunting, his fury unrequited.

When he got to the back corner of the structure and turned, still hunting a new victim, Victor saw the dimly lit doorway and charged toward it.

He took two steps, then his foot broke through the old flooring, and he fell about eight feet to smash onto a cold stone floor. He sat up, glaring around in the dark, and a glinting silver light caught his eye. He stared at it for a moment, and then the red started to bleed from his vision, and his berserking rage began to cool. The air was cool and moist, and as his mind came back to him, Victor realized he was sitting in a shallow puddle; water dribbled in from between blocks in the walls. "From the river," he said aloud, his voice hoarse.

Victor glanced around, confused at first about where he was, but then he saw the hanging, broken floorboards and dimly remembered falling. When he looked at the hole in the ceiling, he realized it was limned in a silvery light and remembered what he'd seen while under the influence of his rage. He jerked his head to the far corner, and there, stretched out as though it was reclining against the stone blocks, was a long, yellow-boned skeleton of a humanoid. Around its neck was a silvery pendant that shone with a white-silver light. Victor didn't stop to think; he just stood up and rushed over to the skeleton, briefly noting the alien shape of the skull with a small crown of black horns protruding from its brow, and lifted the necklace over its head. The chain caught on one of the horns, but he wiggled it free.

He heard the clash of combat, though it seemed distant, and remembered that he was supposed to be watching Captain Lam's back. "I am, though. Didn't I just kill something?" Using the light from the amulet, he looked around the skeleton and saw that it had a ring on its long, bony middle finger. He pulled it off the bone, marveling that both it and the amulet were shiny and untarnished. Nothing else remained of the skeleton's possessions, though some matter beneath it that he took for moss might have been badly decayed clothing. Not wanting to get caught with his loot, Victor stuffed the amulet and ring into his pants' pocket and then moved over to the hole in the ceiling. He jumped up, grabbed hold of an intact beam, and pulled himself up.

Victor saw the crumpled, shadowy form of whatever he'd been fighting and moved over to it. He could still hear Lam fighting in the distance, so he risked a quick reveal of his amulet to shine its light on the creature; it looked like a huge, black-furred rat. Victor stuffed the amulet back in his pocket, grabbed one of the rat's hind legs, and dragged it out of the smashed doorway into the cavern proper. He pulled it farther away from the building, toward the bridge, and then threw it against a different building's wall. He'd acted on impulse, but when he thought about it, he realized he didn't want to leave evidence that he'd been in the building with the skeleton. There was no way he was going to tell anyone about the amulet or ring he'd found.

He was standing with his hands on his knees, gathering himself, when Heng came charging across the stone bridge. He saw Victor and ran over. "That's a big one! Jumped you on your way over, huh?"

"Yeah, got me by surprise! Had me by the shoulder and was dragging me around like it wanted to bring me home for dinner."

"You don't look hurt," Heng said, eyeing him up and down.

"Yeah, I had to use my Berserking ability. It healed me up, but I lost track of myself and where I was until it wore off."

"You missed a hell of a fight. Captain had to break almost every bone in that thing's body before it stopped trying to fight."

"Nothing else jumped you guys?"

"Nah, I think other rats and stuff nearby got scared from the racket. C'mon, Fenlale's butchering that beast. The captain wants some of its organs for some reason." Victor followed Heng over the bridge, avoiding the half where the stones had fallen into the river, then down the far side of the bank to the scene of the captain's battle. The huge creature looked smaller in death, deflated and limp with most of the fluid it had once held running down the stones and into the river. Fenlale had carved a yard-long window into its abdomen and pulled out the entrails, which instantly brought Victor to his knees, retching, when he smelled them. "Ha ha, get it out, kid. We've got more carving to do."

Heng said Captain Lam had left as soon as she'd finished killing the beast without explaining where she was headed. She didn't make an appearance until they'd finished butchering and taken turns washing the guts and blood off themselves in the cold river water. She moved quietly, and Victor didn't notice her presence until her voice rang out from behind him, saying, "Fenlale. Where's the bag you put the organs in?" The mute man jumped to his feet and pulled a small pouch from his vest. He ran over to the captain and handed it to her. "Good. All right, let's move out. I'm done here for now. Good news for you, delvers: I'm going to need to take a trip to town tomorrow, so I'll give you a day off. You can use the time to turn in quests, rest up and train."

"Yes!" Heng clapped Fenlale on the back, and Victor couldn't help grinning. He had a lot to do, and a day off would serve nicely. He'd find a quiet place where he could try to inspect his secret loot, he'd turn in his quest, and he'd spend some time trying to figure out what was up with his Core. Had he had an entire day to himself since coming to this world? He decided he better not count his chickens before they hatched; just because Captain Lam was leaving didn't mean the other veterans would leave him alone. He could hope, though.

# 26

⊰⊱

# SOUL SEARCHING

Victor groaned and collapsed onto his narrow, scratchy mattress. He felt as he did after his first day at summer wrestling camp as a freshman. In a way, it was a good clean feeling of having worked his ass off, and, on a deeper level, he'd accomplished some things that had ignited a little flare of hope in his chest. He reached his hand into his pocket and felt the hard, cool metal of the ring and amulet, and a slow smile crept over his face as he drifted into a deep, heavy slumber.

"Victor," a gruff voice said, and someone shook his shoulder. Victor's eyes popped open, and he rolled onto his back, blinking rapidly in the bright light of the barracks. Heng leaned over him, his jowly, furry face just inches away. His thin, black lips spread into a broad smile, showing off lots of pointy teeth, and he said, "Hey, Captain kept her word. We're free for the day. Me and a couple others are going to turn in quests. You wanna come?"

"Mm, yeah!" Victor yawned while he spoke, then sat up. "Gimme two minutes to take a piss and get my boots on."

"Right, we'll be out front." Victor stood and slipped his boots on, then stepped through the door to the "jacks," as the veterans called the long, narrow room, where wooden toilet seats sat above holes in the ground. Two of the toilets had wooden partitions, but he was the only one there, so he just used one of the open ones. When he finished washing his hands and splashing water on his face, he walked outside to join Heng, Fenlale, Gris, and a Vodkin woman he'd seen fighting but hadn't ever spoken with. They hiked to the central cavern where the Settlement Stone rose from the ground, joking around about how lucky they were to have a day off and what they'd do with all the extra time. Heng joked about taking Sullya, the female Vodkin, to dinner, and she punched him in his belly, making his blubber quiver and jiggle. Victor laughed and dodged out of the way when Heng took a swipe at him.

They didn't have to wait long to access the stone; most of the other teams of workers were busy elsewhere in the mine, so the lines were short. When Victor put his hand on the stone and selected the "quests" menu item, he navigated to the section to turn in completed quests and was surprised to see more than just his slaying quest update:

| Quests for Victor Sandoval in Greatbone Mine: | |
|---|---|
| 1. Slay 100 denizens of the deep | Complete! Reward: 240 credits. Accept reward? Y/N |
| 2. Recover Energy-rich materials | Turn in sunsteel ring for 1000 credits? Y/N<br><br>Turn in artificed amulet for 1000 credits? Y/N |

Victor briefly considered selecting the yes option for the 2000 credits, but he figured that the items might very well be far more valuable to him than Contribution Store credits. He also didn't know if the stone kept track of stuff like that, and he didn't want to answer questions about how he'd gotten so many credits. He turned in the slayer quest and picked up another one, this time requiring him to slay 200 denizens. "Do they always go up in number? The slayer quests?" he asked aloud.

"Nah, if you finish 'em fast, they do, but if you struggle with one for a long time, the next one will be lower," Gris answered.

"Ahh, thanks," Victor said, switching over to the Contribution Store menu. His worn-out, mismatched boots were starting to chafe his feet, and he wanted to see if he could get a new pair and some socks. After a bit of surfing through the menus, he found what he wanted and bought four pairs of wool socks and a pair of sturdy "mining boots" that looked like hiking boots but had steel toe guards. Standing there holding the socks and boots that had appeared in a yellow-blue mist, he also decided to buy a small "miner's pack." The pack was similar to his old school backpack but made of smooth oiled leather and with fewer pockets. He'd only spent thirty-five credits altogether, so he shopped through the menus a bit more. There were many clothing options, but nothing could match up to his black self-cleaning, self-repairing shirt and pants. He bought a few pairs of underwear and a leather breastplate that cost him a hundred credits. He figured he'd use his next quest turn-in to buy an upgraded weapon.

He stepped back from the stone and stuffed most of his purchases into his new pack, then he pulled the hard-leather breastplate over his head, fastening the three straps into their shiny brass buckles. "Not bad!" he said, rapping his knuckles against the stiff leather.

"Yeah, delvers that don't die make a lot more credits than the other crews," Heng said, stuffing some jars of pickled fish he'd purchased into his own pack. Watching him stow away his treats, Victor noticed a coil of rope which gave him some ideas. He still had more than a hundred points, so he put his hand back on the stone and bought a twenty-five-foot rope, a flint and steel, and a flask of lantern oil. He figured he might as well buy a few supplies whenever he could so that he'd be ready if the right opportunity arose. His pack nice and plump with purchases, he stood off to the side, waiting for the others.

On the way back to Lam's barracks, Victor slowed to walk next to Gris, who was bringing up the rear. "Hey, man, what else you got going on today?"

"Hmm? Oh, I'll probably play some dice with the others, then just lounge about. Captain didn't give Fath any instructions for us, so he'll probably leave us be."

"Um, you know I've got a fucked-up Core, right?"

"Yeah, you told me."

"Well, it's tough for me to concentrate and do the tiny bit of cultivating I'm capable of. Is there a place near the barracks I could chill and meditate without any racket?"

"Ha, yeah, there's a cave behind the barracks. Just follow the crevice; you can't miss it. It opens into a quiet place where some veterans go to cultivate. No one talks in there, so don't be making any noise 'cause some of 'em will use it as an opportunity to practice their more violent skills."

"Right, thanks." Victor walked along trying to formulate a game plan for how to escape the mines but was unable to think beyond a few hours. How would he get out? He still had a collar on his neck, there were guards everywhere outside, and he didn't even know what direction to run in. He had a lot more to learn before making a real attempt.

"Victor!" Heng shouting his name brought him out of his daydreams about bolting free of the mines, and he trotted up to the big Vodkin.

"Yeah?"

"Tell Sullya about the rat that almost ate you."

"Oh, yeah, well, it was about as big as Gris and covered in black fur with bright red eyes . . ."

"Hey! Are you comparing me to a rat?" Gris interrupted, marching up to the others.

"No, Gris! You're much better looking than that rat and at least twice as hairy," Victor laughed.

"You believe this? Kid's been here a couple days and is already making jokes?" Gris laughed too, though, and gave Victor a friendly shove. They continued walking, ribbing each other, and Victor found it easy to blend in. In the back of his mind, he was pissed at himself for acting as if everything was all right, but he also knew that he had to fit in and make the most of whatever situation he was in. Sulking, moping, and alienating the people sharing his plight wouldn't get him anywhere.

When they got back to the barracks, Victor didn't go inside, saying he wanted to go try to work on cultivating. Gris nodded, and Heng shrugged, but Sullya scoffed as though he was wasting time. He didn't think she was referring to his weak Core but that she was just one of those people who didn't see the point in pushing yourself, especially when you were being forced to work for other people.

When they'd all stepped into the barracks, Victor walked around the exterior, noting the smooth path worn into the packed dirt and rock of the cavern floor. Behind the barracks, he found that the smooth trail continued toward the jagged rocky wall of the massive tunnel and disappeared into a dark cleft in the stone. He followed the path into the darkness, and as his eyes adjusted, he saw that a faint orange light glimmered up ahead. Walking toward the light, he realized it was one of the glowing Energy orbs that Captain Lam tended to place around on paths she scouted. Victor passed three more glowing orbs following the crevice before stepping into a dome-shaped cave about a hundred feet wide.

The cave was light with more of the softly glowing orange globes, and Victor could see that it had a very smooth stone floor with rounded boulders scattered in every direction, varying in size from a basketball to a mini-van. Fuzzy green and blue moss covered most of the stones, and a pool the size of a large bathtub occupied the center rear of the cavern. The occasional drip of water falling from the ceiling into the pool was the only sound. Glancing around, Victor could only spot one other person—a large blue Ardeni man meditating with his back against a mossy boulder.

Victor tiptoed over the mossy cavern floor to the far wall on the opposite side of the cavern from the other man. He moved over to one of the larger boulders and sat down behind it, facing the cavern wall. He had only been partly lying to the others; he did want to work on his Core, but first, Victor wanted to see what he could figure out about the items he'd found in the ruins. He slipped his hand into his pocket and wrapped the warm, hard shape of the ring in his fist. He'd been thinking about how he'd been told to "bond" with the storage sack that Sergeant Fath had given him to clean up the beetle bodies. Is that how you activated any sort of magical item? Gripping the ring tightly, he pushed a trickle of rage-attuned Energy out through his pathways and into the warm metal.

Victor felt the ring absorb his Energy, but nothing more happened; he didn't suddenly become aware of a dimensional space as with the sack or any other special effect. Glancing around over his shoulders, he risked a quick glance at the ring. Pulling it out of his pocket, still ensconced in his fist, he cupped his other hand over it and slowly peeled back his fingers. The ring sat in his palm, glowing with a warm orange-red radiance and pulsing with heat. Victor clasped his fingers closed and stuffed the ring into his other pocket. He didn't know what it did exactly, but the ring seemed to absorb Energy and become a source of light and warmth. He wondered if there was more to it, but he decided to put it aside for now.

He reached into his other pocket, leaving the ring to pulse warmly over his left hip, and wrapped his hand around the medallion. It was round, about half the width of his palm, and he could feel the raised bumps of some sort of pattern on the metal. He wanted to pull it out and study it, but he knew it glowed with silvery-blue light and would be far too conspicuous for him to feel safe. It was cool in his palm, and gripping it, he felt a slight tingle pass into his flesh. Once again, Victor pushed some Energy out through his pathways and into the item in his fist. Suddenly a surge of ice shot up his arm and into his mind, and he felt it pressing against his mind, his spirit, his very self.

Victor grunted, then scowled; what was this fucker trying to do to him? He could feel the foreign presence spreading, and he bore down on it, turning his mind inward as when he studied his Core, but this time focusing on the icy presence in his mind. He began to squeeze it, pushing it back, cutting it off from the amulet, and compressing it with his will. As he drove it into a tiny corner of his mind and began to apply more and more pressure, a strange, metallic voice sounded in his mind: *"I yield! Please stop!"*

Victor was so startled by the voice that he did stop; he pulled back on the pressure, and the icy presence shot down his pathway and back into the amulet. Again, the voice sounded in his mind, *"Thank you! I am honored to serve one with such a strong will."*

Victor opened his mouth to ask who the fuck was talking to him, but then he clamped it shut. He didn't know who else might hear, and the voice was definitely inside his head. He was thinking about how he was meant to reply when the voice came again, *"I can feel you trying to formulate a response; worry not, I cannot read your mind, though if you think clearly of a statement directed at me, I'll understand it. As long as you maintain contact with me, that is."*

*"Who are you?"* Victor clearly "thought" the words, actually picturing them in his mind.

*"I am Gorz, a spirit bound to the amulet you hold. When bound, I was given the faculties necessary to perform the duties of a personal attendant and majordomo."* Victor's mind reeled at the strange voice's revelation. For a few reasons, he was skeptical and decided to "voice" his concerns.

*"What's a majordomo, and how can you be helpful if you're an amulet? Also, why the hell were you trying to take over my mind?"*

*"Ahh, I see you've never bonded with an intelligent item before! Sir, I must warn you: when dealing with a bound spirit, there's always a struggle of wills. No spirit is forever content to remain in its prison, and the instinctual desire to move to a more spacious and self-determining host is not easily resisted. Now that you've proven your will is sufficient to contain me, I shall not attempt another such struggle. The duties of a majordomo vary from managing a household, to managing accounts, to keeping track of important facts and dates. As for how I can aid you, my mental faculties are quite acute! My previous master used me for making maps and memorizing texts."*

*"Maps?"* Victor's heart began to race.

*"Oh yes! My previous master was quite an explorer. I've memorized thousands of miles of wilderness, cities, even dungeons!"* Victor thought about where he'd found the skeleton with the amulet, and his fingers began to drum with excitement.

*"Do you know where you are right now?"*

*"One moment."* The amulet, always a bit chilly to the touch, surged with coldness for a moment. *"Oh, yes. We're some twelve hundred feet above and three*

*point four miles east and south of where my last master perished. I've not been to this location before."*

"So, your last master didn't get to that location through the big mining tunnel?"

"No, sir. He accessed the Sheev-nagh ruins through the Barrowdon dungeon." Again, Victor's heart sped up.

"There's more than one way out of the ruins, then?"

"If what you told me is true, I'm aware of at least two, yes!"

"How far is this 'dungeon' you mention from where your old master died?"

"Slightly more than thirteen miles through caverns, tunnels, and along an underground river."

"How long ago did your old master die? And what was his name? I'm tired of calling him your old master."

"His name was Reevus-dak, and I'm not sure how long. Something more than a hundred years; I'm afraid I slumbered for much of the time in order to maintain my sanity."

"So, assuming the tunnels and caverns still exist, you could guide me to this 'dungeon?' Can you explain the dungeon to me?" Victor had an idea what the spirit meant by dungeon, but he wanted to make sure.

"Of course! If the path exists, I can direct you. As for the dungeon, sir, it was filled with undead denizens ranging in strength from high Tier Two to middle Tier Three. My master, er Reevus-dak, learned of the dungeon from a man named Polro and gained entry by solving a riddle. The entrance was near a village called Steampool Vale—a quaint place with provincial citizens who make a living gathering the minerals near naturally occurring geysers and, well, steam pools."

"So the 'dungeon' is a place filled with monsters?"

"Yes, sir. Someone of your physical nature would definitely consider them to be monsters."

"And I need to make it through at least thirteen miles of ruins filled with God-knows-what even to enter the dungeon?"

"I'm not familiar with that turn of phrase, but I think I take your meaning, sir. Yes, you'd need to brave the denizens of the deep. My master had an easy time of it at first but met his match, as you no doubt have surmised."

"All right, enough with the 'sir' and 'master' talk. Just call me Victor."

"Very well, Victor! Thank you! Though please forgive me if I slip; I'm not used to such familiarity." Victor heard some movement behind him and realized he'd lost track of time and his surroundings while speaking with the spirit.

"All right, listen. I'm not supposed to have you. Can you dim that light you give off?"

*"Of course, Victor. I'll do my best to remain undetected!"*

*"Also, can you tell me anything about the ring Reevus was wearing?"*

*"Naturally; I cataloged all of his belongings. Let's see, at the time of his death, Reevus was wearing a sunsteel ring and an artificed silver ring of storage."*

*"What? I only found the sunsteel ring!"*

*"During my periods of wakefulness, I was aware that Reevus-dak's corpse was set upon by scavenging creatures more than once."*

*"Well, what does the sunsteel ring do?"*

*"The sunsteel ring is tremendously sensitive to Energy and can store it with minimal leakage over time. Should you desire to, you would be able to build up a large amount of Energy within it and draw upon it as needed."*

*"All right, I'm going to let go of you now, and I don't feel safe wearing you, so I'll just keep you in my pocket."*

*"Until we speak again, then, Victor!"* Victor let go of the amulet and felt the cool tingling in his hand fade away. He could tell that he'd lost connection to the spirit; there'd been a sense of it in his mind, even after he'd won their contest of wills, and now it was gone. He felt his entire body buzzing with the excitement of what he'd learned; there was a way out of this place, and he'd be able to get to it without anyone knowing. They'd assume he was dead if he disappeared in the depths, just like all the delvers he'd already helped bury.

He didn't think it would be wise to make a break for it right away, though; according to Gorz, the dungeon was filled with Tier Two and Three monsters, and he was still only Tier One. Sure, he'd won some pit fights with Tier Two fighters, but what if he ran into two, three, or fifty higher-tier monsters at once? No, he needed to grow stronger, and part of that was figuring out the problem with his Core. He still only had roughly half the Energy he'd had before its fracturing.

Victor closed his eyes and sat the way that Yrella had taught him. It felt like so long ago that she'd teased him about cultivating. Sighing, he turned his mind inward and studied the space where his Core pulsed and slowly revolved. It looked solid and vibrant, filled with the red rage-attuned Energy. Still, there were tiny droplets and pools of white-yellow Energy all around it, and they refused to budge when he tried to cultivate them. Suddenly his eyes sprang open as he had a thought. He reached his hand back into his pocket, gripping the medallion where Gorz resided, and mentally asked, *"Hey, Gorz, do you know anything about Cores?"*

"*Naturally, Victor. I had one when I was alive, and Reevus-dak made me memorize several texts on the subject.*"

"What about Spirit Cores?"

"*Yes, one of the texts I memorized had several chapters on such Cores. What can I help you with, Victor?*"

"All right, a while back, this guy had a tentacled spider dude rip apart my Core. He said he was destroying it, but later, when I looked, the System status screen said it was fractured. I've been able to rebuild it partially, but it's only half as strong as it should be, and I have lots of little pools of Energy around my Core that I can't seem to cultivate or add to it."

"*Fascinating, Victor! Give me a moment to examine my memory.*" The amulet grew cold again; a signal Victor was starting to realize meant it was doing something. A moment later, he heard Gorz's voice again. "*Victor, according to my texts, Spirit Cores are highly resilient and difficult to destroy without killing the host entity. Your description of the pools of unattuned Energy around your Core sounds like a partial attempt at gaining a second affinity.*"

"What do you mean?"

"*How many affinities do you have, Victor?*"

"Just one—rage."

"*Oh my. Well, when someone with a Spirit Core wants more than one affinity, they can split off part of their Core and gather it with the new affinity. It sounds like you had the splitting done for you, but you don't have the second affinity with which to gather the remnants.*"

"Am I screwed then? Can I still get an affinity?"

"*Oh, odds are excellent that you have more than one spirit affinity. When you formed your Core, you probably just focused on your strongest one. You need to do some soul-searching and see if you can glean another strong affinity with which to begin the process of gathering your Core fragments.*"

"Any tips on how to do that?"

"*Yes! You should meditate and focus on strong emotions and ideals. Be sure to avoid thinking of things that enrage you; you're trying to find a new affinity, not your existing one!*"

"*Thanks, Gorz,*" Victor thought and let go of the medallion. He stood up abruptly, too anxious to focus, and looked around the cavern. He saw a few other veterans sitting around the quiet space. They looked to be meditating, and none of them were facing him directly, so he took a few deep breaths to relax and then sat down again. He cleared his mind and turned his eye inward, watching his Core and the space around it. Another affinity, huh? What did Gorz say? Focus on strong emotions?

Victor concentrated and tried to think of times when he'd been very emotional. It was hard because he kept coming back to times when he'd been angry. The more he struggled not to think of a time when he was angry, the more they kept popping into his head, and the more frustrated he became in the present, which jerked him out of his meditation again and again.

Trying to meditate, Victor struggled with his mind wandering, and at one point, he thought about when he'd been fighting the beetles, thinking everyone was going to be overwhelmed, and then Captain Lam had streaked down on her glittering wings to smash into the horde of creatures. He remembered how his arms had been leaden, his lungs burning, and he'd been on the verge of collapse, but when he saw her start to swing that massive hammer, he'd had a surge of strength, of hope, and he'd begun to believe that they could win. Something made him concentrate on that feeling, that spark that had ignited in his heart and allowed him to keep fighting. What do you call that? Hope? No, it was more than just hope; he'd been inspired. Yes! That was it—inspiration!

Victor zeroed in on the way he'd felt inspired by Captain Lam's presence, savoring that feeling, not because he was often inspired or inspiring, but because it had had a profound effect on him and his life. When he examined that emotion, he realized he'd felt it before, but not so clearly. He'd been inspired by coaches and older wrestlers when he was new to the team. He'd been inspired by Vullu and how he'd stood up to the asshole pit fighters who wanted a piece of Victor. He'd been inspired by Yrella and how she'd been kind to him regardless of their terrible environment.

The more Victor focused on that feeling, and the more he realized he wanted to be like that, the clearer it became, and then something happened— a warm, tingling spark ignited in the pit of his stomach. Victor turned his attention inward again, stopping the kaleidoscope of memories and images playing across his mind's eye, and there, pulsing softly next to his hot rage-attuned Core, was a smaller, second star. It shone with a steady white-gold light, and as he watched, one of the tiny Core fragments drifted into it, and it grew just a fraction larger.

# 27

## INSPIRATION

Victor wanted to spend more time cultivating and building up his smaller inspiration-attuned Core, but he hated feeling that he was being watched all the time and was having trouble concentrating. He took a look at his status sheet, for probably the thirtieth time in the last hour, marveling at the fact that he was finally making some real progress:

| Name: | Victor Sandoval | | |
|---|---|---|---|
| Race: | Human: Base 4 | | |
| Class: | Spirit Champion, Advanced | | |
| Level: | 14 | | |
| Core: | Spirit Class: Base 5 | | |
| Energy Affinity: | 3.1, Rage 9.1, Inspiration 7.4 | Energy: | 358/358 |
| Strength: | 31 | Vitality: | 48 |
| Dexterity: | 21 | Agility: | 21 |
| Intelligence: | 10 | Will: | 38 |
| Points Available: | 14 | | |

His Core was no longer "fragmented," and he had a new affinity—inspiration. He didn't know exactly how that would work or what he could do with it, but he was happy, nonetheless. His Energy levels were on the rise, and he knew that as he built up his second affinity Core, he should be able to get back to his old levels, if not higher. Victor contemplated the fourteen attribute points he was still sitting on. He'd gotten them from when he'd leveled fighting the beetles, and he felt he was being dumb, not spending them.

"Am I dumb?" he asked himself, taking a second look at his intelligence attribute. He didn't feel stupid; in fact, he'd always done well in school when he applied himself. "Yeah, but I didn't apply myself very often—that's not exactly smart."

"Shut up, kid." The gruff voice came from the other side of the boulder, and Victor clamped his mouth shut. He furtively glanced around, then stood up and briskly walked out of the "meditation cave." There were a lot more people in there cultivating than when he'd started. As he walked down the narrow cleft leading to the greater tunnel, he wished for a more private place. While he was wishing, he decided to wish that Yrella was still alive and that he could talk to her for some advice. "Fuck it," he said and dumped ten points into intelligence and the other four into strength.

He didn't know if he was making a big mistake, but he felt that he could benefit from a little bit faster brain and some better decisions, and strength had never done him wrong. As the strange sensation of warmth flooded into his head, he almost fell to one knee, catching himself on the rough stone wall. It didn't hurt, but it was disorienting, and when it faded, Victor felt pretty damn good. He didn't notice any immediate changes in how he thought about things, but he hoped it would be a subtle difference that would pay off over time. He did see a sizeable increase in his maximum Energy, however. "Yrella wasn't lying. Intelligence definitely bumps Energy up."

As he strode from the crevice into the enormous mine tunnel, Victor almost wanted to whistle or sing; he was in an uncharacteristically good mood. He stopped himself, though, making sure not to make a spectacle. The last thing he wanted was for people to notice his gains. He slouched his shoulders and screwed his face up into a scowl, and kicked some rocks as he walked down the very slight incline toward the barracks.

He was coming at the barracks from an angle, and when he got to the rear left corner of the building, he heard soft murmuring and movement coming from the shadows near the far corner, and he directed his steps to take him closer. When he came around the part of the barracks that housed the low-ceilinged kitchen, he nearly stumbled into a couple of other delvers locked in an embrace and making out as if they were outside a high school dance. When he saw Edeya's eyes pop open and stare at him over the shoulder of whatever guy she was kissing, he blurted, "Oh shit! My bad!" and turned on his heel, quickly walking back around the other corner toward the front of the barracks.

"Well, that was fucking awkward," he muttered, shaking his head. He was having a hard time finding privacy to work on his Core; he could only imagine trying to find a private place to be intimate with someone. "Poor suckers." He wondered if there were rules about that. He doubted the mine operators wanted people running all over the place having sex and dealing with all the things that came with it. In the end, he decided it wasn't his problem; he had enough on his plate.

Victor stood in front of the barracks, briefly vacillating between going inside or doing a bit of exploring. As far as he knew, he still had several free hours before he should hit the sack. He imagined Captain Lam would be back at it bright and early, so he didn't want to miss dinner or lights-out, but he figured it wouldn't hurt to explore a bit. He knew there might be some side tunnels or caverns back toward the main settlement area, but he figured his chances of finding some privacy would be better if he snooped around toward the deeper parts of the mine.

He took a few minutes to cross over the tunnel to the far side and walked along that wall, skirting boulders and piles of rubble that had been left behind during the mining process. Victor could see and hear groups of miners and delvers moving down the center of the tunnel every now and then, but he was concentrating on trying to find side tunnels or crevices that led away—something like the one that led to the cultivation cave near Lam's barracks. After one promising shadow after another proving to be nothing more than an indentation in the tunnel wall, he was getting ready to turn back, but then he saw a jagged, dark cleft behind a large pile of boulders.

Victor poked his head into the crevice and saw that it opened up into a long, high-ceilinged tunnel with bumpy exposed rock walls. He pushed forward in the dark for a while, but when he looked over his shoulder and could no longer see the light of the larger tunnel, he decided to risk taking out his glowing sunsteel ring. The ring was warm in his hand and gave off a friendly luminosity that only shone for a few feet in any direction. Using its light, Victor followed the tunnel for another hundred feet or so before it opened up into a small cavern with a ledge that hung over a dark abyss, the depths of which he couldn't discern. "Well, it's the end of the road for me, but at least I have some privacy here."

"Oh, aye, it's nice and quiet in here." Victor spun around, adrenaline flooding his body as he heard the gruff voice coming from the tunnel behind him. A large Vodkin stood there, a wooden cudgel in one hand, leering down at Victor.

"Hey, man. Sorry if this is your space; I'll head out."

"Nah, this ain't our space, but we figured we might see what you was doing here." The Vodkin stepped forward, and two more men stepped out of the tunnel behind him. They both were wearing leather armor and wielding delver batons. Victor wasn't dumb enough to think these guys wanted to chat; they were going to mug him or worse.

"Hey, guys. Don't fuck around, all right? Captain Lam is expecting me, and I can't be late, you feel me?"

"Oh, Captain Lam, is it?" the big Vodkin sneered. "She know you got that shiny bauble?" Victor's heart almost stopped at the words. He called himself an idiot in his head, but he snorted out loud.

"Of course, where you think I got it, dumbass?"

"I don't buy it, Chem," one of the other guys, a narrow, tall Shadeni, said.

"Nah, me neither. Let's see what this little pup's got in his backpack."

"Hey, asshole! I'm not little, and if you three come at me, I'm going to go fucking apeshit. I won't be able to keep from smashing your skulls in!" Victor stuffed his glowing ring down on his middle finger and then hefted his baton, menacing the trio. The smallest of them began to chuckle, and Victor noticed the bright gleam of his collar. He held a hand out toward Victor and made a fist. Before Victor could do anything, the stone under his feet suddenly erupted and wrapped around his ankles and knees in a vicelike grip.

Victor roared and activated Berserk, panicking at his immobility. He screamed again, his vision going red, and he thrashed and pulled with all his might, trying to yank his feet out of the stone, but while he concentrated on getting free, sharp pain erupted over his left eye, then another spike of pain exploded in the back of his head, and suddenly he was drifting in blackness.

"Oh, *Madre!*" Victor woke in utter darkness with a throbbing skull and a cold, shivering body. He pulled his arms close to his chest, realizing he didn't have his shirt on. "Where the fuck am I?" He tried to piece things together, but everything was jumbled in his head. He remembered waking up; hadn't he gone down to the Stone to turn in his quest? "Oh, man." He reached up and rubbed at his head, gingerly feeling for what was wrong. The back of his skull was tender to the touch, but other than that, the pain was mainly on the inside.

He felt around himself in the blackness, trying to get some idea of where he was. He was lying on hard stone, fragments of rock and dust everywhere. He patted along his body, relieved to find he still had his pants on, but his boots and socks were gone. That's right! He'd bought socks. What else? He'd gone back to the barracks, and then he'd gone to find the cultivation cave! He started to remember snippets—his new Core, seeing Edeya kissing some guy, wanting to find a secluded spot to work on his Core and talk to Gorz. Oh, fuck! Gorz! Victor shoved his hand into his pocket, and there, as if it were waiting for his grasp, was the cold disc of metal on its chain.

*"Victor! Thank Baz-chemeil! I thought you perished, and I was doomed to lie in a dark hole for another millennium."* Victor pulled the chain out, hoping to shed some light on his situation, but none shone forth.

"Gorz," he said in a dry, raspy voice. "Can you please turn your light back on?" Almost instantly, the silvery-blue light stabbed forth into his eyes, and he had to squint them shut for a moment. Slowly he peeled his eyes open to find himself on a stone ledge, not five feet from a black abyss. Was he still in the place where those assholes jumped him? "Oh yeah—now I remember. Fuck, but those guys fought dirty." He looked around and was dismayed to see a sheer stone wall behind him. He looked up and saw, very faintly in Gorz's light, another ledge about twenty feet up. "How the fuck did I get here, Gorz?"

*"Those ruffians threw your body off after they stripped most of your belongings. Luckily, you told me that you weren't allowed to have me, so I made myself very unnoticeable."*

"Ungh," Victor grunted as he pushed himself into a sitting position, his back to the stone wall. "Well, that's some good news, at least. Nice job, Gorz."

*"I was partially being selfish, Victor; I had no desire to have to spend time conversing with those brutes."*

"All right, but why didn't they kill me?"

*"Oh, I believe they thought you dead. Victor, even in your pocket, I heard your skull crack. Then, of course, they rolled you into an abyss . . ."* Gorz trailed off, obviously thinking his point was made.

"Yeah, I get it. Huh, I've never been knocked out while berserking, and I'm sure I've been hit in the head before." Victor lifted the chain and slipped it over his head; he wanted both hands free. Gorz's cool disc rested against his breastbone, and he shivered, suddenly remembering how cold he was. "At least those assholes left my pants on me. How long was I out, Gorz?"

*"Just over four hours, Victor. Whatever kept you from dying wasn't able to keep you conscious."* Victor felt his head again, unable to even find a lump.

"I think my Berserk ability was still active after I got knocked out; it mended the wound then wore off. Well, that's my guess, anyway."

*"Plausible, Victor. Now, I detected a drop of around seventeen feet; can you see the ledge above?"*

"Yeah, I saw it. Chill, man. I need to get my bearings." Victor closed his eyes and rubbed at his neck, trying to remember the fight. Jesus, that guy's fucking spell really screwed him over, and then he'd used Berserk too early; he'd been so enraged about his feet being stuck he hadn't even tried to defend against their attacks. What was that big guy's name? "Chem. Remember that, Gorz. I'm going to pay those guys a visit one of these days."

*"Noted, Victor!"*

"Right, now, let me see here." Victor stood up and stretched his arms up, pushing them against the stone, gauging how high he'd have to jump to grab the upper ledge. With his arms stretched out and on his tiptoes, he was still a good nine or ten feet from the ledge. "Well, I'm a hell of a lot stronger than I was on Earth," he muttered, shaking out his arms and squatting down a few times to loosen up his legs. He squatted and, with all his might, leaped up, reaching out with his arms, trying to grasp the ledge. He still fell short a couple of feet.

*"Excellent effort, Victor, I felt your vertical traversal, and it was nearly six feet!"*

"Yeah, if I can make it back to Earth, I'm going to have a hell of a career in sports. Well, unless I lose my new strength and stuff."

*"Is Earth the name of your home world?"*

"That's right; there's no Energy there."

*"You'd keep some residual benefits, but without Energy to sustain your enhanced attributes and Core, you'd slowly return to something more typical of that world."*

"All right, I need to jump higher; I think my Berserk ability will work, but I'm not sure I'll have enough sanity to remember to jump up there."

*"Yes, berserking is a fraught talent. I'm afraid if I try to guide you while you're in such a state, you're as likely to throw me into the abyss as listen to me."*

"Yeah, good point."

*"Do you have any other abilities that might help?"*

"Yeah, just a minute," Victor replied, concentrating on his Sovereign Will skill and using it to boost his strength. Once more, he squatted, then jumped, reaching toward the ledge.

*"Excellent, Victor! That was seven additional inches!"*

"Not enough. I'm running out of ideas, Gorz."

*"Victor, perhaps share some information about yourself with me. What sorts of abilities do you have? Were you successful in mending your Core?"* Victor realized he had never spoke to Gorz again after getting his advice about his Core.

"Damn, I can be a prick sometimes. Sorry, Gorz. Let me fill you in." He told Gorz about what he'd done with his Core and told him about his spells.

*"So, you have some inspiration-attuned Energy?"*

"Yeah, I do, but no spells that call for it."

*"Why not try a new spell? One way to innovate Energy abilities and spells is to cast a known spell with a different attunement. Reevus-dak used the exact same spell to cast Fiery Burst and Wind Gust; he just fed differently attuned Energy into the spell."*

"How do I give my spell different Energy? It just happens."

*"It's an act of will. You need to clamp down on the Energy that your spell calls for and push forth the Energy you want to use."*

"Hmm, all right," Victor said softly, turning his attention inward to his Core, where the two suns of his attunements pulsed next to each other. The white-gold orb of his inspiration-attuned Energy was about half the size of his smoldering red sphere of rage Energy. Still, both Cores looked rich and healthy. "Do I have more than one Core?"

*"You have a multi-faceted Core. The shape of a Core's manifestation is often determined by how a mind perceives it. Some people with multiple affinities might see swirling bands of color around a single sphere. Others might see multiple orbs rotating each other. There are as many Cores and shapes of Cores as there are people."*

"So, these two pulsing orbs are my Core. Together?"

*"Yes, that seems to be the type of Core you have, based on your descriptions, of course."*

Victor looked back at his Core and concentrated on holding the red, rage-attuned Energy locked down, and he pulled forth a strand of the warm, bright, inspiration Energy, then he started to cast Berserk. He'd never watched one of his spells take shape before, but this time, while he stared at his Core, he saw the complex, wild spell pattern start to form in his pathways. He felt the rage Energy surge, trying to push past his mental barrier. Victor bore down with his will, holding the Energy in place and coaxing the tendril of warm, golden-white Energy toward the pattern. Suddenly the Energy was sucked into the spell pattern, and a torrent of it pulled out of the shimmering white-gold part of his Core to finish the spell.

***Congratulations! You've learned the spell: Inspiring Presence, Basic***

***Inspiring Presence, Basic. Prerequisite Affinity: Inspiration. You infuse your being with the power of inspiration, filling yourself with potential and bringing forth the potential of nearby allies. Energy cost: minimum 75, scalable. Cooldown: long.***

Victor felt a surge of positivity and power pour into his limbs. His vision grew bright, the silvery-blue light of Gorz seemed to sharpen into daylight, and everything seemed clearer, closer, easier to reach.

He brushed aside the notifications, let out a whoop, and backed up two steps, so the backs of his heels were hanging into the abyss. He looked up at the ledge; it wasn't even that far! He took one huge, jumping lunge, then leaped off his front foot, stretching out with one arm. His fingers curled over the ledge's stone lip, and he caught on, laughing. He slapped his other hand onto the ledge and pulled himself up, bounding onto his bare feet. He laughed again, danced a quick shuffle, then ran back toward the main mining tunnel through the crevice.

Victor made it about a dozen steps outside the dark side tunnel when the Inspiring Presence wore off, and he stumbled to his knees, suddenly feeling very heavy and dull. "Oof! That's a hell of a comedown, Gorz." He slapped a hand to his face, feeling drunk and sleepy.

*"Describe your spell to me, Victor!"* Gorz sounded a little hysterical. Had he been trying to speak to him while Victor had been high on inspiration? Victor told him about the spell, and Gorz chortled, *"Oh, well done, Victor! Well done! I'm sure the effect will be incredible when you push it past advanced."*

"All right, thanks again, Gorz. Hey, can you stay hidden if I wear you? I mean, like you hid from those assholes?"

*"Most definitely if you wear me under a shirt, but I'd have a hard time hiding on your chest like this in the open."*

"Oh, all right, then I'll put you back in my pocket. I'm about to go to the barracks, and I doubt I'll slip in unnoticed."

*"Speak with you soon, then, Victor."*

"Right," Victor took the amulet off his head and stuffed it down in his pocket, then he stood and stretched. He was starting to feel normal again. He broke into an easy jog, angling straight for the barracks. He knew he was late for lights-out, so he figured he'd be in trouble. He tried to open the doors quietly, but of course they creaked and rattled. Sergeant Fath was standing in the aisle between the bunks, arms folded and staring at Victor when he stepped inside. He raised one hand, beckoning Victor with one finger, then he turned and walked up the aisle and through the back door, where Captain Lam kept her quarters.

Victor followed behind, padding softly on his bare feet, feeling as if he was walking to the principal's office. Snorts, loud breathing, and farts sounded in the barracks as he walked between the bunks. When Victor got past the sleeping delvers and walked by the long, wooden table, he snatched up a half-eaten piece of bread someone had neglected to clear and stuffed it into his mouth. He was struggling to swallow the dry mouthful when he stepped through the doorway into a surprisingly well-appointed sitting room. Captain Lam lounged on a plush burgundy chair, her legs up on a matching stool. Behind her and on both sides of the room were bookcases positively stuffed with scrolls, loose papers, and books of all shapes and sizes. She was sipping from a crystal glass half full with a thick amber liquid.

"Thanks, Sergeant. I'll let you know if you'll be needed again." Sergeant Fath nodded and walked out, pulling the door closed behind him. "All right, delver. Explain to me why you're late coming to my barracks, half-naked and caked in dried blood."

"Uh." Victor honestly hadn't thought of what he'd say. He'd had a tiny sliver of hope that he could slip into his bunk unnoticed, but he supposed Fath had gone on high alert when his bunk had been empty. "Well, I was out looking around, kind of exploring nearby, when some assholes jumped me. Took all my stuff." He gestured to his bare feet and held his arms out in a shrug. Fath sat up, setting her glass on the little table next to her chair. Victor noticed she wasn't wearing her armor; he didn't think he'd ever seen her without it. When she put her feet on the ground, her knees jutted up, reminding him how tall she was.

"Who jumped you?"

"Some delvers, I think. Not ours; I didn't recognize them, but they had batons."

"You don't know who they were?"

"Nope." Victor shrugged. There was no way he was going to rat out that fucker's name—no way he'd let Lam have the satisfaction of dealing with him. Captain Lam studied him for a long moment, then she sat back, putting her feet back up.

"I hope this was a good lesson for you, Victor; life is cheap in the delve. You're too weak to be wandering around alone, especially wearing nice clothes. I don't like the idea some scum think they can lay hands on one of my squad, but I really don't have time to take you around to the other delver units and try to find them out. We're heading into the deep in just a couple hours."

"Oh, I learned a good lesson, believe me." Victor reached up and scratched at his forehead, sending flakes of dried blood fluttering down in front of his eyes. Captain Lam grinned at him and beckoned him closer.

"All right. I'll give you a new baton; I've had plenty of delvers die on me over the years and have a pretty good collection. She reached over to a sizeable rune-inscribed leather bag sitting next to her chair, and a dull gray baton appeared in her hand. It was larger than Victor's old one and had a few strange letters carved into the metal. "This one has a momentum enchantment; it'll swing faster than a normal baton, and you should be able to reverse your swings more easily." She held it out, and Victor took it. The baton was heavy, at least twice as heavy as his old one, but it felt almost alive in his hand. He wanted to swing it around but knew that would be a dumb move in the captain's sitting room.

"Um, thanks, Captain Lam."

"You're welcome. I'm glad you didn't die, Victor; you've got some talents I find useful, and my unit is already understaffed. Don't be so stupid again, all right?"

"Yes, ma'am."

"Now go to the supply chest and dig out some boots and a shirt."

"Right, thanks again." Victor turned and moved to the door, pulling it open. He wanted to steal another glance at Lam's sitting room or at Lam and all the cool things she had around her, but he forced himself to keep his eyes forward and stepped out, feeling her gaze boring a hole in his shoulder blades. He closed her door and walked down the short hallway to the supply chest. At least she wasn't going to make him walk around barefoot as a lesson.

# 28

## GUARD DUTY

Victor's new boots pinched his feet around the toes, and he frowned, thinking of the nice new boots and socks he'd gotten to enjoy for all of a few hours. He was tired, dirty, and sore but otherwise felt all right as Lam's delvers made their way back to the forward camp they'd set up for the miners. Edeya had given him funny looks as they'd started out marching, and Gris had gruffly asked where the hell he'd been, but Victor just shrugged it off and said, "Ran into some assholes, but Captain Lam let me off easy, don't worry."

When he'd dug around in the chest, he'd come up with a large vestlike sweater that had originally been rust-colored, so the bloodstains from the previous owner weren't very noticeable. It was scratchy but warm and fit him well enough. After that, he'd stepped into the jacks, into one of the partitioned toilets, and slipped Gorz on under his vest. Having Gorz to mentally "talk" to helped the march go faster, and Victor had learned a thing or two about his attributes.

First of all, Gorz had been enthusiastically in favor of Victor putting points into intelligence, which made Victor feel better; he'd had some doubts after that snap decision. He'd also told Victor that his class awarding him "unbound" points at every level was quite rare and that he'd get a chance to "refine" his class at Level Twenty, but it might be best to keep the one he had.

Another thing he learned was that Gorz really did remember just about everything he "observed," and he assured Victor he'd know it if he got close to the delvers who'd jumped him. Gorz explained that, to him, every Energy user had a signature that made telling them apart very easy. Victor had told Gorz to stay on the lookout because he wanted to find out where those assholes had their camp.

"Victor!" Sergeant Fath called out from the barricade. Victor looked up from his daydreaming and jogged over to him.

"Yeah?"

"Lam wants to take some of the veterans to explore around the latest ruins she found. We're leaving you with a few others to guard the miners. Shouldn't be too bad."

"The miners aren't even here yet."

"That's right. Keep the place tidy while you wait, and don't let the miners get slaughtered by rats or something. We'll be gone a while, probably till quitting time." Victor opened his mouth to object but realized this was one of those moments when the proper response was probably to say something positive.

"All right, I got it."

"That a lad. I knew you were up for it." Fath held out a fist, and Victor bumped it.

*"Excellent news, Victor! It seems this low-ranked authoritarian has deemed you worthy of some responsibility,"* Gorz piped in with his tinny, mental voice.

*"Huh, go figure."*

Lam, Sergeant Fath, and ten of the veterans left through the barricade a few minutes later. Victor was left behind, somehow in charge, with Edeya, Tyge, the rest of the new recruits, and two veterans who apparently weren't worthy of any responsibility. He didn't know if he should try to give directions or just watch everyone to make sure no one did anything really stupid. He decided that, for now, he'd be one of those hands-off managers and just watch, making sure nothing came over the barricade to surprise them.

While he stood on the low rampart, looking out into the dark tunnel, he "talked" some more with Gorz. *"Is there any way to create more spells without altering one of the ones I have?"*

*"Yes, though it takes an adequate knowledge of spell patterns. I know some patterns, but it would be very hard to describe them to you verbally, and I'm unable to write with ordinary utensils; Reevus had a special slate that I was able to interact with."*

*"Damn, what are the odds we could find the rest of his belongings near his corpse?"*

*"Not good, I'm afraid, though some of his belongings were consumed or carried away by giant vermin as they ate his flesh; we might find some near their nest, should we locate it."*

*"Hmm, something to think about, that's for sure."*

"Just gonna stare into darkness until they come back?" Edeya had come up behind him, and Victor turned to smile at her.

"Sure. That's where the monsters come from, right?"

"I guess so, but Trilla says guarding miners rarely has any action. She said the big fights always happen when we claim new territory, like when we first came here."

"Who's Trilla?"

"That tall Ardeni girl, one of the vets they left back with us."

"Well, Sergeant Fath didn't leave her in charge, so she's not worried about getting her ass chewed out if something goes wrong. I'll keep an eye on the dark."

*"Wise, Victor!"*

*"Quiet, dude. You'll make me say something dumb out loud."*

*"Of course; my apologies."* Victor almost chuckled at the contrite tone Gorz had taken.

"Um, thanks for not saying anything when you saw Beal and me behind the barracks yesterday." Victor looked back at Edeya; her eyes were down, and she was fidgeting nervously.

"What? Nah, none of my business. Don't even worry about it. I'd be careful, though; I doubt Fath or Lam want people fucking all over the place."

"Fucking?"

"Yeah, er, having sex." Edeya's face got very red at his words, and she stammered out a few attempts to speak, then she shoved Victor against the railing and walked away with a disgusted explosion of breath. "What did I say?" he called, but she didn't turn.

*"I'd say your friend found your choice of words rather crude and insulting."* Victor almost told Gorz he was being too sensitive, then he frowned and shook his head.

*"I'm an idiot sometimes."*

*"Perhaps so, but nothing some practice won't fix. Why not apologize to the lass? It seems she is sensitive about her reputation and doesn't consider her dalliance with young Beal to be a part of a larger pattern of behavior."*

*"Well, I will, but I'm still not sure why she got so pissed; just because they were only making out doesn't mean they weren't horny for more."*

"*Yes, but your implication was crude; be logical.*" Victor thought about those words, "be logical," and had to admit they were effective. If he looked at his words without any emotion, they really were something an asshole would say.

"All right," he said aloud, turning from the darkness and looking around for Edeya. He saw her standing on the stone incline that led to the upper chamber. The miners still hadn't arrived, and the other delvers were spread all over the place doing their own things. He saw red-haired Tyge sitting with another delver playing with some carved bone dice. Tyge had been the first guy he'd met among the delvers, and Victor hadn't gotten to know him at all. He determined to remedy that as soon as possible. "Tyge!" he called.

"Yeah?" the smallish Ardeni man called back.

"I need you and your friend to come up here and watch the tunnel. I'll relieve you soon."

"Um, all right." Victor watched as Tyge and the other delver picked up their dice and climbed the ramparts.

"You guys know how to use these big bows?"

"The ballistae? Yeah, just crank the string back, put in the bolt, and pull the trigger."

"All right, I'll be back soon." Victor hopped down and walked over to the ramp where Edeya was sitting. "Hey," he said as he walked up. She definitely had the whole sulking thing down—back to the wall, arms crossed, frowning and looking anywhere but at him. "Look, I'm sorry. I have a problem with putting my foot in my mouth. I wasn't trying to say anything about what kind of person you are."

"Well, it was insulting to say that! Even if I liked Beal like that, it doesn't mean I'm going to 'have sex all over the place!'"

"Yeah, I know. Look, I'm stupid, all right? We've already talked about how I talk funny, right? Can we just forget I said it; if anything, what I said speaks more about me than you, right?" She finally turned to look at him, meeting his eyes, and then a grin quirked at the corners of her mouth.

"Yeah, it does! It says a lot about you!"

"Right." Victor wasn't sure he was making the kind of progress he wanted with her, but it seemed good that she was at least smiling. "We okay? Cause I don't want you pissed at me when we're fighting, all right?"

"All right. Thanks for the apology."

"Yeah, you're cool. No worries." Victor gave her shoulder a little punch. Her smile broadened, and she gave him a return punch.

"Right on, that's the spirit. Man, where the fuck are those miners?" He looked up the stone slope, seeing no sign of them.

"I don't know! I was wondering that while I was standing over here feeling mad at you!"

"You think they ran into trouble in one of the upper caverns? Like where we fought the stickmen?"

"Maybe. Do you think we should check on them? Would Captain Lam get upset if we go anywhere?"

"Well, I think my instructions were to stay put . . ."

*"Victor, your superior's words were specifically 'don't let the miners get slaughtered by rats or something,'"* Gorz piped up in Victor's mind.

"Hmm, actually, I think our number one duty was to keep the miners alive, not to guard this shithole barricade. Hey, go get that veteran you were talking to; what was her name?"

"Trilla; I'll get her." Edeya ran over to where a group of three delvers sat around talking next to the amber-ore vein. A moment later, a tall, thin Ardeni woman stood up and strode over with Edeya in tow.

"You wanted me?" As she drew closer, Victor realized she wasn't really very tall; Edeya was just short as hell. Her voice had a slight nasal quality, and she wore a perpetual sneer. Victor looked into her bright yellow eyes and nodded.

"Yeah, I'm heading up to the next cave to check on the miners. I need you to guard the barricade with Tyge and that other guy."

"Who made you boss?"

"You heard Sergeant Fath! He's in charge!" Edeya snapped from behind Trilla.

"Whatever. Yes, sir, Boss!" She sketched a mocking bow and turned to walk over to the barricade. Victor looked at Edeya and shrugged. He brought his fingers to his lips and whistled. When the other delvers looked at him, he motioned them over. They came slowly at first, but then with more urgency as Victor clapped his hands and said, "C'mon, hustle!"

"Listen, I think something's happened to the miners. We need to head up and check things out. I'm leaving those three"—he gestured to the barricade—"to watch the tunnel; we're going up. Let's move!" He tuned out their questions, allowing Edeya to field them, and started climbing the ramp. He wasn't sure why, but he felt that he needed to hurry. He reasoned it could be that he'd built up some imaginary emergency, and he'd find nothing, but it felt strange that the miners were taking so much longer than the delvers to get down to the dig site.

He was a much faster climber than the other four delvers, and by the time he climbed the ramp far enough to see out of the chasm into the next cavern, he was a good fifty yards ahead of them. A rumbling cracking cacophony signaled something going on up above, so he gripped his new baton tightly and crouched low as he approached the opening. He could hear the others scrabbling along behind him as he peered over the lip of the cleft into the upper cavern.

There, among the tumbled ruins where the delvers had fought the stick-men, Victor saw the backside of a fighting retreat taking place. The miners were being pushed back through the tunnel leading up to the next cavern by a frenzied, clicking mob of little men that seemed to be made of stone. They didn't speak or scream or anything else you might expect of stone monsters, but their bodies ground and rumbled as they moved and clacked against the stone of the cavern floor. Conversely, on the far side of the frenzied battle, Victor heard the miners grunt, scream, and roar as they tried to beat the crea-tures back with their mining picks.

Victor was planning a charge when he felt a cool hand grip his arm, holding on to his tricep. "Those are stone imps! They'll slaughter us!" Edeya hissed in his ear. He looked down at her and raised an eyebrow.

"Bullshit. They don't look that tough."

"Well, they are!" Her eyes were wide and round with fear, and Victor looked at the other three delvers crouching behind her.

"Look, I don't give a fuck that Lam told us to protect these miners, but I'm not someone who can slink away while some folks are getting jumped by monsters. Fuck that." Without really thinking about it, Victor stood up straight and cast Inspiring Presence. Once again, he felt the surge of well-being and the brimming potential all around him. He spread his mouth into a wide grin and laughed. "Come on! You want to live like a bug in a hole? Let's fucking kill these things!" Everything was brighter, everything seemed easier, and he could tell that his delvers felt the same way; they stopped cow-ering and gripped their batons.

"Let's do it!" Edeya said firmly.

"Fuck yeah! Hit 'em in the back while they don't see us!" Victor turned and charged, not waiting to see who followed. He jumped over the broken landscape, hopping low crumbled walls and sliding around boulders. Before he knew it, the stone imps jostling and pushing toward the retreating miners were right in front of him, and he jumped into the fight, swinging his baton with heavy, whooshing blows that cracked into their rigid bodies, breaking off pieces of hard flesh and shattering little limbs. Victor howled and pushed more Energy into his Inspiring Presence, extending the duration and bolstering the ragged, battle-weary miners. His arms seemed to sing with power, and he started to laugh.

He was aware of his delver companions joining the fray, but his attention was on the dance of combat. Fighting under the influence of Inspiring Presence was a lot different than when he cast Berserk. While berserking, he was aware of his enemies and his need to destroy them, but he could focus on little else. Now, fighting among the stone imps with his delver friends, he was aware of everything; he could see the movements of the imps, the way their stiff joints seemed to follow a rigid movement pattern, and he was mindful of the best way to block them and slip past their slow, clumsy guard to smash their hard little heads. He concentrated on maximizing the efficiency of his movements and had enough cognizance left over to help a fellow delver with a missed parry or stumbled footing.

The miners and other delvers benefited also, and as their tempo of attack increased and their actions went from harried and fearful to bold and precise, they began to shatter the resistance of the stone imps, who had to fight now on two fronts. Soon they'd reduced their number to just a few, and though Victor's Inspiring Presence wore off, leaving everyone feeling hungover and sluggish, they managed to pulverize the last of the little creatures with no further loss of life among the delvers or miners. As they all stood around panting over the corpses of the stone imps, a thick carpet of Energy motes started to form over the battlefield and began to stream into them. Victor savored the rush as the Energy poured into him, refreshing his exhausted limbs and wiping away his hungover haze.

***Congratulations! You've achieved Level 15 Spirit Champion. You have gained 7 will, 7 vitality, and have 7 attribute points to allocate. Congratulations! You've learned Bludgeon Mastery, Improved.***

"Thank the Ancestors you all came up here!" a grizzled old Ardeni miner with white and red peppered hair said, walking up to the panting delvers. Victor stood up and reached out to shake his hand.

"Yeah, we figured you all were taking a bit too long to get down, so we came to see what the holdup was. Did you lose any?"

"Aye, a miner and our foreman, but it would've been a lot worse. Thanks again." He turned to gather up the surviving miners, eleven of them, and then they all stood around looking at Victor. Victor looked at his delvers, making sure none were seriously hurt, then nodded.

"Well, that was a good fight. Good job, everyone. Let's get down to the ore and get to work."

"Ahh, shit on that idea! We just had the piss beat out of us!" one of the miners said, stepping forward.

"Who's in charge of you miners?" Victor asked, frowning at the stocky, pickaxe-wielding Cadwalli.

"As I said, the foreman died," the older, friendly guy said.

"All right, well, get this straight; Captain Lam doesn't give a shit how tired you are. You've got work to do, and I do too. Do you think Lam will let me slide if I tell her I sent the miners home because they were tired and scared? Now get the fuck down that ramp and get to work."

"What about the bodies?"

"We'll deal with them on the way out. Right now, I need you to hustle down because I've got three guys holding down the fort, and they could need our help at any minute!" Victor didn't know where his sense of authority was coming from or how he was standing up to all these older men and women, but he didn't care. He was sick of going with the flow, and as long as he was in charge, he was damn well going to do things the way he thought was right. "C'mon, let's go!"

"Yeah, quit arguing and get moving!" Edeya said, moving behind the miners to help shepherd them down. Victor nodded, and the whole group got moving. There was some grumbling, but the miners were generally glad to be alive, so they moved with the delvers down the ramp and to the ore vein and got to work. Victor checked in with the three delvers they'd left, and they reported no action.

"Figures you guys would get to have an easy battle while we sat around twiddling our thumbs," Trilla groused, but Edeya wasn't having any of it.

"Easy? Easy? Have you ever fought stone imps? If it weren't for Victor, the miners would be dead, and we'd be down here hiding, hoping they didn't come this way after they killed them all."

"Relax, girl," Trilla said dismissively.

"Everyone relax," Victor said, putting a hand on Edeya's shoulder. "It's good we fucked up those imps, but let's stay cool in case more stuff comes our way." A loud crack interrupted him, and he turned, flinching out of reflex, to see the miners had somehow split off a considerable section of the amber-ore vein and were starting to tap off chunks with their picks. "Shit, that startled me. Are those picks enchanted?"

"Of course," Trilla scoffed, but she turned and stared into the darkness over the ramparts, and Victor took that as a sign that she was willing to let things drop. He turned and checked in with the rest of the delvers, then he spent some time watching the miners work.

He knew there had to be more to this operation than just slaves running around with picks. No, it was slaves running around with *magical* picks and with bags that could hold thousands of pounds of ore. "Magic sure makes shit easier," he muttered.

"*Indeed, Victor. Speaking of which, I had an idea you might like to try,*" a slightly metallic voice said in his head.

"*Oh yeah?*" he thought.

"*Yes. There's a spell that all Energy-using children are taught, and it requires no prior knowledge of patterns. It's a light spell, and, though you don't have any unattuned Energy, I think it will still work for you, perhaps with an added effect because of your attunement.*" Victor walked over to the ramp leading out of the cavern and sat down on a square-topped boulder, keeping the miners and the barricade in his field of view. "*All right, lay it on me.*"

"*Well, children who have developed a Core and pathways are often taught to channel some Energy into their palm, using their will to form and compress it into a ball. With pure Energy, this creates a yellow sphere that casts light. If one's will is strong enough, it can be made to float around the caster.*"

"*And with my spirit Core? My attuned Energy?*"

"*I speculate that it will still cast light, though in a different shade, and it might have an emotional impact on those caught in its glare.*"

"*All right, let me see here.*" Victor turned his mind inward and looked at his Cores, but then he stopped himself. "*Hey, I have seven points to spend. Any advice?*"

"*Will would help with this process, though your will is already quite good for your level. You should weigh that against your immediate survival needs. It seems you're destined to fight a lot, so perhaps more physical attributes. I'm sorry I'm not more help.*"

Victor thought about Gorz's advice, and thought about how he'd spoken to the delvers and miners up in the other cavern. What had made him stand up so firmly? All the fights for his life? His will? His frustration? His inspiration or rage Energy? It seemed that a lot of factors were working to influence his demeanor. Demeanor? Where'd he pull that one from? "*It seems like mental stats are pretty important for survival too. My most powerful abilities require Energy to cast, and I think they're helping me use words to influence people.*"

*"That's an excellent point; sometimes the best victory is attained by avoiding the battle."*

*"Right,"* Victor decided to put four points into intelligence and three more into will. The effects were subtle but, in his mind, undeniable. Then he returned to the scrutiny of his Core. He watched the pulsing, throbbing red light of his rage-attuned Energy, then he coaxed a thread of it loose and pushed it through his pathways and out into the palm of his hand. It seemed easy to him, and he figured that his high affinity and will were responsible. As the thread of Energy started to dissipate into the air, Victor concentrated on it and pushed it back down, willing it to ball up and press together.

He kept coaxing more Energy out and adding it to the ball in his palm, and then it seemed to ignite with a bright red light, bathing him and the area around him in a pulsing, baleful glare. He felt a surge of heat in his chest, and a growl rumbled up out of his throat.

\*\*\*Congratulations! You've learned the spell: Enraging Orb, Basic.\*\*\*

\*\*\*Enraging Orb, Basic: You create an orb of rage-attuned Energy that will bring forth anger in those who behold its light. Energy cost: 50. Cooldown: minimal.\*\*\*

The notifications caught Victor's attention, and he let the orb of red light dissipate, breathing a sigh of relief when it was gone. Suddenly some golden motes coalesced out of the air around him and rushed into him, much like after a battle.

*"Oh, nice! I got Energy for creating the spell like when I learned fighting skills."*

*"The System rewards innovation with Energy. I'm sure you got some when you made the Inspiring Presence spell, as well; you were just too preoccupied to notice."*

"Well, that's cool," he said aloud. Victor looked around, wondering if anyone heard him, but didn't see anyone paying him any particular attention. One of the miners eating a sandwich nearby gave him an odd look, but he figured that was because of the light he'd just made, not his words. *"Probably better chill out with the spell casting for a while,"* he thought to Gorz.

*"Excellent job on creating that light spell, Victor!"*

*"Thanks. I want to try it with inspiration Energy later. Hey, is it possible to cast a spell with more than one Energy type?"*

*"Indeed! That's how elementalists create meta-elements. I don't have any information on combining spirit attunements, but I think it should be possible."*

*"All right, add that to my list of things to try out."*

*"Noted, Victor!"*

Several hours passed with no other incidents, and the miners made good progress on the ore vein. Not long after the miners took their second meal break, Captain Lam and the other delvers returned. Victor walked toward her as she came through the barricade and approached the miners. "Where's Foreman ap'Thell?"

"He died," the older, friendly miner said, sitting up from where he'd been taking a break. Captain Lam whirled around, and her eyes zeroed in on Victor.

"What happened?" Her voice was sharp, but she didn't seem particularly angry. Still, Victor tried to choose his words carefully.

"Well, you'd been gone a while, and the miners were still not here, so I started to get worried. I took some delvers up to the next cavern, and we found the miners under attack by stone imps." Lam stared at Victor for a moment, then she turned to the miner.

"This is true?"

"Oh, aye. We'd have lost a lot more if your sergeant here hadn't come up to the rescue."

"I'm not a sergeant . . ." Victor started to say, but Lam cut him off.

"Huh, good initiative, Victor. And none of you died in the fight?"

"Nope, we caught 'em from behind, and the delvers fought well. The miners made a good showing, too." Victor shrugged, and Captain Lam studied him for another minute, narrowing her eyes. Then she smiled and clapped him on the shoulder.

"Well, I'm going to authorize some extra contribution points for all of you that rescued the miners!" she announced. "You'll find them added to your balance at the Contribution Store." More quietly, she said, "Victor, I'd like a meeting with you when we get back to the barracks."

"All right," Victor said, though he couldn't tell if that was good news or bad. As Lam moved to inspect the mining progress, he thought, *"Gorz, you think I'm in trouble?"*

*"Not necessarily, Victor, though her Energy aura is quite powerful. I'd be surprised if she didn't sense something about you."*

# 29

⟞⟡⟝

# REVELATIONS

With dread heavy in his heart and butterflies swimming in his stomach, Victor approached Captain Lam's study. They'd been back for an hour and had a meal together as a unit, then Victor and some others had decided to head to the Contribution Store. He'd barely gotten outside, waiting with Gris for Heng and Edeya, when Sergeant Fath had come out and said, "Victor, I gotta go fill in paperwork for some recruits. The captain wants you to talk to you in her study. Hurry up!"

"Good luck," Gris had said with a wry grin, probably just glad it wasn't him.

Victor sighed and knocked on the door. A clipped "come" sounded from within, and he opened the door, stepping into Lam's study for the second time. She was sitting at a small round table this time, and she motioned to a stool on the other side of the table. "Take a seat." Victor stepped into the room and squatted down on the stool, feeling silly with his knees poking up under the table. He cleared his throat nervously. "All right, Victor. I've looked over your mess of a contract a dozen times, and nothing makes sense. Tell me about yourself." She gestured to the paper in front of her written with half a dozen different inks, lines scratched through, and signatures scribbled in odd places.

"Um, what do you want to know?"

"Everything. Let's start with where you're from."

"Originally? From a planet called Earth. I don't think the names of my country or town would mean anything to you."

"And how did you end up in my unit?"

"Um, when I got to the mine, the foreman sent me to the tent where . . ."

"No. I mean, how did you wind up with this contract? Why aren't you free?"

"Well, I wish I could explain it. One minute I was in my *abuela's* house; the next minute, I was standing in a barn with some fucking wackos. They took me to the city and sold me to the guy that runs the pit fights there."

"This was in Persi Gables? Yund is the man who bought you?" She pointed to Yund's name up near the top of the contract.

"That's right."

"Tell me about your time with Yund and how you ended up in the mines with a broken Core." She sat back and took a sip from her crystal glass, waiting for Victor to speak.

He started slowly, haltingly, unsure of how much detail she wanted, but with her encouragement, he began to tell her about his time at the Wagon Wheel. He told her about Yrella and Vullu, and his eyes welled up with tears for the first time in a long while. He wiped them away and kept talking, telling her about his Core and some of his fights and how Yund had made the contract with him. He told her about being the "Justice" for the Lady, then he told her about how Yund sold him out to the nobleman that had tried to destroy his Core. Finally, he told her about waking up in the wagon and finding out he'd been sold to the Greatbone Mining Consortium and how the foreman had sent him to the tent where he'd been randomly assigned to Lam's unit.

Lam drummed her fingers on her table as she regarded Victor, then she reached behind her to her bookcase, picked up another crystal glass, and set it on the table. She produced a dark bottle from somewhere and poured an oily amber liquid into both glasses, then the bottle disappeared, and she gestured to the new glass. "Take a drink; you deserve it."

"Um, thanks." Victor picked up the heavy glass and took a sip; he'd tasted whiskey before, and this was similar, though it had a faintly sweet aftertaste. "It's good," he said, smiling.

"All right, Victor. You've been given a raw deal. What's happened to you in this world isn't fair, and it isn't right, but life isn't fair. That's one thing I know about you. Another thing I know about you is that you're a lot stronger than people think. Your Core either isn't broken like it seemed, or you've figured a way to heal it." She held up a hand as Victor opened his mouth to object. "As far as I'm concerned, the two facts even out the scales a little." She paused again to regard Victor, making sure her words sank in. "I don't care how strong you get. I don't care if you escape from this shithole someday. I just want you to know that I won't tolerate any violence to those under my command, and I hope you'll work with me for a while. I'd like to see what you can become."

"Seriously?" he asked, completely dumbfounded.

"Seriously. I don't work for the Greatbone Mining Consortium. Sure, I have a contract with them, but I'm not here *for* them. You understand?"

"Yeah, I understand. Um . . ." Victor had to look down, squeezing his eyes shut. He didn't know why he was so overcome with emotion, but he felt as if someone had taken a huge weight off his back. He blew out a heavy, shuddering breath, then he tried again, "Thank you, Captain."

"Finish your drink, and then go spend some of those contribution points. You need a clean shirt and some boots that fit. Just don't get jumped again, all right?"

"I won't," Victor said, taking another drink, savoring the way the liquid warmed his throat and belly. He smiled and shook his head. "I knew you were cool from the first time I saw you, Captain."

"Cool?"

"Yeah, like awesome, great. I mean, aside from all this." He put a finger under his metal collar and gave it a tug.

"All right, all right. Flattery won't get you another drink. As far as those collars go, yes, I feel some guilt about associating with the mine operators, but these ruins are a rare opportunity. The world's cruel, you know? Anyway, go on, get out of here. We're going deeper tomorrow, and I'm bringing you with us this time." She gestured to the door, smiling, and Victor stood up, almost light-headed with relief, and buzzing slightly from the drink, as he set the glass down. He waved awkwardly, moving to the door and out. When he closed it behind himself, he stood there for a moment, trying to gather his racing thoughts, but all he could do was grin stupidly.

"*Congratulations, Victor! It seems you've gained a powerful ally!*" Gorz's voice piped into his head, and he jerked in surprise, looking around nervously.

"*Thanks, Gorz. You fucking startled me.*"

"*My apologies, Victor!*"

"*It's all good, man. It's all good.*" Victor walked briskly through the barracks, noting that most of the delvers were gone, and then out the front door. Of course, his friends were gone; he'd been talking to Lam for a long time. He turned toward the central settlement and broke into a jog, passing by groups of delvers and miners. There was a lot of traffic at that time of day as groups of workers finished their shifts, returned to their camps and visited the Settlement Stone to turn in quests. He was about halfway to the main settlement cavern when he heard Gorz's tinny voice again.

*"Victor! I can sense the Energy aura of one of the thugs that tried to kill you!"* Victor stumbled as the words hit home.

*"What? You're sure? Just one of them?"*

*"Yes, I'm quite sure. He's just twenty yards away, moving in the same direction as you."* Victor looked ahead and saw the figure that Gorz must have meant. A small, slouched figure was walking briskly toward the tunnel entrance. There were a lot of other people moving about, though, and Victor, no matter how badly he wanted to beat that guy's ass, wasn't going to throw away all the progress he'd made. He didn't need to get flagged by some mine employee and have his collar activated to melt his head off.

He looked around, noting the wooden shanties and occasional larger building, and wondered if whatever delver unit those guys were with was stationed nearby or if he was going to visit the Settlement Stone. *"Gorz, keep track of that guy; how close do I have to stay to him?"*

*"I can't sense him if you're much farther away than this, Victor."*

*"All right."* Victor kept moving, careful to stay well behind the guy, and when the crowds grew thicker and he lost track of him visually, Gorz kept him informed of his movements. As they came into sight of the vast settlement area, the guy turned to the left, and Victor followed him.

*"Victor! I sense another of the thugs, just ahead of where the first thug is; they're not thirty yards ahead and to the left."* Victor moved cautiously to a low ramshackle building and looked around the corner. Sure enough, there was Chem, talking to the guy that Victor had been following. He clapped him on the shoulder, and the two of them turned and walked into a large wooden building with a black star painted on the door.

*"I think we found their barracks, Gorz. Take a note of it."*

*"Done, Victor!"*

"Good job," Victor said softly, then turned and made his way back toward the cavern's center and the tall Settlement Stone. While he walked, he spoke softly to himself, "What a fucking productive day."

When he got to the Settlement Stone, he didn't see his friends right away, and he wondered if he had missed them while he'd been preoccupied following Chem's friend. *"Gorz, can you spot Edeya or Gris?"*

*"Not in the immediate vicinity. I'll keep a lookout, though."*

*"Perfect. Thanks, Gorz."* Victor waited in line to access the Settlement Stone, and when his turn came, he was pleased to see that he'd gotten another five hundred contribution points. He wondered how many Captain Lam was allowed to dish out like that but figured she probably had shitloads; it wasn't like she needed any of the junk for sale on the Contribution Store. Once again, Victor bought himself a backpack, new boots, new socks, and two new, long-sleeve cottony shirts. After all that, he still had plenty of points left to buy a hardened leather breastplate and some leather bracers.

He took his goods off to the side of the stone and started sorting through them. He was paranoid about changing his shirt out in the open where someone might see Gorz, so he stuffed most of his clothes into his backpack. He took the time to swap out his boots and put socks on, though, and his feet thanked him. He also put the hard leather bracers on, pulling the laces tight with one hand and his teeth.

With no sight of his friends, Victor turned back toward the barracks and got ready to leave, but just as he was setting off in a jog, he caught a whiff of something good. He followed his nose to the other side of the Settlement Stone, where a guy was selling skewers of meat from a rolling cart. His cart was made from wood but had a sizeable cast-iron insert in the middle of it where coals smoldered. Hanging above the coals were the skewers of marinated meat, and the scent made Victor's mouth water. He walked over to the cart and got in line behind a few other customers, watching as they each went up, exchanged something with the cart guy, and walked away with some meat skewers.

"What do you charge for them?" he asked when it was his turn.

"Five for a bead, and yes, I know that's robbery, good luck finding another merchant in here."

"A bead . . ."

*"I can teach you how to make Energy beads, Victor,"* Gorz piped in.

"All right, maybe later, thanks," Victor said, stepping back. *"What's an Energy bead?"* he thought.

*"It's a physical manifestation of Energy. Anyone with Energy affinity can make one, but the greater your affinity, the easier it is, and the faster you can do it. They're often used as currency in System-influenced worlds because the System will take them as currency at Town Stones."*

"So, there's nothing wrong with it? Like, I won't get busted for making them?"

*"I doubt that man could trade for them if it were illegal in the mines, Victor."*

"Yeah, that makes sense. Duh. All right, what do I do?"

*"You'll want to be somewhere you can concentrate and where you won't be interrupted, especially for your first one."*

*"All right, I guess meat skewers aren't on the menu tonight. Maybe next time."* Victor turned and started back to the barracks, staying toward the center of the tunnel and keeping alert; no way he was getting jumped again for his boots. He'd only been walking a couple of minutes when he caught sight of Edeya and the others, so he jogged up to them. "Yo, guys! I was wondering if I'd find you."

"Victor! You live! The captain too hard on you?" Gris asked.

"Nah, man. She was fucking cool. She just wanted to talk to me about my contract; all good."

"That's good, Victor," Edeya said, "I was afraid we were in trouble for leaving the barricade or something."

"No way! She was glad we did that. We're good. Hey, did anyone else get some new kicks? Check these out." Victor held one of his new steel-toed boots up.

"Hmm, seems to be a popular model!" Heng said, laughing; all the veterans had the exact same boots.

"Hey, we're allowed to make Energy beads, right? I wanna try to buy some of those meat skewers next time." The older vets looked at each other with big smiles, and Edeya made a gagging sound. "What?"

"You have any idea what kind of meat that was? You don't see any holbyis around here, do you?" Gris asked.

"What's a holbyis?"

"It's a herd animal. The point I'm making, Victor, my boy, is that the meat you're drooling over is probably some kind of monster. Probably giant rats."

"Well, it still smelled fucking good."

"Ha, if you're determined, then yes, it's perfectly fine to make Energy beads; just don't go flaunting them around, 'cause that'll get you robbed. Again." Gris laughed, and Heng joined in. Edeya looked at Victor as if she felt sorry for him. Victor couldn't feel any irritation; he was in too good a mood from his talk with Captain Lam and everything else that had happened that day. He just grinned and shrugged.

They got back just in time for Fath to return and announce lights-out. For a moment, Victor wondered about Sergeant Fath—was he an employee of the mine, or was he loyal to Captain Lam? He certainly seemed to have Lam's trust, but Victor was wary of anyone who didn't wear a collar in this place. When the lights went out, and he lay down in his scratchy cot, Victor realized just how bone-tired he was, and he couldn't spare any more thoughts about Sergeant Fath, collars, or anything else.

He woke as he heard some of the others stirring, and Victor scrabbled out of bed to clean himself up. He managed to get a partitioned stall in the jacks, so he changed his shirt, keeping Gorz nicely hidden, then joined the other early risers for a quick breakfast. It was the first time he'd gotten up in time to eat, and the warm cereal filled with bits of sweet, dried fruit came as a pleasant surprise. He'd just finished wolfing down his food when Sergeant Fath stood up from the table and said, "Wake up the rest of these slugs; we're heading out in five minutes."

Victor took particular pleasure in waking up Edeya, lifting the foot of her cot off the ground and giving it a good shake. She thrashed and sputtered and looked around with wild eyes. When she saw Victor, she bared her teeth and said, "I'll pay you back for that!" They laughed, though, and soon the column was marching out, chanting another marching cadence about a boy who hated his mother's cooking so much that he signed up to work someplace called the Impfire Forges.

Victor hadn't seen Captain Lam yet that day, but he figured she would come flying from behind, or she was already deep in the ruins scouting around. While they marched, Gorz tried to explain to him about Energy beads. *"You see, the System seems to crave Energy-rich materials, and you can create such materials by manifesting the Energy that you cultivate. It's a process very similar to what you did when you made your rage-attuned light; you simply channel your Energy out through your pathways and condense it with your will. You're aiming to create something far denser than your light orb, though, and as it takes shape, you keep adding to it until it's the appropriate size. You start to get a feel for that the more you make. Some places trade in tiny beads, the smallest possible physical manifestation. They only take about one-tenth as long to create as a standard Energy bead."*

*"And it doesn't matter that my Energy isn't pure?"*

*"No! In fact, the System pays more for attuned beads. Why, you can even create beads with multiple attunements, which increases their value!"*

They talked for a while more about the process, and by the time they arrived at the forward camp, Victor felt that he had a pretty good grasp on the concept. Just as he'd half-expected, Captain Lam was already waiting for them. She was all business when they walked up. "I'm heading out with Victor, Heng, Thayla, and Fenlale. Sergeant Fath, make sure the miners don't slack off; we'll be gone most of the day."

"Yes, ma'am!" Sergeant Fath turned to the delvers, "All right, you dogs! I need four on the barricade and four watching the ramp!" Victor walked over next to Captain Lam, happy that she'd kept her word about taking him with her today but also annoyed at himself for being worried that she wouldn't. The other three delvers she'd named also gathered with her, and Victor bumped knuckles with Heng when he held his fist out.

"Victor?" the tall Shadeni woman named Thayla asked.

"Yeah."

"You're the one that got jumped the other day, right?"

"Yeah, that's me."

"Guess you can take a beating. That's good."

"All right, let's get moving," Captain Lam said, looking up from the journal she'd been studying. She strode away, and they all fell in line behind her. This time, Victor took the lead. Something about the way Lam had spoken to him and, more importantly, listened to him made him feel more enthusiastic about helping her. He felt as if having her on his side made his chances in this world a hell of a lot better, and he planned to take advantage of the opportunities she was giving him.

They reached the point where Victor had fought the rat and found Gorz, and, once they'd all shimmied down the rope to the ruined structures, Lam fluttered down and said, "All right, I have a tunnel I'm going to explore. The rest of you split up and dig around these ruins. Listen, I've already been through most of the larger structures, but there are plenty of buildings with lower levels that I haven't been through. You'll probably run into hostile creatures, so I want you working with a buddy. On that same note, I am giving you all some trust here. Don't blow it. If you find something interesting, bring it back here for me to check out. If it's too big to carry, make a note of it, and show it to me when we meet up here. Speaking of which, we'll gather back here in two hours. Victor, you're with Thayla. Heng and Fenlale, you're a team as usual."

"Captain?" Thayla asked.

"Yeah?"

"Can we make it interesting? Any reward for the team that finds the most stuff?" Her lips curled in a grin, exposing her sharp canines, and Victor had to admit, he liked her nerve.

"Thayla, Thayla, Thayla," the captain said, shaking her head with a rueful smile. "All right, if it will keep you all honest, I'll let the team with the best finds take a choice from items I don't want." Fenlale slapped Heng on the back with a big smile on his face. Thayla whooped, and Lam continued, "All right, everyone take a light stone; you'll need it in the ruins." She produced a handful of leather cords with glowing yellow stones affixed to them, passing them out to each delver. "Now, get going!"

"Let's go!" Thayla gave Victor a shove, and he followed her into the crumbling ruins, taking the opposite direction from Heng and Fenlale. She ducked into a narrow "street" between ruined buildings and hurried between several others, seemingly heading somewhere in particular.

"Where are you going?"

"I know what buildings they searched yesterday; I'm taking us to a big building we didn't get to yet."

"Oh, sweet!" Victor supposed Heng and Fenlale had similar intel, but it didn't change the excitement he felt at the prospect of exploring old ruins looking for treasure. "How does Lam keep delvers from trying to keep stuff they find?"

"Ha. If you're dumb enough to try to cheat Lam, then good luck to you."

"Right. I'm not that dumb, and I don't want to cheat her, anyway." Victor meant his words; he respected Lam to a degree—as much as he could respect someone who used indentured servants as fodder to fight monsters while she hunted for treasures. Yes, he wanted to grow stronger and escape, but he didn't want to make an enemy of her. Thayla paused in front of a large building and looked at him; she had long black hair tightly bound to her red scalp in a bunch of braids. Her eyes were angled in such a way that she seemed angry or ready for a fight all the time, but she regarded him calmly for a moment, then shrugged.

"Yeah, I doubt Captain Lam would've brought you along if she thought you were scum. I heard you did a good job protecting the pickers yesterday, too."

"Ha, pickers." Victor snorted and followed Thayla as she stepped through the ruined doorway. The structure must once have been at least two stories tall; some of the upper floor was still standing, though the ceiling was falling down in various places. Something stood out among the tumbled stone blocks, though—steel girders with huge bolts with X-shaped heads holding them together. "Wonder who built this place so far underground."

"Who says it was underground when they built it?"

"Well, we're pretty fucking deep. Not sure how all these buildings could get down here otherwise."

"Hmm, well, the System managed to combine four worlds into one, so I don't think it would be too hard for it to put a town into a cave." She reached forward and lifted a thin stone slab, peering under it while speaking.

"Good point. So, this world used to be four?"

"So they say. C'mon, look around!" She gestured around the ruined building, and Victor moved over to a half-fallen wall and peered over it. Nothing was there but more rubble, so he started sifting through it, looking for anything other than old building materials. He kicked through some dusty, rotted doors and dug through piles of petrified wood, all the while hearing Thayla doing the same in other parts of the building. He was climbing through another old, rotted door when he heard Thayla whoop.

"Victor! Come here!" she called, and Victor turned and hastily retraced his steps. Her excitement was palpable in her tone, and it was hard for Victor not to reciprocate it. He could see the path she'd taken over the dusty stone floor and followed it, wending through broken walls, doors, and around corners. She called twice more, urging him to hurry, and he did, bursting, finally, through another broken doorway into a large, mostly intact room. That's when he saw something was wrong.

Thayla sat against the far wall, her legs stretched out, and her chin hung down to her chest. When Victor saw she wasn't moving, he scanned the rest of the room and saw a dark shadow lurking in the corner to Thayla's right. Movement caught his eye, and he saw a gray tendril of vinelike material twitch along the floor. He traced its length to see that one end of it was hidden in the shadow cast by Thayla's light stone, and it seemed to be wrapped around her neck. Then Thayla's voice came out of the corner where the larger shadow lurked, "Victor! Hurry! I found something!"

Victor stepped back behind the crumbled doorway, his heart racing. What the hell was going on? He peeked around again, staring at Thayla. Was she breathing? He thought he could see her chest moving ever so slightly. "Victor! Hurry!" her voice called from the far corner again. Should he run and try to get Captain Lam or the others? What if Thayla was dying? What if that thing was slowly choking her or draining her life away? His mind began to run away, imagining all sorts of horrifying scenarios.

*"Gorz, any idea what's happening?"*

*"No, Victor. I'm sorry."* Victor wished he could see better, but neither his little light nor Thayla's could reach that far corner. Then it hit him—his light spell! He didn't want to send a rage-attuned light in there, though. He concentrated on his Enraging Orb spell, turning his mind inward so he could

focus his will on holding back his red rage Energy. When he saw the spell pattern start to form, he pushed some inspiration-attuned Energy toward it and was pleased when a white-gold orb of brilliant light began to form above his outstretched hand.

\*\*\*Congratulations! You've learned the spell: Globe of Insight, Basic.\*\*\*

\*\*\*Globe of Insight, Basic: You create an orb of inspiration-attuned Energy that will help those within its radiance see the potential in their surroundings. Energy cost: 50. Cooldown: minimal.\*\*\*

Several things happened at once when the globe of warm light finished forming above his palm: motes of Energy formed out of the air and surged into Victor, the light shone brightly into the room where Thayla lay against the wall, and something screamed with rage and indignation from the dark corner. Having never experimented with moving around his orb with just his will, Victor thrust his hand into the room as if to throw it toward the dark corner.

He watched as the orb sailed through the air, banishing the dark shadows and exposing the long, twisted, gray tendril that snaked over the ground and wrapped around Thayla's neck. Another such tendril was already groping its way over the ground toward Victor, and he lifted his baton in preparation to bat it away when the light uncovered the creature lurking in the corner. It looked like a gray, fleshy tree trunk with stubby limbs and a wide mouth at its center. The gray tendrils or fleshy roots were slithering forth from its base. Unbidden, Victor's uncle's favorite expression slipped from his lips: "*Madre de Dios!*"

His orb had stopped mid-air near the center of the room, and its bright light revealed Thayla's purpling flesh and the weak twitching of her limbs. No longer considering fleeing as an option, Victor charged toward her, skirting away from the other probing tentacle-root, and slammed his baton against the one that held Thayla. He smashed it hard against the stone ground, and though he couldn't cut the thing with this blunt weapon, he felt something give inside it, and the creature screamed again. The screech came from its gaping, gnashing maw. When Victor flinched from the sound and looked toward its source, he saw the mouth was filled with little razorlike teeth and a dozen probing slimy tongues.

Victor shuddered and pounded on the vine, again and again, madly grinning, when he saw the gray flesh start to pulp and break apart. The creature continued to scream, and its other probing tentacle finally caught up to Victor, snaking around his ankle. He tried to yank his foot away, but it tightened like a vise, pressing the leather of his boot into his flesh and grinding his bones together. He hadn't expected it to be so strong! Victor hesitated for a moment, weighing his options, but then the tentacle jerked, pulling him sideways, and he panicked, activating his Berserk.

Red lust for violence filled his mind and clouded his vision, and Victor stopped resisting the pull of the tentacle-root, charging headlong at the gray, fleshy thing in the corner. He cackled as he brought his baton down onto the broad expanse of pallid, damp flesh, smashing it into the creature as hard as possible. Frustration fueled his rage when nothing much happened as a result of the mighty smash. The flesh jiggled, the maw screamed, and the tentacle wrapped further around his leg.

The creature's maw was large enough to snap Victor in half should he fall in, but, even in his madness, he used his left hand to brace against the trunk-like exterior of the monster and continued to pound his baton, to little effect, with his other. All the while, the gray tentacle continued to snake up his leg and around his waist, and then a shiver of panic broke through Victor's rage, and it began to fade. He felt the creature's enormous strength as it continued to squeeze, then he felt a dark, invading Energy creep into his pathways through the flesh at his waist, where the tentacle was in direct contact with his skin.

Victor raged against the intrusion, pushing hot red Energy toward the foreign presence, and he managed to shove it back for a few seconds. Then he began to weaken, his guts squeezed so tightly that he was having trouble taking a breath. His pummeling of the monster degenerated into pathetic slaps, and darkness crept around the edges of his vision, and once again, the invading Energy began to push into him. Then something strange happened in Victor's mind; he stopped panicking and wondering what to do next. Instead, he thought about Yrella and Vullu, then he thought about Belsa and wondered what had happened to her. He'd never know, he realized.

Something wet and hot hit Victor's face, and the squeezing lessened slightly. His ears had long been overwhelmed by the creature's screaming, so he didn't notice anything different when it continued to shriek, perhaps with a slightly higher pitch. Again, wet, hot fluid splashed him, and again, the tentacles loosened, and Victor felt blood rush up to parts of his body that had been deprived. He managed a gasping breath and opened his eyes. Another splash of hot fluid accompanied by a feminine grunt greeted him as he jerked his head from left to right, trying to see what was happening.

Thayla was swinging a broad-bladed axe against the creature's trunk, showering herself and Victor with gore with each swing. Her latest chop had severed much of the tentacle, and Victor managed to stumble back, falling onto his butt. Not knowing how else to help, Victor channeled his inspiration Energy into Inspiring Presence, and suddenly Thayla stood up straighter and began to hack in earnest, more precisely placing her strikes. Victor, for his part, felt a surge of well-being and scrambled to his feet, instantly spotting his fallen baton. He scooped it up and was about to lay into the monster, regardless of the ineffective nature of his weapon, when Thayla stepped back, grinning.

"It's done," she said, panting. She reached toward her chest, slipping a finger behind her leather vest, and suddenly the axe disappeared.

"Nice job," Victor panted, rubbing his sore leg and waist.

"If you mention my axe or my dimensional storage, I'll kill you in your sleep," Thayla said matter-of-factly. Victor genuinely felt insulted and was about to tell Thayla that he wasn't a snitch when a massive current of Energy poured forth from the dead monster into them both, and he lost himself in the exhilaration of it.

***Congratulations! You've achieved Level 16 Spirit Champion. You have gained 7 will, 7 vitality, and have 7 attribute points to allocate.***

# 30

❦

# THE WELL

'm sorry I said that," Thayla said after the rush of Energy faded. "I know you risked yourself to get that thing off my neck, but I don't want to get killed because I showed you my secret."

"You think Lam would kill you for having that axe?"

"Ha, no, not Lam. She's the one who gave me the storage ring I have hung around my neck. This stuff makes me a big target, though, and I'm not looking to get jumped, if you know what I mean." She gave Victor a funny look, and he realized she was trying to make a joke.

"All right, all right. Yes, I know exactly what you mean. I promise I won't mention it. How'd this thing get you around the neck like that, anyway?" Victor looked at the red, blistered marks above Thayla's collar.

"I was looking through that trapdoor, and I called for you, then that damn vine or tentacle thing dropped from the ceiling and grabbed my neck." She pointed to a wooden square in the stone flooring, and Victor realized it was the trapdoor she was referring to.

"Oh shit! So you did find something? Let's check it out!"

"All right, but use your light orb." She pointed to the Globe of Insight still hovering in the air where Victor had "thrown" it. He looked at it and tried to send out his will to make it move toward the trapdoor, but it felt like trying to grab a globe of water with his fingers; he could feel it, but it kept slipping from his grasp.

"Promise not to laugh?" he asked Thayla.

"Sure, why?"

"Well, I don't know how to move that orb."

"Hah, get closer to it. When you're learning to manipulate Energy constructs, it helps to gesture with your hand; my mother told me that people are used to moving things with their hands, so we subconsciously visualize our will as a projection of our touch."

"Really?" Victor walked over to the orb and held out his hand, "pushing" it toward the trapdoor. The orb floated effortlessly ahead of his hand and stopped when he pulled it back. "Holy shit, that was easy. Your mom's a genius!"

"Well, she was pretty smart and a great teacher. I miss her all the time," Thayla said, shrugging and moving to lean over the trapdoor. "All right, get your baton ready. I'm going to open this thing." She pushed her hands through a large gap between the rotting timbers and yanked the trapdoor up. It moved easily, probably because she'd already forced it earlier, and Victor's light shone down onto more gray stones and the rotten remains of an ancient ladder. "Hmm, lots of cobwebs and some mold, but I don't see anything dangerous," Thayla said quietly, poking her head into the hole. "Push your light down there."

"All right," Victor said and, using his hand to guide it, lowered his floating orb and pushed it down into the space beneath the floor. Thayla still had her head hanging through the opening, and when his light moved past it, she took in a deep breath.

"We're going to win for sure!"

"What? What is it?" Victor knelt to try to poke his head through the opening.

"Crates! Lots of crates! They're preserved, too. Whoever stored this stuff cared enough to enchant them!" She grabbed the hole's edge, giving Victor a bit of a shove to make room, then she dropped down. "Nothing here but some old dead spiders! Come down," she called up. Victor took one more look around the room, focusing on the hunched corpse of the gray thing and, seeing nothing to worry about, dropped down.

The room below was a low-ceilinged stone galley about ten feet wide by fifty long, and both walls along its length were stacked with wooden crates, each about two feet square. Thayla was prying open one of the crates with an iron crowbar that she'd presumably pulled out of her storage ring. Victor went over to help. The wooden crate was made of good solid wood, and the nails holding the top down weren't the least bit rusty. "Someone really enchanted these so they wouldn't decay? Would that be expensive?"

"For me or you, yeah. For some rich noble, not at all." She grunted and gave the crowbar another heave, and Victor pulled the wooden lid. With a screech, the nails pulled free, and the contents were exposed—stacks of dull red metal ingots. "Whoa," Thayla said, putting her crowbar away and lifting out one of the ingots.

"What kind of metal is that?" Victor asked, also picking one up. It was heavy, maybe heavier than steel, but he wasn't sure. The red color was interesting, though, and it had a weird, shifting sheen in the light of his orb.

"I don't know. It's not amber ore, steel, or any other metal I've seen. Maybe it's valuable. Forget that; it's definitely valuable. I just don't know how valuable."

"All right, let's take one back to the meeting spot, eh?"

"Yep, Captain Lam will know what it is, I'm sure." Thayla set the lid down and then walked up and down the row of crates, counting them. "Twenty-four ingots in a crate and a hundred and twenty crates. Ancestors! If these are very valuable at all, Captain is going to love us." Victor couldn't help smiling; he'd almost died a few minutes ago, and now he was discovering a hidden hoard of possibly magical metal—the huge, sudden swings in his fortune couldn't be good for his mental state, but he felt good, anyway. Was it the Energy he'd gotten from the kill? Was he still buzzing from it?

They climbed out of the storage cellar and made their way out of the ruined building and back to the meeting point. He and Thayla were the first to arrive. Then Lam came swooping out of a dark tunnel halfway up the wall on the far side of the cavern. Her wings trailed glittering motes as she descended to land in front of them. She was clearing her throat to speak when Heng came jogging out from behind a building, Fenlale a short way behind with a rotten wooden trunk cradled in his arms. "We got something good, I think, Captain!" Heng hollered as they strode forward.

"What about you two?" Captain Lam asked while they waited for the two men to close the distance. Thayla held out the ingot, and Captain Lam took it, weighing it thoughtfully in one hand while she produced a leather-bound text with her other. Heng and Fenlale arrived while she was studying the ingot, and Fenlale let down his burden with a heavy clatter of wood and metal.

"What's in the chest?" Thayla asked.

"Weapons, and most of 'em not even rusted. Artificed, I'd wager."

"Huh, nice. Might have won, too, but I think we've got you beat," Thayla said, a sly smile stretching her lips.

"Hmm, this is an alloy. See how the light makes those rainbow swirls in the metal?" Victor leaned close, looking where she pointed. "And it's hard; I can't scrape it with my steel dagger. I'd say this is a mixture of amber ore and bronze. According to my book, amber ore, tin, and copper require less heat to combine than steel and amber ore, but they still produce a tough alloy. It's valuable for sure, but let me take a look at these weapons before I determine who won." Victor looked at Thayla, and she held a finger to her lips and winked.

Captain Lam lifted the lid off the old wooden box and whistled appreciatively. The box was full of knives and short swords. The knives ranged in size from small four-inch blades to much longer daggerlike weapons. There were only four short swords, but they all gleamed in the light of the glow stones, their matching blades dangerous looking even to Victor's untrained eye. "Yep, very nice blades—artificed for sure. Sorry, Thayla and Victor, but I think Heng and Fenlale win!"

"Oh, but you haven't seen all that we found," Thayla said, grinning at Heng, who'd just started to whoop and raise a fist in the air.

"You have something else?"

"Well, not exactly; we have something more—over a hundred crates of those ingots." Thayla nodded to the ingot still in Lam's fist.

"What?" Lam stood up, and her eyes widened. "Crates?"

"Yep, and each crate has twenty-four ingots," Victor added, holding out a fist for Thayla to bump. She gave him a funny look, but then she laughed and gave his knuckles a good punch.

"Show me!" Lam said, sweeping the box of daggers and swords into her dimensional container. Heng groaned, and Fenlale sighed heavily, but they all started to follow as Thayla scampered through the ruins, leading the way to the cellar full of ingots. Victor clapped Heng on the shoulder and grinned, shrugging his shoulders, and Heng groaned again, more loudly.

"Don't rub it in, kid!" He shrugged out of Victor's grip, and Fenlale smiled broadly, shaking a fist up and down, which was something Victor had learned he did when he wanted to laugh.

It turned out the horde of amber-ore alloy was more than even Captain Lam had hoped for. She had to use three different dimensional storage devices to scoop it all up, and even then, she was in a hurry to get out of the mines and cash it in because two of her storage devices were so full that she was worried about their stability. She'd promised Victor and Thayla a reward but then marched them double-time back to the barricade and the other delvers. As they arrived, she called out, "Sergeant Fath!" The angry-looking Ardeni man hustled over, his deep baritone voice booming a reply.

"Yes, Captain?"

"I have to hurry to the surface. Make sure the miners wrap up their work, then bring the unit back to the barracks. Tomorrow will be another day off."

"Yes, Captain!" As Fath saluted, Captain Lam launched into the air, steaking up the crevice to the next cavern. Fath turned to the four delvers and grinned, "Found something good, eh?"

"Aye, some weapons and a huge haul of amber-ore alloy. I'd say Lam just made more money than the entire mine will produce in the next week," Heng said, scratching at his chin.

"You don't say," Sergeant Fath said, shaking his head ruefully. "The privilege of command, eh? Which one of you found it? Or did the captain find it?"

"Me and Fenlale found the weapons, but these two found all the ore," Heng replied.

"All right, you all take it easy, seeing how you got everyone a day off tomorrow. We'll head up in a couple of hours." With that, Sergeant Fath moved over to the ore vein and began to excoriate the miners about their progress. The four delvers moved off to the side and sat with their backs to one of the cavern walls. Victor took his pack off and dug out an old roll he'd tucked away and began to gnaw on it.

"That what you brought for lunch?" Heng laughed at him. Victor just shrugged and continued to chew the hard, dry bread. Thayla snorted and tossed him an orange fruit that looked like a peach.

"Hey, thanks," Victor said, taking a bite; it was sweet and reminded him of an apple.

"You're welcome."

"Hey, can I ask you guys a personal question?" Victor looked around the small group.

"How personal?" Thayla asked, tilting her head and frowning. Heng just snorted and shrugged, and Fenlale, as usual, just ignored Victor, munching away on some sort of grain mix he had in a small sack.

"Well, I mean, I'm trying to figure this whole Energy thing out, and I was wondering what kinds of Cores you all have. I was told my kind of Core is unusual among 'civilized' people—it's a Spirit Core."

"Yeah, I knew something was weird about your Energy because I felt your light orb affecting me," Thayla said.

"Well, yeah, my Energy is attuned; that light orb had inspiration-attuned Energy in it."

"Hmph," Heng grunted, chewing on a hunk of dried meat.

"I don't have any attunements. I have a Pearl Class Core; it's pretty simple, and I only have pure Energy." She held out a hand, and a small ball of shimmering yellow light formed over her hand. "See? My light spell is just a light."

"Are attunements rare?"

"Nah," Heng said, finally having swallowed his mouthful of dry meat. "But, and I'm not trying to be insulting here, Spirit Cores are more common among primitive people like Urghat or the tribes on the Beneset Steppes. Lots of Ardeni and Shadeni have different sorts of attunements or affinities, as most people call them. Many have some elemental affinity, but they usually also have some pure Energy in their Core. Your Energy is all attuned?"

"Yeah, as far as I can tell."

"That's interesting," Thayla said, taking a bite of cheese. "At least you have a nice attunement; it seems inspiration could be pretty useful. My aunt has a Sapphire Class Core and affinities for decay and air; she's been able to create a lot of powerful spells mixing the two."

"Huh, that's cool." Victor tucked into his fruit, finishing it off in a few bites, then he heard scuffling feet, looked up, and saw Edeya had walked over.

"Hey, everyone! I heard you found something good? We get the day off tomorrow, again!"

"Aye, Captain probably has to go into town to deal with her new riches," Heng said, a chuckle in his voice.

"What's up, Edeya? You guys have to fight any demons or anything?" Victor asked.

"Nah, it's been so boring here! The miners just chip away at that vein, and we stand around picking our butts."

"Least you didn't have your life almost sucked out of your neck by a creepy gray tentacle tree," Victor grinned, giving Thayla a nudge.

"Why are you talking? That thing was about to pull you into its mouth when I saved you!"

"True, true." Victor laughed, motioning for Edeya to sit next to him.

"I can't sit; Fath is going to scream at me any second now. Talk to you all later!" Edeya waved and meandered toward the barricade.

"You say your Energy is inspiration-attuned? It seemed like you went crazy during that fight with the beetles, and didn't I hear Lam telling you to use your Berserk ability?" Heng asked while he dug around in his pack for something more to eat.

"Oh, yeah. I have a second affinity: rage."

"Really?" Thayla regarded him more closely, then turned to Heng. "Isn't that what the Corran Blood Ragers are famous for?"

"Hmm, yeah, now you mention it. I think they use blood magic, too, though. Blood and rage affinities."

"Blood's not a spirit affinity, though, is it? My aunt had classmates at the academy who had blood affinity."

"I dunno." Heng shrugged, looking at Fenlale, who also shrugged. Thayla looked at Victor.

"I don't know either. I wish I had a teacher or something."

*"Victor, I'm happy to inform you that a blood affinity is not a spirit-based affinity."* Gorz piped up in Victor's mind. He tried to process the info without looking strange.

"I don't think it is. How could someone have a spirit affinity and a different kind of affinity at the same time?"

"Some kind of specialty Core, I guess. Probably tricky to form or something. It might require a certain bloodline or a secret process," Thayla said.

*"That's correct. I don't have the specifics, but one of the texts I read mentioned in a footnote that some spirit-casters, as the author labeled them, had traded potency for versatility by forming specialty Cores allowing for such diversity."*

"Interesting."

"What?" Thayla asked.

"Oh, just the idea of having spirit affinities and other affinities."

"I thought your Core was damaged, anyway," Heng said, pointing at Victor's iron collar.

"Oh, yeah, but I can dream, can't I?" Victor stuffed the last of his hard roll into his mouth. Their conversation drifted to more mundane topics—what they'd get for dinner, how close everyone was to their quest completion, what they'd do with their free time the next day, and that's when Heng said something interesting.

"I'll probably volunteer at the well." Fenlale shook his head at these words, and Thayla's face got serious.

"What's the well?" Victor looked at Heng.

"It's a deep pit where creeps come crawling out at all hours of the day," Heng replied. The mine uncovered it about fifteen years ago. They sent a few expeditions in, but none of them got to the bottom without having to retreat. Now they just let volunteers kill the things that come up out of it."

"Really? Is it worth it?"

"Ancestors, no!" Thayla said. "Who wants to fight imps and demons and fire hounds on their time off? I've had at least two friends go to 'volunteer at the well' and never return."

"Bah, it's not that bad!" Heng said. "Not to mention, you get credit toward your quests, and the Energy for killing that stuff isn't bad. How you think I made it to Tier Two in here?"

"Well, I'm not going," Thayla said with a snort.

"Who says I invited you?" Heng laughed, and Thayla threw the pit from her fruit at him.

"Do people really get free time that often? Where they can be volunteering to fight at some endless pit of monsters?" Victor didn't think it made that much sense.

"Well, we get time off now and then when Captain Lam makes a big find; it's the same deal for lots of the delver units. Some people in here don't need much sleep, either, thanks to racial advancements. Those people come to the well and slaughter monsters regularly. Guess who keeps getting stronger?" Heng chuckled, obviously thinking of some particular people he knew.

"Can I come along, Heng?" Victor asked, his impulsive thought blurting out of his mouth.

"Sure, Victor." Heng bit off another chunk of his dried meat and then threw the rest of it to Victor. "Better eat something besides fruit and old bread."

When they got back to the barracks that evening, Heng told Victor they'd head out after breakfast. Victor decided to spend some time that evening working on his Core, so he made his way to the cultivation cave. He was a lot more relaxed this time, not worrying about hiding what he was doing; Lam had told him she didn't care what was going on with his Core, and he figured anyone who took too much interest in him was just going to report what they saw to Lam or Fath. That said, he still found a somewhat secluded spot in a far corner of the cave behind a boulder.

"*Gorz, what would happen if my strength was a lot higher than my agility or dexterity? Do I even need dexterity as a fighter? Isn't that, like, fine motor skills?*" Victor was asking because he still had seven points to spend, and he was thinking about putting them into strength; he might not have an axe, but if he were a lot stronger, his bludgeon might have hurt that gray tree thing all the same.

*"With regard to fighting, having a strength that far outweighs your other physical attributes can cause you to have trouble controlling your weapon. Strength provides power and speed to your swing, but agility allows for movement and hand-eye coordination. Dexterity also plays a role in finer adjustments for targeting, blocking, and weapon manipulation. You wouldn't see a real problem unless your strength was two or three times your other attributes, though."*

Victor looked at his attributes:

| Energy Affinity: | 3.1, Rage 9.1, Inspiration 7.4 | Energy: | 578/578 |
|---|---|---|---|
| Strength: | 35 | Vitality: | 62 |
| Dexterity: | 21 | Agility: | 21 |
| Intelligence: | 24 | Will: | 55 |
| Points Available: | 7 | | |

In his opinion, he was getting dangerously close to having an overbalanced strength. He decided that, as long as he was surviving based on his ability to fight, he'd have to add his free points to those physical stats, being careful not to pump one too much higher than the others. That said, he put three of his free points into strength and two each into dexterity and agility.

Looking at his status screen again, Victor was reminded that he still had a lot of work to do with his second affinity; his pool of Energy had recovered a lot since having his Core fractured, but most of that was due to his increased intelligence and will. There were still lots of little Energy pools and fragments floating in the space around his Core. "Time to get to work," he said, beginning his cultivation drill, focusing on gathering up the little remnant fractures of his old Core and pulling them into the white-gold heart of his inspiration Energy.

Victor lost himself so thoroughly in the process, running through his drill again and again, that when he'd gathered up the last of the little fragments and opened his eyes to study his status screen, he realized he'd been at it most of the night. Still, the results spoke for themselves:

| Energy Affinity: | 3.1, Rage 9.1, Inspiration 7.4 | Energy: | 904/904 |
| --- | --- | --- | --- |

He stood up, stretched massively, and hurried back to the barracks. He knew he'd missed lights-out, but he also knew that lots of people had seen him in the cultivation cave. If Sergeant Fath were looking for him, he'd have figured it out pretty quickly. When he crept through the big double doors and slinked into his cot, no one challenged him, and no angry Sergeant Fath stood in the aisle waiting for him.

Victor closed his eyes, knowing he'd only get a couple of hours of sleep but still feeling good about things. Since he'd eaten that fruit from the noble-woman and advanced his race, he had trouble sleeping more than four or five hours, and, in his mind, a little sleep deprivation to fix his Core wasn't a big deal. So, it was with a wry smile and a yawn that he greeted Heng the next morning as the older man shook him awake.

"Ready?"

"Sure; can I grab some food?" Victor sat up on the side of his cot, stretching.

"Yeah, but make it quick; it'll take us an hour to walk there, and I don't want to spend the whole day fighting. I'd like to have time to do some shopping at the Stone."

"Right," Victor said, standing up and going over to the big table where he jostled for a seat and grabbed a plate of scrambled eggs, a hunk of bread smeared with butter, and a big mug full of watery wine—it was the only drink they ever served in the barracks. After wolfing down his food and doing his business in the jacks, he followed Heng outside and toward the big central settlement.

They'd only made it a few dozen steps when rapid footfalls came from behind them, and Victor turned to see Edeya running up. "Wait up!" she called, and Heng stopped to regard her.

"What's up?" Victor asked.

"You guys are going to the well?" Heng nodded in response to her question. "Can I come?"

"I don't own the well," Heng shrugged, "you can come or not—up to you."

"Yeah, I don't care," Victor added. "Is it crowded there, Heng?"

"Nah, and if it is, we'll fight down to one of the platforms, so we don't have to compete for kills."

"There are platforms?" Edeya asked as they started walking again.

"Yeah, the mining company tried quite a few times to make headway down the well, and they set up forward camps—carved 'em right outta the stone."

"Huh," Victor grunted, matching Heng's quick pace. Edeya walked a little behind them, and she was unusually quiet during their walk. Victor thought about trying to draw her out, but, as usual, he was struggling with what to say without putting his foot in his mouth. Finally, he blurted, "Hey, why so quiet today, Edeya?"

"Hmm? Oh, nothing, just thinking about home. I've kind of lost track of the days, but I think it's my sisters' birthday. They're twins."

"Ahh, jeez, that sucks. I bet you wish you were there."

"Ha, you think so?" she asked, and Heng snorted.

"Right." Victor stopped talking; that's what he got for trying to be understanding. He could tell Edeya wanted to talk some more, but he carefully avoided looking at her as they made their way through the big central settlement, this time taking a right through a narrow tunnel in the massive cavern wall. This new tunnel opened up into another huge tunnel, about half as big as the main central one, and they followed that for a while, past more shanties and ramshackle structures. They turned again and again, and soon Victor was wondering if he'd find his way back.

Heng hadn't been lying; after about an hour of travel, they finally came to a stone wall with a massive metal door mounted to it. The door was designed to slide open on two steel beams about as wide as Victor's thigh bolted to the stone. It was open about two feet when they arrived, and a sizeable Ardeni man in a mining consortium uniform was standing by it. "He's there to close the door if the fighters get overwhelmed," Heng explained. The Ardeni nodded to the three of them as they stepped through, and then Victor got his first look at the well.

The first thing he noticed was the high stone ceiling with two giant yellow Energy globes hanging from chains, making the room as bright as noonday. Then he saw the well—a pit in the stone about a hundred yards across with a stone ramp winding around its rim, leading into the depths. The ramp started about twenty paces from where they'd entered and sitting around the top of the ramp were a dozen or so weary-looking delvers. The men and women held their batons in their fists and had eyes only for the pit, completely ignoring the newcomers.

"Pretty good crowd," Heng said, "We might be heading down a bit." He strode forward, and Victor and Edeya followed, their earlier bickering forgotten.

# 31

※※

# GRINDING

When they got to the carved stone ramp that led down around the pit in a spiral, Victor had a sudden surge of vertigo. The ramp was about as wide as a one-lane road back on Earth, but there was no railing, and it had a fairly steep slope. What was worse, he could see out across the pit to the ramp winding down around the ledge, growing smaller and fainter the farther he looked. Hanging in the air, at the center of the "well" about a hundred, or a thousand for all Victor could tell, feet down, mist clouded the air, reflecting the bright yellow lights from above.

Some of the gathered delvers snickered when they saw Victor stumble and hold out his hands for balance when he walked up. He looked around, scowling, but the assembled characters weren't intimidated by his glare. All sorts were there, lounging or standing idly, tapping their batons in their fists. He saw a huge, bulky Ardeni that made even Ponda seem small. He saw a pair of Ghelli women, their wings glittering—not as large or as brilliant as Lam's wings, but they looked a lot more functional than Edeya's. A cluster of four Vodkin brought his mind back to Ponda, yet again, as they laughed at some joke, their big, furry bellies jiggling with the motion. Then there were the usual red-skinned Shadeni and normal-size Ardeni—some were kitted out in armor and looking ready for action, and some looked more like Victor or Edeya, their gear cheap and patchy and their eyes hungry.

"When was the last wave?" Heng asked, glaring around. As far as Vodkin go, Heng wasn't a very big guy, but he had a look that gave people second thoughts about being rude. A tall Shadeni woman who was all legs and long arms walked up and clasped his hand.

"Heng!" she said. "Been too long!"

"Aye, Captain's kept us busy. Anyway, when was the last wave?"

"Not gonna introduce me to your friends?" she asked, ignoring his question again. She turned to Victor and Edeya and said, "I'm Shar. Heng used to be my lover." Heng groaned and slapped a hand to his furry head. Victor snorted out a laugh before he could catch himself, but Edeya stepped forward and held out her hand.

"I'm Edeya! So nice to meet you! This tall guy is Victor." Edeya clapped a hand on Victor's shoulder, and he smiled at Shar.

"Good to meet you."

"Come on, Shar, how long since the last wave?" Heng tried for the third time.

"Oh, you're no fun, Heng! It's been about fifteen minutes; we'd just thrown the bodies over when you all walked up."

"What was it?"

"Stone imps—only about twenty of them."

"Think we're going to head down a bit. This crowd's a little much." Heng started walking toward the ramp, and Victor looked at Edeya before following. Her eyes were wide, and he caught her licking her lips nervously as she began to follow after Heng.

"Heng, don't do that! Some of us don't want to go deeper; you know what happened to Trennet!" Shar called after Heng.

"Who's Trennet?" Victor asked Shar.

"A friend of ours who went to the second platform. Never heard from him again. Heng's stubborn, though, and he won't want to share with this many. Ahh, well, guess we can loaf about until he gets bored." Victor looked at the other delvers and saw that a handful were standing up and starting to follow after Heng. Still, the vast majority were grumbling and looking toward the door, apparently unwilling to go deeper for action but not wanting to hang around waiting for Heng and his group to come back up.

"So, people that don't want to go deeper will just sit here and twiddle their thumbs?" he asked.

"Ha, funny guy, aren't you? 'Twiddle our thumbs?' I like it!" She reached forward and gave Victor's shoulder a squeeze. "You are a big one, aren't you?"

"Um, yeah. I better go catch up to Heng." Victor awkwardly pulled away and hurried after the smaller group of delvers moving down the ramp. He could hear Shar's laughter following after him, and his ears started to burn. Why was he running away? What was wrong with a friendly woman? He shook his head, cursing his awkwardness.

"She a little too forward for you?" Edeya asked, and Victor realized she'd been watching the exchange.

"Aw, c'mon. I know when to steer clear of drama, and she seemed like more than I could handle." Victor shrugged.

"Mmhmm." Edeya was walking backward, talking to him, and looked as if she would steer herself right off the curving ramp.

"Watch where you're going, *chica*!" Victor snapped, wincing at the image of her tumbling into the bottomless well. She turned and scooted farther from the ledge.

"Glad to know you care," she laughed. "I'm not an idiot, though; I wasn't going to walk off!"

"Ugh, this fucking well is giving me the creeps. No one has ever been to the bottom?"

"Yeah, from what I hear. If anyone's seen the bottom, they never made it back out again."

"What about Lam? She ever try?" Victor couldn't imagine Captain Lam struggling to kill anything that might be down there.

"No idea! I've been in her unit as long as you have!"

"Right." They'd caught up with Heng and the other five delvers who'd followed him, but they were still walking along the ramp. Victor couldn't see any sort of platform yet. "How far is the first platform?"

"Few more turns," Heng said, spitting a gob of black saliva out toward the well.

"What you chewing, man?" Victor asked. Heng dug around in his belt and produced a square brass tin. He held it out to Victor.

"Yiil weed. Want some?" Victor took the tin and lifted off the top, taking a sniff of the black, moist powder within. It smelled bitter and pungent, but it made Victor's mouth salivate, so he took a pinch of it and stuffed it into his lip as he'd seen ballplayers do with chew. It burned a little, but it was spicy with a sweet aftertaste, and it gave him a little buzz almost immediately.

"Disgusting," Edeya said, and Victor laughed, trying to pass her the tin. She huffed and increased her pace, walking quickly past Heng. Victor spat some brown-black saliva toward the edge and passed Heng his tin.

"Thanks," he said. Heng nodded and tucked it into his belt. They'd made a couple of steep rotations of the well, and the air was cooler, and the light from the enormous globes up above was less bright.

"What's the deepest you've been, Heng?"

"When I was newer here, I followed some real heavy hitters down to the third platform. We held that position for a long time, and I got a lot of Energy by just throwing a few shots here and there. Haven't been past the first platform since, though."

"Incoming!" A stout, black-haired, hooved Cadwalli guy shouted, pointing to the far side of the well with his baton. Coming up around the steep, spiraling ramp was a throng of large, lumbering creatures that looked like a cross between a two-legged bear and a beetle.

"What the fuck?" Victor exclaimed, tightening his grip on his baton.

"Oh, this ain't lucky," Heng said softly. Then he yelled, "Form up a line—backs to the wall; they'll throw you off. Don't try to run! They're twice as fast as you!"

"What the fuck are they?" Victor asked, finally voicing his question coherently.

"Deep hulks," Heng grunted, following his own advice and putting his back to the wall. Edeya squeezed in next to him as the others jostled for a spot. The hulks were in view on the ramp now, coming up around the bend; there had to be ten or more, and they were huge, maybe seven or eight feet tall, with broad, heaving bodies and long arms that dragged on the floor as they lurched along.

"If you get thrown over, try to slide down the wall! You'll land on the ramp below," a big, bald-headed Ardeni yelled. Victor looked down at Edeya; her entire thin little frame was about the size of one of those thing's legs.

"You got this, *chica*. Come on, get ready! Get fucking pumped!" Victor yelled, digging deep to make his voice loud and hoarse and slapping his baton into his hand. The hulks heaved closer, their grunting, coughing breaths audible now, and the red gleam of their beady eyes apparent. Victor struggled to categorize them; they had hairy legs and arms, but their chests were gray-spotted brown carapaces. Their long arms ended in three digits, each sporting a black claw wedged like a carpenter's chisel.

When they were just a few paces away, Victor shouted, "Come on! Kill these fuckers!" and activated his Inspiring Presence. Shouts of enthusiasm echoed his words to his left and right, and suddenly everything seemed possible. Sure, they were big, but they were slow, and look how predictably they swung those hooked claws. Victor stepped under a swipe and brought his baton down in an overhead smash, directly into the face of one of the hulks. His baton, far heavier than it felt, thanks to its enchantments, cracked something vital in the hulk's face, and it fell away, scrabbling at its head and roaring in pain.

"Yeah!" Victor howled and laid into the hulk that was pressing toward Edeya. She was gamely holding out her baton, ready to try to deflect the hulk's swipes, but Victor had its flank and, fully inspired, used Channel Spirit to drive rage-attuned Energy into his arms and his baton and laid into the hulk with a combination of three deadly, red-tinged blows. His bludgeon shattered carapace and bone with each hit, and the hulk stumbled back into Heng's devastating overhead smash, which opened a two-inch split in the creature's skull. It fell like a four-hundred-pound sack of dog food.

Victor whirled around, high on victory, only to see that five hulks had wholly overwhelmed the three delvers that had been to his left and, chisel-claws dripping with gore, swarmed toward him. "Stay back from me!" Victor took a moment to shout at Edeya, then he activated Berserk and dove into the pack of monsters. Somewhere in the tiniest part of the back of his mind, Victor worried that he was biting off a lot more than he could chew, but he was still inspired, still high from the exhilaration of combat, and he couldn't spare any room for doubt. He squashed down that little voice and roared as his vision darkened with blood-red rage, and his body cried out for violence.

One of the hulks immediately smashed a massive claw into his left shoulder, sending him flying five feet through the air to crash into the wall of the well. Victor maniacally laughed as he stood up, the flesh where the claw had gouged knitting together. He'd smashed his forehead into the wall, but the contusion was mending before he could even register the pain. Victor didn't wait to take stock of his body's state, launching himself at the nearest hulk, sliding under its hacking swipe and coming up on its flank. He drummed his baton into it with mad abandon, trying to crack every hard surface he could see, sending flakes of chitin flying and causing the bulky brute to stumble into the hulk next to it.

He was vaguely aware that other things were happening around him—he saw sparks and heard concussions. Wails of pain and roars echoed off the walls of the well, but Victor had eyes only for the hulk in front of him. His rage had fully supplanted his inspiration, and his moves became reckless but horribly violent. When a hulk fell before him, he didn't stop pounding it until another hulk charged him and bore him to the ground, both of them sprawling away from the wall and near the edge of the well.

Victor had absolutely no concern for his precarious position; his mind had one thought—kill the thing that had interrupted his smashing. The hulk had tackled him, its long arms around his waist and its bulletlike head pressing into his stomach. The monster was heavy, but Victor didn't care; if this fucking thing wanted to wrestle, he was game! He jammed his right forearm under the hulk's scrabbling left limb, pushing his hand through to grasp the thing's smooth, hard head, then he leveraged himself up to wrap his legs around the monster's torso. He bent and twisted with all his might, fighting with rage-fueled strength against the bulky creature's natural muscles.

They rolled and tumbled, and Victor roared in triumph as he finally got the creature's back and hooked his arm around its throat, pulling with an arched back. The monster flailed its long arms in panic, and Victor's mad laughter accompanied its frenzied thrashing, and then Victor was weightless, and he and his wrestling partner were falling through the air, skipping against the stony face of the well. They fell for three or four heartbeats, then they smashed into the hard stone of the ramp, much farther down in the well.

Luck was with Victor; in their tumbling descent, he'd wound up on top before the crash, and the hulk broke his fall. Still, the concussion of the sudden stop sent him sprawling away from the monster, and he blacked out for a moment. When the veil of darkness lifted from his vision, and he saw the hulk grunting and limply flailing with one working limb, he stood up, annoyed to find that his enraged self had let go of his baton when he'd decided to get into a wrestling match.

He stalked over to the thrashing hulk and delivered several brutal stomps to its round, half-chitin, half-flesh skull. He stomped until the chitin was broken, and fluid began to ooze from the monster's orifices. When it stopped twitching, Victor looked around, out of breath and sore all over. He couldn't see anything moving nearby, but he could hear sounds of struggle up above when he listened carefully.

Victor turned to the upward slope of the ramp and started running. It took him a minute or two of hard climbing to round the curve of the well and start up the slope to the original scene of the battle. He saw slumped, twitching forms, both hulk and delver, on the ground, and he saw one hulk, still standing and swinging its hooked claws at Heng's big, furry form. Heng looked exhausted, laboriously swinging his baton to block the hulk's clumsy swipes. The monster was clearly injured as well, with dark spots of oozing fluid all over its carapace and head.

Victor pumped his legs harder, using Sovereign Will to improve his strength and Channel Spirit to flood the pathways in his legs and torso with rage-attuned Energy. Then he smashed into the side of the hulk like a linebacker catching a quarterback by surprise. Something in the monster's torso cracked, and it flew several yards through the air to land on its stiff back and slide over the edge into the well. In the silence that followed the end of combat, Victor heard the monster smash into the stone below with a resounding crack that echoed off the sides of the well.

"Thanks," Heng said, panting and resting his hands on his knees. Victor didn't hear him, though; his heartbeat was in his ears as he surveyed the battlefield. His eyes slipped over the forms of dead hulks, over the writhing and still bodies of the delvers he didn't know, looking for Edeya. Finally, he saw her slight frame half-buried by the bulk of a fallen hulk, and he hurried over to her.

Adrenaline and panic fueled his muscles, and he didn't need any spells to help him grab the hulk and yank it off of her. He was leaning to feel if her heart was beating when a surge of Energy poleaxed him and knocked him to his knees.

***Congratulations! You've achieved Level 17 Spirit Champion. You have gained 7 will, 7 vitality, and have 7 attribute points to allocate.***

When he regained control of himself, he was relieved to see that Edeya was flushed from her own influx of Energy, and her eyes were blinking rapidly as she came back to herself. "Damn! You had me worried, missy!"

"Oh, Ancestors! Imagine waking up to this sight!" she giggled, and Victor stood up, tsking.

"That's the thanks I get? I shoulda left you buried under that thing!" He snorted but held his hand down for her. "Can you move?"

"I think so," she said, wincing and reaching to take his hand. Victor pulled her to her feet, her small hand warm in his.

"I'm glad you didn't die," he said.

"Same; I saw you fall off the edge."

"Yeah, but I had a big squishy cushion."

"Hey, you two, help me get these others up; we need to cut our trip short. Bad luck running into hulks first off," Heng said gruffly, trying to help the big Ardeni to his feet. The man's left leg was twisted in the wrong direction, and he groaned in misery.

"What about the dead guys?" Victor asked, looking at a couple of mangled delver corpses. He stepped past them to the stout Cadwalli; he was leaning against the wall, nursing a stump where his left hand used to be.

"Leave 'em; we gotta get out before another wave comes," Heng replied.

"You good? Can you walk?" Victor reached down to pull the guy up under his arms.

"Ugh, yeah, but I'm screwed for delver duty; they'll put me in the mining crews now that I'm missing my main hand."

"Sorry, bro." Victor patted his hairy shoulders. Edeya was helping the only other survivor, another Vodkin who'd been clubbed unconscious by one of the rampaging hulks. He was dazed but able to walk, and the little group started struggling up the ramp. Before he started after them, Victor looked around for his baton. He saw it over by the edge of the drop where he'd been wrestling with the hulk.

When he scooped it up, he looked around the fallen corpses again and had a brief macabre thought of checking the dead delvers for anything valuable. He wrestled with the idea for a moment but ended up leaving. He had to admit that part of his reluctance was that he worried about what the others would think if they saw him doing it. He was also strangely reluctant to touch their corpses. "Pretty weird considering all the corpses I've made," he muttered.

Despite his resolve, he did look very closely at the one body between him and the others while he walked by. The smaller Ardeni male had died from having his skull caved in. He wore thin leather armor and had a plain, standard-issue baton lying next to his corpse. Victor didn't see anything of note on the body, so he felt better about his decision as he hurried to catch up to the others.

Victor, for all his bumps and bruises, was feeling pretty good. Whenever he got a big influx of Energy like that, he seemed to heal up a lot more than some of the other delvers. He was tempted to ask about it, but then he decided such a question might raise more questions from them about him, so he asked Gorz instead. *"Gorz, why do I heal more than some of these guys from the Energy I absorb after a fight?"*

*"Victor! I tried to talk to you while you were fighting, but I don't think you heard me!"*

*"Sorry, yeah, my mind was occupied."*

*"You most likely have a higher Energy affinity than those others you speak of. Energy affinity has many secondary effects, the main one being how much your*

*body can use Energy to improve and heal. Someone with high affinity will gain levels faster than someone with low affinity, and as you noted, a body with high affinity will apply that Energy toward repairing tissue more readily."*

"*Thanks, Gorz.*" Victor thought about that and realized he probably had a pretty huge advantage over people with lower affinity. He gained a level almost every time he fought, though he doubted that would continue forever. Right now, though, he knew he was as strong as just about anyone in Lam's unit, and he'd only been in this world a month or so. Sure, he'd been fighting almost nonstop, but the fact remained—his upper limit had to be a lot higher than someone with a low Energy affinity. "*Gorz, what's the highest level person you've known of?*"

"*Reevus-dak was Level Forty-seven. He spoke of his master, alluding to him being of the Sixth Tier and the strongest mage on his continent.*"

"*Was that on this world?*"

"*No, Reevus came here through a portal.*"

Victor was about to ask another question when he realized they were on the last stretch to the top of the ramp, and some of the loafing delvers were running down to help the wounded out. Shar was among them, and she stopped by Heng and scooped an arm under the Ardeni's other arm to help him walk. "That was a quick trip, Heng!"

"Aye, hulks first off."

"Ouch, bad luck. At least you survived." Heng just grunted in reply, and Victor wondered at their strange relationship. She seemed to genuinely like him, but Heng was as reticent with her as he was with anyone. Maybe she liked it?

Once they'd gotten through the massive metal door and dropped off the survivors, Heng turned to Victor and Edeya and said, "I'm going to visit some old friends since we've finished early. Sorry, I'm not in the mood to head back into the well."

"I've had enough for today," Edeya said. "I think next time I'm going to stay up near the top; I'm not meant to be fighting things like hulks."

"Smart." Heng nodded and turned to walk away.

"Later, then," Victor called after him. He looked at Edeya and shrugged, "What now?"

"You aren't even tired, are you?"

"Nah, not really."

"You should go fight at the top of the well for a while; the stronger you get, the safer the rest of us will be down in the deep delves."

"You sure you don't want to hang out? I'll do most of the work, and if hulks come, you can run for the door." Victor chuckled at the image.

"No, thanks, Victor. I don't have your stamina or Energy affinity, I think. I'm feeling really weak, and my head hurts from when I got knocked out."

"You okay to walk back?"

"Yeah, it's nothing. I'll stop for some food at the Settlement Stone."

"All right, then." Victor held out his fist, and Edeya gently knocked his knuckles. "That's the spirit. Chin up, *chica*; you fought like a boss!" That got a smile out of her, and she briefly waved as she turned to walk away. Victor turned back to the big metal door and walked back into the well.

As he walked over to the dozen or so other delvers waiting for action, he called up his attributes:

| Strength: | 38 | Vitality: | 69 |
|---|---|---|---|
| Dexterity: | 23 | Agility: | 23 |
| Intelligence: | 24 | Will: | 62 |
| Points Available: | 7 | | |

He hadn't gained any new insights since his last level, so he decided to do the same thing as before, three into strength, two into dexterity, and two into agility.

"Back for more, handsome?" Shar strolled over from a trio of Ghelli she'd been talking to.

"Uh, yeah, figured I'd try to get some more fighting in. Grind out another level or two."

"Ambitious! Not going down again, are you?"

"Nah, I'm cool hanging up here."

"Cool? What a strange dialect you have. Might I ask about your heritage? Let me see, part Ghelli, part Shadeni?"

"Huh? No, I'm a human. I'm not from this world."

"Ahh, that explains the lack of wings. Most part-Ghelli have at least some wings."

"Yeah . . ."

"Incoming!" a short, very stout Cadwalli hollered from the top of the ramp. "More Herd-damned stone imps!" Victor's face spread into a grin; he enjoyed cracking stone imps with his baton.

"Come on, Shar! I bet I can get more kills than you!" Victor charged toward the top of the ramp, his baton at the ready and his Inspiring Presence primed.

# 32

❧

# JUSTICE REDUX

Victor shattered yet another stone imp skull, sending the rest of the creature's crumbling gray body tumbling down the ramp with a kick of his
heavy boot. "Seventeen!" he howled, looking to the side to see if Shar or any
of the other delvers defending the ramp had heard him, though he didn't
know if they even cared; maybe he was the only one keeping track, but he
didn't mind. His spirits were high, and he was having real, genuine fun for the
first time in a long while.

The imps were just alien enough that he felt no qualms whatsoever bashing them apart. Their emotionless faces and grasping stony claws did nothing
but creep him out; no empathy for these things could be mustered in Victor's
heart, and so he was free to revel in their destruction.

The pack of imps had been dense, stretching down the ramp and around
the curve; there had to have been over a hundred of them, and they pressed
into the abattoir that Victor and the other delvers had set up for them. They
walked and scrabbled over the corpses of their kin, and Victor, surging with
inspiration Energy, led the delvers in their systematic dismantling.

Now, the last stragglers climbed, stumbling on the stony remnants of the
dead imps, to the waiting clubs of the delvers, who mopped them up with
little difficulty. In the end, Victor counted twenty-two kills, and he shook his
baton in the air whooping his triumph. Shar laughed at him, and many of the
other delvers smiled, finding it hard to be grumpy with someone purposefully
acting the fool just to lift their spirits. Victor knew he was being crazy, and

part of him wanted to stop and get serious; why would he want people laughing at him? On the other hand, he didn't give a shit; he was having fun and confident in his capabilities—what did it matter what all these other delvers thought? Let them laugh.

"Nice one, Shar! I saw you shatter that last guy!"

"Oh, handsome and sweet! I'm going to talk to my captain about getting you transferred," she purred, matching Victor's exuberance with her own brand of craziness, and he couldn't help but laugh.

"Better quit flirting with me, Shar! Trying to get Heng to beat me up? How many kills? Come on! Was I the only one keeping track?" Victor looked around, and Shar laughed.

"Oh, fine! I think I had seven or eight," she relented. "Are you happy? Not like you're going to win something!" As she spoke, though, golden motes began to coalesce over the crumbled remains of the stone imps and then stream toward the delvers. Victor's column of Energy was much wider than anyone else's, and as it flooded into him, he grinned, nodding to Shar.

"Yeah, I'd say I won something."

***Congratulations! You've achieved Level 18 Spirit Champion. You have gained 7 will, 7 vitality, and have 7 attribute points to allocate.***

"Hey, Victor, is it?" another delver asked, stepping closer. He was a thickly built Vodkin with sleek black fur and a funny snaggletooth that hung down over the left side of his mouth under his moist-looking black nose.

"Yeah."

"Hey, nice job beating the hell out of those imps. I gotta ask, though— you seem strong; why'd they give you that joke of a collar?"

"Um." Victor reached up to touch his cold iron collar self-consciously. "I'm good at fighting, but my Energy skills are lacking. Way to rub it in, dude." Would that work? Could he play it off?

"Ha, no offense. My Energy skills are worm dung too. At least you have that ability that gave us all some combat zeal. That was great!" He reached out with a big meaty paw to clap Victor on the shoulder, and Victor smiled in relief.

"Hell yeah, bro. Anyone know how long it usually takes between waves?" He looked around at the delvers going through the broken bodies of the imps, tossing pieces out into the well.

"It seems rather random," a thin Ghelli man with terribly notched wings said. "Sometimes a few minutes, sometimes an hour or more."

"All right, thanks." Victor nodded to the Ghelli, then looked at the scavenging delvers. "What you guys looking for?"

"Sometimes they have gems in their bodies," one of them said, kicking through a pile of imp rubble.

"Like this!" another one exclaimed, holding up a glittering red gem half encased in rough gray rock.

"Lucky find!" Shar said in a breathy whisper, impulsively reaching toward the gem. The little Ardeni pulled it back with a grin.

"Ah-ah, you know the rule—finding's binding." He deftly tucked the gem into his vest and moved back into the rubble. Victor shrugged and also started sifting through the imp remains, throwing pieces of rock into the open air of the well as he went. He never found any gems, but it kept him occupied until the next wave of monsters came, this one a heaving, hissing swarm of centipede-like monsters, ranging from the size of his arm to a dozen paces in length.

The bugs were bright yellow with black patterns on their carapaces, and when Victor and the others smashed them with their cudgels, they bled in glowing orange goo that left stinging welts if you got it on your skin. At the end of the battle, Victor was covered in sore, raised red spots, and his clothes and armor were sticky and filthy with the stuff. All save his pants; his wonderful, enchanted pants slowly cleaned themselves, and Victor lamented the loss of his matching shirt.

The bug fight wasn't enough to give him another level, but just as they were mopping up the last of the twitching, hissing creatures, a horde of beetle riders came clicking and howling up the ramp. "Damn, that was fast!" Victor yelled, getting ready for the fight. He hadn't used his Inspiring Presence in the last battle, but looking around, he saw that his fellow delvers were tired, sore, and not quite ready for another round. He stepped ahead of the line to face the other delvers and activated his spell, shouting, "Come on! Are you tired? Who cares? Those scrawny beetle riders aren't any match for a delver, tired or not! Let's beat these little shits back and throw them into the darkness!"

His words might not have been eloquent, but the effect of his aura made up for it. The delvers howled with renewed vigor and determination, and when the beetle riders met their line, they were smashed and pummeled into broken submission. The horde was a lot smaller than the one that Lam's unit had encountered at the amber-ore vein, but the battle still lasted quite a while, and Victor once again started to rack up scratches and bruises and even a few minor stab wounds from beetle rider spears. He wanted to activate his Berserk ability, but he held himself back, afraid that he'd kill a fellow delver or get himself thrown over the edge in his mania.

Still, he used his Channel Spirit ability liberally, especially after the Inspiring Presence wore off, filling his arms and weapon with rage-attuned Energy. So effective was the spell that he was almost guaranteed a kill when he smote a beetle or its rider. His baton tore through carapaces and shattered bones alike, and by the time the horde dwindled to a few stragglers, he was sure he'd killed dozens of the creatures. This time, when the Energy rose from the battlefield and streamed into him, he saw the notification he'd been hoping for:

***Congratulations! You've achieved Level 19 Spirit Champion. You have gained 7 will, 7 vitality, and have 14 attribute points to allocate.***

On top of the level, he could feel his wounds closing up and his aching bruises fading away. "Fuck yeah!" he said, not as quietly as he intended.

"Another good victory," Shar said, her demeanor a lot more serious than Victor was used to. He looked at her and saw that she was covered in gore and sporting quite a few shallow cuts. Her face was drawn, and her eyes looked tired.

"You all right?"

"Oh yes, just tired. I used a lot of Energy in the last two battles—more than I recovered from the victory. I'll be fine after some rest."

"Ahh, yeah," Victor looked around, seeing that many of the delvers were in a similar boat, and quite a few were leaving. He also saw some fresh faces and realized a new group had arrived during the beetle fight. "I need a watch," he said suddenly, realizing he'd lost track of time quite a while ago.

"A watch?"

"Um, a timepiece? Something to keep track of the hour?"

"Of course, I know what a watch is; your statement just caught me off guard. You can buy one at the Contribution Store."

"Good call! I think I'm going to call it a day. Nice meeting you, Shar." He turned and waved at the remaining delvers. "See you guys around. Maybe next time my captain gives us a break."

"Bye, handsome," Shar said with a weary smile. "Tell Heng to come see me, will you?"

"Sure, I'll pass it on." Victor walked to the door, waving as some of the other delvers said goodbye, waved, or thumped him on the back. It felt good hanging out with all these guys and not having any sort of boss around—just fighting for the glory of it against enemies he didn't feel guilty killing.

*"Victor, am I correct in assessing your current level at nineteen?"*

*"Dammit! Gorz, you startled me again!"*

*"I'm sorry, Victor."*

*"Anyway, yeah, I'm nineteen now."*

*"Are you aware that most races receive a class refinement option at Level Twenty?"*

*"Yeah, my friend Yrella told me about it, back when I was just figuring shit out. I don't quite get it, though."*

*"You'll be offered a choice to modify or change your class based on your actions and growth since your last selection."*

*"Right, but if I don't like the options, will I get to keep my current class?"*

*"Yes, usually."*

*"All right, well, is there anything I can do to prepare?"*

*"If you were wealthy and had means and access, you could eat natural treasures to improve your attributes and race, and even gain enhancements to your refinement choices. I don't believe those are options for you, Victor."*

*"No shit. All right, Gorz, I'm lost. Can you please guide me back to the Settlement Stone?"*

*"Of course, Victor."*

Victor followed Gorz's instructions and returned to the Settlement Stone cavern without incident. He was disappointed to see he still needed to kill another forty-three "denizens" of the deeps to complete his quest. Still, he had enough credits to purchase a watch. When it coalesced in his hand out of a cloud of yellow and blue smoke, he was pleased to see that it was an old-fashioned, metal-cased pocket watch. When he opened it, though, the little watch hands were floating freely over a shiny brass backplate, seemingly suspended and moved by magic. "Energy," he corrected himself.

He saw the street vendor selling meat skewers again, and he groaned in frustration. *"Gorz! I still need to learn how to make those Energy bead things."*

*"Yes, Victor. Perhaps this evening, unless you get yourself busy again."*

*"Yeah."*

When Victor returned to the barracks, it was nearly time for the evening meal, and he saw Heng sitting at the table next to Fenlale. He was gesturing widely with his hands and laughing, and Victor wondered if he was recounting the tale of their battle with the hulks. He looked around for Edeya but didn't see her. He started to walk over to the table, but he felt a hand grip his elbow. He turned around to see Thayla standing behind him, her face even more severe than usual. "Where's the little one? Edeya?"

"I don't know. I stayed at the well fighting for a few hours; she came back a long time ago."

"I had promised her some training, but she never sought me out," Thayla said, her frown deepening.

"Did you check around back? Talk to her boyfriend?"

"Boyfriend?"

"Yeah, um, a guy she hangs out with. What was his name? B something."

*"Beal, Victor,"* Gorz supplied.

"Um, Beal."

"Beal . . ." Thayla's expression clouded more, and she stalked toward the table, and Victor saw her target—a thin, young Ardeni man with curly, bright-green hair. Victor hadn't ever spoken to the guy, but he'd seen him around. He hadn't gotten a good look at him when he'd run into them making out behind the building, so he'd never put the name to the face. He watched as Thayla leaned over him, her long black braids falling down the sides of her head and obscuring Victor's view.

A moment later, Thayla stood and stalked back toward Victor. "He hasn't seen her all day. What did she tell you when she left?"

"She said she was tired, her head ached, and she wanted to come back to the barracks." Victor's mind started to race—first with worry and then with guilt; he'd let her walk back, feeling sick, through dark tunnels, past tons of unsavory assholes, while he fucking had a good time hanging around bashing on monsters all day. "Fuck!" He smashed his fist into his hand.

"You should know by now about walking around the mine alone!" Thayla growled.

"Yeah, buddy system," Victor said lamely.

"Ugh! I blame Heng, too. Ancestors! Lam isn't going to let us go looking for her this late."

"Is Lam back?"

"Yes, she returned an hour or so ago."

"Let me talk to her. She owes us a reward."

"True . . ." Thayla turned and stalked toward Lam's private door, and Victor hurried after her. Heng laughed and waved when Victor walked by, but Victor hardly registered it. Victor couldn't stop thinking about Edeya and imagining her lying in some dark tunnel, broken. He felt heat rising in his face, and, for the first time in a while, he felt his grip on his emotions starting to slip. He only managed to get himself under control enough to keep from yanking Lam's door open when he realized he wasn't picturing Edeya—he was picturing Yrella's broken, twitching form. The image burned into his mind when he'd seen her die kept coming to the surface, and he realized he was losing it.

Victor gripped his hands into white-knuckled fists and forced himself to stop walking and breathe. When he had calmed a little, he strode purposefully to Lam's door, where Thayla was already waiting for a response to her knock. After a few heartbeats, Lam's voice called, "Come." Thayla opened the door and walked through, Victor close behind.

"Hello, you two. Here for your reward?" Captain Lam's smile faltered when she saw Victor's face. "What is it?" She was sitting at her little table, a thick ledger book open before her, which she closed with a solid *thwap*.

"Something's happened to Edeya," Victor blurted. Thayla looked over her shoulder at him with a frown, but she turned back to Lam and elaborated.

"You know, the little Ghelli girl? She went to the well with Victor and Heng and left hours ago, but she never made it back."

"And? She has an hour or so before lights-out. Maybe she went somewhere else?"

"No, something's wrong," Victor said through clenched teeth. "She was sore, had a headache. She told me she was coming back to the barracks hours ago. I fucking let her walk back alone." Lam's face clouded a bit as her white-blonde eyebrows narrowed.

"I don't like the idea that some unsavory sort has taken or harmed one of my delvers, but there's little chance we can find her. I wish you hadn't let her go alone, Victor." Victor groaned as his guilt surged again.

"I know! I'm an idiot! Captain, let me go look for her, please! I have a way to track her."

"Oh?" Both Thayla and the captain looked at him with renewed interest. Captain Lam raised an eyebrow, waiting for further explanation, and Victor stammered for a second, trying to explain without getting himself in trouble.

"I, well, it's my Core. I can sense certain types of Energy, and I think I can tell if I get near Edeya. I'll hunt around for a sign of her."

"An interesting talent," Captain Lam said. "Wouldn't that make it possible for you to find those that nearly killed you?"

"Maybe." Victor decided to keep his lying to a minimum. "I know Edeya a lot better, though."

"I'll allow it. Thayla, go with him. If it's another delver group and their captain is present, I want you to channel some Energy into this stone." Lam produced a small black stone and handed it to Thayla. "I'll deal with their captain. If not, if some filthy dreck have taken her, taken one of *my* delvers, I want you two to make an example of them."

"Thank you, Captain," Victor turned to leave, pulling the door open.

"Victor, don't let the mine personnel see you if it comes to a fight. I'd hate for them to activate your collars." Victor paused at her words, but Thayla pressed a hand against his shoulder blade, pushing him forward, and he resumed walking, his heart full of urgency and determination and his mind full of guilt and worry.

Thayla didn't say anything as they hurried down the main tunnel, jogging toward the central Settlement Stone. Victor's mind was running away from him, images of terrible things happening to Edeya flashing through it, followed by darker, vengeful, violent fantasies. He shook his head and tried to get focused. *"Gorz, please keep an eye out for Edeya's Energy signature."*

*"Of course, Victor. I'm already doing it."*

*"Thanks."*

*"Victor, I might suggest spending your remaining attribute points."*

*"Right."* Victor was too preoccupied to vacillate about his choices, so he simply followed his latest pattern: six into strength, four into dexterity and agility.

"You can really find her?" Thayla asked as they started to pass by some of the outlying shanties and closed on the main settlement cavern.

"Yes, I'm going to be running around, seemingly at random, but I'm just trying to get a feel for her. Stay with me." With that, Victor picked up the pace and started running. He passed by a lot of people, but most ignored him—people were often late for one thing or another in the mine, and supervisors were rarely forgiving of tardiness. Seeing a couple of delvers running pell-mell through the mine wasn't all that unusual. Soon, they were in the Settlement Stone section of the massive tunnel, cutting through alleys, jumping over piled scrap wood, and skirting around crowds of miners and delvers.

Victor realized he was heading to the building where he'd located his assailants. He had no reason to believe they were the ones who had done something to Edeya, but he knew they were creeps, so why not check? *"I'm sorry, Victor. I see the signature of one of your enemies within the building, but no sign of Edeya."*

"Dammit," Victor spat, running past the building and continuing his meandering circuit of the cavern. He was working his way around the outer perimeter of structures toward the tunnel that led to the well. He cut in and out of alleys, got cussed at by quite a few filthy miners that he pushed through to get past their smoky, stinking cookfires, and finally finished his first circuit around the settlement space.

"Nothing?" Thayla asked as he paused to get his bearings.

"No, fuck!"

"Relax. You can't do any good if you lose it. Get it together; plenty of time for guilt later."

"All right." Victor took a deep breath, trying to calm down. She was right; there had to be a smarter way to handle this. "Where do creeps go in this place? I mean, unless Edeya is dead, they took her for a reason, right? Where do fucking assholes go to, you know, take advantage of people?"

"I don't know! I don't spend time with that type."

"I have an idea." Victor turned back toward the building with the black star painted on the door, the building where the assholes who'd jumped him hung out. He ran full out, and he knew Thayla was struggling to keep up, but he didn't care. "Gorz," he said aloud. "Tell me if that fucker is still there alone."

*"I will, Victor."*

Victor charged between buildings, ran past several crowds of miners drinking from big, well-used tankards, and finally came around the corner in front of the building. *"Yes, Victor, I sense several Energy signatures within, but only one of the fellows who jumped you."*

"Get ready," he said to Thayla, then he stalked up to the door with the star painted on it, grabbed the handle, and yanked it open. Sweet smoke billowed out, and he had to wave it away to see the interior of the building. He stepped over the threshold, and finally, things resolved in his vision—several wobbly tables with chairs, a group of four men sitting at one of them, smoke wafting into the air from their pipes, piles of glittering marblelike gems on the table, and some dice. Everything was illuminated by low, red-tinged Energy orbs.

"Sorry, game's full," said a one-eyed Cadwalli. Victor scanned the other faces, but he didn't recognize them. Something caught his eye, though: the thin Ardeni man with the smug smile on his face wore a collar that glinted brightly in the red light. It was made of shiny silvery metal and studded with several clear crystals. Here was a serious Energy user, a man that might conjure the very earth against his enemies.

"No worries. I just need to talk to one of you." Victor said, a fake, rather insane-looking smile on his face as he strode toward the table. Thayla stepped along behind him, her hand gripping the baton still in her belt.

"We're rather busy, friend. Wait outside till after the game, will ya?"

"Oh, sure. Yeah, sorry to bug you," Victor said, now only three feet from the table. Suddenly he used Channel Spirit to absolutely flood his pathways with rage-attuned Energy. His body veritably lit up with a red halo, and he exploded over the remaining distance with one stride and had his hand around the throat of the thin Ardeni, lifting him like he was made of straw out of his chair and squeezing him to the point where he could feel the tendons straining not to pop under his grip. "Make one fucking move to cast a spell, and I'll take your head off!"

Chairs screeched on the wooden floor as the other room occupants moved back or stood up, reaching for weapons. "Ah-ah!" Thayla said, waving her baton at the three of them. "We've got no problem with you guys. Let my friend deal with his problem, and we'll be gone in a moment. You don't owe him, do you?"

"Don't kill him! He's losing this hand," the Cadwalli said.

"Depends on him. You ready to talk, asshole?" Victor growled, struggling to contain his fury with all the rage-attuned Energy in his pathways. The Ardeni moved his lips like a fish out of water, and Victor realized he couldn't speak. He reached forward and grabbed the man's wrist with his other hand, squeezing until the bones ground together, then he loosened his grip on his throat. The man sputtered and coughed.

"You've made a mistake," he wheezed.

"Spare me. Now, answer this simple question: Where would someone who kidnapped a pretty young girl take them in this fucking mine?"

"What? I didn't kidnap any girl?"

"Stop! Think about the question I asked you and fucking answer it, or I am going to pull this arm out of the socket. No more warnings." Literal steam was coming out of Victor's mouth with his growled, guttural words, and his vision was growing more and more red by the second.

"Maybe the northwest tunnels, toward the well. Some groups sell sex there."

"Good. I'm in a hurry, but you and I aren't done. I owe you," Victor growled, and, as he turned to leave, he yanked the man's arm with such force that his body flopped forward, and his head smacked onto the wooden table with a resounding crack. "If he owes you for the game, take what you want," he growled to the Cadwalli as he turned and ripped the door off its hinges in his haste to get out of there. He was already running toward the well when he finally managed to push his rage-attuned Energy back into his Core, and he heard Thayla yelling.

"A little warning would have been nice!"

"I told you to get ready!" Victor snapped.

"Don't take it out on me, Victor," Thayla replied. Her voice was grave and heavy, and Victor knew what she was thinking—they were too late. Edeya had been missing all day; what horrors had she already endured? Victor screamed in rage up at the cavern ceiling, and several nearby miners scrabbled to get back from him as he ran past. He ducked into the tunnel leading to the well, and when he came out to the large, open passage, he scanned the wall on the left, looking for further tunnels. It didn't take long to find, especially running as he was, and soon he was blindly charging through a warren of twisting tunnels, passing through small caverns filled with little shanties and tents.

"*Here, Victor!*" Gorz's tinny, metallic voice suddenly shrieked in his mind.

"Where?" Victor scanned the cavern as Thayla ran up behind him. He saw a dozen small wooden buildings and half as many large canvas tents. Grubby, disheveled miners lingered around little cook pots, drinking whatever homemade swill they used to blind them to their misery.

"*Twenty-seven meters ahead of you and slightly to your right.*"

"Get ready; she's here," Victor said, striding toward the big brown canvas tent in the direction Gorz had indicated. Thayla hefted her baton, looking around to ensure no mine employees were present. Victor couldn't remember seeing even one the entire time they'd been searching, so he wasn't particularly worried. There weren't any guards watching the flaps of the big tent, so Victor walked right up, yanked the flap aside, and walked into the tent.

The cavern outside had been very dim, so he had to squint his eyes at first against the bright yellow light in the tent. He'd just started to look around when a haughty voice said, "What are you doing here, delvers? Get back to your units." Victor saw the speaker was wearing a Mining Consortium uniform, which gave him pause, but when he saw the cage behind him, filled with chained, bruised, bleeding people, his rage pulsed hotly in his Core. He took another step forward, studying the faces of the prisoners. When he saw Edeya crumpled in the back of the cage, blood dripping from her nose and one of her wings bent and broken, he turned to glare at the thin, mustached Ardeni with bright yellow hair.

"The fuck is going on here?"

"Nothing for you to worry about. I told you to go back to your units." He pulled a thin metal rod out of his belt. "On second thought, drop your batons." Victor heard a thud as Thayla dropped her baton to the dirty yellow rug. "You too, big man." He waved the thin rod at Victor, raising an eyebrow. When Victor didn't move fast enough, he shrugged and said, "You've seen too much anyway."

Suddenly Victor's collar began to grow warm, then hot, and his mind registered what was happening. This asshole was going to kill him. Without thinking about it, he unleashed his hold on his Core, flooding his body with rage and inspiration-attuned Energy, using Channel Spirit to power his arms and hands. He dropped his baton, his whole body suddenly limned with red and white flickering, pulsing Energy.

"Too late for that," the man snickered, watching as Victor's baton rolled to clatter against Thayla's. Then Victor reached up and grabbed his hot, burning collar, and he pulled with both hands. Metal screeched as he stretched and tore it apart like taffy. He threw the broken, deformed pieces at the feet of the mine employee, then he let his fists do what they'd been aching for.

# 33

---

# INTO THE DEPTHS

Victor! Victor, stop!" Thayla's voice finally cut through his fury, and Victor looked up from the pulverized face of the mine employee he'd been battering. His hands were painted red to his wrists, and spatters of red decorated him, the canvas of the tent, and the faded yellow rug. "We have to get out of here!" Thayla urged, pulling at his shirt.

"Not yet," Victor said, his voice thick with emotion. His neck was raw and burning, and only now that he was coming out of his fury did he notice it. "Let me search this asshole," he finished. He moved to the side, unsure when he'd straddled the man to better beat his face, and as he did so, thick motes of Energy rose from the body, confirming that he was dead, and surged into him. He didn't level, but the influx did wonders for his scorched neck and calmed his mind even more.

"Keep watch," he grunted, glancing to see Thayla regard him askance for a moment, then turn to the tent flap, pulling it aside slightly to peer out. Victor ripped the man's yellow and green uniform shirt open, sending polished wooden buttons scattering over the blood-spattered rug. "No necklace." He wasn't sure why, but he'd imagined the key to the cage hanging on a chain around the kidnapper's neck.

"Get us out of here, please!" One of the cage's occupants had gathered enough wits and confidence to speak up.

"Quiet! I'll help you in a minute," Victor snapped, afraid that more of the prisoners would start to clamor for release, and he didn't know who might be listening from the neighboring tents. The man didn't have a pack or pouches on his belt, so Victor looked at his hands, spotting a silvery band with carved black stone inset along its center. Victor pulled and twisted at the ring, finally getting over a knobby knuckle, then he trickled some Energy into it, just as he had with the storage bag they'd had him use in the delves to collect insect parts.

Suddenly Victor was aware of an enormous space inside the ring, along with quite a few objects therein. He scanned through the items quickly, figuring he could spend more time with them later. He saw a baton, some knives, clothes, a cloak, quite a lot of different kinds of food, a sheaf of folded papers, a notebook, writing utensils, a belt, some boots, several pouches full of Energy beads, a ring with an onyx blackbird inset on a silver face, several sets of manacles and collars, and a ring of keys.

Victor grabbed the key ring out of the space and slipped the storage ring onto his finger. He walked over to the cage and unlocked it, but before he opened it, he looked around at the prisoners, at least the conscious ones, and said, "Ladies, I'm going to let you all go, but please wait until we're all ready to move out. Let's get everyone on their feet."

"You heard him," the woman who'd spoken before said. "Come on, let's help get everyone up. Sir, you should know he had some soldiers with him earlier. He sent them to get someone."

"Let's fucking hurry, then." Victor strode through the crowd of women and knelt before Edeya. Her eyelids were half open, but she didn't seem to recognize him. "Edeya, you there? Come on, *chica*, snap out of it."

"Don't call me girl," she said, limply lifting a fist to prod at his chin. Victor smiled.

"That's the spirit, c'mon. Up you go; everyone's waiting for you." Victor stood and pulled her to her feet. She was shaky, but when she grabbed onto his arm, her grip was tight, and she followed him when he walked out of the cage.

"Nobody coming yet," Thayla said. She'd collected both of their batons, probably while Victor was pounding on the mine employee, and she held Victor's out to him now. "You gotta do something about your collar; it'll raise questions if someone sees you like that." Victor felt up to his bare neck and nodded. He looked down at his stretched and broken collar and picked up one of the elongated halves. He lifted it to his neck and bent it around, so the two ends met in the back, then he gave Thayla a questioning look. "It'll pass at a glance. Let's go."

"All right, everyone, be safe; please don't mention me to anyone," Victor said, glancing back at the crowd of women, some propped up by others, and then he hooked an arm around Edeya's shoulders and ushered her out of the tent, Thayla hot on his heels. *"Gorz, please guide me on the shortest route back to the barracks."* He felt a little bad taking off and leaving those other women to their own devices, but he felt as if he'd just robbed a bank and needed to get the hell out of sight.

*"Of course! Take your next right,"* the amulet's slightly metallic voice replied. Victor walked quickly, trying to keep to the shadows and avoiding the crowds of miners they passed here and there, but no one challenged them or came running behind them. Edeya shuffled along under his arm the whole while, her eyes downcast. Victor had to lift her while they walked to keep her moving fast enough to keep up, but it wasn't hard; she felt smaller than ever.

They were back to the main settlement area and passing through a narrow alley of shanties when Edeya jerked against his arm and looked around with wild eyes. "Get off me!" she cried, pushing against him. Victor let go and held his hands out.

"Easy, Edeya. It's Victor; you okay?" She looked around, her eyes wide and her hands out, ready to fight, but then something clicked, and she looked back at Victor.

"You got me out?"

"Me and Thayla," Victor said, nodding to the tall Shadeni woman. Edeya looked at Thayla, then a sob escaped her lips, and she crumpled against Thayla, who grabbed her in a hug.

"You're all right, Edeya. You're all right," she said softly, stroking her hair, careful not to squeeze her broken wing. "Come on, little bird. We need to get back to the barracks; there'll be people looking for Victor and probably me, too." Edeya took a long shuddering breath, sniffed, and nodded. Then they all started walking again, Edeya holding an arm tightly around Thayla's waist this time.

"You think they'll know it was us?"

"Yeah, I'd say. How many women did we spring from that cage? Nine? Ten? They won't all keep their mouths shut, and then the mining company will send an investigator. They'll do some scrying, and we'll be deep in the roladii shit."

"Of course—magical world means magical investigators." Victor smacked a fist into his palm. "Well, maybe you'll be fine. I'm sure whatever they see with their scrying will be something like me beating the shit outta that guy, not you."

"Depends on how thorough the investigator is, and the mine can afford good ones."

"All right, well, let's just talk to the captain and see what she thinks."

"You sure we should? The captain works for the mine . . ." Thayla let her voice trail off.

"You know the captain; she has her own rules. I don't think she'll fuck us over." Thayla didn't reply, so Victor looked at her, and when their eyes met, she nodded over the top of Edeya's head.

Listening to Gorz's directions, Victor led them through the alleys and out into the main tunnel. After ten minutes of quick walking, avoiding the eyes of the strangers they passed, they were in sight of Lam's barracks. Walking up, they were greeted by the presence of Sergeant Fath, pacing back and forth in front of the building. When he saw them, he strode forward quickly and, in his baritone voice, rumbled, "You found her! Captain wants you to bring her in through her private entrance. Come on." He turned and strode around the side of the barracks, and Victor, glancing at Thayla, who nodded, followed after.

Victor didn't remember any side doors to the barracks, so he was only slightly surprised when, rather than a door, Fath led them to a ladder. He gestured for them all to climb it to the barracks' roof, and Victor did so first, reaching down to help Edeya up after him. Thayla came next, and then Fath came up, pulling the ladder after him. He pointed to a square of light near the rear of the barracks, and Victor walked to it, realizing it was an open trapdoor. "Drop in; she's expecting you." Something about the whole situation was making Victor nervous, but he couldn't see another move; he supposed he could make a run for it, but if Lam wanted him, she could catch him, he had no doubt. He moved to the trapdoor and peered through.

It wasn't Lam's study. The floor was carpeted, and he thought he could see the foot of a fancy four-post bed. "Her bedroom?" he muttered.

"Hurry, drop down," Fath said. Victor glanced at Thayla and Edeya. Their faces were pale in the cavern light, and Edeya wouldn't make eye contact with him. Thayla gave him another quick nod, so he stepped forward and dropped onto the carpet. Sure enough, it was a nicely appointed bedroom. The bed was large with a fluffy, white quilt, and the carpet was rich and clean. The walls were plastered a creamy white and lined with backlit display cases. Victor had just started to examine the contents of one of the display cases, some sort of manuscript pressed between glass, when Lam cleared her throat behind him.

"Victor, move so the others can come down." He whirled to see Lam sitting on a low, padded sofa, watching him from behind a glass of liquor. He stepped toward her, but she held up a hand.

"Your collar."

"Yeah, we ran into some trouble." A thud signaled the arrival of Thayla behind him, then the soft sounds of Edeya being helped down. Then the trapdoor was closed from above, and Victor heard footsteps moving away over the roof.

"Best explain to me, and quickly," Lam said, taking another drink, her face not betraying her mood.

"We . . ." Victor started, but Thayla stepped forward and cut him off.

"It was a mine employee. He had a cage full of abused women, and when Victor and I saw it, he activated his control rod to kill Victor and probably would have killed me, too. Victor ripped his collar off and beat him to death." That got a reaction from Captain Lam; one of her wispy pale eyebrows lifted, and she actually smiled.

"I knew they messed up with that collar!" She stood up and brushed past Victor to grab Edeya by her shoulders, leaned over, bent nearly in half to make eye contact with the girl. "Are you okay? I'll tell you what I told Victor when he got attacked off by himself: I hope you learned something."

"I'm okay," she said softly. "They only had me a little while."

"Tut, look at your wing. Come here." She glanced at Victor and Thayla and said, "Wait here." Then, she led the diminutive Ghelli to the far side of her bed and helped her to lie down. She produced a small vial of glowing amber fluid, and Victor could just barely hear her say, "Drink this down; you'll wake up feeling like a twirler on Starleaf Night." A few moments later, Captain Lam came back from around the bed and sat down in front of Thayla and Victor. "You're likely in a bit of trouble."

"Can you do anything?" Thayla asked bluntly.

"Oh, I imagine I could figure something out. Let's think on it a moment. Back up and tell me the whole story. How you found Edeya, who witnessed your actions, everything."

"All right," Victor said, taking the lead. He didn't want Thayla trying to cover for him or worrying about revealing too much, so he started from the beginning. He told Lam about questioning the guy at the gaming hall, searching the tunnels, and what he did when he found the man in the tent. He didn't leave much out, mostly just his secret conversations with Gorz.

"How'd you know the gambler would be able to lead you to Edeya?"

"Just a hunch; I knew he was a scumbag, so I figured he might know where to find other scumbags."

"Victor, do you want my help?" Lam asked suddenly. He nodded, and she continued, "Stop being evasive. You're holding something back, and I'm not going to stick my neck out for someone who's not honest with me."

"All right. The guy in the gambling hall was one of the assholes that jumped me. I tracked them down a while ago, figuring I'd give them a taste of their own medicine one of these days." He glanced sideways at Thayla and saw that her eyes had widened, but she didn't say anything. Captain Lam's lips spread into a wide smile, though.

"You keep surprising me. All right, next question: what did you do with the body?"

"Um," Victor started, then shrugged.

"We left it," Thayla finished.

"Oh, Great Forest!" Lam sighed. "Was he alone? Are you sure?"

"Actually, one of the women said he had sent his guards or soldiers to get someone."

"Soldiers? He had soldiers? Did you catch his name by chance?"

"No, but he was a smug one; he seemed full of himself," Thayla added. Lam studied Thayla and then Victor for a moment while she thought. Her eyes fell to his twisted, broken collar, then down, over his body to his hands.

"You took that ring from him?"

"Uh, yeah," Victor said, shrugging.

"What's in it? Anything to identify him?" Understanding dawned on Victor like fireworks going off, and he turned his mind toward the space in the ring, producing the sheaf of papers and the blackbird signet ring. He put them onto the low table in front of Lam's couch. "All right, let's see here." She bent to pick up the ring and turned it over in her hand, a frown deepening the curves of her mouth. She set it down without a word, though, and picked up the papers, removing the cord binding them all together and opening the top one.

Victor began to grow nervous the longer Lam read through the papers without saying a word. He wanted to ask her what they were about, but he knew she'd say something when she finished, so he just stood there, fidgeting and wishing he could stand stoically without saying a word or even looking nervous like Thayla. Finally, after reading through more than half of the papers, Lam looked up and said, "My options for helping you are slimmer than I thought."

"What does that mean?" Thayla asked plainly.

"The Greatbone Mining Consortium is run by a group of families—merchant families grown so wealthy over the decades that they might as well be nobility. In fact, they own many of the nobles in the Ridonne Empire. Well, the man you killed was a member of the ap'Yensha clan, one of those families. He wasn't skimming; he was here to collect prospects for service in a new venture they were starting in Gelica."

The dots started to connect in Victor's mind, and he said, "So if he'd been some random employee stealing girls to make money on the side, you could have gotten us out of this mess, but seeing as he was a member of some powerful family and he was here on business they condoned, we're fucked?"

"I can help you slip free of the mine, but I can't protect you beyond that. I'm strong and wealthy, but nothing compared to those families. They can afford to hunt you to the ends of the world."

"Would they? Just to avenge that one asshole?" Victor asked.

"I don't know. Maybe? If he was well-liked, then yes, they will hunt you. If you'd made him disappear with no witnesses, it would take them a lot longer to figure out what happened to him. As it is, there's a good chance his soldiers are already combing the area for witnesses, and a scryer is en route. Also, there's one more nuance: according to these papers, another of the families, the ap'Bale clan, wasn't on board, and this fellow was taking these women under their noses. I'm not sure if that would help you or cause more problems, but I can assure you the ap'Yensha don't want others finding out about this, so they're motivated by more than just revenge."

"What if we disappeared into the depths?" Victor asked suddenly.

"You mean killed ourselves?" Thayla scoffed.

"No." Victor licked his lips, nervous all of a sudden, but continued, "I've heard there's a dungeon that leads out of the mine. If we can find the entrance, we could escape that way. They'd probably assume we were dead if they scry us down there, right?"

This time it was Captain Lam who scoffed. "You think you can find a dungeon down there? You know how long I've been digging around for treasure and hidden things in those depths? If you have something more to tell me, I'm listening."

"I saw a map. I saw a map in the home of the asshole that tried to destroy my Core. He caught me studying it, and that's why he did it—fractured my

Core and sold me to the mine. I didn't even really know what I was looking at at the time, but when I went into the depths with you, I started to recognize the layout of some of the caverns. I think I could find the dungeon, or at least get heading in the right direction. It has to be better than what's in store for us if those families get ahold of us, right?"

*"Clever ploy, Victor. I like this captain of yours, but she may well want to take me from you,"* Gorz piped in, startling Victor enough to make his heart hammer in his chest.

"I won't lie, Victor." Lam looked at Thayla and continued. "And Thayla. I'm not excited about going up against those families, and if you were to disappear into the depths, that would be one less headache for me to deal with. I hate to see you both throw your lives away, though. How good is your memory, Victor? You've continued to surprise me, so I'd love you to prove me wrong about this."

Victor glanced at Thayla, and his heart hammered even harder—he saw hope in her eyes. God, what if he was wrong? "I think it's pretty good, Captain."

"All right." She produced a large sheet of thick, hexed paper and a set of charcoal pencils. "If you can draw the route, and if I recognize any of it as being accurate, I'll help you get started. Start with lift fourteen-A." She took one of the pencils out of the wooden case and held it out to him.

*"Gorz, time to work your magic. You need to describe what I need to draw in very fucking fine detail, please."*

*"Understood, Victor, though it would be much easier if you had my old slate."*

*"But I don't, so please help me here."*

*"All right, Victor. We'll treat each hex as ten feet. For the lift room, draw a box near the top of the page that is eight hexes by eleven. Then draw an arrow down from that room that is exactly twenty-seven point five hexes long."* Gorz continued with his instructions until Victor had covered most of the sheet with winding tunnels and chambers, and when his drawing took him to the edge, Captain Lam handed him another sheet to continue on. By the time he was finished, the map covered three large sheets of her hex paper.

"Victor, do you have some sort of genius for maps? Do you remember everything you see?" Lam quietly asked as he set the pencil down.

"I'm good with maps, but no, I don't remember everything I've seen."

"If you're right, you've got more than ten miles of ground to cover down there; it's going to be dangerous and take you days. What about this long wide tunnel with the little squiggles in it?"

"That's an underground river. I think there's room along its bank to walk, though. If I remember the map correctly," Victor finished lamely. Lam gave him another squinting examination but shook her head slightly.

"I don't think you're suicidal, so I'm going to go ahead and hope for the best. Are you going to try this crazy plan with him, Thayla?"

"Do I have a choice? I'm sure I'll show up in the scries at the scene, and witnesses saw us running around together. Looks like I'm going to have to trust Victor."

"Victor, I'll make a deal with you. I already owe you and Thayla a reward for your ore find, so I'll give you each something before I send you on your way. But if you manage to escape through that dungeon, I'll reward you again for any information you can give me about what you find there. Thayla, if you get to safety, just use that stone I gave you; I'll be able to find you."

"All right, it's a deal," Victor said.

"Let me get you some supplies; I don't want the other delvers to know you came back here, so sit tight." Captain Lam stood up and slipped through the door, closing it behind her.

"We're going to die down there," Thayla said, stretching and cracking her neck.

"Maybe, but it's a chance." Victor shrugged.

"Can we trust the captain?" Thayla asked softly, a whisper that Victor could barely hear. He looked at her and saw the doubt in her narrowed eyes and how she pressed her lips together.

"If she wanted to betray us, she'd just beat us into submission. She's higher than Tier Four, right?" That simple statement seemed to send a wave of relief through Thayla, and she suddenly grinned, shaking her head.

"Good point."

The door opened again a moment later, and Captain Lam came through, quickly closing it behind herself. Her hands were empty, but Victor knew that didn't mean anything when you considered magical storage devices. Lam sat down again, oblivious or uncaring that Victor and Thayla had been standing for their entire meeting. She began to stack items on the table—wrapped sausages, loaves of bread, sacks of fruit, several long lengths of thin, sturdy rope, a package of those self-sinking pitons that Victor had seen her use before, four glow lamps, and two bedrolls. She motioned to the pile of supplies and said, "Split it up in case one of you dies or gets lost."

"Thanks, Captain," Thayla said, starting to deposit some of the items into her hidden ring. Victor followed suit, taking half of the supplies into his new ring.

"I'm not done; you two don't know the fortune I'm going to make off those ingots. I wasn't joking when I said I'll reward you for more information. Here." She was suddenly holding a long, silvery-red metal spear. She handed it to Thayla. "This is artificed to pierce armor. It's self-sharpening and nearly weightless in the hands of its bonded owner." Then she turned to Victor. "You don't strike me as a finesse-type fighter, so I'll give you one of my first truly good weapons. I haven't used her in decades, so I figure I'll give her a chance to see some action. Treat her well, Victor." Suddenly she was holding a black-bladed axe with a polished cherry-colored haft. The blade was bearded and gleamed along the edge like liquid silver.

"Wow," Victor said, eyeing the heavy, wicked axe head.

"This is Lifedrinker, and she has a heartsilver core. Those she strikes suffer as she takes their Energy. Her thirst is great; I've never been able to sate her, but some say that given enough Energy, heartsilver will start to grow conscious." She held out the axe to Victor, and he gingerly took hold of the haft. It was long enough to wield with two hands, but he could easily swing it with one.

"Thank you, Captain. I, I hope I don't lose her down below."

"You passed the first test; never call her an 'it.' Can you promise me that?"

"Yes," Victor said with a gulp, realizing he'd already thought of the axe as a thing in his mind.

"Very well; she wasn't mine when I was given her to use, and now she's mine no longer," Lam said. "Are you ready? Fath tells me the mines are abuzz with the search taking place. I think you should be gone soon."

"What about Edeya?" Victor glanced over at the slumbering form.

"You don't have to worry about her. She reminds me of a friend I had." She glanced around and down at herself, then continued. "Before all of this. I think I'll buy her contract and get her some training. I'm not saying I'm going to coddle her, but she won't have to worry about someone nabbing her, if that's a concern for you."

"That's pretty great," Victor said, but his face fell slightly, and he frowned down at the carpet, avoiding Lam's eyes.

"I'm ready," Thayla said, still holding her new spear.

"Not quite," Lam said, looking at the tall woman. She held out her hand, and Victor saw that she held a control rod like the one all mine employees carried. She held it out toward Thayla, and a moment later, a click sounded, and Thayla removed her collar, now spread open at an invisible seam.

"Ancestors! It feels good to have this thing off."

"I imagine," Lam said, a slight smile twisting her lips.

"Don't you see how wrong it is?" Victor blurted.

"Hmm?" Lam scowled slightly, looking at him.

"Captain Lam, you've been very good to me, but don't you see how wrong this all is? People being forced to fight and die while you dig around in the ruins? Look at Edeya! You seem to care about her, but she could die tomorrow protecting some miners while you dig around for treasures." Victor wanted to kick himself or slap himself or something, but the words just came flooding out.

"Strange way of thanking someone," she said, standing up, clouds behind her eyes.

"I am grateful, truly, but I feel like you're better than this!"

"Victor, you don't know me. You know a few things about me, but you don't know me. I didn't get where I am because I was coddled. I know what I do seems selfish, but that's simply because it is: I work to improve my own power. Some power comes with Energy and levels, some power comes with connections and politics, and some power comes with wealth. I do care about Edeya and others, but I also know they have their own struggles to get through. I might tip the scales in their favor from time to time, but I'm nobody's savior. Not Edeya's, not yours. I'm helping you because it won't cost me much, and it might pay off someday. Don't mistake my aid for something it isn't—I'm fond of you both, but I won't risk what I've gained to carry you out of your challenge. You've got to do that on your own. Now, it's time you both got going. I hope I hear from you someday."

Lam had been pacing the whole time she spoke, and now she stopped under the trapdoor leading to her roof, and she motioned for Thayla and Victor to come over. Thayla got there first, and Lam, having opened the trapdoor, placed her hands on Thayla's hips and boosted her up so that the Shadeni could scramble up onto the roof. Victor stepped up next, still holding Lifedrinker, and he said, "I didn't want to insult you, Captain. Thanks for your help." She nodded, grabbed his hips, and when he hopped up, she boosted him like he was a child, and he found himself on the roof.

"Close the trapdoor, please," Lam called softly from below. Thayla gently lowered the wooden trapdoor, careful not to slam it, and then the two of them padded to the edge of the barracks roof and dropped down.

"You have a death wish?" Thayla asked as they hurried off into the darkness of the tunnel.

"What?"

"That woman could kill us with a thought, and you decided that, after she gave us her help, you were going to lecture her about her morality?"

"My mouth gets away from me. I had to say something, though—I might never see her again, and I want to like her, but I can't get past all the evil in this place that she turns a blind eye to."

"As she said, we don't know her whole story. Let's be grateful for what we got, agreed?"

"Yeah, agreed." Victor hefted Lifedrinker and almost put it into his ring, but then he decided not to. If he was going to think of the axe as alive, then he shouldn't put it into a storage container. "Her," he corrected himself aloud.

"What?"

"Just thinking about this axe. Can you believe these weapons? I feel better about our chances already."

"Yeah, they're nice, all right." Victor saw that she'd already stowed her spear in her ring, which glinted with a golden luster on her hand.

"You moved your ring to your hand," he said.

"Quicker to access things like weapons." She shrugged. "I'm not trying to hide anymore."

"Good point," Victor said, stopping suddenly. He reached up and grabbed the ends of the twisted collar on his neck and pulled them apart, flinging the strip of metal to clatter among the stones of the tunnel. "Let's go. It's all downhill from here!" He laughed at his own wit, and Thayla, though she didn't seem to get his humor, smiled along with him. Sometimes, Victor figured, you just had to laugh in the face of the shit coming your way.

# 34

## REFINEMENT

Thayla held a finger to her lips as she peered around the corner. They were almost to the chamber where Victor had first gone with Lam on her little exploration and where he'd found Gorz. Thayla, crouching ahead of him with her spear leveled, had hissed at him to be quiet and then slunk into the shadows to peer around. Victor wasn't sure what she'd heard, but he'd grown to respect her senses in the short time they'd been sneaking through the dark together.

Twice, she'd warned him ahead of an encounter with giant insects crossing their path, saving them from having to fight an unknown number of the creatures. She'd even spotted a group of stickmen lying in the shallows of an underground pool they had to skirt. To Victor, they'd just looked like deeper shadows, but Thayla had spotted their creepy, shiny eyes blinking in the lights that Lam had left behind.

Victor gripped Lifedrinker tightly in his fists; his hands choked up near the bearded blade in the tight tunnel. Thayla looked back at him, her long braids flicking lightly on her shoulders and her dark eyes glittering in the light of his glow stone. She slowly motioned with her left hand to come up beside her. As he started to move, she gestured at her chest, her hand over her glow stone. Victor copied her, plunging the tunnel into darkness, the only light coming from Lam's hanging orb up ahead.

When he got close to her, he saw the old piton and rope Lam had placed for everyone to climb down. Out past that, he saw the little stream crossing the cavern, the pile of ruins where Lam had killed the rot fiend, and rummaging around the battle site, several large, hunched humanoids. "Are those deep hulks?" he whispered.

"I think so. Five that I can count." Thayla's voice barely made a sound.

"All right, do we try to sneak past? Do we kill them?"

"Hmm. It would be a tough fight."

"Yeah, maybe." Victor couldn't help looking at Lifedrinker; he wanted to fight with her so badly, he could feel it in his bones. Thayla gave him a searching look, then shook her head.

"We should try to sneak around."

"Just a sec; let me think," Victor said. *"Gorz, what exit from this next cavern do we take? Is it feasible to sneak past those hulks?"*

*"Victor, the tunnel you want is halfway up the far wall, slightly to your left. You'll be quite exposed climbing up, if my memory serves."*

"Our exit is that tunnel halfway up the far wall. We're going to need climbing equipment. How can we do that while sneaking? We gotta kill those *pendejos*," Victor said softly in Thayla's ear.

"Ugh, this is going to hurt," she said, but she started creeping forward to the rope and piton. Victor crouched in the shadow, watching the hulks shuffling around, scooping their claws under rocks and hunks of fungi, and depositing whatever they came up with into their maws. Thayla stowed her spear, grabbed the rope, and silently shimmied down it.

When the hulks didn't react or look their way and Victor was sure she was down, he crouch-walked up to the edge, hooked his axe through his belt, lifted the rope, and dropped over the edge. He was halfway down, using his feet to spring away from the cliff face while he let the rope slip slowly through his hands, when a loud grunt, followed by roars and splashing water, told him the hulks had spotted him.

"Hurry!" Thayla hissed, and Victor looked down to see he was only twelve or so feet from the ground, so he let go and landed in a crouch.

"Get ready!" Victor said, yanking Lifedrinker from his belt.

"You tell me to get ready a lot! *You* get ready!" Thayla said, brandishing her red spear, its silvery streaks winking in the bright light of the overhead orb. Victor just laughed, lengthening his grip on his axe, ready to make use of the wide space in the cavern. "Put your back to me if they surround us," Thayla said, and Victor didn't see a reason to argue. The two of them stood, side by side, waiting for the hulks as they crashed through the ruins. "You're ready to try that axe out, huh?"

"Damn right, sis." Victor grinned, preparing to cast Inspiring Presence. He took two long, controlled breaths, and then the first of the hulks was on them. Victor unleashed his spell, and before he could even fully realize the surge of Energy and possibility that flooded him, he was stepping forward and bringing Lifedrinker down in an overhead chop. He'd aimed for the hulk's round, smooth head but missed, splitting its shoulder and tearing a long terrible groove down through its carapace. Lifedrinker carved through its flesh and shell like it was papier-mâché, and Victor crowed at the difference a good weapon made.

Shards of shell and gouts of yellow-green fluid burst from the wound, and Victor felt Lifedrinker buck in his hand as it seemed to pulse with Energy. The hulk squealed through its mandibles and fell back, causing the two on its heels to stumble. Victor lifted his axe for another hack, but Thayla's spear was suddenly sprouting from the eye of the hulk he was aiming at, and it fell away, scrabbling at its face. With a minor adjustment, Victor brought Lifedrinker down in a sideways angled cleave into the next hulk, catching its neck and nearly removing its head. It fell, twitching, to the rubble-strewn floor.

The light was so bright, the angles so clear, and the axe so smooth as he sliced through the air that Victor felt as if he was performing some kind of dance rather than fighting with huge, monstrous creatures. When a long, hooked limb came his way, he backed up a step and brought Lifedrinker down through the jointed wrist, relieving the monster of its appendage.

Thayla was like a machine with her spear, using its length to keep the monsters at bay as she filled them with deep, weeping wounds. It and Lifedrinker had no trouble with their carapaced torsos, slicing and punching through them easily, exposing the hulks' weakness to sharp weapons. When the massive monsters tried to use their bulk to overwhelm them, Victor met their charges with heavy chops, and Thayla let them drive themselves onto her spear.

It helped that the hulks had come at them in a staggered line, never having the chance to surround them fully. The first kills came quickly, then the two of them slowly hacked and stabbed the others into broken submission. Victor never had to use any rage Energy, so he kept his wits the entire time. He noticed Thayla's spear glowing brightly and moving more quickly from time to time, and he made a note to ask her what sort of spell she was using— maybe he could copy it.

After just a few minutes of violence, the hulks were reduced to broken, bleeding mounds, and Victor and Thayla stood over them as the Energy surged out of the gathered motes and into their Cores.

***Congratulations! You've achieved Level 20 Spirit Champion. You have gained 7 will, 7 vitality, and have 7 attribute points to allocate.***

***Level 20 Class refinement is available. Class refinement is permanent. Human Energy cultivators will next be offered a class refinement selection at Level 30. To view your options and make your selection, access the menu through your status page.***

"Oh shit! I hit twenty! Time to upgrade my class!"

"It's not always an upgrade—sometimes it's smart to keep what you've got," Thayla said, trying to wipe the gore off her spear with a scrap of leather.

"Are you Tier Two?"

"Just barely. Been Level Twenty-one for a while now."

"Did your class change?"

"Yeah, I went from a brawler to a skirmisher—it's advanced, so I get better stats than my old class, and I can improve weapon skills more."

"Nice," Victor said, wondering how lucky he'd been to get an advanced class at level ten. "You have some Energy attacks?" he asked as they started walking to the half-collapsed bridge; their exit tunnel was on the far side of the stream.

"Yeah, Flash Strike. It lets me channel my Energy into an attack, so it moves faster than normal. It makes it hard as hell to dodge or parry." Thayla hopped over a gap in the bridge, nimbly scampering to the far side. "It uses a lot of my Energy," she added with a shrug as Victor followed her over. "That inspiration thing you do is amazing, though. I swear I'm twice as good when it's active."

"Yeah, I think it helps you get insight into your skills, too. Let me know if your spear skill advances faster than you think it should while we're together."

"Maybe if we find a secure place to camp, we can do some sparring." She moved toward the cavern wall, passing between some crumbled ruins not far from where Lam had killed the rot fiend.

"You think they'll chase us down here?" Victor asked, gesturing vaguely toward the upper mine.

"Maybe. I'd be surprised, but they might. I figure they'll keep scrying to see if we're down here and maybe send some hunters, but if we can get into the dungeon, they might lose track of us—figure we're dead."

"That'd be good," Victor said. They'd reached the rocky wall leading up to the exit tunnel, and he thought he could see enough handholds to make his way up. "Looks like we might not need ropes or those spikes."

"You first, then," Thayla said, gesturing to the wall.

"I kinda want to look at my refinement options, but we're like sitting ducks in this cavern. I'll do it later," Victor said, jumping up to grab a low ledge and pulling himself up. A few more hops followed by pull-ups, and he was in the tunnel mouth. Thayla was watching from below, and when he turned to wave at her, she grinned.

"Now toss me a rope!"

"Oh, I see how it is," he laughed, calling one of the ropes out of his ring and unraveling it down the rocky cavern wall. He held it tightly while Thayla pulled herself up, walking her feet up the wall. He grabbed her by the wrist when she came close and pulled her up beside him.

*"This tunnel meanders for about half a kilometer, Victor. Just stay with it and don't take either of the side passages you'll see,"* Gorz said as Victor turned to regard the low-ceilinged, narrow tunnel they were in.

"Looks like we follow this one for a while. My neck and back are going to be killing me." He stood up and thumped a fist on the ceiling, his back partially stooped.

"Yeah, tight quarters. You want me to go first?"

"I don't care. Nah, I'll go first." Victor had pulled the rope up and stowed it. Already getting used to the convenience of the storage ring, Victor had stored his backpack and its contents within. It was just too easy to think about what he wanted and have it appear in his hand; he knew if he weren't so busy, he'd probably have been messing around with it like a kid with a new game. Taking a deep breath and steeling himself, he walked into the tunnel, his light stone illuminating the darkness for about ten strides. He held his axe, grip choked up close, out in front of him as he stalked, stooped over down the dusty, rubble-strewn passage.

They ran into a trio of giant rats about halfway down the tunnel near a branching side passage, and Victor, using Channel Spirit, hacked the head off one of them as it charged, Thayla, from just behind him, drove her spear in the throat of the second one, and the third turned and ran. "Smart little stinker," Victor said, watching it scurrying away, dust clouding its passage.

"Let's get out of this tunnel! Keep moving," Thayla said, giving him a nudge. Victor grunted acknowledgment and kept moving through the low-ceilinged, narrow, windy passage. According to Gorz, he was almost to the exit when they came to a very tight portion, and Victor stopped, looking at Thayla.

"I'm going to have to slither through on my belly to get through that." The idea of sliding through a narrow passage with a million tons of rock and earth above him was starting to freak him out.

"Yeah, I hope you can fit," Thayla deadpanned.

"Are you trying to freak me out?"

"Claustrophobic?"

"I didn't think so, but that looks too fucking tight for me!"

"Ancestors! I'll go first, and that way, I can pull your arms if you get stuck."

"Not helping!" He saw the grin on Thayla's face and getting that reaction from her usual reticent demeanor was almost worth his genuine discomfort. He watched as she crawled forward into the narrow portion of the tunnel, and then she was on her belly, slithering through. A few moments later, her light shone back toward him.

"Your turn," she softly called.

Groaning, Victor crawled forward as far as he could, then he stretched his arms into the tight passage, holding his axe out in front of himself, and began to worm his way forward. At one point, his hips caught, and he almost panicked, but he felt Thayla's fingers wend their way around his wrists, then she tugged with surprising strength. His shoulders strained, and he pulled and wriggled, then he broke free and slid through the last portion of the cramped chute. "That sucked!" he said, sitting up and brushing the dirt off himself.

Thayla didn't respond to him right away, and he saw why when he looked around. They were in a small cave, about ten-by-ten paces, but rounded with a high ceiling. The only other passage from the cave was a similarly small tunnel leading from the far side, but that's not what had Thayla's attention—the walls were littered with little crystals that reflected their glow lamps, creating a bright, almost cheery space. "We should take a break here," Thayla said.

"I guess so; it's not like we've had any sleep in the last two days, and we can watch these two tunnels pretty easily."

"You should check your class refinements anyway, especially before we run into something a lot tougher than a deep hulk."

"That's a good call. Can you keep an eye out while I'm distracted?"

"Yep. I'm gonna have a snack, too." Thayla sat down on a rounded stone, with both tunnel openings in clear view, then she started taking things out of her ring: some sausage, some bread, and a tall, narrow wine bottle.

"Damn, save some for me!" Victor laughed, finding a comfortable stone to sit on. Before opening his status screen, he glanced around the sparkling cave and said, "Do you think these crystals are valuable?"

"I think they're just quartz, but I'm no expert. Maybe?"

"Huh." Victor shrugged the thought aside; they didn't have time to be chipping cheap crystals out of stone. He called up his status sheet and then selected the option for class refinement, reading through his five options:

***Class refinement option 1: Spirit Weaver, Advanced. Prerequisite: two or more spirit affinities. You have begun to unlock the secrets of the spirit. This refinement will allow you to continue that progress, searching out the depths of your inner-self and melding your aspects into powerful Energy workings. Class attributes: Will, Intelligence.***

***Class refinement option 2: Battle Caller, Epic. Prerequisite: Inspiration affinity. You exemplify excellence on the battlefield, inspiring your comrades and turning the tide with powerful tactical boons. Class attributes: Will, Intelligence, Agility, Unbound.***

***Class refinement option 3: Herald of Carnage, Epic. Prerequisites: Spirit Core, two or more affinities, one of which being rage or terror. Walk the path of carnage, driving your foes ahead of you, breaking their spirits, and reaping their Energy. Class attributes: Will, Strength, Unbound.***

***Class refinement option 4: Battle Zealot, Epic. Prerequisites: Spirit Core, two or more affinities, one of which being inspiration, and one related to fear, anger, or shame. Continue to develop your battle-calling abilities. Whip your comrades into a frenzy and drive your foes mad with your exhortations. Class attributes: Will, Vitality, Strength.***

***Class refinement option 5: No Refinement. You are pleased with the path on which you find yourself and choose to continue until your next refinement option.***

"*Jesus,*" Victor said softly, frowning and shaking his head at his blasphemy.

"What?" Thayla asked around her mouthful of sausage. She took a swig out of her wine bottle and cocked an eyebrow at him.

"Uh, I have a lot of options, and they seem *loco* as hell."

"Crazy?"

"Yeah, like fucking 'Battle Zealot,' um, '. . . whip your comrades into a frenzy and drive your foes mad . . .'"

"Hah, that does sound a little crazy! Spirit Cores are something different, I guess."

"*That's an interesting option, Victor. Do you mind sharing more details?*" Gorz asked, once again startling Victor; he jerked his head to the side before he registered that it was Gorz. Thayla kept watching him while she slowly chewed her food.

"Let me know if you want any advice," she said. "I'm not an expert, but I might have an idea or two."

"All right, let me study these some more; just a minute," Victor responded aloud while he began to read the refinement options to Gorz silently.

*"Those are all excellent options, Victor. Your choices with unbound attributes are far more numerous than is typical."*

*"Really? Why do you think that is?"*

*"Most likely a result of you having a Spirit Core and having a base class with unbound attribute points. It's uncommon to have refinement options that don't build upon your base class."*

*"So, when you say it's not typical, you mean in your experience?"*

*"Ahem, yes."*

*"Any advice?"*

*"If you're torn between options, remember that greater rarity, or, in this case, the epic options, will give you more attributes per level but take a bit longer to level. Also, look at the attribute distribution: the first attribute listed is usually the one with the greatest increase per level."*

Victor looked at his options again, deciding to discount options that didn't have unbound attribute points. He liked the idea of the Spirit Weaver class, thinking it might lead to more control over his Core and perhaps open the door to more affinities. Still, he didn't like that his only attribute improvements would be in will and intelligence for at least the next ten levels. Battle Zealot, while sounding strong, also didn't allow for any unbound attributes, and it also seemed just a little too crazy for Victor's taste. "Well, not any crazier than going berserk, I guess."

"What?"

"Oh, just thinking out loud. The Battle Zealot sounds kind of nuts, and I was just debating with myself about it."

"Mmhmm, all right."

"Well, what do you think? Herald of Carnage, Battle Caller, or keep my current class?"

"Tell me more than their names," she said, taking another long pull of her wine bottle.

"Take it easy. You're supposed to be keeping watch, not getting drunk," Victor said.

"This weak stuff? I'm not going to do more than get a little buzzed if I drink this whole bottle. My vitality is too high."

"Oh, right." Victor cleared his throat and then described his class options to Thayla.

"I don't know. Battle Caller sounds more support-oriented, and the other one sounds like you're going to be leading the way into fights. Which one sounds more like you? Based on that fight with the beetles the other day, I'd say you should pick the, um, carnage one."

"What about my current class?"

"Well, if I had the option for an epic class, I'd take it. My levels have slowed a lot since I got to Tier Two, but I'm still holding out hope for an epic class at Level Thirty."

"All right, fuck it. Herald of Carnage it is."

*"I think you and your friend have demonstrated excellent logic, Victor,"* Gorz said.

*"Heh, thanks, Gorz."* Victor scrolled to the option and touched the "select" button.

***Congratulations! You've refined your class: Herald of Carnage. Class skill gained: Project Spirit, Improved.***

***Project Spirit, Improved: Send forth a wave of your attuned Energy to influence the minds of those in front of you negatively. Energy cost: 200. Cooldown: medium.***

"Hmm, that's wild. I got a new spell that will use my attuned Energy to impact those in front of me negatively. How could my inspiration Energy affect others negatively?"

"I'm not sure; remember, I don't have any affinities." Thayla shrugged.

*"Victor, spiritual affinities, like other affinities, can be altered in your pathways to reflect different aspects of the same affinity. Imagine you had a water affinity; you could cast spells using liquid, ice, or vapor. With the right pattern, your inspiration-attuned Energy can be twisted into discouragement."*

*"What about my rage?"*

*"Just as your rage can give you great strength and fortitude, it can be twisted to deliver madness without those benefits."*

*"Damn! Good to know. We need to spend more time talking, Gorz."*

*"Indeed, perhaps you'll have more free time now that you're sneaking through the deep delves and preparing to enter a dangerous dungeon."*

*"Was that sarcasm, you little* pinche?" Victor laughed, and Thayla gave him another strange look.

"Care to share the joke?"

"*Did you enjoy my humor?*" Gorz asked at the same time.

"Oh, just thinking about driving my enemies nuts while I hack at them with Lifedrinker."

"Yeah, you definitely picked the right refinement. I'm glad you're on my side." She shook her head, then passed her wine bottle to Victor. Victor took the bottle with a grin and chugged a good third of it down. It wasn't watery like the wine at the barracks, and Victor was no wine expert, but to him, it was damn good.

"Doesn't taste bad to me," he said, passing it back to Thayla.

"I found a couple of crates of this stuff about a year ago—no idea how old it is."

"Seriously?" Victor knew wine lasted a long time in the bottle, but the ruins down in the depths seemed ancient.

"Yes, the bottles are enchanted to preserve the contents. Lam doesn't know I found them, and I didn't think she'd reward me enough to give them up." She shrugged and took another drink.

"What are you gonna do? If we live through this shit and make it through that dungeon?" While he asked, Victor stood up and hefted a boulder about the size of a basketball, setting it in the center of the little tunnel they'd come through.

"I'm not thinking that far ahead. I doubt we'll even get to the dungeon entrance—there's stuff down here that even Lam won't fight."

"Come on," Victor grunted, hefting another boulder and stacking it next to the first. "Be positive. Say we make it; where would you go?"

"Well, probably to Gelica first. If we live, there's a good chance we'll have some treasure from the dungeon and gain some levels. Gelica's a big enough city where no one would notice a Shadeni woman coming into town to sell some things and resupply." She watched, kicking her feet out while Victor piled yet another stone into the tunnel entrance. "Hope we don't have to make a hasty exit that way."

"Hah, you serious? Nothing hasty about me trying to worm through that tiny tunnel. I'd rather die on my feet than have something eat me from the ass up while I'm stuck in there."

"Lovely image," Thayla laughed.

"What about after Gelica? You got family? Got a home?"

"What's with the interrogation? Let's just take it one day at a time, all right? I don't think you should know all my plans, anyway. Suppose they catch up to us and I get away, but you don't? Think I want them going to my hometown looking for me?"

"Huh." Victor stacked a fifth boulder into the little tunnel, completely blocking it off. "All right, suit yourself."

When he felt satisfied that anyone crawling through that tunnel would find progress nigh impossible, Victor sat down and ate some of his food. The sausage was fatty and salty, but it tasted delicious after all the hard work he'd been doing. While he sat and ate, he decided to spend his seven attribute points the same way he had the last few levels. He figured when he gained his first level as a Herald of Carnage, he could revisit the pattern. Besides, his current distribution gave him an even fifty strength—it felt good. "You want to sleep for a couple of hours?" he asked, closing his status display.

"Not really. I'm too wound up. Let's put another few tunnels between us and whoever might be coming after us. I'm hoping that passage you filled up with rocks will discourage them enough, but you never know." She stood and brushed herself off, then peered into the exit shaft. "This one widens up after just a few feet."

"All right, I'm right behind you," Victor said, once again hefting Lifedrinker.

# 35

## MONSTERS AND RIVERS

I don't know." Victor took a slow, steadying breath, scanning the wide, low-ceilinged cavern again. "I don't see anything."

"I heard something, though; I'm sure of it," Thayla hissed. Once again, Victor scanned the cavern, running his eyes over the substantial fungus sprouts and the mossy rocks. Moisture hung in a vaporous cloud along the low ceiling, and the air was hot and fetid. Ever so slowly, he moved his gaze over the ground, past the stinky, bubbling pool at the center, and then to the far wall where their next tunnel opened.

"I'll go first," he said, at last, unable to see anything but not wanting her to have to rely on his judgment—she'd wanted to stop and watch until whatever it was showed itself, but he was tired of the wait.

"And if you get eaten by some Tier Five monstrosity? I'm just on my own, then?" Thayla's voice was petulant and irritable, and Victor knew she was tired. They'd had to practically dig their way through the last half mile of narrow, muddy tunnels, and if she were half as dirty and exhausted as he was, he didn't blame her.

"Yeah, I guess," he said and started prowling forward, Lifedrinker gripped in both hands. The ground was mushy, and it squelched with his steps, so he tried to move slowly, letting each foot sink silently before taking the next step. He was about twenty paces into the cavern, skirting the edge of the steaming, stinky pool, when the ground rippled, and he fell to one knee, the wet, spongy fungus soaking into his pants. He froze there, looking around.

When he glanced back at Thayla, he saw her narrowed brows and angry eyes and knew she was cussing him out.

The ground didn't shudder again, and nothing moved, so Victor carefully got back to his feet and started moving again. He'd just passed the pool when the ground surged again, and he was on his butt. Then, one of the slender, slimy fungus sprouts started to move, stretching upward and peeling back like some kind of nightmarish sex organ to reveal a three-foot-long, bone-colored spear. The long tentacle of fungus turned in the air, pointing its talonlike tip at Victor, and shot forward. He rolled to his right, narrowly dodging the stabbing thing.

Suddenly the cavern began to shake in earnest, and more and more of the fungi sprouts rose into the air, peeling back their gray, moist skin to reveal those bone-white spears. Victor heard Thayla's voice from behind him: "Run!" Then she was tearing past him, running for the far tunnel. Victor cast Inspiring Presence and started to run after her. Suddenly the waving tentacles with bone-spear tips didn't seem so numerous, and he thought he could spot a route through them. Thayla leaped to her right, avoiding a stabbing tentacle, and then Victor lost track of her as he began to dance with the seven or eight tentacles in stabbing range.

He couldn't help the bubbling laugh that started to roll out of his throat as he dodged the stabbing, weaving spears. They sank into the ground over and over, and, inspiration guiding his arm, Victor started to cleave the tentacles off as they stabbed into the mossy floor. Before long, he was standing amid a cluster of writhing, waving, gore-spraying tentacles sans spears. He turned to the far tunnel, ready to make his way out of the creepy fungus trap when he saw Thayla's spear sticking out of the spongy ground.

Icy panic gripped his heart, and he whirled around, looking for a sign of the tall, red-skinned woman. When his eyes fell on the pool at the center of the room, he saw the surface bubbling and something thrashing within. "Thayla!" he roared and charged to the bubbling water. As he got close, his inspired mind ran through a dozen plans to get her out, but then his eyes fell on the edge of the pool, and he noticed the way the ground seemed to surge up and down, and it reminded him of a mouth sucking on a straw. "Oh, hell no!"

Victor brought Lifedrinker down on the gray flesh surrounding the pool, hacking a terrible wound in the quivering surface, and gouts of red-black blood began to seep out. Lifedrinker throbbed and pulled and seemed to sink deeper of her own accord, and Victor knew she'd found a deep well of Energy to draw from. The ground of the cavern quivered and bucked, and if he hadn't been holding tight to Lifedrinker with his legs wide, Victor knew he'd have fallen into the pool. "Spit her out, you fucker!" he screamed, and then he tried something new—he used Project Spirit, and a surge of rage-attuned Energy pulsed out of him in a cone-shaped, palpable red haze.

He hadn't consciously decided to use rage Energy with the spell, but it seemed to do the trick; the gray, oozing flesh surrounding the little pool puckered and then began to convulse, stretching up out of the ground like an unhoused section of intestine. As it stretched, heaving and spewing gouts of the fetid liquid within, Victor swung Lifedrinker in a wide horizontal cleave, opening a terrible, yard-long gash in the side of the protuberance. Gouts of thick black blood sprayed forth, along with more of the liquid that had been bubbling in the "pool."

The cavern floor shook, and the swaying, bleeding, stabbing tentacles went wild in their attempts to reach Victor. None of the nearby ones had their spears anymore, and most had been shortened by his axe to the point where they couldn't even slap at him. Victor turned to hack one that was still long enough to flail at him, liberally soaking him with black-red ooze. He cleaved it in half, leaving a stump that could only thrash and splash him with more blood.

Victor cast Sovereign Will, pumping up his strength, and also Channel Spirit, filling his arms and Lifedrinker with rage-attuned Energy. Then he went to work, hacking at the now two-meter-tall, writhing, pulsing, bleeding protuberance. Lifedrinker ripped considerable gashes in the thing with each swing, and soon the top half was just a deflated flap of loose flesh, and the bottom was pouring gouts of liquid and blood with each convulsion. Victor was about to deliver another terrible chop to an existing cut when he saw a glimpse of shiny, wet red flesh.

He let go of Lifedrinker with one hand and plunged it into the gaping wound, feeling around. Immediately, Victor's fingers began to burn, but he shoved his arm in farther until he felt something solid, then he grabbed on and yanked with all his rage-fueled strength. As his arm and hand emerged from the gash, he saw that he had a grip on Thayla's ankle, and he pulled, backing up a step, delivering her through the slash like a nightmarish birth. She slid free in a splash of foamy liquid and red gore, and Victor stood stunned for a moment when he saw her condition.

Thayla had an oozing, puckered puncture wound through her chest under her right collarbone. Her clothing was frayed and gore-covered, and, worse, her flesh was raw, and beneath her red skin, he could see exposed muscle tissue in many spots, including her cheeks—the thing had been dissolving her.

Victor's heart began to hammer in panic and anger, and his hand tightened on the haft of Lifedrinker until his knuckles were white. He stood over Thayla, wondering if she were dead, wishing he could heal her somehow, but struggling to contain the urge to turn and keep hacking at the monstrosity living under the cavern floor. "*Pinche,* motherfucker!" he growled, turning back to the bucking, quivering, fleshy tube.

As he struggled to contain his rage and turned, trying to force himself to pick up Thayla and run from the cavern, a thought occurred to him: she might not have as much Energy affinity as he did, but she still would heal some if he got her a big Energy influx. A wicked grin spread on his face as he turned back to the gray intestine thing. "You must be worth a lot of Energy, asshole!" Somewhere in the back of his mind, he heard Gorz's tinny laugh.

Hefting Lifedrinker into a two-handed grip, Victor stopped holding back his rage and let it flood his pathways, pushing himself to Berserk. The dim light in the cavern grew darker as a shade of blood-red filtered over his vision, and the only thing he could see was the heaving, pulsing, gore-spewing monstrosity. He screamed, spittle frothing his lips, and launched himself at it, whipping Lifedrinker in heavy side to side arcs, tearing through the thick, springy flesh of the tube effortlessly. The cavern floor continued to roll and tremble, and the spear tentacles waved about madly, the ones shortened by Victor spraying gore all over the place, painting the room with more red. Victor laughed.

The huge gray tube continued to thrash its way higher out of the springy cavern floor, then the ground cracked around it, and a ropy tentacle with a clawlike hook on the end pushed out, sinking into the ground and pulling. Victor hacked it in half, and it sprayed forth a much brighter shade of blood. The sight of it fed Victor's fury, and he continued his rampage. As he worked his way around the tube, hacking it to shreds, he came within range of one of the tentacles with a spear still intact. It stabbed him through the back of his thigh, and he screamed in pain and fury, whipping Lifedrinker around and cutting it in half.

The tentacles' waving and thrashing caught the attention of his enraged mind, and, after he yanked the spear from his leg, he went on a rampage around the cavern, running from one spear tentacle to the next, cleaving them off as close to the ground as he could. He felt his rage cooling at one point and pushed more of his prodigious rage-attuned Energy pool into his pathways, extending its duration. Whether he could have chosen not to do so wasn't apparent or of interest to him; killing and the madness of combat were all he craved. The stab wounds he accumulated in his rampage mostly healed over, and the pain served only to drive his fury to new heights.

He was standing over one of the truncated spear tentacles when the cavern bucked again, almost knocking him over. He caught himself against the cavern wall and spun to see the source of the cracking, screaming, hissing sound that had disturbed him. At the center of the cavern, not far from where Thayla lay, the huge, massacred, intestinelike protuberance was now horizontal, and the creature from which it sprang was worming its way out of the ground. It heaved itself with a dozen of those hooked tentacles, pulling its enormous, sluglike body out of the ground, inch by inch.

Victor charged through the inch-deep layer of red-black blood, splashing with each step, and launched himself through the air, Lifedrinker over his head, bringing her down with a tremendous chop along the side of the quivering, gray-white horror. Puslike ooze sprayed in the wake of Lifedrinker's blade, and he felt the axe pull at his hands as she seemed to surge through the flesh, and Victor saw currents of purple-black Energy rushing toward the axehead through the puckered flesh of the creature.

A handful of the hooked tentacles released the ground and swung toward Victor, and he danced back, waving Lifedrinker in front of himself to ward them off. He nimbly sprang toward the rear of the exposed slug body, out of their reach, and began to hack into the top of it where it was just coming out of the hole. Again, Lifedrinker cleaved through the pulpy flesh, pulling runnels of that purple-black Energy into herself. Victor watched the process, cleave after cleave, and realized his rage had faded and that the monstrosity was only weakly thrashing, its hooked tentacles mostly lying limp.

"Die! Just fucking die!" he screamed, moving around it, hacking great gashes into its side and severing tentacles whenever they came within reach. Finally, the thing shuddered, and a massive gout of bilelike fluid poured out of the mangled intestinal protuberance, and then it collapsed, slipping slowly down its hole.

Large, baseball-size motes of purple-gold Energy started to wink into existence in the air above the gaping hole. Then they began to coalesce into streams—a broad, riverlike ribbon flowed toward Victor, and a much narrower but still significant one, toward Thayla.

***Congratulations! You've achieved Level 21 Herald of Carnage. You have gained 10 will, 8 strength, and have 10 attribute points to allocate.***

\*\*\*Congratulations! You've learned the skill Axe Mastery, Improved.\*\*\*

\*\*\*Congratulations! You've learned the skill Berserk, Improved.\*\*\*

As the notifications filled his vision, Victor realized he was floating off the ground slightly. He stretched, arching his back and letting the rush fill him, then he dropped to the ground lightly. He looked toward Thayla and saw that she was stirring, groaning softly. "You gonna live?" he asked, walking toward her.

"Ugh, am I dead?" She pushed herself up to a sitting position, and Victor was relieved to see the flesh had mended on her cheeks and arms. "I leveled? How? Last thing I remember was a spear hooking me and dragging me toward . . ." she paused and looked at the hole where the monster had slid into the darkness. "Wasn't there a pool there?"

"Yeah, it was the mouth or throat of some kind of giant, underground, tentacled slug. It was gross as hell. You were almost dead, that's for sure. Good thing that big, stinky, slithering butthole was worth a lot of Energy." Victor reached out, taking Thayla's hand and helping her to her feet.

"You have a way with words," she said, examining her frayed leather vest and the nearly dissolved shirt she wore underneath.

"Well, I'm not trying to be rude, but your braids are soaked with that thing's spit or whatever, and you kind of stink."

"My hair!" Thayla was suddenly holding a half-full bottle of wine and pulling the cork out with her teeth, then she started pouring it over her hair and braids, trying to rinse the acidic fluid away.

"You don't have water?"

"No!"

"Shit, me either. I have the watery wine the captain gave us, though." He, too, produced a flask of wine and started helping Thayla.

"You realize you're covered in gore, too, right?" she snapped, though there was relief in her voice as she began to realize her hair was holding up quite well to the acidic fluid.

"Doesn't seem likely we'll find a shower down here, though we will pass by a river soon, I think."

*"That's right, Victor."*

*"Thanks, Gorz."*

"This cavern is fucking disgusting; let's get out of here." Victor started walking toward the exit tunnel but stopped when he saw something shiny winking in his glow stone. "What's this?" He was walking through the shallow puddle where the creature had vomited up its guts as it died, and, as he advanced, he began to make out glittering objects. He saw rings, bracelets, a necklace, and quite a few gemstones. Larger lumps of metal looked as if they were once pieces of armor or weapons, though they hadn't fared as well in the creature's belly as the objects made of denser gold and silver.

"Treasure!" Thayla said, scooping up a gold chain.

"Let's gather this stuff up on that flat rock, and then we can go through it." Victor had already started, fishing out a couple of rings and a large red gemstone. Thayla and he, their urgency to leave forgotten, spent the next several minutes sifting through the disgusting effluence. In the end, they had a little pile of gold and silver rings, some of them with gemstones, some plain, and several necklaces and bracelets. They'd gathered a pile of metal armor, mostly worn down to uselessness, but one piece seemed perfectly fine.

Thayla held up the silvery bracer and said, "This thing's artificed for sure; see the runes? Mind if I try it on?"

"Go for it. What about those blades?" Victor gestured to the pile of sword, dagger, and spear blades they'd found. "Any of them magical?"

"I think one of the spear blades is. It's perfectly sharp and doesn't seem decayed." She pointed, and Victor picked it up. The blade was eight or ten inches long with two razor-sharp edges. He could see the part where the old spear haft would have been mounted, but there was no trace of the wood. Still, the blade was covered in bright silvery runes, and it veritably hummed with Energy.

"All right, I'll take this spearhead, and you take the bracer. Then we can split the rest up?"

"Hold on, let's see if any of this jewelry's enchanted," she said, smiling at how the shiny bracer hugged her wrist. Victor nodded and began sorting through the pile of rings. He found two with runes inscribed on them and set them aside. Thayla shook her head after going through the necklaces and bracelets.

"How do we tell what these rings do?"

"Bond with them—I'll do one, you do the other."

Victor picked up the larger ring, a thick silvery band with a yellow gem mounted on a square facet. He trickled some of his Energy into it, and suddenly a description in System text appeared before him:

***Ring of the Guest: Once per day, the wearer of this ring can knock upon a mundane lock, and it will open.***

"Weird! I got a notification describing the item."

"That happens if an artificer takes the time and effort to give the item a description," Thayla said. "This ring had one also. It's a ring of whispers, or so the artificer labeled it. It says it can allow the wearer to overhear distant conversations."

"That's pretty cool. This one allows the wearer to open locks once per day."

"Want to trade? Or do you want to keep that one?"

"Let's just keep what we've got for now," Victor said, then pointed to the other piled valuables. "Let's take turns picking these others. You go first." Thayla nodded, then she scooped up a large red gem. Victor followed her lead and picked a glittering blue gem. They continued like that until all the objects were gone, and Victor ended up with eleven rings and necklaces and seven precious-looking jewels.

When they left the putrid cavern and walked a short way down the narrow, much cleaner tunnel, Thayla sighed loudly and leaned against the wall, taking several deep, exaggerated breaths. "Ancestors, it feels good to breathe some clean air again."

"Yeah, that creature was nasty." Victor, too, took a deep breath, groaning at how sticky with gore his body still was. He rubbed his hands vigorously, trying to rub away some of the dried blood. Even his neck was tacky, and he rubbed at that, too. "I'm dirtier than ever, even worse than when I was fighting in the pits."

"You were a pit fighter?"

"Yeah, when I first got summoned to this world . . ." Victor's heart started to race, and he said, "Wait! What if those rich assholes try to summon us?"

"What?" Thayla scoffed loudly, "Good luck! My will is plenty high to resist an unwanted summon. Is your will that low?"

"No, it's my highest stat!"

"You'll be fine, then! When you were summoned before, was your will lower?"

"Ha, yeah—I was Level Zero."

"There you go. Don't worry about getting summoned."

"Really? Just like that? What would happen if they tried?"

"You'd feel them pulling at you, and you could pull back. It's a thousand times harder to pull someone through space than for that person to simply hold their ground. Summons work differently than portals or teleportation skills. I don't know why—it's way past my level of expertise."

"How do you know that? Did someone try to summon you?"

"No. It's common knowledge; even little kids know it. My favorite nursery story involved a witch that gave people poisoned pies so that they'd fall asleep and be unable to resist her summon spell. Then she cooked them into more pies which she fed to their families."

"Goddamn! That's a twisted story! That was your favorite?" Victor raised his eyebrow, giving her a searching look.

"Well, there's more to it! One little girl she summons escapes and makes friends with the witch's pet forest troll. The troll saves her in the end."

"Troll? There are trolls in stories from my world, too."

"Really?" Thayla straightened up, and the two of them continued down the tunnel, talking quietly about fairy tales, which brought to light the fact that fairies were a thing in this world also. Victor was telling Thayla about wendigos when she held up a finger to her lips and touched her ear. By now, Victor knew that meant she'd heard something, so he slowed his breathing and tried to hear it also.

At first, he couldn't separate the sound from the normal echoes and scrapes that seemed ubiquitous in the deep, but after listening for a few moments, he heard it—a constant rushing, rumbling sound. "The river," he hissed softly.

"Right!" Thayla started moving forward again, Victor close behind. The temperature began to drop, and the stones in the tunnel wall grew cool, and soon, the rush of the river was unmistakable. They came to the mouth of the passage and saw that it opened onto an enormous tunnel with a quickly flowing river at its center. The tunnel floor was stony with patches of actual sand here and there in depressions. Victor wondered if the river swelled during certain seasons, and if that was why the tunnel was so much wider than the current flow.

"Look," Thayla said, pointing along the river, and Victor could just see, in the light of their glow lamps, that though the tunnel narrowed, there was a clear, open path along the river in both directions.

"That's the way we need to go to get to the dungeon," he said, gesturing to the left.

"You think there's anything terrible lurking in that water?" Thayla was slowly moving closer to the rushing river.

"It seems to be moving too fast for something to be lurking," Victor replied, also moving closer. He knew what she was thinking: it would be very nice to get cleaned up.

"I'll fill up some empty wine bottles, and we can rinse off back on the shore so the blood doesn't get in the water," Thayla said.

"Good thinking! I saw a documentary about sharks once—they can smell blood in the water for like a mile."

"Sharks?"

"Yeah, um, monsters that live in the ocean."

"Right, well, here." She handed him an empty bottle. "Faster if we both fill them." She held out another, and he took it. The two of them moved up to the flowing river and quickly filled their bottles, then scurried back toward the tunnel wall. They poured the water over themselves, scrubbing away dried blood and grime. Victor saw Thayla fish out a clean shirt from her ring, so he turned away and kept scrubbing at his gore-matted hair.

It took him another two trips to the river to fill his wine bottles before he felt clean, and by then, he was shivering from the cold, his clothes, all but his pants, soaking wet. Once again, Victor silently praised the person who crafted his miraculous black, self-cleaning, self-patching pants.

"Ready?" Thayla asked, her teeth also chattering.

"Yeah, we need to get moving and build up some heat!"

"We'll be fine! Do you feel that breeze blowing along the river? We'll be dry in no time."

"Hmm, yeah, good point." Victor nodded and started walking along the river. According to the map Gorz had helped him draw, they were more than halfway to the dungeon now. He was beginning to feel a lot better about their odds of making it.

"Victor, do you see that?"

"What?" Victor peered ahead into the darkness and noticed a bunch of little yellow lights or maybe reflections of their glow lamps. He stared at them for a moment, but then he noticed they kept winking on and off, and then it hit him—they were blinking eyes.

# 36

## TUNNELS AND STAIRS

Thayla stepped up beside Victor, her spear leveled and pointing toward the creatures lurking in the darkness. "What are they?" she hissed.

"How would I know?" Victor held Lifedrinker sideways in front of himself, waiting and watching.

"Yellow eyes, short, or crouching. Yeksa? How could Yeksa survive this deep?" Thayla's words were hurried, rambling, and Victor realized she was speaking in a stream of consciousness, panic tinging her voice. Thayla panicked? That didn't make sense.

"Chill, deep breaths. Hang on," Victor said, then he cast Globe of Insight, and the dark, stony riverbank was suddenly bathed in white-gold light as the ball of Energy formed in his palm. He concentrated on moving the globe and then lifted and "threw" it with a motion of his hand. It sailed forth and shed light on the scurrying owners of the eyes—dozens of huge, black-furred rats.

Thayla took a deep breath and said, "Thanks; the not knowing was freaking me out. I think I'm still shaky from almost getting digested earlier."

"No worries," Victor said, watching the rats scramble back toward the shadows, avoiding the pool of light cast by his orb. "They don't like the light."

"Let's keep pushing forward; you can drive them ahead with your light."

"Sure, if they stay scared. They're as big as mastiffs, so I'm hoping they don't all suddenly get a backbone." Victor started walking, and when he got up to where his orb hovered, he put his hand up behind it and shoved it forward again. The rats continued to scurry ahead of the light. Victor noticed a reflection off to his right and realized some of the rats were in the water, rushing past them with the current. "Watch our backs!" he hissed, pointing to the rats in the water.

Thayla spun with her spear, shining her light back behind them, then she said a word that didn't translate and screamed, "They're rushing up behind!"

"Steady, Thayla! They're just fucking rats!" Victor roared and cast Inspiring Presence. Suddenly the golden light of his orb seemed to permeate the entire massive underground tunnel, and Victor saw all the black-furred, scrabbling shapes of the rats in front of them, in the water, and behind them. There were hundreds. "Thayla! We're going to charge the ones in front of us! Come on! Stay with me!"

Victor glanced at her to make sure she registered his words and was happy to see a grin on her face and brightness in her eyes; she was also inspired. Victor rushed past his orb, nimbly leaping up and batting it forward so that it sped along the river, over the humping, wriggling mass of rats. Then he was in front of them, unleashing more inspiration-attuned Energy with Project Spirit. A visible wave of black-tinged, sickly yellow Energy rolled out in front of Victor onto the rats, and their narrowed yellow eyes suddenly grew wide and round. They squealed in a much different pitch and turned away from him, scrabbling back and jumping into the river.

Victor knew more rats were on their heels, so he kept pushing forward, shouting, "Keep moving!" He swung his axe in narrow cleaves, catching a few slower rats with the edge and dampening Lifedrinker's edge. He saw Thayla jabbing her spear to the side and in front of them, and he couldn't help exulting in the rush of battle with a high-pitched howl. To his surprise, Thayla picked up the howl and ululated in a perfect counterpoint.

As they broke through the crowd of rats and stretched out their legs, really moving, Gorz spoke up in Victor's mind. *"Victor! Another five hundred meters, then you'll want to take the passage on your left!"*

"Come on, Thayla! Five hundred more meters before we turn!" They tore along the hard stone riverbank, skidding through the little depressions holding sand and silt, and put more distance between them and the pursuing rats. Victor knew he was in better shape than when he was on Earth—he had numbers on his status screen to prove it, but his empirical evidence was pretty strong, too. This sprint, for instance—he knew he had to cover five hundred meters, but it was only a matter of thirty or so seconds before Gorz was screaming in his mind.

*"Here, Victor! Turn here!"*

"Here, Thayla," Victor yelled, cutting in front of her and dashing toward a dark cleft in the stone tunnel wall. He found himself charging through a narrow smooth-walled passage, his glow stone shedding just enough light for his charging, bobbing progress to throw crazy shadows up and down on the high walls. He could hear Thayla's heavy breathing behind him and, farther back, the clawing skittering progress of their pursuers.

Suddenly he burst out of the high-walled, narrow passage and into a round, stone chamber with a crazily steep set of stairs winding up the curved walls. *"Your next passage is three hundred meters up this shaft,"* Gorz said helpfully.

"Thayla, get up the steps a bit; I'll be right behind you. Let's make a stand here; you can stab around me, and I'll hack any rat that comes up!" Victor said, slowing to pull her arm and propel her up the steps. "C'mon! Run up a ways, so they can't pile on each other to flank us!"

"Right!" Thayla said, taking two steps at a time with her long strides. Victor was hot on her heels, and he could practically feel the rats scrabbling at his back as they climbed. When they'd mounted a good fifty or more steps, he panted, "Here! We gotta make a stand, or they'll run us down!" Victor spun, arcing Lifedrinker in a downward, sideways cleave, anticipating the rats right behind him. He hadn't been wrong; two rats met their end at that moment as the axe's gleaming, silvery edge tore through their snouts in a wet, crunching gash.

As Victor recovered Lifedrinker's momentum, Thayla jabbed her spear beside him, catching another rat on the point and flinging it down the steps into the bucking, thrashing river of giant, hissing, growling rodents that were scrabbling up the narrow steps after them. Victor lifted his axe and ended another rat, but a dozen more were scrabbling at him as he lifted the blade. Wanting to give himself some space, he cast Project Spirit again, this time with rage-attuned Energy. The closest pile of rats went into an absolute mad frenzy as the wave of shimmering red Energy rolled over them. They began to bite at each other, screaming in their madness, turning the stairs into a slick, blood-soaked, self-serving abattoir.

Victor backed up a step and breathed heavily, enjoying the break as the rats ravaged each other. "They have weak wills," Thayla said, behind him, also watching the mad rat melee.

"Fuck yes, they do," Victor replied, still holding his axe sideways, ready to smite any rats that broke out of the frenzied, snapping, clawing ball of vermin. One rat did slip free and lunged at them, but Thayla stabbed it in the air, knocking it off the stairs to fall to the blood-soaked stone at the bottom.

By the time the madness left the rats' eyes, dozens were dead, and they were so drenched in blood and battle frenzied that it took them a while to redirect their aggression on Victor and Thayla. By the time they did, Victor was ready with a fresh Inspiring Presence. He and Thayla cut apart five, then ten, then twenty rats as they bounded up the steps and leaped at them. Blood and rat parts liberally soaked the steps beneath them, and as their footing grew gory and crowded with corpses, he and Thayla slowly backed up, higher and higher, leaving a trail of broken, twitching, screaming rats and corpses.

When Inspiring Presence wore off, Victor was ready with another projection of rage Energy, and the ensuing mad melee gave him and Thayla another breather. "I don't see any more coming out of the tunnel. This is it, just what's on the stairs—we can do this!"

"Yeah," Thayla said, breathing heavily beside him. "I can't believe we've killed so many already." It was true; the number of dead giant rodents was staggering. A huge mound of black, twitching fur rose at the base of the stair, and the steps were slick and cluttered with guts, blood, and corpses.

"Gimme a drink, please," Victor said, holding out a hand. He had a hankering for some of her wine, and Thayla got the idea, grinning and pulling out a bottle. She drank half of it and gave him the other half, and Victor quaffed it with a grin, watching the rats maul each other a few feet down the stair. Just as he stowed the empty bottle in his ring, the rats seemed to recover their senses and redirect their frenzied rage on him. His Inspiring Presence wasn't off cooldown yet, but he and Thayla were rested and ready, and the fight was on.

By the time the last of the growling, yellow-eyed beasts died with Lifedrinker in its head and Thayla's spear in its breast, they were painted red and exhausted but exhilarated. Victor fell back onto an empty step, and Thayla collapsed on the step above. They both were panting and sweat-soaked, but it was a good kind of bone-deep weariness they felt, the kind that came with victory, and Victor couldn't help looking back at Thayla and grinning. "We fucking did it! We killed a damn army of rats the size of pit bulls!"

Golden motes of Energy started to gather on the mounds of dead rats along the stair and piled at the base, and soon it was all flooding into Victor and Thayla.

***Congratulations! You've achieved Level 22 Herald of Carnage. You have gained 10 will, 8 strength, and have 20 attribute points to allocate.***

"Shit, I forgot to spend my attribute points from the last fight!"

"You get free points? Mine all go into strength, agility, and vitality."

"Yeah, my class gives me some 'unbound' points to spend each level." He looked at his gore-covered arms and sighed. "So much for that bath we just had."

"You're much filthier than I am. It's a benefit of having a longer weapon."

"Yeah, I guess." He looked at the scene of the slaughter beneath them, noticing the heavy reek of expended bowels and souring blood now that the adrenaline of combat was wearing off. "Let's move up a ways, then I want to rest for a minute and look at my attributes."

"Agreed." Thayla stood and started stalking up the steps, her spear still held ready. Victor tried not to focus on her ass, and he knew it was creepy even to realize he was doing it, so he pushed his gaze past her, up around the turn of the spiral, making sure there weren't any ambushes in wait. He hadn't really thought of Thayla that way—she was so damn tough and angry most of the time. It wasn't like his current life had room for romance, anyway. He laughed to himself softly, imagining it.

"What?" Thayla glanced back at him over her shoulder.

"Nothing. Laughing at my own idiocy." He thought of something else and tried to steer the conversation. "I'm not going to get a chance to get revenge on the jerks who robbed me and tried to kill me."

"In my hometown, there's a saying: 'life's roads aren't made in straight lines.' You never know if your path will bring you back to the mine, or it might lead you to those people in another place; not everyone is destined to die in this pit."

"You're sounding more optimistic; think we have a chance to make it through that dungeon?"

"Oh, don't spoil the mood by making me be realistic." Thayla chuckled.

"This is good; I can't smell the corpses anymore." Victor turned so his back was to the wall and then sat on a step, contemplating his attributes. Thayla sat just above him and also seemed to be staring into space. "Did you level, too?"

"I did. Fastest level I ever gained—I think those rats were tougher than the usual huge rats we run into in the delves."

"They were tough for rats, but we showed them who was boss, right?"

"Sure, but I think your inspiration abilities had a lot to do with that."

"Teamwork," Victor muttered, trying to figure out what to do with his attribute points:

| Strength: | 66 | Vitality: | 90 |
|---|---|---|---|
| Dexterity: | 33 | Agility: | 33 |
| Intelligence: | 24 | Will: | 103 |
| Points Available: | 20 | | |

His class made sure his will and strength were going to keep going up, and his vitality was already solid. Did he want his strength to outpace his dexterity and agility so much? Gorz didn't think it would be a problem until it was "two or three" times his other attributes. "My strength is twice as high as my dexterity and agility."

"Strength is important, but so are speed and skill," Thayla muttered, clearly preoccupied. Victor knew his intelligence wasn't as crucial for physical fighting, but it bugged him that it was so "low." *"Gorz, I don't feel stupid, and my intelligence value is more than twice what I was born with. I'm not going to start feeling dumber or something if all my other stats keep growing but my intelligence doesn't, will I?"*

*"Not exactly, Victor, though you will eventually run into people with much higher intelligence than you, and their thoughts will be faster, they'll have more raw Energy, and they could prove to be very dangerous to you."*

*"So you're saying there's no easy choice. Why can't anything ever be easy?"*

*"Oh, surely there will be times when things will seem easy, Victor. Look for the brightness after the storm."*

*"Ha, I love it! My talking necklace is giving me counseling."* Victor started to smile, but then his face sobered. Thinking of counseling made him think of Ms. Marshal and how she'd seen his potential and helped him graduate. Had he let her down? How many people knew he was even gone? His girlfriend, for sure. His *abuela*. Did any of his "friends" care or notice? Did people think he'd just run away? God, what if his grandma and aunties were looking for him? What if they'd gone to the police and put up missing person flyers? They probably had.

"What's wrong with you?" Thayla asked suddenly, and Victor realized she had moved up a step and was eating a piece of bread and staring at him.

"What?"

"Your face. You look like you just ate something sour."

"My mind ran away from me. I've been so busy surviving that I haven't spent a lot of time thinking about what everyone in my life would do after I disappeared. My grandma, she, well, she didn't have a lot going on; I think making me dinner and asking me about my day was about all that kept her going."

"That's hard." Thayla shook her head, and Victor appreciated that she didn't try to cheer him up. He sighed heavily and then allocated his attribute points. He put five into intelligence, five into dexterity, and ten into agility. He didn't want to let his minor attributes stagnate, but right now, while he was fighting for his life, he figured agility was slightly more important.

He sat back and basked in the warmth of the Energy that flowed into his body as his allocations took effect. There wasn't anything he could do about his family and what they thought of him. Marcy hadn't been that serious, and he didn't worry about her. His aunties probably were convinced he'd run away to his mom's side of the family. Hopefully, they'd convince his *abuela* not to worry. If he couldn't find a way to travel home, maybe he'd find a way to send a message. This world was full of magic; surely there was someone who could help. "Are there a lot of wizards in Gelica?"

"People with the actual Wizard class? Or do you mean just strong Energy users?"

"I don't know. Both?"

"Well, that's the answer; there are both. Hundreds of thousands of people live in Gelica."

"Awesome. You ready?"

"Mmhmm," she said, and Victor looked at her again. She'd leaned back against the stone wall and was chewing her last bite of bread with her eyes closed. She had spatters of dark, dried blood on her red cheeks, but she looked relaxed and peaceful, and Victor wished they could rest longer.

"This isn't a good spot to rest, I'm afraid," he said, grunting as he stood up. "Let's go a bit farther." He thought, *"Gorz, is there any good spot for resting coming up?"*

*"If nothing's changed, Victor, you're going to be traversing a lot of constructed hallways and rooms soon. Ancient ruins. You should find a suitable space."*

*"All right, thanks."*

"Yeah, I'm coming, I'm coming." Thayla opened her eyes and lithely stood. Victor started up the stairs, Lifedrinker held crossways in front of him. The axe's wide, bearded blade gleamed in the light, and Victor realized he'd never seen blood linger on it. On her, he corrected himself.

"You're a thirsty lady, aren't you?" he asked the axe suddenly, on an impulse, and he swore that Lifedrinker shuddered slightly in his grip.

"Are you talking to me?" Thayla said from behind him.

"Nah, Lifedrinker. You think it's true what Lam said? Do you think she can gain consciousness? Like, come alive?"

"Maybe. I don't know; I've never heard of whatever she said it was made of. Some kind of silver?"

"Heartsilver, I think."

"Add it to your list of things to check out when we get to Gelica."

"That's the spirit! *When* we get there!"

*"The passage you want to exit through is coming up, Victor."*

*"Right. Thanks again, Gorz."* Victor lifted Lifedrinker into a more ready position and kept climbing, focusing ahead now, ready for anything that might be lurking in the upcoming passage. His precautions proved unnecessary; the passage was a smooth stone tunnel that led away from the stairway, dust thick on its floor and no monsters in sight.

"How much farther do we have to go?" Thayla asked, looking into the tunnel.

*"You're more than two-thirds of the way, Victor."*

"We're about two-thirds of the way there. I think we'll find a good spot to rest soon."

"Okay." Thayla nodded, adjusting the grip on her spear.

Victor started into the tunnel, carefully watching the dusty ground as his glow lamp illuminated it, searching for signs of previous occupancy. Nothing seemed to have disturbed the dust in a very long time, and soon, the two of them came to a wooden door that was rotted off its brass hinges but still propped crookedly in the doorway. Victor looked back at Thayla and motioned with his head toward her spear, mouthing, "Ready?" She nodded, and Victor grabbed the door between two of its old warped boards and yanked. When it flopped open, he regripped Lifedrinker and peered into the room beyond.

It was a square, stone room about twenty paces across with dusty piles of broken, rotted furniture partially obscuring the space. Victor thought some of them looked like old bookcases or cabinets. He stepped forward, Thayla right behind him, and a warbling shriek was the only warning he had before a heavy creature with lumpy yellow skin smashed into him. It shrieked as Thayla's spear bit into its side, and Victor pivoted, pushing his axe between him and the creature, using his lowered center of gravity and prodigious strength to shove it back.

The monster looked like a bulky, naked, boil-covered old woman. Her skin was yellow, her nose exceptionally long, and her eyes crazed and red. She waved her long, claw-tipped arms about in a frantic, warbling display of insanity. Her strange dance made her long, narrow sacklike breasts wave about, and the pus-filled boils that liberally coated her thick, wrinkled skin erupted and oozed with her gyrations. "Fucking hell!" Victor recoiled away from her, imagining the pus splashing onto his face.

Thayla hadn't withdrawn her spear, and she drove forward, pushing the disgusting creature across the room. It wailed and shook, dark blood pouring out of the wound Thayla had inflicted but seemingly more concerned with its strange dance than with getting away from her. Victor wasn't an expert on monsters or their tactics. Still, he had a bad feeling about whatever she was doing, so he used Channel Spirit to ignite his arms and axe with rage-attuned Energy, then he took two long steps forward and brought Lifedrinker down on the hag's skull. He split the monster from forehead to breastbone, and the quivering body shook for a moment, then stilled. Lifedrinker pulsed in his hand, and Victor saw rivulets of green-yellow Energy flowing into her sunken edge.

Moments later, golden motes rose up from the hag's horrible corpse, and Victor knew she was dead. Neither he nor Thayla leveled from the encounter, and the monster's body was so offensive to their senses that they decided to quickly vacate the room. They had a choice of three doorways, but with Gorz the choice was easy, and Victor led the way through the broken doorway to the left, Lifedrinker at the ready.

"That thing was disgusting," Thayla softly said as they advanced down yet another long, stone passage.

"Yeah. I fucking need a bath like never before. She was practically hugging me." He shuddered at the thought but kept moving. Soon, Gorz directed him to turn down a side passage, and they continued that way for a while until they came to a large, empty hall with several small rooms lining one wall. Broken, rotten furniture littered the space, and most of the small rooms stood empty and open, but two of them had mostly intact doors. With Thayla at his back, spear ready, Victor opened each door, revealing mostly dust in the first one and an ancient, partially collapsed table in the other.

"Let's rest in one of these," Thayla said.

"Yeah, I'm beat." Victor went into the room with the old table, pleased that its long, polished top was still quite solid. "This one. We can barricade the door with this table." Thayla helped him close and barricade the door, then they sat down on the dusty stone floor and shared some of their food. "How much more of this wine do you have?"

"Eleven bottles."

"Nice. I filled the empties you gave me with water from the river. You think it's safe?"

"Why wouldn't it be?"

"I don't know—bacteria, monster piss, rat shit?"

"Well, that's disgusting, but we'll live. No one with as much Energy as we have really gets sick from things like that."

"Seriously?"

"Yeah. Haven't you noticed? You heal faster? You're more resilient? The more Energy you have suffusing you, the more that will happen. Someone who made it to Level Ten or higher hardly ever gets sick. Well, unless they're dealing with some nasty attuned-Energy attack."

"Still, I prefer the wine." Victor grinned and bit into one of the sausages Lam had sent with them.

"I notice you don't drink or eat as much as I do. Have you improved your race?"

"Yeah. I won a big fight for a rich lady. She gave me a fruit that advanced my race a few levels."

"Seriously? How many?"

"Three."

"Wow—quite a prize."

"Yeah, the asshole that held my contract was pissed. I think he saw it as a waste of money."

"He'll be surprised if you come knocking after clearing your way through a dungeon, hmm?" Thayla grinned, her eyes closed, and Victor saw her long, sharp canines. Was she imagining him taking revenge and savoring the image?

"I wouldn't mind paying him a visit someday, I guess." If he were being honest, Victor hadn't hardly thought about Yund, but he definitely owed that big asshole a thing or two. He'd sold Victor out at the first opportunity. He might have been scared of the nobility, but he could have handled it a hundred different ways. How about a heads-up? Maybe Victor could have "escaped." Who was he kidding? Yund wasn't sticking his neck out for anyone, least of all one of his slaves. "Yeah, I've got a few people in Persi Gables that I need to pay a visit to one of these days."

Thayla didn't respond, and Victor realized she was sleeping. He sat back against the wall and watched the door, letting his mind drift. He thought

about home, about the Wagon Wheel, and about the mine. He remembered
his glimpses of Persi Gables when he'd been led around to different fighting
venues and imagined walking those streets a free man with money in his
pockets. A smile spread on his lips as he thought of meeting Vullu and taking
the goat-man out for a meal. Then he frowned, thinking about the people in
the cages at Yund's and all the ones who died during every Pit Night.

Victor had ideals, but he wasn't stupid, and when he thought of trying to
stop the whole system that allowed the pit fighting and all the other things
that went with it, like selling people to the mines, his mind spun at the com-
plexity of the problem. Like Edeya had said, what was he going to do, take
on the whole Ridonne Empire? "Maybe not, but I can help a few people and
see what happens from there," he whispered to himself.

When his eyes grew so heavy that he grew worried he'd fail to keep watch,
he shook Thayla's shoulder. Her eyes sprang open, and she looked panicked
for a second, but when she saw Victor's face leaning over, she sighed and
nodded. "Your turn."

Victor slept a few hours, and when Thayla woke him, he felt stiff but
ready. His neck and back were sore, but he figured a bit of walking would sort
him out. "Ready?" he asked Thayla after they'd picked up their belongings
and stowed them away.

"Yeah, feeling a lot better. I was practically sleepwalking earlier."

Victor nodded and moved to slide the table out of the way when he heard
a sound like boards clattering onto the stone floor in the next room. He held
his finger to his lips, and Thayla nodded. He moved to the side of the table
they'd propped in front of the door and pressed his ear to the wood, holding
his breath. He didn't hear anything at first, but then the sound of something
snuffling came to him. It reminded him of the sound a dog makes when it's
sniffing around at the ground for a bit of food you dropped, but it was deeper
and slower as if coming from a much bigger nose.

Victor turned to Thayla to whisper what he'd heard when a howling roar,
loud enough to vibrate the wood of the door and table, broke out in the next
room, then the door rattled as something big hit it. Victor threw a shoulder
against the table, trying to hold it in place, but the door rattled and shook,
and the table kept bouncing into him as if it was being hit by a charging
linebacker. "Something fucking big is hitting this door!" As he hollered, a
flash of red light erupted on the other side of the door, bleeding through the
dark cracks in the door, and then three long, knifelike claws speared through
the wood and slid through it like paper, pulling away long hunks of wood.

A moment later, a big round orange eye with a vertical black pupil peered through the hole.

Another howl erupted from the monster, shaking the wood and making Victor's ears ring, and he backed up, holding Lifedrinker. "This thing's coming through. Get ready!"

"Stop telling me to get ready! What do you think I'm doing? Sleeping through this?" Thayla snarled, stepping up beside him with her spear ready.

# 37

## THINGS UNKNOWN

Another red flash bled through the gaps in the door, and the claws ripped away another considerable chunk of the ancient wood. The opening was large enough now that Victor could see the scaled, horn-bedecked head that housed the livid, bulging orange eyes. "The hell is that thing?"

"I don't know!" Thayla said, her voice shrill with stress. The monster howled again, a deep, reverberating siren sound that hurt Victor's ears, then it smashed into the mangled door, which burst open in a shower of broken planks and splinters. Victor was ready, having prepared a Project Spirit spell, and he sent out a sickly wave of black-tinged yellow Energy that gave the hulking monstrosity pause.

While the hulking beast hunched, struggling against the urges Victor's spell put into its mind, Thayla dove forward and put her spearhead deep into its thick, scaly neck. Victor, shaking off his bewilderment at the sight of the monster—a hunched, broad-shouldered, hound-shaped lizard complete with thick scales—chopped down with Lifedrinker. The monster's scales parted for the axe's shiny edge, and she bit deeply into its flesh, carving a gouge between its neck and shoulder, and spilling hot, steaming blood onto the dusty stone floor.

The two wounds seemed to break the stalemate between the creature's will and Victor's spell, and it shook its head, roaring and exposing a double row of pointy triangular teeth. It lunged at Victor, and he held up Lifedrinker like a shield, trying to press her edge into the monster as it crashed into him, but he couldn't measure his success—he'd been driven back into the wall, and the gaping snapping maw of the monster grunted heavily next to his ear, centimeters from his flesh. Victor screamed and used Channel Spirit to fill his limbs with rage Energy, still trying to push the monster back.

He couldn't see Thayla because of the monster's bulk, but he knew she must be going to work with her spear because the beast seemed distracted, shifting left and right as it struggled against Victor. It drove him farther toward the corner as he strained to keep his neck and head out of its snapping maw. He finally remembered to cast Sovereign Will as his shoulder jammed into the corner, and his muscles surged with the additional twenty-five strength. His sudden burst of vigor, combined with whatever Thayla was doing, allowed Victor to slip around the creature's side and use its momentum to drive it into the corner where he'd been pinned.

Victor chopped and chopped with Lifedrinker, cutting huge gaping wounds in the side and haunches of the monster before it could get turned. One of his chops opened the soft side of its belly, and glistening entrails slipped free of the gash like a mass of giant shiny worms. Thayla was on the other side, pointy teeth bared in a fierce grimace as she, too, drove her weapon into the monster, over and over. The beast thrashed and moaned, smashing itself into the wall in desperation, but its death throes were short-lived—they'd done too much damage to it.

When the bear-size lizard-hound was finally still, Thayla and Victor stood leaning on their weapons, panting and sweating, then the purple-tinged golden motes of Energy that rose from the dead monster surged into them.

***Congratulations! You've learned the spell: Sovereign Will, Improved.***

***Sovereign Will, Improved: As an act of concentration, you can apply up to 33% of your total Will to any physical attribute.***

"Nice!" he said, reading the description.

"Level, already?"

"No, but one of my skills improved."

"Ahh, good . . ." Thayla's further words were cut off by a howl that echoed through the dark chamber beyond the outside hall. It sounded distant but far too familiar for Victor's taste.

"Another one of these things? Let's get moving; what if this thing had a big family?" He turned and started walking, and Thayla was right behind him. *"Which way, Gorz?"*

*"Take the tunnel straight ahead, and then the first left, which will put you in a tunnel you'll follow for quite a long distance."*

Victor followed Gorz's instructions, and soon they were hustling down a long, winding tunnel with a slight downward slope. The howl was repeated a few times in the distance but didn't seem to be growing nearer.

"I think that monster was Tier Three," Thayla said suddenly.

"Why?"

"First, its strength and vitality; I put enough holes in it to kill five bull roladii by the time you threw it off. Second, the Energy we got from it had some purple in it. I've never seen that killing Tier One or Two monsters."

"The slug monster under the ground that almost dissolved you gave a lot of purple Energy."

"No wonder it healed me so well," Thayla said, a shudder in her voice.

"Well, good thing we can handle a Tier Three monster." Victor looked at Thayla and grinned.

"Why?"

"Well, the dungeon we're going to is full of Tier Two and Three monsters. Or that's what I heard when I learned about it, anyway."

"What? That's pushing our luck, Victor! Do you know anything else?"

"Um, yeah, let me see," Victor thought back to Gorz's words, trying to remember what he'd said about the dungeon before the little amulet spirit piped up and reminded him. "I think the monsters in the dungeon are undead."

*"That's right, Victor!"* Gorz said.

"Tier Three undead? Oh, Ancestors!"

"Not good?"

"Not good! I'm lowering our odds at success; we're going to be worm food, I'm sure."

"Aww, come on! What do we have to worry about from some zombies?"

"Zombies? I thought you said Tier Three?"

"Uh, yeah."

"So, more like crypt horrors and blood ghouls."

*"That sounds familiar,"* Gorz added.

"Ahh, I get it. Well, try to stay positive—probably some good treasure in there, and we're tougher than we look, right?" He gave her shoulder a nudge with his elbow, grinning.

"Speak for yourself! I look tough!" She growled at him, displaying her sharp canines, and he laughed.

*"Una mujer peligrosa,"* Victor said, with a low whistle.

"I *am* a dangerous woman! Remember it!" She chuckled, too, and they kept walking, both of them occasionally looking over their shoulders to

ensure no giant lizard-hounds were stalking their tracks. Victor followed
Gorz's directions until they came to a tunnel that opened onto a ledge over-
looking a wide, perfectly round tunnel that crossed their path. Hung from
brass-colored chains, hexagonal glow lamps were regularly spaced in the long
tunnel, shedding an eerie, pale green light. Victor looked left and right and
saw no end to the enormous, lighted passage.

"What the hell? How long have these lights been burning down here?"

"No idea." Thayla shrugged.

*"Reevus-dak, too, remarked about those lights; he called them 'strange, deathless
lampposts from an ancient era.'"* Gorz's tinny voice was hushed as though he
were being reverent. *"You and your companion need to cross to the far ledge and
continue along this narrower passage."*

"We need to get across—over to that far ledge." Victor pointed to the
ledge that matched the one they stood upon, perhaps twenty normal strides
away, should there have been a bridge over the gap.

"Too bad we can't fly." Thayla began looking around over the ledge. "We'll
need to drop down and climb up to the other one—it's only about ten feet
to the ground." She sat, hanging her legs over, and moved to drop, but Victor
grabbed her shoulder.

"Wait!" He'd seen a shadow lurch in the distance to the right, and as he
watched, it did it again. He lay flat on his belly, using the ledge to hide from
anything moving below, and Thayla quickly pulled her feet up and lay next
to him. Soon a sucking susurration came to their ears, and a slithering night-
mare came into view.

A pale, round body the length of a passenger bus, but lower and narrower,
with stalks along its lengthy bulbous body, each housing an eye that blinked
around at the surrounding tunnel, came slithering toward them. The front end
of the eyestalk-covered slug was dominated by a large, round mouth that per-
petually opened and closed like a puckering sphincter lined with hornlike teeth.

Victor and Thayla inched back from the edge of their ledge, and they
both held their breath without any consultation. Thayla's black irised eyes
were wide with fear or disgust, and Victor couldn't blame her—that monstrosity wasn't something he wanted to tangle with. They lay there in silence,
utterly still, while the slithering horror inched its way past. Thayla slowly
let out her breath at one point and drew in another, but Victor managed to
hold his breath for what must have been a world record back on Earth. He
supposed it had to do with his improved racial level, much like his reduced
reliance on food and sleep.

Finally, the thing was far enough down the tunnel that they couldn't see the shadows its eyestalks cast on the walls. After studying the other direction for several moments to ensure another wasn't coming, they hopped down and hurried across to the other ledge. They both leaped up, caught the shelf, and pulled themselves up. Then, after one last glance at the creepy slug highway, they continued down the narrow, stone passage.

*"How much farther, Gorz?"*

*"Victor, you're getting very close; just a few more turns and short passages, and you'll be in the room where Reevus exited the dungeon!"*

"We're getting close, Thayla."

"Pretty great trick you have, memorizing maps and whatnot." She glanced at him sideways, and Victor felt a surge of guilt for having lied to her for so long.

"Listen, I haven't been totally honest with you."

"Oh really?" She stopped walking and turned to face him, amusement on her face. "Do you think I've told you all my secrets?"

"No, but have you been lying to me?"

"Oh, so you're a liar? You want to clear some guilty conscience? What's your big secret, then?"

"I'm not a liar," Victor said through clenched teeth, her reaction starting to piss him off.

"Well?"

"Fine, I didn't memorize a map. I have an artifact that told me about the dungeon. I found it while I was with Lam, and I didn't tell you about it because I didn't want her to take it or kill me for keeping it. I mean, at first. I should have told you after we both were on the run."

"Really? What kind of artifact?" She suddenly sounded more intrigued than angry or judgmental, and Victor didn't know if that was a good sign or a signal to watch out.

"It's a necklace that remembers everything you tell it and can keep track of every place it's been."

*"You reduce me to those simple words?"* Gorz sounded hurt.

"No, Gorz, sorry. It also has a nice personality and is good at listening to my problems." Victor grinned at Thayla, trying to make light of things.

"It's called Gorz? It's listening to us all the time?" Thayla looked down at Victor's chest. "Let me see it."

"All right." Victor pulled Gorz out from under his armor, twirling the silvery medallion on the chain. Thayla peered at it for a while, then shrugged.

"That's a lucky find. I'm guessing its previous owner came through this dungeon, and that's how it knows about it?"

"Right."

"Well, any other big secrets?"

"Well, sure, but they have more to do with dance moves and kissing." His attempt at humor struck home, and Thayla snorted, unable to fight off her smile. "All right, what about you? I told you my big secret; what are you hiding?" Thayla's face got solemn suddenly, and then she shrugged and turned away from him, starting to walk again. "Hey, I was just joking, kind of, but now I'm really curious—you *do* have a secret, don't you?"

"You really want to know?" She whirled to face him, and Victor was dismayed to see tears welling in her eyes.

"I do, but not if it's going to upset you like that. Look, I'm sorry, I was just messing around." He was a little surprised at how much her troubled face bothered him.

"No, I'm all right. These tears—" She wiped at her eyes. "They're more because I have some hope now. My big secret is that I have a daughter. I'd resigned myself to missing her childhood while I was in the mine, but now I'm ever-so-slightly hopeful we might make it through that dungeon, and if I do, I'm going to find her."

"Oh, damn! Seriously? How old is she?"

"She's six years old now. I last saw her when she was two."

"Fuck. I'm sorry, Thayla. That's rough as hell. Is she with your family? With her father?"

"She's with a friend, a friend the Greatbone Mining Consortium doesn't know about, and that's enough said on the matter, all right?" She sniffed and wiped her eyes again, and Victor nodded.

"Hell yeah. 'Nuff said. Let's get through that dungeon, right?"

"Right," she said, favoring Victor with a normal, non-murderous smile.

Following Gorz's instructions, they made their way through several more tunnels, up a short set of crumbling stone stairs, then into a new sort of passage: a square, stone-block tunnel constructed of perfectly cut and fitted granite blocks. *"This is the final tunnel, Victor. The entrance to the dungeon is just over seventy meters ahead, though it's in a large cavern, and Reevus met with combat when he stepped out of the portal."*

"Gorz says the dungeon is seventy meters ahead, but there might be monsters around the entrance. His old owner had to fight when he came out."

"All right, let's proceed slowly and quietly," Thayla whispered, gripping her spear and raising an eyebrow for confirmation.

"Yeah, no going back now." Victor hefted Lifedrinker, and the two of them began slowly to stalk up the square, stone corridor. The stone floor wasn't very dusty at the center, but Victor saw clear scuff marks along the walls where the dirt and accumulated grime were thicker. As they advanced, the far end of the tunnel came into focus, and Victor saw a large space beyond backlit by an oscillating pale green and blue light. He crouched lower and closer to the wall, creeping forward with Thayla hugging tight in his shadow.

Coming closer to the corridor's end, he started to notice shadows moving about in the open space beyond, so he continued as cautiously and slowly as he could until his next step would put him out of the shadow and into the light, bleeding into the corridor's open mouth. Peering from eight or so feet back from the opening, he had plenty to observe.

A stone dais rose in the center of an enormous, natural cavern, and pulsing at its center was a large oval disc of smoky green and white-blue light that seemed to hang in the air. He could only assume it was the portal. Hooded figures milled about in the cavern, some kneeling and rhythmically bowing their heads to the ground as they faced the portal, while others walked around the room performing some unknowable task, moving as if in a fugue state. Victor counted eleven of the black-robed individuals. He felt Thayla squeeze even closer to him and heard her barely uttered whisper, "Do we fight or make a run for the portal?"

"You sure we have to fight? What if they're just, I don't know, a weird cult that worships this thing?" He glanced back at Thayla and saw her arched eyebrow, but he didn't take it back.

"Seriously? Black-robed weirdos deep underground, bowing to a dungeon portal and walking around like they're mind-controlled?"

"I know, I know. Let me walk in; if they attack me, you can surprise them. If we're getting our asses kicked, we run for the portal. Agreed?" He stared into Thayla's dark eyes until she nodded. Victor nodded and stood up, lifting Lifedrinker to his shoulder and letting her rest there, one hand on her handle. Then he strode out of the corridor into the stone cavern, walking right for the portal but watching closely for a reaction from the strange hooded people. He pushed inspiration Energy into his pathways, getting ready to cast Inspiring Presence or Project Energy.

He'd only made it about seven paces into the cavern when one of the figures milling about to his right jerked its head his way and let loose a long ululating cry. As soon as it started its high-pitched wail, lifting its head to project the sound, Victor caught a glimpse of its too-wide jaw and tightly packed jagged teeth. Worse, he saw its eyes and that they were pale white orbs, devoid of irises. As the creature pulled its hands out of its robe and extended a finger to point at Victor, he saw the long, black claws and gray-tinted skin and knew he wouldn't be negotiating access to the portal.

He immediately cast Inspiring Presence, and the room brightened in his eyes, revealing the frayed, tattered state of the figures' robes, how they moved in a jerky, uncoordinated fashion and seemed more afraid of him than threatening. This wouldn't be so bad! He hefted his axe and screamed, "Come on, then!" Suddenly a weight was pressing on his mind, and he had an urge to drop Lifedrinker and prostrate himself, supplicating for mercy. Victor lowered Lifedrinker, but then a thought sparked in his mind: "Supplicate? What the fuck?" He shook his head and glowered at the cluster of figures in front of the portal. "I don't think so!" With an effort of will, he pushed back the notion and strode forward, Lifedrinker once again held high.

He was aware of the figures flanking him, but he kept moving forward, increasing his pace to a long-strided jog. He kept them in mind but trusted in his speed and Thayla's upcoming surprise attack. Soon he was bearing down on the four cultists or ghouls or whatever they were near the portal, and he was sure they were the source of the mental attack he'd shrugged off. It was like their projected will was a palpable thickness in the air, and he was slicing through it—an icebreaker through a thin, frosty expanse of water. When he was just a few strides away, he cast Sovereign Will, boosting his agility, and Channel Spirit, filling Lifedrinker with rage-attuned Energy, and dashed into their midst, rapidly cleaving left and then right.

Whether the cultists were too busy concentrating on their attempt at a mental attack or were too slow to combat his sudden violent burst, he'd never know, but Lifedrinker felt no mercy or pity as she split shoulders, cleaved necks, and separated limbs. Victor saw and felt a couple of the creatures attempt to claw at him or bite at him, but he was so fast and their attacks so obviously projected that he simply stepped around them and continued his constant flow of hacking attacks. Dark blood sprayed out on his backswings and spattered as he buried Lifedrinker in their robed bodies, and Victor felt her pull herself deeper, draining Energy with each solid hit.

When the four original targets were down, along with two others that had come to their aid, Victor whirled around. He scanned the room, looking for more targets and Thayla. He saw her back by the tunnel mouth, backing up slowly, her spear in front of her, warding off the remaining five robed figures. "Dammit, you were supposed to surprise them," Victor said, starting to charge toward her.

He felt something then, tickling his mind, and he shook his head, unable to discern what was happening. It felt different from when they'd tried to make him drop Lifedrinker; there was no command, just an unpleasant presence. Suddenly he realized his distraction; he'd stopped running, and now he heard Thayla screaming. He shook his head and looked to the cavern entrance. He couldn't see Thayla, only the robed figures standing in a circle, clawing with their hands at something in their midst and throwing gore and blood into the air. "No!" Victor screamed and started running again.

As he charged toward the melee, something wavered in the air, and he felt that tingling presence in his mind again. Something wasn't right, and he didn't like that feeling in his head. He stopped again and screamed, "Get the fuck out!" He flooded his pathways with rage-attuned Energy and pushed at the presence. Suddenly the light shifted, and the scene at the tunnel mouth was very different: three unmoving cultist corpses lay on the stone floor, and two others were pressing Thayla, trying to flank her as she backed slowly toward Victor. "What the hell? On your left!" he yelled, running past her and burying Lifedrinker's gleaming, silvery edge into the cultist's chest. She bucked and pulled, and Victor saw dark, black Energy flow in little streams to the axehead.

"Thanks!" Thayla said, standing over the last cultist, pulling her spear out of its round, bulging white eye.

"Sure," Victor said, about to describe how they'd messed with his mind, but then he saw something strange happen to Thayla's face. Her expression changed from grim pleasure to panic, and she whirled her spear around and started breathing rapidly, eyes wide and unfocused. "Thayla! Something's fucking with your head." Victor backed away and scanned the cavern. Something was still out there, and it had a grip on Thayla's mind.

Victor cast Globe of Insight, and the globe appeared in his hand, brightening his immediate surroundings and pushing back the strange, sickly light of the portal. "We need more of this," he grunted and pumped every ounce of inspiration-attuned Energy he had into the orb, swelling its size to that of a cantaloupe and then a basketball. It pulsed and glowed with brighter and brighter light as his Energy flooded it. It became hard to see any of the green light through the white-gold radiance of his orb, and when Victor pushed the huge, swollen globe into the air, all the shadows in the cavern were banished. Then Victor saw what had been hidden—another black-robed figure lurked behind the portal, this one wearing a twisted silvery crown.

As his orb had grown and bathed her in its light, Thayla's face had lost its panicked expression, but she still stood, listless, her spear hanging limply in her grasp. Victor didn't waste any time, turning from where he'd thrown his orb to charge at the hunched figure. The cultist or monster was scuttling away from the portal toward the far wall of the cavern as if to get away from Victor's orb. "Where are you going, asshole? Think you can fuck with my mind?" Victor felt violated, outraged, even, not just for himself but for Thayla; it was one thing to have someone come at you openly, trying to open you up with their creepy claws, but having someone hide in the shadows and slip into your mind—that wasn't all right with Victor.

At the last minute, when Victor was bearing down on its back, Lifedrinker raised, the cloaked figure whirled, opened its oversized mouth in a croaking hiss, and pushed dark wispy tendrils of Energy out of its outstretched hands. The waves of dark Energy coursed at Victor while he charged, but he nimbly dropped into a slide. He skidded over the dusty stone ground, right past the cultist, under its attack, and, as he passed, he chopped Lifedrinker through the cultist's robed leg, and she parted the cloth, the flesh, and the bone, as easily as woodsman cuts a sapling.

The creature fell back, screaming, and its metal crown clattered along the stone floor. Dark blood gushed from the severed leg, and Victor stood up, watching as it writhed. "Can you talk?"

"Fool," it hissed, then Victor saw it reach a hand toward a pouch tied to the robe's belt, and he stepped forward and put Lifedrinker through its neck. The cultist's head rolled away, a wide-mouthed gasp of surprise forever written on its face. A clatter made him jerk his gaze from the gory sight, and Victor saw Thayla's spear rolling on the ground while she held her hands to her head. He walked over to her and squeezed her shoulder just as a surge of golden motes flooded into them both.

***Congratulations! You've achieved Level 23 Herald of Carnage. You have gained 10 will, 8 strength, and have 10 attribute points to allocate.***

***Congratulations! You've learned the spell: Globe of Insight, Improved.***

***Globe of Insight, Improved: You create an orb of inspiration-attuned Energy that will help those within its radiance see the potential in their surroundings. Overcharge the spell with extra inspiration-attuned Energy to drive back confusion and mind-altering influences. Energy cost: variable. Cooldown: minimal.***

When the effects faded, Victor saw that Thayla's eyes were clearer, and she was standing up more easily. He waved away his notifications and said, "You all right? Their boss had a way to mess with our minds."

"I'm all right, but I didn't like that feeling; it was like someone was in my head with me."

"I know exactly what you mean."

"Nice job fighting it off. I felt your inspiration orb cut through the madness, but I still felt trapped until you killed that thing."

"Any idea what they are? That one called me a fool." Victor pointed to the dead cultist leader and started walking toward it.

"No, I don't. They weren't very tough, other than, you know, taking over my mind."

"Yeah," Victor said, nudging the corpse with his toe. "I think it had something in that pouch; it was reaching for it when I removed its head."

"Also, the crown," Thayla said, walking over to it.

"Careful. That thing gives me the creeps." Victor didn't like the sickly silvery-green metal of the crown, and the twists and whorls in the metal gave him a decidedly uneasy feeling in his gut.

"Really?" Thayla frowned briefly, then said, "Come stand closer and put your hand over it. Don't touch it." Victor shrugged and did as she asked. When he held his hand close to the metal, he felt a burning, crackling sensation in his skin, but it seemed fine when he pulled his hand away.

"It feels like it's drying my skin out or something. Definitely unpleasant."

"I think your higher affinity is picking something up; maybe it's a dangerous attunement or a curse. Maybe it has an evil spirit within. Let's be careful with it until we can get an expert to check it out, hmm?"

"Yeah, sounds good. Any ideas?"

"Sure." Thayla produced an old burlap sack and held it open next to the crown. "Flip it in here with a stick or something." Victor fished out an empty wine bottle and used it to scoot the crown into Thayla's sack, which she closed up and put into her storage ring. "All right, you check out the pouch." Victor untied the leather pouch, and when he lifted it away from the corpse, he saw that it was covered in dark runes.

"Dimensional container?"

"I think so." Thayla nodded.

"Here goes." Victor trickled some Energy into the pouch, and suddenly he was aware of the enormous space within. He could see a large pile of meat in various states of decay, some smooth and pale, some dark and furry, but all of it quite disgusting looking. He saw a stack of smooth stones with various runes carved into them. Next to the runes was a little pile of green-tinged vials, and next to those was a single, dirty, torn black robe. "He didn't have a very diverse set of interests. I see potions, rotten meat, dirty clothes, and some runestones."

"Maybe throw out the meat and dirty clothes, and we can have the runestones and potions checked out sometime?"

"Yeah." While Victor dealt with the more unpleasant items in the cultist's bag, Thayla inspected the other corpses, coming away with nothing but unpleasant memories. After they came back together, Victor said, "So this is a portal, huh?"

"Yes. I'm not sure how it will work—I've only heard of dungeons having one entrance. Will this take us to the dungeon entrance, or does it have more than one starting point? Maybe it will put us near the end, and we'll be killed instantly by some powerful dungeon boss."

"I love the positivity."

"Do me a favor, will you?" She glanced at him, and Victor nodded. "Make your inspiration orb and keep it up in there. Higher-level undead can mess with our minds, kind of like this guy did." She pointed at the leader's corpse.

"Sounds good. We've got this, Thayla. Just a little dungeon between us and freedom, now." Thayla gave him a weary smile. "One sec." Victor called up his attributes, not wanting to walk into his first dungeon with unspent points:

| Strength: | 74 | Vitality: | 90 |
| Dexterity: | 38 | Agility: | 43 |
| Intelligence: | 29 | Will: | 113 |
| Points Available: | 10 | | |

He decided to leave it to his class levels to keep bumping up his strength and will, and he put five points into agility, three into intelligence, and two into dexterity. "All right, I'm ready."

"Your orb." Thayla smiled.

"Right," Victor used his improved spell to summon a substantial, softball-size globe of inspiration Energy that glowed and pulsed with a pure, warming white-gold light that pushed back the sickly green of the portal. He found it a lot easier to control now, simply willing it to float above and behind them.

"Perfect," Thayla sighed. Victor nodded, and together they stepped into the portal, letting the cold, shifting Energy wrap around them, and pull them to an unknown destination.

# ABOUT THE AUTHOR

Plum Parrot is the pen name of author Miles Gallup, who grew up in Southern Arizona and spent much of his youth wandering around the Sonoran Desert, hunting imaginary monsters and building forts. He studied creative writing at the University of Arizona and, for a number of years, attempted to teach middle schoolers to love literature and write their own stories. If he's not out enjoying the beach, you can find Gallup writing, reading his favorite authors, or playing *D&D* with friends and family.

# DISCOVER
# *STORIES UNBOUND*

PodiumAudio.com

Made in the USA
Middletown, DE
18 November 2023